This book is a work of fiction. Names, Characters, places, and incidents are either the product of the author's imagination or are used fictitiously, and any resemblance to actual persons, living or dead, events, or locales is entirely coincidental.

The following story contains mature themes, strong language and sexual situations. It is intended for mature readers.

All characters are 18+ years of age and all sexual acts are consensual.

Content Warning: Violence, Gangs, Organized Crime

Tabby

Tabby Williams was once an outgoing, all-American girl, but when a conniving bastard broke her heart, she was left in shambles. Heartbroken, she vowed to never rush into a relationship again. But when she meets a handsome new city councilman with a troubled past, she realizes some promises are meant to be broken.

Patrick

When Patrick McCaffery meets a young and desirable Tabby Williams, he finds out that he's not the only one with secrets in the closet. A handsome, up-and-coming city councilman with a questionable past, Patrick has ambitious plans to clean up his city. But with a girl that's every bit as mysterious as he is at his side, he finds himself biting off more than he can chew.

Table of Contents

Chapter 1
Tabby

My fingers were beating a staccato rhythm on my desktop as I waited for the call I'd been expecting all afternoon. I'd expected the news around one or two, and it was now nearly four o'clock. Three times in the past hour I had to be reminded of phone calls or other things on my schedule by my secretary. "Miss Williams, your appointment is here."

"Eh? Appointment?" I said, looking up. Vanessa, who I had just hired two months prior when I was appointed head of MJT Consolidated Holdings, kept her best professional demeanor. I appreciated it. "Who with?"

I had hired Vanessa Montenegro because, at thirty-four, she already had fifteen years of experience as an executive assistant. She'd worked with all sorts of companies, from healthcare to manufacturing, and in each instance she'd gotten rave reviews from her former employers. In fact, three of them had told me they would hire her back in an instant with a hefty pay raise if she'd take the job. When I asked her why she kept changing jobs instead of taking the pay raises, she impressed me, not only for her insight, but for her bluntly put honesty.

"I'm an INTJ Architect personality type, which normally isn't good for the type of job I do. According to the online profiles, I should be working as a freelance project-type person, like in software engineering, or maybe as a lawyer. But for me, I see this sort of work as my calling. I come into a company, and while I don't like the spotlight, I really focus on doing what I can to help the company set up the structures it needs in order to be successful. Once that framework is in place, I tend to get a bit itchy-footed and move on. No offense, Miss Williams, but I doubt I'll be around for more than four or five years. I'd say less, but you're so new at this, you'll be providing me with plenty of challenges and ways to help out for a lot longer than some of my other jobs."

Now, two months later, I understood what she meant. Vanessa was a real help around the office, the sort of person who helped a twenty-five-year-old like me get a handle on a company that, on the books at least, was worth well over a hundred million dollars, on a staff of (again, on paper) two people—three if you counted the cleaning guy I hired to come in three times a week. I never have understood the idea of making your secretary clean up after you, and while I kept my office pretty neat, I wasn't going to make someone like Vanessa do dusting.

Of course, all of that was on the books. Off the books, well, MJT was a lot more. Funded by well-scrubbed blood money, MJT was in reality three people, and the company had access to nearly three hundred million dollars if needed. I wasn't even the head of MJT—that honor was held by Matt Bylur, nee Marcus Smiley, nee Mark Snow, The "M" in MJT. Once the best hitman in the city, and perhaps in the country, Mark has killed a lot of people. Just how many I don't really know, but I could go the rest of my life without knowing the actual number. It's a weight on my soul I could live without.

I've actually seen Mark in action once, when he saved me from a group of gangsters in a nightclub after they'd kidnapped me. He dropped four men so fast that I barely had time to scream before the last man hit the ground. I'm getting ahead of myself though. Calm, confident, wickedly smart and handsome—in a lot of ways he is a dream guy for any woman. I did make a pass at him once, which he promptly rebuffed—kindly, but with finality.

I don't think of Mark in that way any longer, though, because of the second person in MJT. The "J", Joanna Bylur, nee Sophie Warbird, nee Sophie White, was my best friend all through college and the woman who had become the sister I never had. Beautiful inside and out, being with Mark had really brought her out of her insecure shell and let her understand just how fucking awesome she is. She accepted me for who I am, a weird but outgoing firebird. Then, as if that wasn't impressive enough, she turned the baddest hitman in the city into a vigilante crusader. Oh, and she has about a thousand other little skills that make her the perfect woman.

Which is kind of how MJT (I'm the "T", duh) was born. The rest is history, including how Mark and Sophie took down the two largest criminal networks in town. After doing so, Mark needed to disappear. On the other hand, in order to keep our city from falling into chaos, his money and the influence he wanted to use couldn't. Taking on the identity of Matt Bylur, he and Sophie (now Joanna) got married in Las Vegas and moved back into town as my housekeeper and groundskeeper. I was jealous that they didn't have me at their wedding, but I understood, and they had videotaped it for me. So I had my boss and my best friend—or whatever you wanted to call them—as my house staff. At least, that was their so-called day job. I still have to shake my head about it, and I lived through it all.

This all brings me back to Vanessa, knocking on the door frame of my office with a professionally exasperated look in her eye while I stared at her, totally lost. You see, Sophie had gotten pregnant right before becoming Joanna, and I was nervously awaiting news of her most recent prenatal exam. I couldn't even go with her, as much as I wanted to. I mean, seriously, what CEO goes to the doctor with their maid? On reflection, don't answer that. We might know what kind, usually an older male with a maid who is either scared out of her mind or already counting the money from child support payments.

"Who with?" I asked, blinking and drawing a total blank at Vanessa's comment. I knew I was gathering wool, but I wanted to hear from Sophie. Still, Vanessa didn't know about *Matt* and *Joanna*, other than that they were my domestic help, and I had to appear professional.

"The Padre," Vanessa replied. While she was never one to be as outwardly emotional as I am, she showed her feelings in other ways, usually through the use of nicknames. The Right Reverend Gerald Traylor was one of the people she detested most, and in my opinion, with good reason. The leader of one of the most influential churches in the city, Bishop Traylor's Holy Assembly of the Ever Loving God could brag about holding three services per Sunday, each of them packing in over a thousand people. With services broadcast on a locally owned channel, he swung a lot of weight, especially among the Evangelical population of the city. His fiery preaching and unique blend of gospel, Christian funk music, and a bit of other popular music styles made a good show, if that was the particular brand of Christianity that spoke to you. Considering who I am, and the opposition I had to a lot of his preaching, I couldn't say I was a fan of his.

I would've overlooked all of my issues with Traylor and his preaching if he'd been even halfway as honest as the figure he portrayed onscreen and in public. The problem was that he was as corrupt as a preacher could be. For years—carefully

7

hidden, of course—he'd taken money from the members of the Confederation, one of the two criminal empires that Mark had smashed just months prior. A man who preached humility and the Bible, Traylor lived in a penthouse that was just over four thousand square feet in a high-rise that commanded top dollar per square foot. Hell, the HOA fees alone were nearly twenty thousand dollars per year. On top of that, Traylor owned about a half dozen other properties around the city, two of which he kept his mistresses in while his wife played her role in public. Knowing what I did about his private life would lead anyone who doubted in the existence of God to wonder how the man didn't burst into flames every time he touched the Bible.

And of course, I detested the man for his ministry as well. Hellfire and brimstone, he'd more than once called for people like me to burn in hell because of my sexual appetite. It was kind of the personal cherry on top for making what I was about to do just a little more fun than my average work, which usually consisted of doing a lot of business investing. Turn on the TV show, *Shark Tank*, and you get the idea, minus the reality show dramatics.

"Miss Williams," Traylor said in his broad, well-practiced tone as he entered the office. I had to admit, the man could speak well. He toned down his inflection in private, but still had the sonorous, rumbling sounds that led gravitas to his voice. It wasn't quite at the level of James Earl Jones, but he could certainly make reading your grocery list interesting. "Thank you for meeting with me so quickly after my church's request."

"When one of the leading members of the community makes a request, I do my best to accommodate them as quickly as possible," I said, standing up from my desk and coming around to shake his hand. I didn't want to. In fact, I had to resist the urge to turn around and immediately squirt about three dollops of antibacterial gel onto my hand. I felt dirty just with that light amount of contact.

I was wearing my black suit that day, which went great with my fiery red hair. I had taken a page from Sophie's playbook as Sophie Warbird and had dialed up the volume on my natural auburn hair to an almost fire-engine red, which gained a lot of attention. Actually, the suit was hers, too. We're close enough in height that I just needed to have it tailored a bit. Sophie's a natural D cup, while I'm a C. To offset it, though, I do have a smaller waist, so the effect created by the tight jacket and blouse underneath was similar. Namely, that the so-called man of God's eyes fluttered

8

between my hair and my boobs in an almost metronomic fashion. I think if I'd turned around and let him look at my ass, he'd have blown a load in his custom-tailored suit.

"Please, have a seat," I said, leading him over to the coffee table that was tucked next to the window on the east side of the room. With the MJT offices only having three rooms, my office doubled as our conference room and was rather roomy. I had my desk, an eight-person conference table, and the coffee area which I used for casual meetings. "I have to say, I was surprised at how quickly your request came in. Tell me, have the recent troubles been that significant for your community?"

"Yes, Miss Williams, they have," Traylor said, taking the seat opposite me. I wanted us separated by the table. While I was hoping that my words alone would neuter the man, I was taking no chances. People do stupid things when pushed, after all. "You should see the streets, Miss Williams. Gunfire on a nightly basis, shops closing left and right. Over a hundred of my parishioners have come to me over the past month stating that they have lost their jobs, asking for the church's help. We've helped as many as we can, but the church's coffers are tapped out. Now, I know that your particular organization is not in the charity business, but I do feel that we can be beneficial to each other."

"Oh, and how is that?" I said, leaning forward and letting him see just a bit of my cleavage. I may not be as busty as Sophie, but with a Wonderbra and a button-down, V-neck silk blouse, it doesn't matter. I wanted to keep the Bishop off-guard for when I dropped the bomb on him.

"Your . . . um . . . your company can use good publicity," Traylor replied, unconsciously licking his lips before pulling his eyes back up to my face. "While you have done lots of good for the city, the fact is that there are some who are resistant to what you're trying to do. A good charitable donation to Holy Assembly would go a long way toward easing concerns in the minds of some people."

"I see," I said, sitting back and pretending to consider his idea. He was right, in a certain sense. After investing in over four dozen companies in the city, MJT was becoming a major player in the business and political currents of the city. We were ruffling feathers, some of which were starting to try and push back. "It would be quite helpful. And of course, having the positive word of a man as powerful as yourself wouldn't hurt either."

9

"I'm not the powerful one. I only have what the Lord has given to me in order to further his kingdom," Traylor said, spreading his hands out beatifically, as if he were laying claim to the whole world around him. For all I knew, he was, although not through his holiness, that was for damn sure. "But yes, I can do a lot to ease the concerns of the community."

"And how much are we talking here?" I asked, pretending to read the document that his request had come with. In fact, after discussing the original proposal with Mark and Sophie, I hadn't opened the folder in days, and I honestly didn't care if the folder had contained cut-outs from the most recent issue of *Captain America*. "You left that part blank, I noticed. My secretary wasn't happy about that."

"That depends totally on you," Traylor replied. "Our charity outreach program can cost us upward of a million dollars per year, although I wouldn't expect your company to provide anywhere near that. On the other hand, the more you give, the more good we can do."

"I see." I stood up from the coffee table and walked back over to my desk, wishing that I had chosen a hard floor rather than rugs for the office. Let's face it, the sound of a woman's heels clicking along tile while she sashays around in a tight skirt can send blood flowing to all the right places. I could feel Traylor's eyes glued on my hips and legs as I walked, and I pondered just how easy it was to use my sexuality to totally throw the man off. Funny, really. I had a few classmates in college, self-professed militant feminists, who said that my using my sexiness to get what I wanted was just selling out to the male dominated system in place. To me, I thought it was weird how I was supposedly powerless, but I could reduce these supposedly powerful men to mindless, begging wretches with just a swish of my ass and a glimpse of my boobs.

Getting a pen from the holder on my desk, I turned around and perched on the edge, my face dawning as if I'd come to a sudden realization. "Bishop, I've got it! I know a way for us to both get what we want!"

"What's that, Miss Williams?" he said, taking me in at my full height. I wondered how much of his mind was on what I was saying and how much was mentally undressing me. "I'm all ears."

"Well, Bishop, if you're looking for funding for charity, I have a great idea. What about a new community center, with education and job training programs, a food bank, after school activities, even childcare for working single mothers? I mean, a place that could be a real hand up and not a hand out."

"That sounds amazing, Miss Williams, but such programs are very expensive. When I looked into something similar, I was told it would cost nearly five million dollars just to get up and running after finding a building, performing renovations and similar tasks. I just don't have that amount of funding." He was lying through his teeth, as we'd kept tabs on Traylor's church. His personal finances alone were worth well over ten million dollars, and there was more owned in his church's name that they used, all tax-free under their supposed 'ministry programs.'

"Oh, of course we can get it done," I replied, smiling my best smile. "After all, MJT has more than a few buildings it could outright donate to any such program, and the funding for running it, well, that wouldn't be a problem either. I know just where you could get the funding."

"What do you mean?"

"Well, Bishop, all it would take would be for you to sell that twenty-million-dollar penthouse you have in the Park district that your friends in the Confederation got for you—not in your name, of course, but in your church's—along with the two other condos your mistresses are using, and move into a house more befitting a man of God," I said, keeping the smile on my face. Still, I knew my look had gone from happy to predatory, and the pale expression on the Bishop's face told me my words were hitting home.

"After that, you can sell your private jet that is kept out at the airport—the one that you told your audience was too old for you to continue to do your important work with, and that they needed to dig deep to buy you a new Gulfstream. You know the plane I'm talking about, don't you? The one that is parked in a hangar that was owned by Taylor Broadwell, the gentleman who got himself assassinated, only to have it come out later that not only was he the largest trafficker of illegal items in the city, but he was in with both the Confederation and our recently indicted ex-deputy mayor, Owen Lynch, the same Owen Lynch who I believe you had stand next to you at the pulpit before the last election and stated that he was an honest, hard-working man of God? Ring any bells, Bishop?"

I didn't give him a chance to answer before continuing. "Here's the deal, Gerald. You're going to resign as head pastor of your church. Go to Florida, or to

11

Arizona, Texas—hell, go to Fiji for all I fucking care. But you're leaving this city. As for your charity request, that's already been in the works—it has been for over a month. Tonight's news is going to include the announcement by MJT Consolidated Holdings that MJT is partnering with the owners of the Spartans (the local professional football team), Nike, and Google to build a series of four community centers in the city. Each of them will have exactly what I just described. The Spartans, Nike and Google will fund the actual running of the centers, while MJT is donating the buildings themselves and the renovations. I expect I'll probably have to do some publicity shots of me in coveralls and a t-shirt, hammering wood or laying carpet, but since you've spent most of the time we've been in the same room staring at my tits, I'm sure you won't mind if I make it a tight shirt. You think I'd look good in Spartan colors?"

Traylor recovered well from my attack, or at least he tried to. I doubted many people were willing to really stand up to him, at least not in years. After all, he could command the ears and souls of thousands at a whim. Who would want to piss him off? Well, except for a very committed redheaded woman who didn't care if she pissed him off. He leaned back in his chair and folded his hands in his lap, only the pulse of a vein in his temple exposing how angry he was.

"And if I turn my people against you? It'll be mighty hard to have a good community center when you have street gangs patrolling outside the doors. Let's drop the facade, Miss Williams. I know who goes to my church. One call and you have the Gangster Disciples tossing bombs through your windows."

"You have powerful friends at the street level, Gerald. On the other hand, I happen to have friends at the Justice Department and the IRS. Tell me, Bishop, are you certain you paid the proper taxes for all that you received last year? Because I'm quite certain the IRS would say differently. Just how is it that a Bishop is able to pay for not only your lifestyle, but that of a wife and two mistresses on just the donations of your parishioners? Oh, by the way, how are Carrie, Pauline and Baby Love doing right now? I know Carrie knows about them, but I don't think Pauline knows about Baby Love."

Traylor swallowed but recovered well enough. I had dirt on him, and while he could try and go against me, I had a grip on more than a few sensitive areas of his. "I see. Well then, good day, Miss Williams. I doubt we'll speak again."

12

He got up to leave, buttoning his coat and heading for the door. Reaching for the handle, he stopped when I called his name. "Gerald?"

"Yes, Miss Williams?"

He turned to look at me, and I fixed him with my most menacing look. I'd honed it in the mirror for weeks, Mark coaching me the entire time. It was useful, and I could go from seductive to menacing in about two seconds flat if I wanted. "Don't even think of fucking with me on this. I'm letting you off easy. Take the money you've doubtlessly squirreled away, and your wife, if she'll stay with your cheating ass, and get the fuck out of the city. If I see or hear that you're back in town, let's just say bad shit might just happen to you."

"What do you mean?" Traylor said, his lower lip quivering. "Do you think I'm worried about what you might tell the IRS?"

I let my mouth spread into a smile, but not a friendly one. "No. I have friends too, Gerald. Very efficient friends."

Silently, so as to avoid letting Vanessa hear—she was totally in the dark on the other side of MJT—I formed the word that struck fear in the hearts of the city's evil and corrupt. "The Snowman."

Traylor's eyes grew wide, and he almost ripped the door open getting away from me. I watched from my desk as he hightailed it out of the MJT office, Vanessa still sitting at her desk and watching him go. When he was finally gone, she came into my office, her face still professionally impassive. "Shall I pencil in the Padre for another appointment later, Miss Williams?"

"No, I don't think that will be necessary. And how many times do I have to tell you to call me Tabby?"

"I don't think so, Miss Williams. By the way, Mrs. Bylur called while you were in your meeting. She says she has returned from her doctor's appointment and will still be able to have her work completed by the time you get home."

Vanessa left my office, and I went around to my desk chair, unbuttoning my suit jacket before plopping down. The meeting with Traylor had fired me up, and I was in the swing of things now. If Sophie's message was that she was fine, I could hear the details when I got home that night. I still had some adrenalin to work off, and I figured I could use it to make up for the hour of zoning out I'd done.

Tabby nearly sent the door to Mount Zion off its hinges when she came home that evening, causing Sophie and me to hide our smiles. We knew that when we called and had only gotten to talk to Vanessa, she'd be itching for an update. She's a great front for our company, a great friend, and smart in her own right, but she's a total softie when it comes to Sophie.

"So?" she asked, barely taking the time to toss her briefcase to the side, where it clattered to the floor. I was grateful she didn't carry a computer in her briefcase, as we had her computer at MJT networked with ours at home. While Tabby is hardly as messy as she claims, I do have to admit that I spent about twenty minutes per day picking up after her. Tabby is difficult as hell to get out of bed in the morning, so between waking up and leaving for work, she somewhat resembles the Tasmanian Devil. Thankfully, my new lifestyle allowed me the time, as long as I got into the stock markets on time. That meant that most mornings, while Sophie did the back rooms or got started on her work with the computer, I spent the time cleaning up, finishing just in time for the opening bell on the market.

"Well, the doctor's got some new magazines in his waiting room," I said, stirring dinner. It was a unique setup for our supposed work. On paper, Sophie (excuse me, Joanna, but we used our real names around the house) was supposed to be the housekeeper, and she did do a good amount of housework. On the other hand, as beautiful and talented as my wife is, she's not as good of a cook as I am, so I would often do outside yard work or other things befitting my "job" and then come in to make dinner. Neither woman had ever complained, even when I experimented with new recipes. "I got to read a very interesting article in the latest *Popular Mechanics*."

Tabby replied by making a face, sticking her tongue out and blowing a very loud raspberry. "I'd fire you if you weren't my boss," she mock-complained before coming over and seeing what I was cooking. "Smells good."

"Thanks. Doctor Atkinson said that Sophie needs a bit more Vitamin K in her diet, so we're having sautéed kale as a side dish. Sorry, no pizzas or stuff for a while."

Tabby stood on her tiptoes and gave me a kiss on the cheek. "You're too much, Mathew Mark Bylur," she said in reply. She would call me that at least once a day as practice to make sure she didn't screw up and call me Marcus Smiley or Mark Snow in public sometime. "I swear I'm going to find a company that can just clone you for me. Just need to give him naturally black hair."

"Don't forget that he needs to be more adventurous in the bedroom," I joked back. "I doubt I could keep up with you."

"From what Sophie's told me, I doubt that. So where is our mom-to-be?" Tabby said. It was a strange but by now comfortable adaptation to our relationship. She and I would often talk to each other about subjects that I would never speak about with a woman I wasn't in a relationship with before, yet we were both comfortable with it, more like best friends than anything else. Tabby was just cool with the relationship Sophie and I had and how she fit in. She was even cool with occasionally keeping herself to her portion of the Mount Zion estate to give the two of us some intimate privacy.

"She's in the back, fussing with the laundry. Doc Atkinson's was busy, so sorry about the delay in how long it took us to get you news," I replied as I chopped up some chanterelle mushrooms to go in with the kale.

"Which, by the way, you still haven't told me," she replied. "I'm guessing that is on purpose?"

I stirred the pot and added another splash of olive oil before a pinch of herbs and salt. "Of course. Now go and hang out. Dinner will be ready in twenty minutes."

Tabby nodded and stepped back, taking off her high heels as she did to walk comfortably through the rest of the house. As she did, I watched her go and pondered how lucky I was. Seriously, how many men got to live with two amazing women, both of whom love him in their own way?

I just wondered how Tabby would take the news that Doctor Atkinson thought that we had a little girl on the way.

* * *

That night, after dinner was finished and the ladies were changed into their evening wear—matching silk pajama sets from Victoria's Secret that were very tempting for me to just stay home—I went into Sophie's and my bedroom to change

15

as well. Taking off the jeans and t-shirt that I favored for housework, I pulled out my night time wear.

Stripping down to my underwear, I was surprised when I heard a knock at the door. I turned and saw Sophie leaning against the door frame, the royal purple of her pajamas molding to the swell of her hips and breasts in a way that left my stomach and cock stirring. "You really have to go out tonight?" she purred. "I was hoping we could celebrate the good news."

"You know I want to," I said, walking over and giving her a kiss. Sophie pushed into my arms, and I was left breathless as her lush body pressed against me, supple silk covering enticing curves. When we finally parted, I was unabashedly standing with my cock tenting the briefs that I prefer when I'm going to do something athletic.

"I can tell," she said, reaching out and rubbing my cock through my briefs. She looked at me with desire, but also with a well-humored resignation. "But, you're going to tell me it's been six days since you had a night patrol, and that with what we've learned about the street gang activity, you need to get out there and do some pacification. I know, I know."

"And yet," I said, trying to suppress the groan and the desire to just fall to my knees and make love to my wife right there, "you keep rubbing my cock."

"That's because you look so delicious standing there like that. It's hard, and I mean very hard, to stop," she replied. Finally, when I was just at the point of delaying my patrol, she pulled her hand back, grinning at me. "Use that as motivation to make damn sure you come home in one piece with no fluids leaking out."

The big, shuddering breath that I had to take to regain control told Sophie everything she needed to know, and she kissed me again on the cheek. "By the way, Tabby says thanks for the night out."

"Oh?" I said, trying to distract my mind. It was funny: in the traditionally classic sense, Tabby is definitely a knockout, but talking about her never tempted my libido. I could acknowledge that she was beautiful, but never have I had the desire to sleep with her. That's what Sophie does to me. "What do you two have planned?"

"A silly romantic comedy, then she's going to get some sleep. She's got the press conference tomorrow with the General Manager of the Spartans for the new community centers, remember?"

16

"Gotcha," I said, stepping back and turning toward my patrol wear. First thing I pulled on were the compression undershorts I like to wear, although it was a bit painful tugging the tight fabric over my erection. "You want to watch the TV?"

"I might," Sophie replied. "I just wish I could have watched her castrate Bishop Traylor today instead."

"Well, we can always try and set up a video feed if you want," I said, taking down the black cargo pants that I was wearing. Despite the comic book name, the Snowman didn't exactly go out looking like anything out of the ordinary. Pulling them up over my hips, I cinched the belt in tight, noting that after shifting to mostly healthy eating since Sophie's pregnancy, I'd lost some weight, and not in a good way either. I didn't sport a lot of body fat to begin with, and if I was losing weight, that meant I was losing much needed muscle and strength for my night patrols.

"I think I'm going to add in some more fats to my diet," I noted. "These pants are hanging off of me."

"I still think you look like a million bucks," Sophie replied. "Well, I'll let you finish getting dressed. Just come give me a kiss before you leave for work, okay?"

"Okay."

Sophie left, and I finished pulling on my patrol uniform. Since the downfall of the Confederation, I didn't need to carry quite as much firepower as I did when I patrolled earlier. Still, I was headed into the area of the city known as The Playground, which, despite the innocent sounding name, contained some of the darkest corners of the city. Illuysas Petrokias, the Confederation member that Sophie had put a bullet into, used to own about half of the area, which was now more or less up for grabs. It was one of the most frequent areas I patrolled, as drugs, prostitution and all forms of vice competed with each other.

I pulled on the tactical vest (with integrated body armor) I preferred over top of the long-sleeved, hooded t-shirt that went with the pants, before finishing by lacing up the short boots that worked best for me. There's a time and place for full on tactical or combat boots, but not for most of my patrols. I did enough running and jumping that the extra shoe height wasn't helpful. Instead of preventing twisted ankles, it just slowed me down.

The last part of my outfit was in an electronic safe in the closet, my favored twin 9mm Glocks, which went into holsters against my ribs. Pausing, I double-

17

checked that the safety was on before I slid the first magazine in, but knew I wasn't going to chamber a round until I was in The Playground. No need to be stupidly risky.

Coming out into the television room, I found Sophie and Tabby, both seated on the large bean bags that made up the furniture of the room, with two cups of herbal tea ready for them. "What, no desserts?"

"With those suits I have to wear to work?" Tabby said with a smirk. "You're crazy if you think I can do that. Even working out with you four times a week isn't going to overcome nightly ice cream and cheesecake."

"I hear that," I said, kneeling down and giving Sophie a kiss. "By the way, we're still on for tomorrow evening, right?"

"Yeah, yeah, six o'clock, with Sophie here playing both training partner and taskmaster for us. Now go, have your fun playing around with the criminals of the city, and I'll make sure Sophie's not too tired to reward you when you get home."

I rolled my eyes and kissed Sophie again. "Stay safe," she whispered, looking me in the eyes. Despite all the playfulness of our banter about my *job*, we both knew that what I did multiple times a week was deadly serious, and her eyes were filled with that knowledge now.

"I will," I whispered back, laying my hand on her stomach.

Riding my midnight black Energica Ego sport bike, I focused on the patrol at hand. It was more than just a case of being ecologically friendly. The electric motorcycle was lighter and went zero to sixty in three seconds if I wanted it to. Tonight wasn't so much about actual confrontation as intimidation, although there was one bit of nasty work that I wasn't looking forward to. With my mirrored visor on my helmet and my silent motorcycle, I created quite the figure cruising the neon-splattered, grungy streets. Once it became known that I was in the neighborhood, the streets quickly cleared, and within twenty minutes there was hardly a person in sight. That task completed, I found a dark alley where I could stash my bike and set off on foot. Despite the similarities to television superheroes, I kept my hood up and wore a Kato style mask over my eyes, held on with spirit gum. There were times to be fashion conscious and times to cover my ass.

Stalking down the alley, I made my way two blocks over to a door that was my other main target of the night. There was no sign and no advertisements, but if you were into very hardcore BDSM, Mistress Blood's was the place to go. While BDSM is nowhere near the sort of thing I was into, I have no personal vendetta with it. I understand that there are lots of different things that people do to have fun. Sophie and I have our own little quirks that fall outside the 'norm' that people talk about, and we don't feel guilty about them at all.

What I do have problems with is when some of the 'subs' available for the clients to enjoy were not there of their own volition. Considering what some of the clients did to them, few people in the world would ever volunteer. I knew of at least a dozen people who had been permanently maimed inside the walls of Mistress Blood's, and I believed the rumors that at least two real snuff films had been made within the walls. I'd worked with one man who said he'd disposed of the bodies from Blood's, and that some of them were disfigured in ways that looked like something from a horror movie. I said my mission that night was intimidation, but that didn't mean Mistress Blood's didn't need to be shut down.

I waited until the door opened from inside—there's no way I was taking down an inch-thick, steel-core door, not without a lot of plastic explosives—to make my move. A client stepped out, a man whose face would make the evening news if I had a camera. Before the security guard could close the door, my Glock was in his face, backing both of them inside.

"You, Mr. Bank Vice President, bounce," I hissed to the frightened man. It wasn't just for effect, either. As Marcus Smiley, I'd done a lot of news interviews, and I needed to disguise my voice, although I never did get as ridiculous as Christian Bale did in the Nolan *Batman* films. "And if you value your career, never come back here again. Not unless you want Bill Franklin to know what you do late at night."

The scared executive nodded, his jowly cheeks fluttering as a piss stain started to spread over his crotch before he fled into the night. The guard, a beefy guy wearing leather pants and a good amount of baby oil, was more composed and started backing toward a spot on the wall. "Uh-uh, Gimp Boy," I said, pointing the Glock in my left hand at him. "You've got two options. I can knock you the fuck out, or I can shoot you. Personally, I don't care which."

The guard looked me in the eyes and knew who I was. We were in a small alcove, with almost no chance of anyone hearing us. The rooms were very well soundproofed, after all. It helped with preventing complaints from the neighbors.

19

"You promise I can live?"

"If you play it cool," I said. "I'll tie you up if I knock you out, though."

The guard nodded and thought it over for half a second before lowering his head and turning around. I brought the butt of my Glock down at the base of his skull, and he dropped like a two-hundred-pound sack of rice. Pulling a roll of electrical tape from my vest, I quickly taped his wrists behind his back, along with his ankles before connecting the two. He'd be uncomfortable when he woke up, but he wasn't going anywhere. Fifty meters of electrical tape can bind up just about anyone.

Heading down the hallway, I pulled my other Glock and kept it by my ear, all my senses open. There was a lot that those senses gave me that I didn't want but would deal with later. The cries and whimpers coming from the closed doors, the crack of whips, the hum of power tools, and other things that I didn't even want to consider.

I couldn't even start busting heads, as much as I wanted to, because I knew that, despite the illegality of some of the shit that went down at Mistress Blood's, over half of the subs were there of their own volition. Not that I could understand the appeal of paying someone to cut your back to shreds with a cat o' nine tails, but that didn't mean you needed to die because of it. I made my way down the hall toward the office, knowing what I'd find.

Mistress Blood, long before she had gotten into doing hardcore BDSM, had been an amateur bodybuilder. In fact, it was in an attempt to make money for her bodybuilding career that she'd first gotten into BDSM, doing so-called 'sexy wrestling' videos and smothering men with her muscular thighs. She'd even done submission porn videos before turning her attention to running her own place. With the assistance of Illuysas Petrokias, she'd set up Mistress Blood's.

I found her in her office, wearing the leather and latex that I was sure she used for work. Incongruously, she also wore steel-rimmed glasses while she looked over an account ledger when I opened the door. It was a strange look, kind of dominatrix combined with school teacher.

"Did the Councilwoman come in early? If she did, tell her she needs to pay for last time," she said before she looked up, seeing that I wasn't her security guard. "You."

"Me," I replied. "I assume you know why I'm here."

20

"I suppose it's not just to ask if I've got a part-time job opening," Blood said, sitting back and tenting her fingers under her chin. I had to give her credit, she had more guts than the client I'd chased out of here.

"Not in the least," I said. "Although be thankful that I actually respect you enough to look you in the eye."

For the first time, I saw fear in Blood's eyes. "You're not giving me a chance?"

"After the dozen men and women I've seen carried out of here permanently disfigured? Tell me, Blood, how much did they pay you for the chance to blind a teenage girl, or to literally castrate a man?"

"Quarter million each," Blood automatically replied. "Let's face it, Snowman, you killed people for less. At least those people didn't die."

I nodded, my eyes still not flinching. "And I've lost sleep over each and every one of them. We could argue the morality of killing versus permanently maiming, but it doesn't really matter, Blood. You're going to become just another number."

Blood nodded and stood up, keeping her arms spread. She seemed calm, and I wondered what she was doing. "If you're going to, then do it," she said, kneeling down next to her desk. She looked like a supplicant, someone happy to receive what I was offering. "I've been looking forward to it."

I squinted, surprised. "What?"

"You think I got into this because I like it?" Blood asked me, a haunted smile on her face. "I got into it because it was the only thing I was good at. I got into it because every drop of blood I draw, every little whimper of pain I deliver is a balm on my soul."

I nodded in understanding. I had heard similar stories before and should have ignored hers. But for some reason, I had to know. "How old were you, Blood?"

"*She* was seven," Blood replied. "Carla was her name, and she was sold by her mother to pay off a drug debt. There were three of them, and the whole time she cried, tears mixing with the blood as she was torn open on both sides. By the time the third one was in her, Carla died. I was born, and it was I who killed my mother when I was eleven. Every weight I lifted, every pound of muscle I packed on was to make sure that nobody would ever hurt me again. When the money came in to let me hurt back, it was all too easy."

21

I was tempted to let her go, really. Her story was definitely believable, and it jived with what I knew about her. She'd been a street kid before getting into the weights, and I knew that she had a deep distrust of people, men in particular. But then I remembered something. "I'd believe you if it wasn't for all the girls that came through here, some not much younger than you were when your innocence was taken, Carla. How many of their lives did you ruin, how much innocence of theirs did you exchange for money? You want to comfort yourself with thoughts of revenge? You didn't get revenge. You became your own mother, Carla."

The words struck deep inside Blood, who surged to her feet, anger and hatred in her eyes. She sprang at me, and I pulled the trigger of my Glock, hitting her in chest. She collapsed to the floor, clutching at the wound, her eyes in agony. "Please . . ." she gasped, looking me in the face. "Please."

I nodded. "I'm sorry, Carla."

I pulled the trigger again.

Chapter 3
Tabby

I woke up at about three in the morning, somewhat surprised. Normally, when Mark went out on patrol—and given the way he and Sophie were making eyes at each other—I'd wake up to the normal sounds of them making love, especially as Sophie's pregnancy hormones put her sex drive into hyper-speed. Despite her claims of being demure and restrained, there was something about Mark that turned my friend into a very vocal lover. Our unique living situation gave them a full section of the main house to themselves, and I often slept in the supposedly sound-proofed living room (those bean bag chairs are actually awesomely comfortable), but I could hear them at least once or twice a week. If it wasn't that I loved them both so much, I'd have been upset.

Instead, that night I woke up to absolute silence. I'd planned on sleeping on the bean bag chair, so I stretched, enjoying the rustle of the stuffing under my head.

22

The bags aren't filled with normal foam beads but something else, so they never go flat and dumpy on you. Another one of the effects is that the rustling of the padding inside is quite nice, with none of that plasticky squeal that cheap bags give you. It was somewhere in between leaves rustling and sand scrunching under your toes when you walk on a wet beach. The magic of science, indeed.

Getting off the bag, I wrapped the light blanket I was using around me to ward off the chill of the evening and walked into the hallway. The layout of Mount Zion was rather strange, to say the least, considering it had for years been a church and rectory. The main living area connected to what had been the main sanctuary through my bedroom, which had been the room that housed the choir things as well as the pipe organ. Mark and Sophie used what had been the rectory's living room, while the office was in between and had been converted into our own living room. The kitchen, laundry room, and other things were scattered off of our living room, and considering how rich Mark is, were most likely undersized compared to others in his tax bracket. It didn't matter to us, though, and we enjoyed the whole setup.

The sanctuary itself had been converted into our own gym and was very nice for what three people could use. Behind it, near the front door of the sanctuary, was the entryway, which led to the bell tower. The bell tower was used by Mark and Sophie as a base of operations for his vigilante work.

Coming out into the hallway, I headed toward the kitchen area, expecting at any moment to be warned away by a giggle or repressed moan. Instead, I was shocked to find Sophie in bed, snoring lightly while the other half of the bed was empty. Checking the clock, I was shocked to find that Mark wasn't in bed with her.

Heading back toward my room, I heard a muffled sound coming from the gym. Sticking my head in the door, I saw Mark kneeling over one of his practice bags for martial arts, blasting it with rapid-fire punches. I could see, even in the dim light of the moon filtering through the windows—Mark had replaced the original broken stained glass with triple-paned, clear panels—the dark shine of blood against the blue of the bag and the pale of his knuckles.

"What's going on?" I asked, coming closer. It was then that I knew how upset he was, because one of Mark's traits is an almost inhuman sensitivity to everything around him, details that you wouldn't even believe he would note and react to, giving him an air of super freaky precognition or something. This time, though, Mark didn't hear me, so I waited until there was a pause in his self-mutilation before repeating myself. "Mark, what's going on?"

His head jerked up, and I could see that not all of the moisture on his face was due to sweat. Tears were coursing down his face, and the look he gave me was so full of agony that my own heart threatened to break. Instead of answering, he stopped his punching and wiped at his eyes. "Nothing," he said finally, while I watched blood ooze from his knuckles and trickle down his hand, "just a hard patrol."

I went over to the wall, where there were some hand-held foam shields that we sometimes used, and grabbed one, bringing it over and sitting down. Even in summer, the mats we used were cold at night, and I was wearing thin silk pajamas. "You know you're full of shit," I said softly, "and Sophie's going to tell you the same thing when she sees your knuckles in the morning."

Mark couldn't reply, so I wrapped my blanket around me and looked at him evenly. "Tell me about it."

He shook his head, his hair tossing from side to side. He'd grown it out as part of his disguise as Matt Bylur, and it looked good on him. The chestnut brown mane was regal on him, and I know Sophie enjoyed it. She'd told me so herself. "There's some things that you don't need to be burdened with," he replied to my question, "some dark corners that you don't need to look into."

I nodded, not arguing. There were some things that Mark had done, that he knew about, that were so dark that I couldn't disagree with his statement. He'd once told me during a lighter moment when I'd pressed him about his past, that he had his own little timeshare in hell all laid out for him when he passed on.

Perhaps that was the difference between me and Sophie. She'd be willing to go to those places with him, maybe all the way to hell itself. I guess I would too, if Sophie asked me to. For Mark, however, no. I loved him as a brother and as Sophie's husband, but not that much. Instead, I offered what comfort I could. "It must have been very bad, for you to send Sophie to bed alone."

"It was," he replied, grabbing a towel and wiping his face. For the first time, he winced and noticed the damage to his hands. "Shit. Think you can help me with the peroxide?"

In the gym we kept a small medical kit—not much, really, just some Band-

Aids, cotton balls, and a large bottle of hydrogen peroxide. It was useful with the training that Mark and Sophie did, where small cuts were common. Holding his hand over the tiny bar-style sink he'd had installed, I poured the liquid. We watched silently as it bubbled and fizzed angrily, like it was upset with him for causing such damage to his body as well. "You sure this is all you need?"

"I'll wrap them in gauze before I go to bed to keep the sheets clean," Mark replied. He looked at the ruined, pulpy mass that was his knuckles and sighed. "I wish it didn't have to be this way."

"I know," I said. "I wish there was a way I could help you more."

"You do a lot," Mark said with a rueful smirk. "You free up my time to do what I really need to do, and you help by being the public face. Although Sophie and I both wish we could have been there when you took down Traylor yesterday."

He had a point there. For all of Mark's direct action, my role did some good as well. "It was quite satisfying. You sure you don't want to tag along for the press conference tomorrow? You could be my driver, my maintenance man and my personal chef."

"There are a lot of roles I fill, but no thanks. I think tomorrow will be all about Sophie and me. Maybe after a night's sleep and some thinking, making love with my wife won't feel so damn dirty."

I patted him on the shoulder. "I don't know all the details of what you guys do, but I can tell you one thing from looking at my best friend's face. Nothing you two do can ever be considered dirty. If anything, you guys elevate the whole idea. Now go get some sleep."

Maybe Mark drew strength from my words. Maybe he was just tired and the punches had let him drain the worst of the poison from his soul. I didn't know, but some of the pained look was gone from his face, and he was even able to muster a ghost of a smile. "You too. Unless you plan on sucking down a gallon of yerba mate with your breakfast."

* * *

Mark's prediction of my being sleepy was dead on, even after he had made me a super-strong green tea protein smoothie before he went to bed, chilling it in the fridge for me in the morning with a note attached. "Thanks. Sorry there's no hot breakfast, but if you want, there are Pop Tarts in the cupboard."

25

Eight hours later, I was running on fumes standing outside the first of the community centers that MJT was opening. Rubbing my eyes, I smiled wanly at the General Manager of the Spartans, who, along with three of his players, was dressed in a jersey. He smiled back with an understanding expression. "You doing all right, Miss Williams?"

I nodded, shrugging. "Long night, you know how it is. I'm sure your head coach feels the same way the week of a hard game."

"Why do you think he's not here?" the GM said with a chuckle. "He's getting an hour of sleep before the team starts film and practice this afternoon. Man spends five months per year running on three hours of sleep per night. I'm surprised he doesn't have a mental episode once each season."

I was surprised when another car pulled up, and City Councilman Patrick McCaffery got out. On the job just a few weeks after the shakeup in city politics that had been caused by the downfall of Owen Lynch, Pat McCaffery was a bit of an enigma. Charismatic, he'd easily won his recall election, which by itself wasn't a problem. The problem, at least the one that concerned Mark and me, was that his district included The Playground and other high-crime, corrupt areas. In the past twenty years, nobody had won an election from that district without criminal backing.

Stepping out of the car, he was dressed for the occasion, wearing a Spartans t-shirt along with blue jeans and holding a Spartans jacket. "Sorry for the late arrival," he said, shaking hands with the General Manager. "How are you doing, Gene?"

"Not bad, Patrick," he said with a smile. "Tabitha Williams, I'd like to introduce you to Patrick McCaffery. I know he's got a new job, but I'll always think of Patrick as the kid I had to throw out of the stadium on nearly a weekly basis back when I was head of security at the old Municipal Stadium."

"Oh?" I asked, smiling. "Were you a bit of a rule breaker back in the day?"

McCaffery laughed and held out his hand. "I break rules nowadays too, Miss Williams. But I've tried to at least reform the reasons I break them. I used to just want to get in for autographs and maybe snag a bit of free swag from the laundry room. Now, I'm trying to make the city better."

"I remember. I saw your posters around the city," I said, smiling professionally. Up close, I had to admit that Patrick McCaffery was pretty cute. A little over six feet, he was bigger than Mark by about twenty or thirty pounds, I'd say

26

coming in at a solid looking two hundred and ten pounds or so. With black hair and green eyes, he was definitely handsome. Thinking back to my comment the day before about cloning Mark with black hair, I could do worse. "I seem to also remember the local news loving your speeches."

"Not so much the news as one particular editor at NBC," he replied with a cocky grin. He knew he was handsome and wasn't shy about acknowledging it. "She sort of has a thing for me."

"Along with half the cheerleaders," the General Manager joked. One of his players, the starting linebacker who had gotten All-Pro awards the year before, came over after wrapping up a news interview and whispered in his ear. "Sorry, the press wants a comment from me before the ceremony begins. Just a moment."

With me and McCaffery left alone, I was able to take a closer look at him, and I realized why he was carrying a Spartans jacket. His right arm was covered in tattoos, some of them ones I recognized from the training that Mark had given me. "Interesting ink, Councilman," I said. "Where'd you pick all that up?"

McCaffery quickly pulled his jacket on and shook his head. "A reminder of a lot of stupid decisions when I was a teenager," he said. "I keep them to remind myself of not making those same mistakes. Still, not exactly the sort of stuff you sport during a City Council meeting."

"I can see that. So how'd you turn things around? You're not much older than I am, right? Those bad decisions couldn't have been all that long ago," I asked, thinking. "Not that I don't have some bad decisions in my past too."

"We all do, Miss Williams," McCaffery replied. "I don't have time to go into it now, though, but if you really want to know, maybe we can get together at either my office or yours? MJT has been doing some amazing community outreach work, and I'd like to talk about ways we could maybe work together and maximize our efforts."

"I don't know. I just had a meeting with Bishop Traylor that started the same way."

McCaffery leaned his head back and laughed. "Yes, I've heard about that. He came by my office to protest and see if he could weasel his way into a podium slot for today's activities. I told him to take your advice and get the hell out of town."

"Interesting choice of words."

"I speak honestly. People only say I have charisma because they agree with

27

what I say," McCaffery replied with a smile.

The press conference-slash-ceremony began, with most of the speeches being made by the Spartans. They were the celebrities, after all, and the local media ate it up. The crowd was especially loud when some of the Spartan cheerleaders came out to lead the assembled group in a few cheers and put on a short little dance performance. The biggest applause of all was for McCaffery, however, who was called to the microphone by the Spartans' MVP quarterback.

"Ladies and gentlemen, I'm not here today as a city councilman," he said, starting his speech. "I'm not even here as a Spartan fan, even though I've been cheering for these guys since I was five. I'm here as that five-year-old, who was born in Mercy General, not two miles from where we stand today, and grew up not in a loving home, but in a series of foster homes and orphanages. I stand here as the kid who did a lot more than just sneak into Municipal Stadium, as Gene fondly recalls. I stand here as the one percent. Not the one percent that a lot of people associate with the term, but the one percent of kids who somehow claw and scratch and climb their way out of places like where I started. I'm proud today, not just of our team, the Spartans, but people like the one I'm going to call up here in just a minute. People who know that there is more to making money than just seeing how large you can make your bank account."

"When I first thought of running for city council, I was inspired to make a difference. I saw that by getting out there and putting your money where your mouth is, you can turn things around. Sadly, he's not here today, but his shoes have been more than adequately filled by his protégé. Marcus Smiley may be gone—and I hope he's enjoying his retirement, or whatever he's doing, since he cannot be here—but we have with us today the lady who is footing most of the bill for this wonderful project, Tabitha Williams of MJT Consolidated."

My reception was polite, but nowhere near as enthusiastic as that for the local celebrities. I was dressed more casually than I normally did for work, in jeans and a t-shirt that had come fresh from the printer's that morning with the logo for the new community centers superimposed over the Spartan logo and the rather simple logo we'd designed for MJT. "Thank you for the flattering introduction, Councilman McCaffery," I said, taking the microphone. "Honestly, I feel a bit nervous being up here after such a great speaker. It's kind of like being the act that follows Bruce

28

Springsteen at our own Summer Ultrasonic Festival."

"You look a hell of a lot better than Springsteen, though!" someone in the crowd yelled, which got a few chuckles that doubled when I visibly blushed. The jokester got some boos as well, which also got a laugh.

"Thanks, but I hope to be more than that," I replied, earning a few smiles from the ladies in attendance. "Councilman McCaffery is right, I'm no Marcus Smiley. I just hope that I can continue his dream of making this city into a city we can all be proud to live in again, a place where everyone has the opportunity to make the most of themselves. We've temporarily shaken off some of the shackles of crime and corruption, and now we are faced with a tremendous choice. We could do the easy thing and drift back toward the way things were. After all, we've done it before. The path is so easy; all it takes is stabbing a few friends in the back or turning away when we see evil acts being done for our short-term safety or profit. Sadly, as a city, that pattern of cleanup and then a new generation of corruption seems to be cynically cyclical."

"That's one path we have before us. Or, we can take another path, a path that is going to be harder, one that takes a lot of risk. That's the path of fighting our way out of the darkness we've been in and back into the light, into a new future. It's somewhat ironic that we have with us today members of the Spartans, a group known most famously for actually losing a battle. But you know what happened less than a year later? The Spartan forces won and led a rejuvenated Greece into a new renaissance. I say that our own losing battle is over, and we're coming into the new battle, the one we can win, and the one that will lead this city, our city, into a new era. Thank you."

The applause that greeted my comments was a lot louder than when I began, and I had to smile when I saw Patrick McCaffery applauding when I stepped away from the microphone. "Nice speech," he said in my ear as the Spartans General Manager stepped back up to wrap up the conference. "Next time I need someone to speak with me, I'll give you a call."

"You don't have my phone number," I replied, causing him to laugh. He looked at me with a subtle challenge to his look, which I returned just as politely. He may have been handsome, but I know I'm decent-looking myself. There was no need to fawn all over him, after all.

29

"Well, maybe this is just my way of asking for it," he said after a second. "Of course, if you want me to just call you at your office, that's fine too."

I looked in his green eyes, which sparkled with humor and just a bit of sexiness, and made a decision. What the hell, it was only a cellphone number. I reached into my pocket and pulled out a business card and a pen, scribbling on the back. "Call me Tabby. And here."

Chapter 4
Patrick

After the press conference, I hopped back in the car I'd borrowed to drive back to the office. I'd ridden the RIST to work that morning, and besides, there was no way I'd turn up at a press event in my real car, not with the way it looked. While being a city councilman in a town where the mayor and deputy mayor have most of the power isn't quite as stressful as, say, being a US congressman, it's a lot more difficult than my last job, bartending. Public perception was important.

I was distracted, though, as I tried to sit down at my computer and work my way through the pile of emails that were waiting for me. I was supposed to be able to hire two staffers to help me with my job, but coming from no party and with no political background, I was still floundering. I was about two hundred unread emails behind, and taking a few hours out for the press conference didn't help.

Neither the local Republicans nor Democrats were willing to help me either, as my grassroots campaign had upset their handpicked candidates as well. Not to mention my positions didn't quite jive with either party. I was far too liberal on the social issues for the Republicans, while the Democrats saw my personal opposition to the city's unions and gun laws as being poisonous to them. They didn't seem to understand that it wasn't the idea of unions in general I was opposed to. I was opposed to the particular unions that had a lot of power in the city, as they were just as corrupt as the Confederation and Owen Lynch's group. So far, the biggest offer for help I'd gotten was from the local branch of the Liberty Bell Party, which I had to look up on the internet to see if they really existed or not.

The city's unions were in the forefront of my mind as I saw that Francine Berkowitz had sent me an email stating that she was due to come by my office about twenty minutes after I read the message. "I've got to hire a fucking assistant," I muttered to myself as I thought about pulling off the gifted Spartans jersey that Gene had given me as part of the press conference. It was emblazoned with my name across the back, along with the number of my favorite Spartans player from my childhood, number 42, Tim "Firetruck" Follows. "Fuck it, if she wants to complain that I'm getting illegal swag, I'll write Gene a check for the jersey."

While I waited for Francine to arrive, my mind kept going back to Tabby Williams. Beautiful wasn't the beginning of words I would use to describe her, with her flame-red hair and creamy skin. She had dressed a lot more modestly for the press conference than she did for most of her press coverage, but she was still the sexiest woman I'd talked to in a long time.

I worked in a bar, and as Tabby had noticed, not all of my associations when I was younger were with the right crowd. I'd covered a lot of the ink up with other designs, but it took time and money to change, and I didn't yet have the money for a full sleeve on my right arm. Thank God I was only stupid enough to get the tats on one arm.

Tabby Williams was smart. I knew that from the research I'd done on her. It's not that I'm a weirdo stalker—I did the research strictly because I wanted to make sure that I was lending my name to a worthy group. When Gene gave me a call and told me about the program the Spartans were doing with MJT, he'd done me a favor. He wanted me to have a good start to my political career, and being involved with a good charitable program was a great leg up.

I knew about the scam charity work people like Bishop Traylor did, and I refused to participate in that sort of fleecing, so I'd done what research I could on her and MJT. Everything I read about Tabby was impressive: a good MBA, and she worked hard at her job prior to becoming head of MJT, with admittedly a bit of luck meeting Marcus Smiley when she did. All in all, she was smart and gorgeous, and she had a dedication to improving the city that hit all my buttons.

I also knew a bit about things she didn't want the public to know about, such as her seduction by Scott Pressman. Like I said, I have a lot of bad decisions to atone

31

for.

I was still thinking about Tabby when a knock at my door interrupted me, and I looked up at the clock, noticing the time. I'd been zoning out for nearly fifteen minutes. "Come in."

Francine Berkowitz—or as I like to call her, Berkowitch, and sometimes Berkobitch—is pretty much everything that Tabby Williams isn't. With a face only a mother could love, she had connived and politicked her way to the top of the city's unions by collecting a list of black marks and dark deeds on each and every person who could be a threat to her power. I knew she would be visiting me eventually, considering who I was. Having a member of the city council in her pocket was useful, after all.

"Hello, Ms. Berkowitz," I said, getting out of my desk chair. The office had sort of old-fashioned chairs that looked like they belonged in a rich man's study or library, appropriate for semi-casual meetings. They were a relic of the old councilmember who'd been indicted for bribery, and I hadn't taken the time to move them or the horrendous coffee table out. At least they were useful this time, as I indicated for her to sit before turning to my little office fridge and grabbing two Jolt Colas. "Care for a drink?"

"Uh, no thank you," she said once she eyed my offering. My tastes are unique. "I must admit, Councilman McCaffery, that I didn't expect a novelty cola. Usually they serve tea or coffee at things like this."

"Forgive my inexperience. I'm still breaking in my office chair," I replied. "In fact, twice last week the security guards stopped me, thinking I must be some sort of guest, not knowing that I work here. So tell me, what brings you by?"

"I wanted to offer my assistance, of course," Francine practically oozed, perching herself on the chair. She ran a hand over the upholstery, which I had to admit was nice, if not my style. "I had such a good time picking out this pattern for your predecessor. I was sort of hoping things could be equally magnanimous between us."

"Considering that Harry Vickers is currently in federal custody awaiting trial, I'm not sure that's a good thing—although I hear he's scraped up his bail money," I replied with a laugh. "Considering he was dirty and all."

"Harry was dirty, but so is most of the rest of the council," Francine said,

32

shrugging off my comment. "He was only stupid and dirty. I'd hate to see such a bright young superstar as yourself make the same mistakes he did."

Damn, the bitch didn't mince words. I wondered if I should set up my office for recording conversations like Nixon did, just to protect my ass. "And what mistakes were those?"

"For one, he didn't have enough buffers between himself and the money he took. Secondly, and probably more importantly, he didn't play ball with the right people."

Spinning the cap on my Jolt Cola, I took a long swig before replying. I wanted to make sure I chose my words very carefully, just in case Francine was trying to get me to say something incriminating as well. I may not have been recording, but that didn't mean she wasn't. "And by the right people, I assume you mean you, of course."

"Among others," she said. "Patrick, this city has been rotten to the core for generations, and the actions of one man, especially one with the unknown background of Marcus Smiley, is like pissing into a hurricane. You're just going to end up covered in stench if you try."

Again, I chose my words very carefully. "So what is your advice?"

"I saw your little press conference on the television before I came over. Very noble of you, by the way. I suspect that, regardless of the buildings that MJT is donating or footing the bill for, they're going to need extensive renovations to be able to pass city codes for fire safety and other issues."

"I suspect so. I haven't talked about the details on that with Miss Williams yet," I said, taking another drink of cola. "Why?"

"Well, this city has a long and rich history of our construction workers and renovation experts having very strong union ties," Berkowitz said, smiling. "I would advise you to of course use only qualified unionized workers for the renovations. After all, better safe than sorry."

I nodded, understanding her threat. In addition to the construction union being under her control, Berkowitz was also head of the union that represented most of the city's workers, including the fire department and the city inspectors. If we were going to get our permits, we'd need their approval. "I see. Well, I'll have to talk this over with Miss Williams, of course. MJT and the Spartans are running things. I'm just providing the political oomph to make sure we get good coverage of this."

"Of course, Councilman. I mean, such a position could be a coup for you. What is it, a two-year term that you have until the next regular election for another five years? Why, you'd be the sort of young face that the city would love to see climb the ladder of politics, free from the constraints of either the Republicans or the Democrats. I would give you one more piece of advice—for free, of course."

"Of course."

"If you do decide to turn this into something more than a gig in between bartending jobs, go and get those tats lasered off. Especially the ones that say you used to affiliate with the Confederation. I doubt the state Democrats would appreciate those."

She stood up and smiled at me, but there was no warmth in that smile, just the bared teeth of a shark that knew it was circling prey. "Good day, Councilman. I'll be in touch."

I watched Berkowitz go and drained the rest of my Jolt in one long pull. I looked at the bottle she had left unopened on the table and put it back in the mini fridge with a sigh. I had to before I sucked the whole bottle down. I couldn't be cruising on caffeine that night. I had work to do, and I couldn't afford a caffeine crash at one in the morning. Sighing, I sat back down at my computer, then pushed the keyboard away.

"Fuck this," I muttered to myself. While reaching for my phone, I pulled out the card that Tabby had given me with her phone number written on the back. Dialing quickly, I wondered if the increased heart rate I was feeling was due to fear from Berkowitz's visit, the caffeine going through me from the Jolt, or nervousness from talking to Tabby again.

"Hello?" a slightly musical, sexy as hell voice said in my ear. Damn, I hadn't noticed that the last time.

"Hello, Miss Williams?" I said, trying to be professional. "It's Patrick McCaffery."

"Oh. Hello, Councilman," Tabby replied. "Please, though, just call me Tabby. What can I do for you?"

The potential answers that ran through my mind were staggering, but I kept it professional. "Well, I kind of need your help."

34

"With what?" she asked. "If you don't mind, I'm going to put you on speaker. I'm heading home early today, taking some work with me. I'm in my car."

"All right, I wouldn't want you in an accident," I replied.

"Okay, so what's up?"

"I'm drowning in emails, and I'm in serious need of an assistant," I said, hoping my real life need would lead to a reason to see her again. "Now, you've been on your job just about as long as I have here at City Hall."

"About three weeks longer, actually," Tabby replied, "but yes, I'm pretty new at this too. You don't have any staff?"

"None at all," I replied honestly, "but apparently I have the budget for two staffers. I asked one of my new colleagues—one of the ones who will actually talk to me—and he said that by tradition, the old staff is supposed to help with handovers or even fill in until the new staff is hired, but they kind of just quit when Harry Vickers was arrested. A lot of people think they ran out of town before the District Attorney got to them as well. So I've been doing this by the seat of my pants."

"Ouch. Well, I don't know a lot about it, but I'll talk to my assistant. She's a real pro at this sort of thing, and she probably knows someone in the city who you can bring in quickly. Although, if I'm not careful, she'd possibly just quit working for me and go over to you. She's into the crusader types."

"Crusader types, huh? Is that what I am?" I asked with a laugh. "Well, I've been called worse. All right. Also, while I have you on the line, would you mind if we got together for a working lunch to discuss this project? I had a visit from a certain union leader, and I think you'd like to be brought into the loop."

"Of course," Tabby said without missing a beat. "How about my office the day after tomorrow? I know I'm asking you to come to me, but there's a place nearby that does great delivery, and you'd love it. If you do, I promise you my assistant will be able to help you with finding some staff for you too."

"Deal. So, it's a lunch date then. Day after tomorrow. Say, twelve thirty?"

"Date, huh? Why, Councilman, you do move fast," Tabby said with a laugh, and I have to admit I blushed. She had a very sexy laugh. "But yeah, twelve thirty is fine. See you then."

That night, just as the clock of St. Timothy's Church tolled in the distance, I stood up from the roof of the convenience store I was crouched on in the Fillmore Heights district. It's confusing to newbies to our city that there are two areas of town called Heights. On one hand there is The Heights, a very rich neighborhood that had been through gentrification about twenty years ago. With lots of big, expensive homes and a few McMansions, The Heights was bordered by Tabby's house, Mount Zion, although some would argue that Zion was actually included.

On the other hand, on the opposite side of town from The Heights both geographically and economically, was Fillmore Heights. As dangerous as The Heights was safe, Fillmore Heights was the sort of neighborhood you didn't walk after dark unless you were either armed, stupidly brave, or in a group of at least four—preferably all of the above. The newspapers had more than once reported on a poor schmuck who had mixed up a friend telling them The Heights and Fillmore Heights, and had died because of it.

Standing on the roof of the low store, I could see a good chunk of Fillmore Avenue, which was the namesake of Fillmore Heights. The city bus that lumbered down the street was empty, the sides covered in graffiti.

Further down the block, I saw movement, which I expected. My targets for the evening were coming to their meeting spot. I was ready.

One of the things that makes Fillmore Heights so dangerous is the gang activity. Fillmore Avenue, at least the northeast quarter of it, was controlled by one of the most dangerous, the 88s. So-called because of the Neo-Nazi symbolism involving the number, they weren't skinheads. They were, however, white supremacists who had formed in the late nineties after a wave of other gangs, spearheaded by the Latin Kings and the Gangster Disciples, tore Fillmore Heights apart in violent turf warfare with the already established Familias and Crips. The white kids of Fillmore, caught between four ethnic gangs that didn't like them in the least, were slowly pushed until a charismatic leader, Bryan Sweeney, formed a gang of only white kids to fight back. Quickly adopting a white supremacist ideology, they countered the larger numbers of

36

their rivals with a ferocity and bloodthirsty lack of restraint that stunned even the hardcore gangsters in the other sets. Soon, the 88s had not only secured their original neighborhood, but they had expanded their territory, taking over most of the northeast side of Fillmore Heights.

About ten years after their founding, however, the 88s had become just as corrupted as the gangs they had fought against—running drugs, protection rackets, and every other form of gang bullshit you can think of. By this point, they were nothing more than racist punks, the type I despised more than any other for personal reasons.

Pulling my face mask down, I kept my eyes peeled as 88s began to assemble in the parking lot of the convenience store, which had the unfortunate luck of being at 8988 Fillmore Avenue. Finally, at eleven fifteen or so, the group for that night was assembled. I listened as they talked normal gang bullshit—nothing important, but I still kept my ears peeled. Two of them went inside to help themselves to free beer, which the poor owner, a Korean immigrant who was barely tolerated by the 88s since his protection money was so high, let them take for free. Better to write off the six-packs on his taxes than to have his entire store destroyed.

There were about six of them outside when I pulled my two sticks from their holders on my back. Similar to an escrima stick, each was actually made of aluminum, with a nasty surprise inside if I needed it, a seven-inch-long, spring-loaded spike I could deploy with the push of two buttons on the handle. So far, in the few weeks I'd been doing this, I hadn't used the spikes yet.

Muttering a quick prayer, I jumped from the top of the building onto the nearest Eighty-Eight, using him to buffer my fall while at the same time taking him out of the fight. Rolling, I swung my left hand out and nailed another Eighty-Eight in the kneecap, with wonderful results as I heard a bone crack and the man collapse in a howl of pain.

The rest of the fight was somewhat of a blur, mainly because someone did hit me in the back of the head pretty hard at one point. I could feel blood trickling down the back of my neck as I stood in the parking lot, sweat and a bit of blood dripping off my mask from another cut over my eyebrow that went all the way to the bone. Putting my sticks away, I looked inside, where the owner was picking up the phone to call the cops. Before he could finish dialing, I took off running to my car, parked three blocks away.

What can I say? Marcus Smiley wasn't the only person inspiring me to try and make a difference.

* * *

Mark

That night, after dinner, Sophie and I were able to get some alone time. "Are you sure your hands are okay?" she asked me as we lay on our bed. It was a nice gesture from Tabby that Sophie and I kept the so-called master bedroom of the house, even though hers was still pretty large as well. We didn't invite people over often, so there wasn't a need for an elaborate deception as to who had what in the house. We just lived as we needed.

The bedroom wasn't super large; we didn't really feel the need for a huge space, but in a nod to Sophie's desire for a comfortable bed, we did have a very large, custom-made mattress with high thread count, Egyptian cotton sheets and an organic merino wool bedspread, all custom made to fit the bed. I was rubbing massage oil between my hands before rubbing down Sophie's back, which glistened in the dim lights of the room.

"They feel fine, really," I said. "It looks a lot worse than it feels, that's for sure. Most of it is just where some of the blood scabbed under the skin, and that will take a few days to work its way out and fade. But I do have to remember to wear rubber gloves until they heal when I cook dinner. The lemon juice on my left hand wasn't too fun."

Sophie turned her head to the side and looked at me out of the corner of one eye. "It was kind of funny to watch you hopping around and muttering curses as Tabby and I tried not to laugh."

"You still did anyway," I noted, working my thumbs in alternating circles down her spine. I was straddling Sophie's upper thighs, both of us wearing nothing as we rejoiced in each other's presence. My erection was already halfway up, nestled in between the soft swells of her butt. Still, I wasn't ready or needing sex just yet. I wanted to focus on Sophie first. She was, and is, the light of my life, and the reason I can do everything I do. "In fact, I think I saw a bit of milk dribble from the side of

38

your mouth when I whacked my hand on the countertop as I was hopping around."

"It's just funny, that's all," Sophie said, before a sigh, groan and giggle all mixed together to interrupt her words. "I've seen you do what seems like superhuman things, fighting multiple men like it's nothing, and then you get reduced to cursing and even, I think, a tear or two from some lemon in a boo-boo."

"Careful there, my love. You keep making fun of me, and you'll find your backside still isn't too tender for a spanking."

Sophie wiggled her hips, which sent a course of electricity through my cock, causing it to harden some more. "I can tell. Then again, maybe your ass isn't too tender for a spanking either."

I leaned over and kissed her shoulder, nuzzling against her silky soft hair. "If you want, my love."

It was perhaps one of the best parts about being with Sophie. Being with her, we'd both blossomed in self-confidence, which sounds weird considering that I had such a reputation as an Alpha Male type before meeting her. But being in her arms, knowing she both accepted me and depended on me, protected me as well as being protected by me, we could both let go of our inhibitions.

Sophie turned her head a little more and smiled. "Really?"

"Really. Just . . . one thing."

"What's that?"

"After last night, well, no more using *Mistress*, okay?"

* * *

Mark

The next morning, as I prepared breakfast for everyone, Tabby came in with a grin on her face. "Hey, guess what?"

"You won the lottery," Sophie quipped, wearing the yoga pants and t-shirt she preferred for indoor work. She didn't look like a normal housewife, that was for sure, but more like some sort of fitness instructor who just happened to be doing laundry or dusting the furniture before her day began.

Tabby, who was wearing one of her business suits, shook her head. While I know Sophie didn't miss wearing the overly constricting and sexualized suits, I had to admit that a part of me missed seeing her dressed up as the naughtiest of secretaries. "Nah, Tabby decided she wants to run off to Tibet and become the Dalai Lama's interior decorator."

Tabby stuck her tongue out at both of us, a familiar reply when we joked with her, and one that said she was in a good mood. "No, but turn on the TV. Seems we're inspiring people in more ways than one."

I reached over and flipped on the small television on the counter, a leftover from Tabby's old apartment that we just didn't want to throw out. It was too new, for one, and it fit perfectly underneath the cabinet in the kitchen as well. Jabbing the button, I turned the channel to the local NBC affiliate, which was Tabby's recent favorite due to their favorable coverage of MJT.

"Wait for it, they said they'd repeat it at the top of the hour," she said. I glanced up at the clock and saw it was five minutes to seven, and finished up breakfast. I plated the eggs with grilled mushrooms and eggplant, along with a kale smoothie for Sophie's Vitamin K needs. "Oh, here it is."

"Our top news this morning: it seems our city has gained another new public figure," Don Thompson, one half of the lead anchors, said. He had been on the air with NBC for nearly a decade, and had been one of the first anchors to break the color barrier in the city. I had met him once when I was Marcus Smiley, and I thought he was a pretty good journalist. His trademark was his smooth voice—a bit more academic than Billy Dee Williams, but still silky smooth. I momentarily compared him to Gerald Traylor's voice, and thought that while they had some similarities, Don Thompson sounded much more calm and educated.

The screen shot changed as Thompson's voice narrated. *"The Fillmore Heights neighborhood is no stranger to gang fights and violence, especially from the notorious group known as the 88s. Here, at one of their favorite hangouts, a group of 88s encountered something new as a masked vigilante seemingly dropped out of nowhere. Security camera footage . . ."*

I tuned out Don's voice as I watched the multiple angles of security video. The attacker had come off the roof, that was for sure, and attacked with a lot of ferocity. I was slightly impressed by what I saw, but there was a lot that worried me.

"This idiot's going to get himself killed," I said as I saw him stagger under a shot to the back of the head from one of the last 88s. "He's brave, I'll give him that, but he's going to get himself killed."

I reached over and switched off the TV when the story shifted to news in Washington, turning around. "I understand your enthusiasm, Tabby. It's good to see that someone is trying to do something positive for their neighborhood, but taking on a mass of 88s while swinging around nothing but a couple of aluminum batons is stupid, even when you're as good as I am. And in what I saw, he's not that good."

"How would you have done it?" Tabby asked, curious. Sophie just hid her smile, knowing that while her best friend knew the results of my nighttime actions, she didn't exactly know the details, and for good reason.

"For one, I wouldn't have just dropped down with nothing but two sticks," I replied, twirling a bid of eggplant around on my plate. "I probably would have started with either a smoke grenade or a flash-bang if I didn't mind blowing out the windows on that Circle K. Anyone that was still up after that I might have taken out with the sticks, but honestly I wouldn't have dropped from the roof. There's too much of a chance of twisting your ankle or blowing out your knee, at which point you're pretty well screwed."

I didn't tell her the unabashed truth, which is that if I wanted to take down a gang like the 88s, I wouldn't have done it with non-lethal force either. I'd dealt with them when I worked for Sal Giordano, and they were one of the roughest gangs in Fillmore. I probably would have gone in with both Glocks pulled if I had to, or maybe an old-fashioned charge of a pickup truck through the herd. Better yet, an AK-47. As the saying goes, when you absolutely, positively have to kill every last motherfucker in the room, accept no substitutions.

"In any case, I hope he doesn't get himself killed," Tabby said, scraping the last of her breakfast onto her spoon and swallowing quickly. "Now, hate to eat and run, but I have a lunch meeting with a city councilman today, and I should probably get some work done beforehand. I'll call you guys if anything comes up."

"Oh, which councilman?" Sophie asked with a grin. "It wouldn't happen to be the cute Pat McCaffery you were telling us about last night?"

"Yeah," Tabby said sheepishly. "I know, I know, he's got Confederation tats, but you said yourself, Mark, that he wasn't active that you knew about any longer."

"Still, keep your eyes and ears open and your Spidey senses sharp," I warned her. "If you have any concerns, give me a call."

Like a whirlwind, Tabby was out the door, and we heard the rumble as her

Mercedes started up and pulled out of the garage. Sophie looked at me with bemusement. "Okay, big brother. Before you start, remember who you are. I married a former hitman, correct?"

Sometimes, I can't win.

Chapter 6
Tabby

The deliveryman got to the office with his steaming containers of Chinese food right at twelve twenty-five, refusing the tip I offered him. As the steam rose out of the bag and made my stomach rumble, he grinned and waved his hands, backing away slowly while displaying almost unnaturally white and shiny teeth.

"Any delivery here is a pleasure," he said, referring to the investment MJT had made in his family's restaurant. In fact, the deliveryman, a nice nineteen-year-old kid named James, had been able to start taking night classes at the community college because of it, since it allowed his family to hire another delivery person for night shift as well as expand their services. "If it wasn't that my Dad knew it would be a waste of time, he'd not even charge you guys."

"Still, James, you came all the way down here in less than twenty minutes," I said. "Come on, at least a few bucks?"

"Nope," James replied, stepping back and toward the door. I knew better than to follow him; one time he'd actually run down the stairs to avoid the tip. I wouldn't give up, though. I'm kind of hard-headed like that. "But if you really want, next time I'll send my sister. Lin's the sort who'd pocket a five without telling Dad."

James disappeared out the door while Vanessa sat at her desk, amused. "You do that at least once a week," she said when the door closed. "I thought you'd have learned by now."

"Come on, Vanessa. I'm getting paid an obscene amount of money to run this place. The least I can do is help the kid," I replied. "Gratitude or not, he deserves an extra little bit for risking the lunchtime traffic to get the shrimp here while it's still hot and crispy. He's on a fifty cc scooter, for God's sake."

"You never know how people will react to generosity," Vanessa replied. "You remember the story about the CEO who raised all his employees pay to at least seventy thousand a year as a gesture of income equality or something? It made the national news a while back, a software company, I think."

I turned away from the door after closing it behind me. "Yeah, I remember something about it. Why?"

"Did you know the average amount of happiness and worker satisfaction in his company actually went down after that? Seemed a lot of people started worrying about if they were really earning their keep, and then there was jealousy and a lot of other issues cropping up. He actually had to rent out a room in his house to make ends' meet for a while, because he had so much turnover and problems that he couldn't get work done and was losing money. I guess what I'm saying is, I know you feel bad about the money you're making. But it doesn't help to spread it around so much. That is, unless of course, you want to buy a very expensive gift for Secretary's Day. I hear that gold is nice, but platinum is all the rage this season for the well-respected executive assistant."

I turned and looked at Vanessa with a smirk. "Okay, okay, point taken, joke noted, and comment filed away for April. Just don't be surprised when you get something that is platinum coated. Now all I'm missing is a city councilman to share this food with."

"Just remember the General Tso's chicken set is mine," Vanessa said as I heard footsteps on the stairs leading up to the third floor. I was slightly surprised; I'd expected him to use the freight elevator. It was very old school, and you had to pull the security gate down, but it had that sort of retro feel that I personally loved using, especially when my legs were tired. "Your cute date is here."

Rolling my eyes, I took a moment to admit to myself that yes, Patrick McCaffery was cute, and yes, I'd had much worse-looking lunch meetings. I went over to Vanessa's desk and pretended to be not looking like I was waiting for the door to open when he came in. "Sorry, I know I'm a minute or two late. I didn't realize that you had a gym downstairs. I got caught up in watching someone do some pretty impressive stuff with the kettlebells. Well, that and I ran into the delivery kid coming down the stairs."

"Then you're right on time, it seems," I replied. I opened the bag and took out Vanessa's lunch. "Vanessa, while I set up the table in the other room, can you give Councilman McCaffery those hints on how to find someone like you to help him out? I'm afraid if you don't, we're going to be failing in our civic duty."

"Of course," Vanessa replied, taking out a three-page document from her desk drawer. "Councilman, I typed this up for you this morning, actually."

"First off, it's Patrick. The only time someone calls me Councilman is usually when I'm not looking forward to the rest of the conversation. As for the document . . ." I heard, before going into my office and setting up the table. It was the same table, I noted, that Bishop Traylor and I had our meeting at. I considered shifting to the conference table but decided against it. The chairs there were too uncomfortable for anything other than straight business meetings, and I didn't want that.

As I arranged the Styrofoam containers, I pondered to myself if I was really meeting with Patrick because he was a member of the City Council, or because of his looks. I had to admit that since Scott Pressman had fucked up my head pretty well, I hadn't been on any dates at all, a record for me since I was fourteen or so. Hell, I was even seeing a guy while getting ready to defend my thesis.

But Patrick ticked a lot of the marks on what I like in guys. Tall, fit, and yes, he had a bad boy vibe about him, and it was more than just the tattoos on his right arm. At the same time, though, he wasn't exactly the same as some of the guys I'd dated. For one, he actually had a job.

I was trying to decide whether to offer Patrick the plastic cutlery or if he could use chopsticks when there was a knock on my office door, and Patrick came in with a laugh. "Thanks, Vanessa, I'll give them a call this afternoon. You've got my unabated thanks."

"I'll remember that next time my property taxes come due," Vanessa replied deadpan, causing Patrick to laugh. He shut the door and came over, shaking his head in disbelief.

"Seriously, she's going to make my life about a thousand percent easier," he said as he sat down. The paper Vanessa had given him was already covered in blue and red pen, and there were a few sections circled. "I'm going to call these people as soon as I can."

"That's good," I replied, not really knowing what Vanessa had told him. I

44

trusted her advice, and I didn't see the need to know what she was telling him. "So other than a lack of staffing, how is adapting to your work coming along? And what happened to your face?"

Patrick touched the small cut above his eyebrow and winced. It looked deep and ugly, but still tiny, like it had been patched well. "Yeah, that's what you get when you decide to try and save money by not leaving your entryway light on and forget that you also parked your bicycle there at the same time. I was happy I could get it stopped with some pressure and a bit of medical tape last night, because I didn't want to go to the Mercy ER for something so embarrassing. As for my work, you mean besides learning that the corridors of City Hall are just about as dangerous and full of people willing to stab you in the back as The Playground?"

"Welcome to the jungle," I teased in reply. "Only difference is, in City Hall, you can't see the knives meant for you."

Patrick waved it all off in good humor before looking around the table. "Damn, what a spread. You expecting a third person?"

I laughed and shook my head. "No, but seeing how big you are, I know that you probably don't eat a single spring roll and call it a day. My groundskeeper is a big guy too, and he eats like a horse."

"Well then, thank you," he said, sitting down. He was wearing tan chinos and a button-down, collared long sleeve shirt, but no tie or sport jacket. "I'd kind of gotten used to leaving lunch meetings feeling more than a little hungry."

"You don't have to worry about that," I replied, grabbing some pepper shrimp and putting it onto my tray of white rice. "I enjoy good food too. Of course, the side effect is that I need to work out like a fiend in order to not swell up to the size of a small car."

Patrick chose the lemon chicken for his first choice and followed my example. I was pleased to notice that he was quite adept with chopsticks; it's another one of those little cues that I use to see if a guy is worth being interested in. No man who doesn't have the patience to learn how to use chopsticks well is going to be able to put up with me, unfortunately. In watching him more, I was actually surprised; he was deft and skilled.

"I've got some Chinese friends who you could give lessons to," I noted as he picked up some rice with his sticks and took in a mouthful. "Seriously, how'd you get

45

so good?"

Patrick chuckled and set his chopsticks down. "I had a lot of practice for a while. Before this I was a bartender, and before that I worked in an Asian buffet place for a while. The owner gave us free lunches, but with the caveat that we could only take thirty minutes to eat, and we had to use chopsticks. I got to the point that I could fit a lot of my daily caloric needs into a thirty-minute window of binge eating while working for minimum wage, no tips."

"Really? You mentioned some of it yesterday, but I have to admit, I didn't really pay attention to your stump speech during your campaign. I live in The Heights right now, and on the north side before that."

Patrick chewed on his shrimp for a moment before answering. "Well, I'll be honest, it's not something I normally talk over with lunch. Think you'd be willing to trade?"

"What sort of trade?"

"I'll tell you about my life, and you tell me about yours. I'll even be the nice guy and start off."

I took a sip of the iced oolong tea that the restaurant had included and nodded. "Sure, why not? But I get to ask questions. If you don't want to answer them, you just have to say so, but no lying."

"Deal. All right, so the basics. Yeah, I was born in Mercy Hospital twenty-eight years ago. I have no idea who my father was, and my mom was, well, troubled. The state took me away from her when I was two."

"What happened?" I asked.

"Abuse, both of me and of herself through drugs. I spent the next sixteen years bouncing through the state systems, mostly within the city. I did get to do some summer camps upstate though, which were fun, but by junior high school the system pretty much didn't give a damn about me. I got into a lot of trouble during my teen years, which carried on until I was twenty-one."

"What happened then?" I asked. "Or is it my turn?"

Patrick shook his head and continued. "A friend of mine got shot down in The Playground, and I missed getting killed at the same time by about three inches. Since then, I tried what I could to get out of the life and keep myself on the right side of the law. I haven't always been able to, but on the other hand, my arrest record is

46

clean since I turned eighteen, mostly due to luck than anything else, considering what I was mixed up with for three years. Your turn."

I chuckled darkly and ate another bite of my food, which had lost some of its delicious flavor. "I'm pretty much the opposite. My family is down in Florida, where my father owns three car dealerships in the upstate area, the biggest near Pensacola. Ah, after high school I wanted to find success on my own, so I came up here. My parents understand, even if Daddy doesn't really like it, but he's got my brother to take over the business when he's ready to retire. I think in a lot of ways they're a bit relieved that I moved up north anyway. I was always a PR disaster waiting to happen with them."

"How so?"

Shaking my head, I smiled and chewed my food. "Sorry, maybe the next time we get together. Let's just say that I don't exactly fit in around the Florida culture, even in the more open-minded places like Tallahassee. But, I came up here, found myself comfortable for the first time, and have stayed. My parents and I don't really talk much anymore, but that's more due to a simple lack of common ground than anything else. All right, my turn. What made you run for city council, and don't tell me my boss."

Patrick laughed and shook his head. "You wouldn't believe me if I told you."

"Go ahead. I've got quite the capacity for tall tales and bullshit. Besides, I may just be able to blow your mind as well with some of the things I've seen and done."

Setting his chopsticks aside, Patrick scooped up some of the leftover orange chicken into his tray, followed by some ginger pork. "Well, like I said, I ran with a pretty rough crowd during my teen years. You noticed my tattoos yesterday, and I regret to say that some of them are associated with the Confederation. I'm ashamed to say that yes, for a while there, I did some stuff for them. Thankfully nothing too extreme, but still, not exactly the sort of tales that I want to tell my future children. Anyway, even after getting out of the life, I worked in bars and around places that some of these Confederation guys would go to, and toward the end there, some of these guys started talking about one of their own who turned on his bosses and had sworn to take them down. This guy, I never met him. He's about three or four years younger than me, and by the end, he was damn near mythical in terms of his aura. They say that even now he patrols through some of the neighborhoods, taking out

47

the trash and keeping the city clean. That, combined with what Marcus Smiley started doing, kind of were the sparks that started to lift the city out of the crap it was drowning in. So when Harry Vickers was caught up in the ruckus, I just thought that it was my turn to start making a difference. I went around to the guys I knew, the folks in the area who didn't think I was a total loser, and found that more than a few of them were willing to sign the petition I needed to have signed to get on the special ballot. Gene, the GM of the Spartans you met yesterday, was actually my first donor, giving me the money out of his own pocket to pay the registration fee, and the rest, well, I'll be honest—it's so crazy I can barely keep track of it all in my mind. I know I've done a lot of talks on street corners, attended a few prayer breakfasts and school PTA meetings, stuff like that. The funniest was when I somehow wrangled an invitation to talk to the members of the Nation of Islam Mosque over in Fillmore Heights. I think I was the first person of Irish descent to speak there in years, if ever."

I laughed and realized I was enjoying my lunch again. "I bet. Not too many McCafferys in the NOI. How'd that one go?"

"Pretty good, once I relaxed. They even had me as a guest for their luncheon afterward, although I didn't get any donations cash-wise," Patrick said laughing. "Put it this way: I'd rather have the NOI come by my office than the visitor I had after our little press event."

"Oh, who was that?"

"Francine Berkowitz. Let's just say she's a lot more dangerous than some of the Confederation people I used to run with."

I nodded. "I've heard. Marcus told me he had a few run-ins with her, but he honestly didn't give a damn. Then again, he only has to worry about money, not vote counts or public polling."

"Exactly."

The rest of our lunch went on with a relaxed, casual feeling, and by the end, we were both giving each other little glances. As we finished the last fortune cookie, I noticed that it was already nearly two o'clock, and that Vanessa had knocked on the door frame twice, dropping off things on my desk. "Wow, the time," I said, setting my drink aside. "I'm sorry if I kept you from any appointments."

"No, I cleared my calendar for the most part," Patrick replied as he also scooted backward to stand up. "Uh, I know this isn't exactly business professional, but I was wondering, would you maybe like to get together some time?"

"You mean like a real date?" I asked, trying not to laugh. "I'd love to. But, one rule."

"What's that?" Patrick asked.

"We never, ever go to a restaurant called Mar de Napoli. Bad memories," I said, shivering.

Patrick gave me a concerned glance, but he shrugged it off and smiled. "No problem. We'll do Thai or something. Tell you what, let me see what I can pull together, and I'll give you a call tonight. Say around eight or nine?"

"Make it nine. I've got a workout scheduled with my housekeeper after work today, and they like to push me hard. I'll need it after this feast."

That evening, when Tabby came in from work, she was practically floating. It'd been a long time since I'd seen that look in her eyes, and the warning lights in my head immediately started flashing. I didn't get to see much of what Tabby had looked like when Scott Pressman had seduced and then screwed with her head, not until he already had her all messed up inside. But I'd seen that look before.

"Uh-oh," I said, setting aside the laundry I was folding. We still had at least a half hour before we did our workout, as Mark was in the other room, catching the last of the day's trading, leaving just the two of us girls. "You've got a look on your face that worries me."

"What look is that?" Tabby asked, smiling that silly little smile she gets every time she starts to like a new person.

"That look that your heart is running way faster than your head, and that a certain city councilman is the one leading it on the way," I said, folding the last of the t-shirts and going to work on the part of the laundry I hated most, socks. Mainly, I hate matching them, because I swear they all run away from me, hiding amongst their similar yet not identical brethren. I had already repeatedly threatened Mark that next time we went shopping, I was going to throw out every sock in the house, and buy nothing but two identical twelve packs for everyone in the house, black for Mark and white for me and Tabby. She and I wear the same size socks, and we'd shared clothes in the past. I never did get around to backing up that threat though. "I guess your lunch went a lot better than you'd expected."

"It did," Tabby said, unbuttoning her suit jacket and setting her briefcase on the kitchen table, plopping down to pull off her high heels. "In fact, he asked me out on a real date right at the end."

"That's not the normal way to conclude a business meeting," I remarked, finding my first matched set, a pair of Snoopy socks that Tabby's had for years. They were nearly worn through, but Tabby refused to throw them out, since they were a gift from me back when we were undergrads together. "In fact, I've never had a business meeting conclude that way."

50

"True, but you met the man of your dreams in a nightclub," Tabby said, massaging her feet. "Not all of us are so lucky, remember."

"I don't want to drag up something painful, Tabby, but the last guy you were with, well, he tore you up pretty bad," I said softly, tossing the first pair of socks underhand into Tabby's basket for putting away later. "Are you sure you're ready to get back in the game?"

Tabby put her feet down and came over next to me, taking my hand. "Do you mean am I ready for the risk of exposing my heart again?"

I nodded. "I'm not trying to be cruel, but you've been protected for the past few months."

I was surprised when Tabby pulled me into a hug, wrapping her arms around me and nearly squeezing the air out of my lungs.

"I've learned more about myself and my heart in the past six months than I have in my entire life," she said softly in my ear. "The best thing was that you've been there for me the whole time. You and Mark, really."

She kissed my temple near my right ear once, then let me go, keeping hold of my hands. "I'll never forget it. But yes, I think I'm ready. Seeing you and Mark together everyday reminds me of what I'm missing."

"All right," I said, realizing Tabby's longing need for love. "You know I love you, Tabs. I just want what's best for you."

"I know," she replied, letting go of my hands and turning to the laundry basket, helping out. "You showed me what real love looks like, having me stay with you and Mark. I've gotten to watch as you two have made something better than anything my parents have. At the same time, both of you have loved me as me, which is also a hell of a lot better than what my family did for me. Also, I'm going to take it slow this time. I know I'm not exactly the best judge of character when it comes to people sometimes, especially men."

"Oh, I don't know about that," I replied, finding the match to the sock Tabby was hunting for and handing it to her. "You did pretty well in choosing me and Mark, after all."

Tabby chuckled and put her head on my shoulder. "I did do that pretty well, didn't I? Okay, I'll say I've chosen two times pretty well. But I can't take full credit for Mark. You chose him, remember? I just got lucky enough to tag along on that one."

"Still, you know that even if this doesn't work out, you'll always have us. This house is big enough for all of us, after all."

Tabby folded another pair, finding one of Mark's pairs and then tossing it unerringly over her shoulder into his basket. How she did it I never could understand; she's terrible at basketball, but hand her a pair of socks or a wad of paper to toss into a trashcan, and she could hit it blind around a corner with three bounces off the wall more often than not. "Even after your daughter comes? You really want a bipolar, sex-starved young woman as one of her role models?"

I dropped my sock and took her chin in my hand, turning her to me. "Well, let's get it right. You're not bipolar, Tabby. A bit shaken up by a master asshole, yeah, I'll give you that. But you're far too strong for that to drive you over the edge."

Tabby looked deep into my eyes, then smiled, her fears reassured.

* * *

That night, after Tabby had retreated to her room to have her phone call with Patrick, Mark and I were in the gym, cleaning up the mats after our workout. After putting Tabby though her paces, the two of us had gone to work with the long staffs, a new traditional weapon for me. Then again, Mark's technique wasn't classical, adapted more for the ad-hoc weapons he might have had to use. As I mopped the mats with a mix of bleach and water, I told him about the conversation Tabby and I had earlier.

"That's good," he said at the end. "I was actually thinking about that a few days ago, after Tabby helped me that night after the whole thing with Mistress Blood's."

"What do you mean?"

"I was thinking that maybe the rest of Mount Zion could use some renovation. Maybe in the future that old mental ward can be torn down for a new house to be put up, or maybe this place can be expanded. Two complete living quarters housed within their own wings or something. That is, if Tabby is willing to stay our neighbor or even in the same house as us. I've kind of come to find her as irreplaceable as you do. What do you think?"

"It's something to consider," I replied. Thinking of something Tabby had said in our conversation, I laughed. "Sure you'd be willing to put up with a bunch of crazy women?"

Mark laughed and nodded. "Of course. But I did have a question, something you said. If you'd like, I could ask Tabby though."

"What's that?"

"You said that we treated her better than her family did. What did you mean?"

"Tabby went through a phase of bisexuality in her early years. Her parents didn't exactly take well to it. She never gave me all the details, but from what I gathered when we were undergrads, her father worried more about how his daughter's reputation would hurt his business than how his attitude hurt his daughter. It wasn't like they disowned her or anything, but he was clearly disapproving of the whole thing. I think he was kind of happy to have her coming up north for college, since she'd be far enough away that she couldn't cause a scandal back home, and that was why he paid for her schooling without any questions at all. Tabby's mother was, in her own passive aggressive way, worse about it, from the little I ever interacted with her. A lot of snippy comments and just kind of a saccharine worry. Anyway, by the time we were seniors, it seemed like she was only interested in men, but the damage was already done, and things were said that could never be forgotten. Have you ever noticed her on the phone with them?"

Mark set his materials aside and thought for a moment. "Nope, never have. I always thought she just used Skype or something and wanted her privacy. I mean, you try explaining to your parents that you're living with your best friend and her husband, who happen to be us. That'd freak out even the most permissive of parents."

"That's true, but in all honesty, I think you and I are about the closest thing she has to family. Not that I'm opposed to that or anything."

Mark picked up his oiling rag and little squeeze bottle of heavy duty synthetic motor oil and went back to lubricating the equipment. "Neither am I. In fact, I might just pay a visit to her potential new boyfriend if he's a dick. He'll find out Tabby's brother-in-law is a real bastard."

"Just think what our daughter is going to be like." I was touched by the term Mark had used to refer to Tabby, but kept my praise to myself. "Her boyfriends are going to be scared stiff of you."

Moving on to the leg press machine, Mark hummed. "Nah, won't be needed. If she's anything like her mother and father, her boyfriends will be smart enough not to try and screw with her. Or else."

Chapter 8
Tabby

The next day, I was in my office when Vanessa knocked on my door. "Miss Williams?"

"I swear, Vanessa, if you don't start calling me Tabby, I'm not buying lunch for you any longer," I countered, setting my pen aside and looking up. "Seriously, though, what can I do for you?"

"You have a visitor," Vanessa said, "not on the schedule."

I looked over my work and noted that for the most part it was just implementing things that Mark and Sophie had worked out the day before. It was a big part of my job, making their decisions look like my ideas. Mark gave me a lot of leeway too, which I appreciated. It made me feel like part of the team and not just window dressing. "That's okay, Vanessa. Who is it?"

"Ms. Berkowitz," Vanessa said evenly, her eyes flickering back over her shoulder. I understood. "From the Union."

It was a rather unique thing about our city, in that while there were many unions, they all tended to align under one association, which after struggling through about a half dozen awkward acronyms just came to be known as the Union, emphasis on the capital letter. The Union was a monolith, and had been very powerful in city politics for many years. Worse, they'd become very corrupt.

Francine Berkowitz was one of the deadliest political enemies in the city. After Marcus Smiley had more or less made a fool of her right before the shit hit the fan with Owen Lynch, she'd laid pretty low on our part, but I could tell she was waiting for a chance to move. Running my hands through my hair, I nodded to Vanessa. "Show her in, please. And if you could, see if we have any coffee or something similar to offer our guest?"

"Of course . . . Tabby," Vanessa said, a worried smile on her face. Hey, it was

54

a start.

Francine Berkowitz came into the office like she was queen of the city, in a Ralph Lauren Black Label shirtdress that cost more than most union workers made in a month. "Tabby Williams, it's a pleasure to meet you," she exclaimed in faux good humor, as if we were sorority sisters who just happened to meet at the steeplechase or something. She even spread her arms out like we were going to do air kisses. I had to resist the urge to pretend to puke, it was so nauseating. "I must apologize in not coming by earlier."

"Ms. Berkowitz, have a seat," I replied, offering my hand. She slowed her approach and took the offered hand, her smile disappearing and her eyes tightening at the gesture. I didn't really care if I wasn't this woman's friend, but I didn't need to make her totally pissed off at me either. "What can I do for you today?"

"I just wanted to come by and congratulate you on your new project," Berkowitz said, taking the seat on the other side of my desk. I wasn't looking to be informal with this woman, and while my desk may not have been as intimidating as something in the Oval Office, it had the advantage that my seat was just a bit taller than hers. She had to look up to me, while I could actually lean on my desk and look slightly down at her. It wasn't originally done on purpose; Mark had chosen the chairs due to their design rather than their height. I just took advantage of the situation when I needed it.

"Why thank you, Ms. Berkowitz. MJT is just hoping to make a difference in the community," I replied. "If anything, the renovations and opening of the centers themselves are going to inject a lot of much-needed money into the community."

"Yes, I agree. In fact, it was those renovations that are the crux of the matter," Berkowitz said. "You must agree that this city has a fine history of construction workers and experts, all under the convenience of the Union banner."

"I'll admit that Union workers have done some impressive work," I replied. "The Financial Tower, the Hamilton Building, and many others I'm sure were done by Union workers."

"Exactly," Berkowitz said with a hint of enthusiasm. "Nowadays, that sort of quality is important. The Union built this city, Tabby. It should have a role in rebuilding it as well."

Vanessa brought in two cups of coffee in our best ceramic mugs, which were admittedly not too much. The MJT offices were built off of functionality, not flashy appearances. Sophie had, in the one time she'd come by after everyone was gone, called it 'dot-com startup chic.' Whatever the case, I happily took the thick handled mug with 'World's Best Dad' written on the side, leaving the plain red mug for Berkowitz. Thanking Vanessa, I offered my guest the bowl of sugar cubes. "We have cream as well. The real stuff, not non-dairy."

"No thanks, I take it black," she replied, while I loaded mine up with cream and sugar. She arched her eyebrow and harrumphed. "Well, I guess having a gym downstairs has its advantages."

"It does," I said, not mentioning that most of the time I worked out at home with Mark and Sophie. "But as to your point, I do agree that Union workers did a lot of good for the city. And, I hope they can be in a position to help with our project as well. It all comes down to their bids, really."

"What do you mean?" Berkowitz replied.

"We're doing an open bid process for the renovations," I replied. "Open to all contractors, both Union and non-Union. The only rules we're using to judge is quality of work, cost, and of course, we will be giving a certain edge to contractors who have their shops in the communities where we are building the centers. What better way to show the disadvantaged people of those neighborhoods that we are willing to give them an opportunity than from the very beginning?"

"I see," Berkowitz replied. "I'm not trying to tell you how to do your job, Miss Williams, but in the city there has been a tradition of letting the Union have first and last attempts on any bid process."

Hmm, I was no longer Tabby, but Miss Williams. Duly noted. "I know, Ms. Berkowitz. However, in planning our outreach program, we are looking for more than just experience. We want to evaluate raw talent, and that means that sometimes we're going to have to look for contractors and workers who may not have the same level of . . . sophistication when it comes to understanding how bids are done for large projects around the city. So instead, each bid will come in sealed, and I will make the decision based off of what I feel is best for the project."

It was the closest I'd come to flat out calling the Union bidding process corrupt. Not that anyone didn't know the Union bids were total lies anyway. Any cost accounting of a Union bid, especially one that was tied to a charity or to a public works project, was automatically inflated by at least thirty percent, if not more. It got so bad at one point that the federal government had to step in when a Union contracted project for modernizing the city's sewer system was ten years and about two hundred million dollars over budget, and that was in nineteen eighties dollars.

Berkowitz's face went from closed to wintry, and she finished her coffee quickly. "Best of luck in your project then. I will forward on your information to our Union members, of course."

Her threat was subtle, but there. It wouldn't just be the construction members who would get the word, but also the police, fire, and other city workers. Basically, I needed to make sure I was driving under the speed limit, and hope no fires broke out at Mount Zion. Not that I ever wanted them, considering the highly illegal arsenal we kept in the bell tower.

"I expect nothing less, Francine," I said, shifting to using her first name. Instead of the condescending familiarity she'd used on me, however, I was simply using it as a way to put her down. It said *I'm not playing your games or kissing your ass. In fact, I think I'm better than you.* And in a lot of ways, I did.

We continued our little chat for a few more minutes, but it was mostly banalities. When she realized that her jibes and threats weren't going to rattle me, she made her exit, closing my door behind her. Vanessa was there a minute later to gather up the coffee cups. Noting my cup, she gave me a look. "I thought you hated cream and sugar?"

"I do, but Berkowitz took hers black," I replied. "Just one of those things, you know."

"I understand," Vanessa replied. "I saw her face when she left. She's not happy."

"Considering she tried the same threats on Patrick McCaffery just a few days ago, I can understand. I've already talked with Gene over at the Spartans, and they're tired of her crap too. They are actually expressly anti-Union, which surprises me. I figured they'd play it neutral in order to keep the fans happy."

"The fans are happy when the team wins games," Vanessa replied. "And the Spartans already have enough union issues to deal with when it comes to the Players' Association."

"Good point."

When Patrick picked me up for our date that Sunday, I was at first surprised when he drove up in a car that looked eerily similar to Sophie's old beater Civic she'd had me sell for her when she was on the run with Mark. "Hi," he said, getting out. He was wearing jeans and a Spartans long sleeve t-shirt, his black hair pulled back and his green eyes shining in anticipation. "I know it's not exactly what you're used to. Sorry about that."

"No, it's okay," I said, running my hands over the roof. "It's just that I had a friend in college that had a car that looked very similar, except the color."

"Really? Yeah, I picked this up from a used car lot when I had to get a real car about six months ago," Patrick replied. "I had a friend paint it for me to cover the worst of the rust spots—it used to be a faded out blue."

"With a rust spot on the right front fender?" I asked, my eyes widening, "Kind of looked like a fish?"

Patrick gaped at me for a moment before nodded, then both of us laughed. "Wow, who'd have thought it? The fates are kind to me, it seems."

"Fate? Perhaps," I replied, "but no offense, I've ridden in this beast before. Unless your friend also did a full mechanical workup on it, how about you drive my car tonight?"

"You serious?" Patrick asked incredulously. "You really want to park your car over at the Stadium?"

"Why not?" I asked. "I'm sure we'll get a good spot. You said Gene got us box seats, right?"

"Yeah, although they're technically in your name," Patrick replied. "Something about donations to politicians or something. I didn't realize the rules were that strict, but I'm cool with it. Guess I'm going to have start paying my bar tab too."

"Most likely," I said with a chuckle. "If I can ask, why are you still driving that old beater anyway?"

"Well, in good weather I drove a moped for years, and I kind of enjoy it, the open air and all. Since then though, I just haven't had the time to go car shopping. I don't even drive this thing to work that often. I'd probably just get harassed by the other city workers."

"Well, let me go grab my keys; we'll take the SUV," I replied, turning and heading back inside. "If you don't mind, my house staff can watch your car."

Ducking inside, I saw Mark standing close to the door, looking out the small side window. "Well?"

"I'll keep an eye on the car," Mark said with a smile. "You have your phone and everything, right?"

"Don't have the gun, but you haven't taught me how to shoot it yet anyway," I wisecracked. "But yes, I'm going to be careful. If anything, it's just a football game."

"I know, but still," Mark said. "Tell you what, let me get his keys from him."

I rolled my eyes and nodded. "Okay, I'll take an extra thirty seconds getting the keys for the SUV. I'll even pull it out so that he doesn't get a look at that electric motorcycle of yours."

I left Mark and headed into the kitchen, which connected to the garage area. Sophie was sipping some cocoa and smiled. "He's just being overprotective; you know how he can be."

"I know. It's actually kinda cool," I remarked, leaning over and giving her a kiss on the cheek. "Just tell him I'll be home by nine, unless the game goes to overtime. Until then, you can become reacquainted with your old car."

"Don't worry, we won't break in the back seat, that car is way too small for that," Sophie replied. "Tabby?"

"Yeah?"

"Be careful."

"I will. Love you guys," I said, grabbing the keys from the hook board by the door and going into the garage. Pulling around, I saw Mark and Patrick in conversation, Mark holding the keys to the car in his hand. It was interesting, as I realized for the first time that Patrick was a little bit taller and bigger than Mark.

"Hey guys. Patrick, this is Mathew Bylur, one of my staff. Mathew, this is Patrick McCaffery."

"We were just getting introduced," Mark said, turning. From the corner of his mouth, the side that was hidden from Patrick with the way he was turned, he gave me a sort of half smile, which I took as a good sign. "I promised the Councilman I'd take care of his car while you two were gone. Would you like me to give it a wash?"

"No thanks, really," Patrick replied. "I'm still embarrassed enough to be driving my date's car to the game."

I shut off the engine and got out. "If you want, I'll drive. We can be very women's empowerment around here if you want."

The stadium was only half full when we got there, but then again it was only a preseason game. The Spartans were coming off a so-so season, and our city's always been rather fickle in terms of fan support. When the Spartans did well, games were packed and just about everyone was wearing Spartan shirts. Meanwhile, when the Spartans were in the division basement, you couldn't find a Spartan shirt just about anywhere, and massive amounts of tickets had to be comped out and papered over to avoid broadcaster blackout rules.

Since the Spartans had picked up some pretty hot free agent talent in the offseason and were sporting a third-year running back that had done some pretty good stuff when he took over as the starter last season, fans were giving the Spartans a chance this year, and we actually had to wait a few minutes in line before we got through the gate. Once inside, however, we were greeted by a VIP usher who led us up to our box. We got there about ten minutes before they did the pre-game activities and settled in.

"So what do you think?" Patrick asked, looking down on the three-quarters-full stadium. "I'll be honest; I've never been able to sit up in one of these."

"I got to watch a game last season," I admitted to him, "just after I started working with Marcus Smiley. It was when I was an intern at Taylor & Hardwick's, and they gave me tickets as a reward for bringing them so much business. Although it wasn't as private as this. We had to share with ten other people."

I could tell Patrick was obviously a bit deflated—he had hoped to impress me—and I reached over, patting his knee. "Don't sweat it, money doesn't impress me, Patrick. Although this is a nice gesture. I appreciate the effort you went through more than any dollar amount."

Patrick looked me in the eyes, a small smirk on his lips. "This is certainly going to be different."

"What's that?"

"Dating someone who makes a lot more money than me. I've spent most of my single life kind of being the guy who gets it done for my dates, through hook or by crook."

"Is that what it is, huh? Dating?"

A pleasant tension rose between us as I waited for Patrick's answer and our smiles mirrored each other. It was like a small duel to see who would admit their attraction first. Finally, Patrick nodded, but before he could say anything, a roar came overhead as three National Guard F/A-18s flew overhead. Both of us jerked our heads to see the impressive aircraft fly past us, seemingly inches over our heads, only to launch into a heart-stopping vertical climb and disappear into the late afternoon sky.

The game itself was your standard preseason game. The stars came out for roughly the first half of the game, which was actually the more boring half. Not wanting to risk injury on a game that didn't mean anything, they played conservatively, and at halftime the Spartans were ahead by only a field goal.

More importantly to me, though, was the time Patrick and I spent talking. The conversation was pretty light, nothing of soul-bearing importance, but just sharing what we liked and our points of view on various things. For example, I was surprised when Patrick stated that he was a big fan of hip-hop music. "I guess it was just what I grew up with down in The Playground, but if I were to put a soundtrack to my life up until now, there'd be a lot of hip-hop involved. I know it comes off as trite, but until recently a lot of my life was hip-hop and slightly older R&B."

"Oh? Any particular acts?"

Patrick shook his head. "You'd laugh if I told you."

"No, go ahead," I said. "I listened to more than my fair share of hip-hop and stuff when I was in Florida. I even remember going to a few junior high school dances to some stuff that was a bit moldy at the time, but still had some good memories for me. First person I kissed was to a Keith Sweat song."

Patrick laughed. "Blackstreet for me. Freshman year of high school, girl named Gwen. Can I ask you another question before the second half kicks off?"

I got up from my seat and went over to the snack table where there were fresh nachos waiting for us, a treat of the VIP section. Picking up a plate, I came back. "As long as it doesn't involve my prior dating life, go ahead."

"Actually, I wanted to ask you if you didn't mind that I'm not as educated as you. I mean, I graduated high school, but most of my so-called higher education has come via the school of hard knocks."

I took a bite of my nachos and offered him some. Our fingers made contact as I passed over the plate, and both of us paused for a second to look at each other at the contact. A few of the tortilla chips rattled in the tray, but nothing spilled. "Don't sell yourself short, Patrick," I said. "Besides, who knows? Maybe you have knowledge and skills that you don't even know about."

The Spartan reserves ended up winning the game by two touchdowns, mainly due to the passionate plays of some of the guys lower on the depth charts who were giving their all for a chance to make the team. Driving home from the stadium, there was none of the nervous tension that I'd felt on a few other first real dates. We both knew we had enjoyed ourselves, and that we wanted to see the other person again, even if we didn't say as much. The only question to be answered was who was going to call or text the other first in order to make that first step.

There was one thing that I liked as our date progressed that I hadn't expected. When I'd first met Patrick, he had a hint of a cocky air about him—nothing too over the top, mind you, but there was a sense of self-confidence that bordered on cockiness. It was the sort of air that a lot of voters would like, but other people would get tired of after a while. Talking with him, though, he opened up more, and I could see that while he was confident in himself, he wasn't cocky at all. He was actually intelligent and perceptive, and he was willing to admit when he needed help or experience.

Pulling into the driveway at Mount Zion, Patrick put the SUV in park and looked over. "Well, you're home safe and sound. I hope your butler doesn't feel the need to kick my ass any longer."

I laughed. "Did Matt threaten you to act like a gentleman?"

"No, just in the way he looked at me and some of the questions we had back and forth. I can tell he cares for you a lot. He gave off that big brother vibe. It was actually both weird and sweet. You seem to inspire a lot of loyalty in your house staff."

"He and Joanna are great people," I admitted, although I didn't tell Patrick just how great. "We've become very good friends as well as them working for me. I was lucky that Marcus forwarded me their resumes and that they even applied. Maybe next time you can meet them both."

"I'd like that very much," he said, taking the keys out of the ignition and holding them out for me. I reached for them, but when our hands touched, the reach became a lean, and the lean became a slow, soft kiss. His left hand came up to trace my jawline, and I responded by feeling the swell of his bicep under his Spartans shirt.

When his tongue traced my lips I responded, both of us tasting the other. I had to admit it wasn't the sexiest taste I'd ever had on a kiss—he tasted like stadium hotdogs—but then again, I'd had a lot of jalapeño peppers on my nachos, so I'm sure I wasn't exactly minty fresh either. We were both so wrapped up in conversation that neither of us thought to break out a tic-tac. Still, our kiss was great, and I could tell when we parted that he was just as happy with it as I was. "Top three, for sure."

"Top three what?" I asked with a small smile, unbuckling my seatbelt.

"Top three kisses I've had," he said with a slightly cocky grin. I could tell he was joking. It wasn't the same sort of cockiness he had before our date, more like a playful cockiness. "But definitely best first kiss."

"Hmmm, well, I won't give you a rank," I replied with a cocky grin of my own. "I mean, I'm not the sort of girl to kiss and tell, after all."

"But maybe it was good enough to get me another date? Say, this Thursday? I'd ask for Friday, but there's a community event I'm slated for, and Saturday is the City Council meeting that's open to the public. And I don't want to wait a week before seeing you again."

I smiled and nodded. "Thursday is good. But let me make the plans, okay?"

"Okay."

Patrick got out of the SUV and came around to open my door, escorting me to the front door of Mount Zion. There, we paused and kissed again, this time even better than the first. While I had told him the truth—I don't rank kissers—he was very good. His hands rested lightly on my waist, and he never tried to move them lower or pull me tighter, even though I could tell he wanted to. It was both passion filled and gentlemanly, the right blend that warmed my belly and sent shivers through me. After Scott Pressman, it was exactly what I needed. When we parted, he had a slightly star-struck look on his face, and I was smiling the entire time as I made my way inside and then to my room.

Driving back to my apartment, I barely avoided driving through red lights twice because I was so distracted. I had told Tabby she was a top three kiss, but that was a vast underestimation. The way her lips felt on mine, the feel of her waist in my hands, everything about her was the sexiest, most beautiful I'd ever felt. Still, I knew I had to be careful. She'd been hurt, and I didn't want to screw it up by going too fast.

Reaching the outer limits of The Playground, I found my apartment and parked. I still lived in the same dump I'd been in months ago when I was just Patrick McCaffery the bartender, and I didn't really see the need to move just yet. The local gangs respected me, more or less, and none of them had tried to start shit because I was now in politics instead of slinging beers.

Opening my door, I stepped in and closed the door quickly before someone looked inside. I had spent a little bit of my pay so far to put another lock on my door, not that it would really stop someone who wanted to break in. I'm pretty sure my front door could be kicked down by a motivated seven-year-old if desired. Still, The Playground seemed to be happy that one of their own had gotten out of the hood while not forgetting where I came from, and my building hadn't had a break-in the entire two months I'd been in office.

I had another reason to close my door quickly, however, and that was what was hanging on my living room wall. I'd have put my outfit away somewhere different, but to be honest, my apartment was seriously lacking in hiding places. Also, I'd just laundered the thing and had to hang it up to dry; the dryers downstairs were all taken up when I'd washed it. Getting blood out of the fabric is kind of important, after all.

Looking over my uniform, I wondered which side of me was more important, or perhaps which was the real me. Was I the newbie politician, who seemed to have the gift for gab that attracted the voters, while at the same time was a little bit cocky, unflappable under pressure from the vested interests of the city?

Was I the masked vigilante who was starting to clean up Fillmore Heights? I'd chosen Fillmore simply because it wasn't the same neighborhood I lived, but was still

64

nearby and needed help. If I'd gone into action in The Playground, I was worried I'd get recognized. Also, I had to admit to myself that busting the heads of the 88s had been thrilling.

Or was I the guy who'd just had one of the best dates of his life, who had intentionally been sensitive and listening, and had found that in listening to Tabby I'd found a deeper level of enjoyment than I'd ever had before with a woman?

As these whirled through my mind, another, darker voice whispered to me, one that I had tried to suppress for a very long time. What if I was the asshole, the player, the criminal I was on the path to becoming in my teen years? What if everything I'd done since then, the years of struggling as a bartender, running for city council, hell, even trying to date a woman as classy and high quality as Tabby Williams was just a front, a desperate attempt to run away from what I really was? What if I was just another kid from the ghetto who'd drunk his first malt liquor before he could do long division, and whose chemistry knowledge depended mostly on how to mix household stuff together to get somebody high? What if I was just another piece of Playground trash?

I looked up at my mask, a simple black hood, and made a decision. If I was trash, then so be it. I'd heard somewhere, I didn't remember where, that sometimes, to combat evil, you didn't need good. You just needed a different kind of evil.

Pulling off my Spartans shirt, I reached for my uniform.

* * *

An hour later, I was crouching in an alleyway in Fillmore Heights, listening as three of the Latin Kings were talking business outside a brownstone apartment across the street. I was using a cheap parabolic microphone, the sort you could get from just about any electronic shop for about a hundred dollars, and had to wince every time a car or bus drove by on the street, overwhelming the microphone and temporarily deafening me. Thankfully, this late at night, few people were stupid enough to try and drive through Fillmore Heights unless they were looking for trouble. The Kings used a lot of code words, but if you grew up in the bad part of town, you knew what was going on.

"*Orale.* After the hit on that group of Eights the other night, El Patron is worried. Thinks Fillmore's gonna cook off," one of the Latin Kings, a short, skinny guy in a black tank top said. "Wants us soldiers to keep our eyes out for trouble."

His compatriots, one bald and overweight while the other was long-haired and looked kind of like a rat, nodded. Rat-face, who had a black and gold Latin King bandanna tied around his forehead, reached between his legs for the forty-ounce malt liquor on the steps and took a pull. "*Es frio*, man. You know the GDs ain't gonna come up here. They're just gonna bark and talk shit like the little bitches they are."

The big man interjected. "They outnumber us, and if they think that the attack on the white boys was done by one of us, they might just find the stones to do more than bark. They could find their teeth."

The three Latin Kings nodded. I'd seen the video, and while my face was never shown, there were enough flashes of skin from my movements that it was easy to tell, even in the cheap black and white security footage, that the attacker wasn't black. If the Gangster Disciples thought that the attack was done by another gang, it would have either come from a Latin King, who were mostly light skinned to light brown Hispanics, or an outside white gang, the nearest of which was on the far side of The Playground.

"I'm more worried if it's the Snowman," One commented, earning alarmed looks from the other two.

"Homie, don't even whisper that shit around here," Big man hissed. "I'm just happy he's stayed pretty much in the Confederation stomping grounds. Fillmore Heights was just an affiliate of them, he's left us alone so far."

"And let's hope he stays that way," Rat-Face added. "I don't need a bomb in my mailbox, or a sniper shot in my grill."

"Shit, that'd improve your looks," one joked, causing the three of them to laugh. The Rat-Face guy was a remarkably ugly man, that was for sure. "Hey, did El Patron have anything to say about when we might get a new load for the streets? My cousin's running low, and a lot of customers are feenin'. I know it's been tight the past few months, but I'm 'bout at the point of whipping up some bathtub crystal if we can't get the good stuff goin'."

A car drove by, so I missed a few seconds of reply. ". . . in about a week. They're just trying to work it all out."

I was so absorbed in what the Latin Kings were saying that I didn't hear the person creeping up behind me until I was dragged back and slammed against the brick wall of the alley, pulling the earphones from my head, the parabolic microphone clattering on the pavement. Staring me in the face was another man, all in black, his face obscured by a glued on face-mask. "You're dead, amateur," he rasped in my face. "You're playing a game that you aren't ready for."

The sound of my scuffle must have reached across the street, because I heard the three Latin Kings stop their conversation and start coming our direction. My assailant, his forearm pinning me by the throat against the wall, jerked his eyes in their direction before looking back at me. "Follow me, keep up. If not, you're going to get your ass killed."

Releasing me, he took off down the alley, with me hot on his heels. It was hard keeping up, partly because I was wearing supportive combat boots while he was wearing a lighter, more flexible shoe, but also because he was at least fifteen to twenty pounds lighter than I was. Even though I was in good shape, he made me feel like a slob as he rounded the corner and vaulted on top of a dumpster, then jumping and grabbing a fire escape ladder that was bolted to the side of the apartment building we were running behind. "Move it!" he called harshly behind him, giving me a single glance back.

I could hear the Latin Kings coming down the alley after us, and I knew they'd be carrying weapons. Scrambling up on top of the dumpster, I barely cleared the jump to the ladder, pulling with everything I had to find purchase for my boots. Finally, my right foot reached the bottom rung, and I followed the masked man up and over the roof, throwing myself over just as two of our assailants turned the corner. I figured the big guy wasn't too far behind, and was most likely bringing up the rear.

"What the fuck?" One of them said, looking around. "You see anything?"

"No, you?"

"Not a fucking thing. Hey, Victor, your fat ass see anything?"

"Fuck you, Ricardo. You know I didn't see shit."

"Still, there was that thing in the alley—someone was there. That sort of shit ain't exactly common."

One of them started to look up, and I jerked my head back out of sight. "What if it was you know who?"

"For fuck's sake, man, he isn't fucking Voldemort. You can say his name, bitch. You think we spooked the Snowman."

They argued for another minute before giving up and heading back to their brownstone, most likely to go inside. I turned my attention to the other man, who was crouched about fifteen feet away. In the hazy moonlight I could see the glimmer of the pistol at his side. At least it wasn't pointed at me.

"Thanks," I said. "But I was doing fine."

"You were unaware of your surroundings and had cut off your hearing to listen on that cheap mike set," the masked man admonished me derisively. "That's twice you've done something stupid and amateurish. I saw your little stunt with the 88s. You got out of that with just pure luck that none of them thought to pull a blade on you."

"You know, not everyone has the resources and training you do . . . Snowman," I said, adjusting to a seated position. He had the drop on me and was already armed; there was no point in useless posturing. "I'm just trying to do what I can on a shoestring budget."

"You could have done the exact same thing from this roof if you'd used your brain," Snowman countered. "What the hell were you doing, anyway?"

I rested my forearms on my knees and sat back against the brick retaining wall of the roof. "What does it look like I'm doing? You took down Owen Lynch and the Confederation, but this town needs a lot more than just that to have a chance, and it's too big a job for one man."

"A big job, but one made more difficult by people who don't know what the fuck they're doing," Snowman countered. "I don't need your help. You're just going to make things harder."

He stood up and holstered his pistol, backing away. As he turned to walk to the edge of the roof, I called after him. "I'm not going to stop, you know."

"You're going to get yourself killed," he replied, turning and walking back toward me. "I may not be the guy who sneaks up on you next time."

"Some things are worth dying for," I said. "You of all people should know that, if the stories about you are true."

Snowman looked at me for a moment—I wasn't sure if in exasperation or admiration—then turned and ran toward the edge of the roof. Jumping just before he reached the edge, he easily cleared his way to the building next door, jogging across and disappearing into the gloom. I waited for him to go, then made my way

68

over to the edge of the roof that overlooked the street where the Latin Kings had been gathered. Unfortunately, they'd either gone inside or run off, leaving me with only a hint of information, and out one parabolic microphone.

Damn.

Chapter 10
Tabby

Monday through Wednesday were pretty routine for me as I dealt with the paperwork for getting the community centers off the ground. The only notable thing was Wednesday afternoon, when I went by City Hall to have a meeting with the mayor. Joseph Williams and I may have shared the same last name, but that was where our similarities ended.

The stress of the past few months had trimmed close to thirty pounds off his frame, and he looked cadaverous as I stepped into his office. He had survived the scandals that had taken down his deputy mayor with his own job intact, but that was about it. I honestly thought that if he wasn't constrained by the term limit law the city had in place, he would have been taken down as well. Instead, the voters were willing to let him serve out the last two years of his term before retiring into obscurity. I felt for him, since according to Mark, he was a man who had been caught up in circumstances beyond his control more than actually being evil himself.

"Good afternoon, Your Honor," I greeted him. I was dressed to impress, but had toned the sexiness down just a touch. There was a time to be drop dead distracting, but I didn't have to always, so the suit coat and skirt were just a bit looser than normal. "I'm thankful you asked me to come by."

"When a company agrees to spend millions of its own dollars for community outreach, I'd be a fool not to," the mayor replied. "But, like I told your boss the last time he and I had a private conversation, can the *Your Honor* and *Mister Mayor* stuff. My name is Joe, except to my wife when she's mad at me, when I become Joseph. Lately, I've been called Joseph a lot."

His fatalistic humor made me smile, and I reached out to shake his hand. "All right, Joe, then please, just call me Tabby. Nobody calls me Tabitha, thankfully. So I'm guessing you've been catching a lot of flak the past couple of months."

I sat down in the chair Joe offered to me, which was in front of a small coffee table. It was a similar arrangement to my office, but much nicer. The table was already arranged with light snacks and teas, which were perfect for the time of day. Joe sat down in the chair next to mine and reached for a small tuna salad sandwich. "As you can tell, I've lost a bit of weight recently, and my doctor has advised me to up my caloric intake, but only with healthy foods. So out with the burgers, sadly enough, and in with the tuna and salmon."

"I understand," I said, pouring myself a cup of tea. "Excuse me if I don't join you too much. These suits I wear leave very little wiggle room for indulgences."

Joe laughed. "Yes, you did continue Miss Warbird's habit quite well. I actually have had two groups complain to me about you. Apparently the University Association of Women Against Patriarchal Oppression think you are, what was it they said? Oh yes, 'encouraging the misogynistic patriarchy to continue the oppression of female executives'."

I laughed, remembering their letter to me at the office. "Yes, their direct letter to me had that and a few more gems. When I scanned the letter and forwarded it to Marcus, he replied that he and Sophie both had quite a few good laughs over that." That was more or less the truth, although I didn't have to scan it to send it to them. They'd read the original.

"I still don't know what exactly they wanted me to do, as you aren't a city employee," Joe commented. He tucked half the sandwich away with a single bite and set the plate aside. "I'd eat more, but I have a disturbing case of indigestion recently. It's part of the reason I invited you over for this chat."

"Oh? No offense, Joe, but I'm not a doctor," I said. "In fact, I don't even have any doctors under the MJT investment banner. About the best I could do for you would be to recommend a couple of our restaurants. I know one of them has a macrobiotic menu that says it is good for overall body health. I can't say anything about that, but their hummus wraps are yummy."

Joe shook his head. "I wish it were that easy. Actually, I had a visit from a certain influential Bishop in town on Monday, which of course left my stomach

70

roiling. In case you didn't know, my wife is an active attendant of his services."

The groan that came out of my mouth was obviously amusing, since Joe nodded his head in commiseration. "Exactly. Now, I personally have no problem with what you did. I think the man's a snake myself, although I've more or less given up on my wife listening to his poisonous crap cloaked in the Word. I figure your boss has more in line with what the Word says than any so-called bishop who wants us to buy him a private jet. However, the reality is, he swings a lot of influence in the city, especially among the people who live in The Playground and Fillmore Heights. By the way, what are the other areas you're looking at opening your community centers?"

"We were going to open one near Spartan Field, and another on the border of the warehouse district. Both are in areas that, while not exactly as bad as Fillmore or The Playground, do need their fair share of assistance. Also, not to put too fine a point on it, it makes for good press for the Spartans to have a center close to their practice facilities. They can send over players almost weekly, which I'm sure looks great when it comes to those spots they put on TV."

"Nice selections. You'll also get a good mix of kids there. I hate to spin everything politically, but you'll be able to get a center in a lot of the different ethnic groups there. I hope you have a plan in place to prevent them from becoming racialized gang centers?"

"We're working on it. I'm following Marcus's advice, and am going to hire some very good center directors and trust their voice. I feel like we're digressing from what is causing you trouble though. What does the Bishop want?" I asked, sipping my tea.

Joe took a moment to finish his tuna salad before answering. "He wants me to more or less throw every challenge I can in your way, starting with your building permits. He figures if I frustrate you long enough, he might be able to position himself as someone who can step in and smooth things over, providing, of course, that he gets lots of publicity and his own stamp on things. I suspect he isn't the only one who might be wanting this, as I've heard that Francine Berkowitz also is not exactly happy with the way you've decided to hand out the contracts on this."

"I've decided to not put up with her corrupt bid rigging bullshit," I said bluntly. Joe half choked on his tea and coughed a few times before he got his cup set

71

down. "Come on, Joe, you and I can speak honestly here. The Union has had a stranglehold on this city's finances for decades. If you oppose the Union, then you've got building inspectors finding excuses to shut you down. I've spent the past week driving two miles below the speed limit or taking the RIST to work simply because I don't want a Union cop pulling me over and giving me a four-point ticket on my license. Who knows what the hell I'll do if Mount Zion blows a water main in the next few weeks?

But it doesn't matter. What these guys have to realize is that I'm not against the unions. Hell, if a union shop gives me a fair estimate for the labor on the centers, then I'll hire a union shop. They've got the exact same chance and opportunity as a non-Union shop. But what I'm not going to allow is the sort of bid-rigging and sloughing off that the Union has allowed for far too damn long."

Joe brushed a few crumbs off his shirt and folded his hands on his lap. "I support you, privately. In public, I'm not going to make any major announcements one way or another. I did want to just warn you, and to offer my private support. And, if you ever do get those centers open, I'm going to be right there congratulating you. If I'm still in office, I'll even give you the key to the city. But you've got a fight on your hands."

"Thank you, Joe," I said honestly. "But I think I know just how to handle at least one of those issues."

Heading back to the office, I waited until I was there to call up Mark on his cellphone. "Hello, Marcus," I said, just to be safe in case anyone heard me.

"What's up, Tabs?" he asked me. I could hear a burring noise in the background which quickly shut off, and I knew he'd been riding his new favorite toy, the riding tractor he used to maintain the lawn. And yes, in true Mark style, he'd had the thing supercharged. He could cover the entire property in an hour if he wanted, which, considering the size of Mount Zion, was saying a lot.

"You think you still have some pull with your friend Bennie?" I asked, careful not to use his full name. Bennie Fernandez had technically never met Marcus Smiley, nor did he know for certain that we had been the source of his information that led to the arrest of Owen Lynch. But still, we could use him.

"I might. Why?"

"Seems our friend, Bishop Traylor, made a visit to the mayor and might be

72

trying to work an alliance with our favorite Union leader," I replied. "Think we might need a hand?"

"That could work. Also, I've got a few anonymous connections with the media as well. Let me see what I can do this afternoon and tomorrow. So, how was the rest of the meeting?"

"Just fine. Joe says hello, by the way." I took off my coat and sat down in my chair, closing my eyes and massaging my temples as the long day started to hit me. "He also says if we can get these centers open, he'll give me the key to the city. He knows we're in for a fight."

"Glad to know it. And did you stop by to see your new favorite member of the city council?" he asked, a clear joking edge to his voice.

"No, Dad," I joked back. "We're seeing each other tomorrow night. Besides, he was interviewing potential assistants today, and I'm sure we'll talk on the phone later tonight."

"Okay. That'll give me and Sophie some free time at least. Anything else?"

"Nah, just wanted to keep you updated. Thanks."

"No problem, Tabs. See you later."

* * *

I was more nervous than ever the next night as I waited outside the theater for Patrick. We'd both decided that the sort of casual, non-dressy dates we'd been on so far were ideal for both of us. Despite our jobs, both of us were laid back, casual types, and we didn't feel the need to get dressed up *all* the time.

I'd even taken the RIST downtown to meet Patrick, forgoing any of the cars in the garage. I was wearing a casual, flirty sort of baby blue skirt with a white top and light jacket, since the evenings were starting to get a bit cooler. I also had one of my favorite little purses, a shoulder bag that was bigger than what I'd take to a club, but nowhere near huge. I've never understood women who carried a purse larger than some people's backpacks. It just wasn't my style.

I didn't have to wait long. Materializing through the foot traffic around the theater, a smile lit up his face as he saw me waving for him. I'm sure I was doing the same as he came closer, jogging the last few feet before swinging me around in an embrace like we hadn't seen or spoken to each other in years.

"Whoa tiger," I joked, giggling with delight. "Are you going to greet me that

73

way for every date we go on?"

"Depends," he replied. "Did you like it?"

"It was fun, but we can't do that after a meal," I joked in reply. I joked because the reality was, I was thrilled by the feeling. Patrick was strong and solid, his arms sturdy enough to carry me around like a little girl if he wanted to. Yes, I was enjoying it, and yes there was a bit of fluttering in my belly, the sort that usually meant I was feeling more than just fun.

We stood outside, looking at the marquee for a few minutes, and another warm chill went through me when Patrick put his arm around my shoulders. Instead of saying anything, I leaned into him, putting an arm around his waist. "You know, I really should get out more," he said after a bit. "I have no idea about any of these movies."

"Me either," I admitted. "I've been so busy with MJT, most of the entertainment I've gotten has consisted of stuff watched on the home theater."

"Really? Sounds like fun," Patrick replied. I could tell he was more comfortable with our respective socio-economic situations, for which I was grateful. After all, just a year prior I hadn't been making much more money than he was. I still wasn't quite used to the money I was making these days. For me, the stuff at Mount Zion was mostly toys that didn't matter compared to the important things, the people inside.

It was that importance that made my next decision easy. "Well, how about we skip this then and head back to Mount Zion? I promise, the home theater Marcus installed is equal to anything short of IMAX, and the seats are going to be a lot more comfortable."

Patrick considered it for a minute, then nodded. "Sure. Uhm, is your staff going to be there?"

"Yes, but I can ask them to give us our privacy," I said. "They do have their own wing of the house they can stay in."

"Okay," Patrick said, "with one request."

"What's that?" I asked as we turned and walked toward the RIST station.

"If you don't have popcorn at home, we stop and pick up some."

Pulling out my cellphone, I typed a quick message to Sophie, who responded within minutes.

74

No problem. Mark's even gone to the store to get you guys some popcorn, he said he'll make kettle corn for you when you get back.

I think he's happy he'll be in the area, I texted back. Sophie's reply was a series of hearts, LOL's, and a laughing emoticon.

I put the phone back in my purse and looked up at Patrick. "Shall we?"

It took us nearly forty-five minutes to get back to Mount Zion, but as soon as we walked in, we were greeted with the most heartwarming site I'd ever seen. Sophie and Mark had dressed up, putting on their best suits (that weren't from the wardrobe of Marcus Smiley and Sophie Warbird), playing the perfect house staff couple. The lights were dimmed, and Sophie had dug out a lantern from somewhere to light the entryway. The candle inside flickered in a welcome, old-fashioned light, casting us all in a beautiful orange-yellow light.

"Welcome home, Miss Williams," Sophie greeted me with a small smile, her eyes twinkling in the candlelight. "If you'd follow me."

Mark, for his part, looked elegant in the twin tail tuxedo that he had put on, taking our jackets and disappearing into the gym area, probably to hang them up somewhere. We didn't exactly have a formal coat check room, after all.

"What is all this?" Patrick whispered in my ear while Sophie led us to the entertainment room. "Last time I saw Matt, he was wearing a t-shirt and looking like a strict bodyguard."

"Careful, he could turn into James Bond at any minute," I only half-joked back, knowing how deadly Mark actually was. "I think they just want us to have a good time."

The entertainment room was laid out perfectly, with the largest bean bag chair positioned in the middle of the room, and two small tables set nearby, both of them currently empty. "Have a seat, I'll bring you your refreshments presently. If you don't mind, Miss Williams, Matt and I have taken the liberty to load the movie for tonight."

"How could I refuse such luxury?" I said, touched more than I could let Patrick know.

Sophie smiled an understanding smile and left the room. "Wow, you've got some amazing staff," Patrick said.

I nodded my head and looked at the door. "Amazing friends, Patrick. Amazing friends indeed."

We settled in, our legs touching on the large bag as Sophie came in with two large cups of root beer, along with a huge container of sweet smelling popcorn.

"Your remote control, Miss Tabby," Sophie said, presenting me with the small device. "Shall I adjust the lights?"

"As you wish," I said with a smile. Sophie bowed and left, turning the control knob to a dim glow as she left. Suddenly, before I could settle back, I stood up and turned to Patrick. "Just a moment, I'll be right back."

"No hurry," Patrick replied. "This is so cool I'm still geeking out."

Rushing out of the room, I found Sophie still in the hallway. "Wait," I said, quickly coming toward her. She stopped and turned, a quizzical smile on her face. I looked her in the eye and tilted my head. "Why? Why all this?"

Sophie took my hands and gave them a squeeze. "Because you deserve every chance at happiness," she said simply. "Enjoy your movie, and if you need us, Mark and I will be in the gym. It's private and quiet for you. Now go and enjoy."

Sophie leaned forward and gave me a quick kiss on the cheek, then patted my arm. "Go."

Blinking back tears of gratitude, I went back into the entertainment room, where Patrick was fiddling with the remote. "I just got excited. I wanted to see what it was," he said, "but I behaved."

"Good to know," I said, plopping down next to him. "Now, knowing those two, we're probably in for a cheesy science fiction movie. Or one of the Star Wars prequels. Meesa like Jar-Jar?"

Patrick groaned and hit the play button. The system was cued up perfectly, as the video screen turned on at the same time and we were treated to the fanfare and drumroll of the 20th Century Fox opening, before the screen dropped to black. A few electronic sounds came out, and the opening credits rolled. "No way," I said, both laughing and groaning at the same time.

"What?" Patrick asked, looking at me and then at the screen. "What is this?"

"You mean, you've never seen *The Princess Bride?*" I asked, incredulous. "Seriously?"

"No," Patrick replied. "I mean, it's what, thirty years old? Why? I've heard some people say it's good, but I never had the big urge to watch it before."

Rolling my eyes, I turned and lay my head on his chest, watching the film.

"Just watch and find out, farm boy," I said, my eyes twinkling in the dim light.

"Farm boy?" Patrick whispered, then glanced at the screen.

"You'll see. Never seen this before . . . inconceivable."

For the next two hours, Patrick and I lay on the large bag, enjoying the classic movie. Patrick loved the film, laughing at the funny bits, adjusting and squirming with the action or the romantic bits. When the final scenes rolled, we let the music play, and I snuggled into Patrick's arm.

"Patrick?" I said, looking up into his green eyes. I knew what I was risking, but it felt so right.

"Yes?" he said, looking down at me. I shifted, scooting up to look him in the eyes. I cupped his cheek, stroking where just a little bit of stubble was growing. It rasped against my fingertips pleasantly, and the butterflies in my stomach took off at the sound.

"Kiss me," I said, leaning forward. He didn't have to reply, his lips finding mine as we slowly kissed, first with a little peck before growing bolder. His left hand stroked my side while his other arm pillowed his head, the two of us just kissing and forging a bond between us. When we finally parted, I smirked at him. "You were supposed to say *As you wish*."

"You didn't give me much of a chance," he teased back. "But if you would like, I'd be more than happy to."

Patrick brushed a lock of red hair out of my eyes, his eyes full of questions. "Tabby," he said, his mouth working as he struggled to form words that wouldn't come out. Finally, he gave up and sighed, letting his hand fall back to his side. "I want to, but I'm worried."

"That I'll say no?" I said, taking his hand and bringing it to my lips. "Patrick, you never know what's going to happen unless you ask."

He looked at me with such inscrutable eyes, as if he knew something and he was making a decision. Finally, he swallowed and looked me in the eyes. "Tabby, would you let me make love to you?"

"No," I replied, "but I would like to make love *with* you."

The momentary fall in his face was replaced almost instantaneously with unspeakable joy as we came together again, our hands roaming over each other. Pushing him back on the bag, I ended up on top of him, my hands stabilizing myself on his shoulders.

I was glad I'd worn a skirt, because it gave me plenty of ability to feel his body between my legs while my hands pulled at his shirt. He was wearing a button down shirt that I worked quickly, kissing the smooth exposed skin with every inch that came to my eyes. Pushing his shirt back, I could see that his tattoos on his right arm extended to his shoulder, and there was one of a gryphon on his right pec, just above his nipple. "What's this for?"

"A promise I made to myself," he said, covering my hand as I traced the mythological beast. "Just a promise."

"For what?"

"Later," he said, reaching up and pulling me down for another kiss. His tongue wrestled with mine, looping and twisting around each other. My skirt was lifted and his strong, still slightly calloused hand ran over my hip to cup my ass. He squeezed, and I squealed with glee as he found one of my most sensitive areas. Unfortunately, he misinterpreted the sound and stopped. "Did I hurt you?"

"No," I giggled, leaning back and undoing the buttons on my top. I shrugged it off and was rewarded as Patrick's eyes grew round as saucers when he saw me in the white lacy bra I was wearing. "I like what you were doing. Think you can keep it up?"

"As you wish." He laughed, letting go of my hips to reach for the clasp on my bra. "May I?"

"Yes," I said, leaning forward to give him a bit of assistance. The bra was clasped in the back, and he struggled a bit with it for a second before getting the catch. Shrugging my shoulders forward, I let him take off my bra, his lips following the fabric so closely I couldn't even register the cool air before my skin was lit on fire from his kisses.

I love to have my breasts pleasured, and Patrick was superb at that. Hearing my sighs and moans perfectly, he set my body on edge as he explored me. His teeth scraped lightly across my nipples and I cried out in a light release, almost brought to orgasm just from his touch.

Not that his mouth was the only thing touching me. His hands, which were still the strong, slightly rough hands of a man who worked with his hands more than sitting behind a desk, wrote poetry on my skin, his left thumb teasing my nipple while

78

his right hand roamed over my back. Beneath me, trapped in the denim of his jeans, I could feel him hard and wanting, bulging against the wet fabric of my panties until neither of us could take it anymore.

I pushed him back onto the bag, grinning wolfishly down at him, and I was thrilled at the touch of not fear, but uncertainty in his eyes. "What have I gotten myself into?" he whispered as I reached for his belt.

"A lot more than you bargained for, and I hope you can handle it," I replied, fumbling with his belt before realizing that it wasn't the normal type. Instead of the typical buckling method, it was one of those GI style web belts with a rolling friction clasp in the buckle, which I quickly undid before unbuttoning his jeans. As my fingers worked, I felt the hunger growing inside me, and I knew that even if Patrick and I didn't end up having a long term relationship, I was ready and needing his body at least for tonight.

I peeled down Patrick's plain boxer-briefs, and what was inside more than made up for the packaging, as his thick, beautiful cock emerged from hiding. He lifted his hips and helped me get the rest of his pants off, and I took a moment to get off of the bag and look at him.

He was very fit, with large swells to his muscles that flowed to a tight waistline and then back out into strong, tree trunk like legs. Not fat, but muscular. His cock stood tall and proud from its base, and I could see that I'd be challenged by his thickness. I love a good challenge.

"Take off the skirt," he said, his confidence growing as he saw how I reacted to his body. I was glad in that, while I enjoyed his initial trepidation, I didn't want to do all the work when it comes to having sex.

I reached for the fastener on my skirt, then let my hands lower. Instead, I raised them and cupped my breasts, and toed off the sandals I'd been wearing. "You do it," I replied, turning my hip to show him where the thing closed. "Please?"

"As you wish," Patrick replied, getting to his knees and crossing the short distance over to me. His hands caressed my calves and thighs, running under the skirt to cup my ass and send more thrills to me. He leaned forward and kissed my belly button, and I felt more powerful than I'd ever been with this strong, handsome man on his knees in front of me, his hands kneading my ass while he kissed my stomach. I stroked my hand through his dark hair, I and knew that, regardless of anything else, this was not going to be a one-night thing.

Patrick let go of my butt to reach higher, finding the waistband to my bikini briefs and pulling them down and off my legs. "Not the standard way, but I like it so far," I teased as he lifted one leg and then the other to free them.

"I like this skirt," he answered, running his hands back up my legs. His right hand turned to go in between my thighs and I parted my knees, giving him access. Blindly, he found my pussy, cupping it in his hand. His eyebrows lifted as he stroked the smooth skin.

"Shaved?"

I shook my head. "Waxed, and a few laser treatments," I half moaned in reply. It was the one indulgence I'd partaken in during the lean years of my student days and early associate days working, and if that made me vain, so be it. Still, I love the feeling of being bare and smooth, silken under a lover's touch. "You like?"

"I love it, all of you," he replied, stroking a finger between my lips. Wetness coated his questing finger and he smiled, bringing it out from under my skirt to admire in the light before licking it clean. "Delicious."

Lifting my skirt, he lowered himself more until my pussy was open to his tongue, and his hands cupped my ass again. With my skirt in the way, I couldn't see anything except the flex of muscles on his back and shoulders as he made love to me with his seemingly impossibly long, deft tongue, which swept from top to bottom on me before probing inside. I couldn't believe how good it was or how amazing he felt, my mind flashing with desire as he licked me over and over.

My legs trembled as he found the hard little button of my clit, flicking his tongue over it. I bent over, trying to keep my balance and leaning on him as he licked and sucked, his strong hands and arms keeping me within his tongue's reach. "Oh fuck, Patrick," I gasped, my hands digging into his shoulders. "What are you doing?"

Pulling back, Patrick's face was covered in my wetness and he stood up, sweeping me into his arms and covering my face with kisses. "I'm worshiping the most beautiful woman I've ever seen," he replied before nibbling on my earlobe. He turned easily and carried me to the bean bag chair, where he laid me on the carpet next to the chair. "I'd use the bag, but I'm afraid we'd be unable to move the way we want."

"You read my mind," I replied, pushing him back. "I'm *very* active in bed."

"Good to know," Patrick said, grinning. "One request?"

"What?"

"Leave the skirt on," Patrick said, as he tore open a package and slid a condom on with a quickness.

Laying down next to him, I lifted my leg and reached for his cock, which was still hard and thick in my hand. With me guiding him, he pushed his way inside me, pausing when he could tell I was getting stretched too much. "You okay?"

"Just go slow; it feels great until the last bit," I said. "It's been a little while, and you're pretty thick."

Patrick nodded, his green eyes looking into mine as he worked slowly in and out. The unpleasant stretching soon melted into wonderful fullness, and I felt more and more of him inside me. It was funny, in that the way we were laying, we were almost in a scissor position. It was a favorite of mine, but with Patrick, it was so different and so much better at the same time. When the base of his cock rubbed against my clit for the first time, I nearly came, I was so close. My fingers hooked into his back and I growled. "Now you promise me," I said, my fingernails threatening to tear his back apart. "You don't stop until you and I both come. And I mean *don't stop*."

"As you wish," he said, pulling back and pushing forward again. Explosions of pleasure tore through me as Patrick stroked in and out, my pussy already quivering from the wonderful oral attention he'd given me. I was delirious, drunk off the heady mix of pleasure and hormones as he pounded me without restraint, his cock filling me again and again.

Part of the reason I'm so adventurous sexually is because for me, orgasms are not just a momentary thing, but rolling, building upon one another. Multi-orgasmic is barely a beginning to describe how I can be, and Patrick's unrelenting, powerful stroking cock was all I needed. In only a minute, maybe less, my pussy clenched and the first wave of my orgasm broke through me, soft cries joining my gasps as I felt myself tense around him.

Patrick's lips found mine as he increased his pace, flowing with me in perfect harmony, like no other lover I'd ever had. The image of Scott Pressman flashed through my mind, only to be shattered and obliterated as Patrick kept going, right there with me. Scott had played me emotionally, set me up. Patrick was doing

81

nothing of the sort, but just staying with me, his body in tune with mine.

Pulling on me, we rolled so that I was on top, filled deeper than ever by Patrick's wonderful cock. Holding my waist, he planted his hips and thrust hard and deep, his eyes still looking into mine. My body tensed again as another wave of orgasm swept on me and I cried out, my body singing joyfully to the universe as pleasure and release shot through me, all the way to the tips of my fingers and back again. It felt like my hair was almost standing on end, it was so electrically wonderful, and still Patrick kept up his thrusts, even as sweat stood out on his forehead and beaded on his chest muscles.

I lost track of time, of the world, of everything except the feeling inside me and the wonderful, stupendous man underneath me. I rode him, pleasured myself on him, feasted on his body and his cock with carnal, unbidden need until I could feast no more. My breath tore from my throat as I lost count of the number of climaxes he gave me, still maintaining iron-willed control, until tears were coursing down his cheeks from the effort of his restraint. I couldn't take any more, and I looked down at him.

"Now," I mouthed, my voice having failed me. "Come for me."

"As you wish," he said through gritted teeth, pulling me tight and rolling me over so that he was on top. His hips sped up even more, and in moments I could feel the trembling in his back and his thrusts that told me he would be mere seconds.

I'll never forget the image of Patrick as he came, the way his eyes flew open like it was a holy, ethereal experience. He came, and my body tensed one more time, coming with him as we found that final level of perfection that I'd never found with anyone before. For the first time in my life, I'd found my total, complete sexual partner and equal, and as we collapsed on the carpet, too exhausted to even disentangle ourselves, I knew that I would forever be bound to this man.

I wasn't so much upset that Tabby was having sex with Patrick in the entertainment room as I was worried. It wasn't about the furniture, mind you.

I was worried because, as far as I knew, the last man before Patrick to have sex with Tabby was Scott Pressman, the Knave of Hearts. His chicanery had left her an emotional and mental wreck, and while she wasn't the same woman who Sophie had brought home and cuddled on the bean bag chair a whole night using classic Ben & Jerry's therapy, I cared about her enough to still worry.

"You knew she had to get back in the saddle eventually," Sophie said the next day after they'd both left. We'd loaned Patrick one of the Mount Zion cars so that he could get to his apartment to change in time for work, while Tabby just called Vanessa to say she was running late. Being the President meant you got to do that sometimes.

"Don't say that," I groaned, trying not to smile. "Because knowing Tabby, she has a literal saddle somewhere that we don't know about. I guess just, after Pressman, I was kind of hoping that Tabby would find a boring, non-criminal past sort of person. Better yet, an accountant who likes cats or something."

We were sitting in my home office, the Dow Jones and Nasdaq numbers running by me, Sophie on her computer composing an email to some of the media outlets we knew. Bennie Fernandez had gotten back to my blind-drop email saying that while he was too busy to deal with Gerald Traylor, he knew a good guy down in Washington with the IRS who would be able to handle the information we'd given him. Hey, when you're hiding two mistresses in million dollar apartments, the IRS will find you if they want to. In the meantime, Sophie was using the media to blow up Traylor's facade even before the Feds got to him.

"I'm sure you would," Sophie joked back as she typed. "That way there'd be no way to have any lingering issues."

I shrugged. "Maybe. I just . . . I'm worried that she's exposing her heart again before it's ready."

Sophie clicked the mouse she was using and stood up, coming over and kissing my cheek. "Mathew Mark Bylur Marcus Smiley Mark Snow, you are the kindest, sweetest, most protective man I've ever met," she said. "But relax. I've seen Tabby before, and yes, Pressman screwed her up bad. But I've watched, and she's been right here with us. I wouldn't have set up the room the way I did if I didn't think she was ready."

"I guess. I suppose you know her better than me, and I know she's like a sister to you," I said.

"While it was a terrible experience, she's become a stronger person now."

I turned in my chair, pulling Sophie down into a hug. "You're too beautiful, you know that, Sophie? Just too damned beautiful."

We held each other for a minute before Sophie kissed me and then patted me on the cheek, climbing out of my lap. "Well, if you want to have more than just a hug, give me a half hour to finish my work. If you can get through the market session, we can do a lot more than just a little playtime too."

"Oh?" I asked, turning back to my computer. "Why's that?"

"Because anticipation makes it all the sweeter," she breathed into my ear, her warm breath sending chills down my spine. "Besides, after listening to those two for most of last night, I'm needing a lot of satisfaction."

She reached between my legs and gave my cock a gentle rub and squeeze through my shorts before kissing my ear. "After lunch, this is mine."

As it was, after lunch playtime lasted until slightly before five o'clock, when both of us woke up from a sex induced nap. Showering quickly, I started a hearty meal and was about halfway through my preparation when Tabby came in the door.

"Hey, bro," she greeted me, setting her briefcase down and giving me a kiss on the cheek. She'd been calling me that a lot recently.

Her eyes were glittering with happiness, and I had to admit there was a bounce to her step that she hadn't had even the day before.

I went back to chopping vegetables and looked over. "By the way, our Traylor issue is on its way to being solved, and I cleared nearly fifty thousand profit on the market today. I wish I could do that every day; we'd make fifteen million a year easy just on the market. So what made today so special?"

"Nothing much, really. Just normal office stuff. I guess, well, you know."

"I do," I replied, "and there's no reason to be shy about it. Listen, Sophie's in the back taking a quick shower, so I'll keep this short. Yeah, I'm concerned. You know why. But I also trust you, and will be there to support you however it happens. If emotions get involved, I hope they're good ones. If not, we'll both be there for you. And if you need the guy's ass kicked, you know who to call."

Tabby laughed and wrapped her arms around me from behind in a hug, leaning her cheek against my back, near my neck. Without her heels on, she is kind of short. "That's why I love you so much, Mark. You're the best big brother I wish I'd had my whole life. Thank you."

Letting me go, she looked down at dinner. "Wow, work up an appetite?"

"I've got a patrol tonight. I need the energy. I studied the pattern of the amateur up in Fillmore Heights, and I suspect he's going to be out there," I said, taking my vegetables and pouring them into the large soup pot I had simmering on the stove.

"Why are you so worried about this guy, anyway?" Tabby asked, leaning against the counter. "He's just a guy trying to do what you do."

"What I do is quiet, although a loud sort of quiet. Nobody talks to the cops, and everyone knows that if I come around, to get the hell off the streets and to stop their stuff. But I'm always safe in what I do. Normal patrols, surveillance, even most of the hits I've done, I've never taken the risky route. This guy though . . . he's flashy and he's rash, which is great for getting attention, but not the type he's hoping for. He's going to get himself killed at some point. When that happens, the cops are going to be on the streets hard, and they're all going to be looking for me. Not because I killed him, but because I'm another rumored vigilante out there, even if the TV doesn't have reports on me."

Tabby nodded, then crossed her arms over her chest. "You sure it's because you don't actually like this guy? He's out there trying, at least, which you have to give him credit for."

I didn't answer, and Tabby chuckled after a minute. "I'm going to change. Patrick's got a community event that he said would take up a chunk of the evening, and if you're going out, I figure I can help Sophie with her load of the housework. Then the two of us are going to sit back and relax, have some girl talk, and think of all the ways we're going to spoil your daughter. After all, I have to spend that two hundred K a year you're paying me on something besides Chinese food for my secretary."

* * *

The early fall air was chilly against my cheek, and I was glad I'd switched to the slightly more thermal compression top I was wearing under my tactical vest. The city, while not one to get tons of snow during the winter, still had more than its fair share of nights that dropped below freezing, and I didn't want to have to worry about wearing heavy garments if I didn't need to. The hood hugged my head more too, which helped with my disguise.

Despite his amateur actions, I had to admit the new vigilante was having a positive effect on the neighborhood as I surveyed it using binoculars from the top of St. Patrick's Church. Its slate roof was slippery, but clinging to the steeple just below where the cross was, I could see a lot of Fillmore Heights, and what I saw was encouraging.

The gangs were spooked, that was for sure. The Latin Kings, maybe as a side effect of our interrupted eavesdropping earlier, were quiet, while the 88s, despite being out, were sticking to their territory.

I played a hunch and headed over to GD territory. The amateur had hit the 88s once, and the Latin Kings once. If he was trying to actually lower the overall gang presence in Fillmore Heights, he'd come after the Gangster Disciples next. After the gang wars of the nineties, they were the last of the big powers left. It was what I would do if I were in his position.

Rappelling quickly down from the steeple, I slid down the church's roof before freeing the rope and then reattaching it to the side of the building and descending to street level. I got on my cycle and drove off, heading toward the east side of Fillmore Heights. The GDs had their headquarters in the east side, and they controlled the area with an iron fist. Part of it was due to their numbers. Vastly outnumbering both the 88s and the Latin Kings combined, the GDs were the oldest of the three big gangs in the area. Mostly African American, they also had Hispanics, especially Puerto Ricans, which for some reason the Latin Kings didn't accept in their ranks. They'd also absorbed a lot of the remnants of the Fillmore Crips at the end of the gang war, boosting their ranks even more.

I stopped my bike while in the border zone between GD and 88 territories, parking it in an alleyway behind a dumpster. I found an old discarded tarp and pulled

86

it over the bike, hoping it would be enough. The electric motorcycle wasn't registered, so if it was stolen there was no way I'd get it back, although the price of replacement didn't worry me. It was the principle of the thing that bothered me. Well, that and having to go rooftop to rooftop or through back alleyways out of Fillmore Heights and then somehow still getting my way to my nearest strike base where I had another vehicle in order to get home.

My bike stashed, I headed up the nearest fire escape to the roofs. Staying near the edge so I could still see the streets below, I took off at a light jog, looking for the GD headquarters.

I was two blocks away when the sound of a car engine below caught my attention. This car was tuned up, whatever it was, and I stopped, dropping down to a knee on the rooftop. Pulling out my binoculars, I caught sight of an old compact car down the street. It pulled into a parking lot and out of sight before I could make a clear identification, but something about it tickled my attention. Maybe it was the shape, but I swore I'd seen a vehicle similar to it before.

Shaking my head, I turned back toward the GD territory, quickly making my way along the rooftops to just across the street from the GD leader's house. Tweak Petersen had been head of the GDs for about three years, after the previous leader had been killed off in an 88 attack. Tweak had consolidated his territory and pulled back, which in the short term weakened the GDs, but allowed them to eventually halt the advance of their rivals. By actively recruiting the young men of his territory, he had plenty of street soldiers.

Tweak was famous for running his operation out of a donut shop that was in his area, which was strange. Not only was the shop fronted by plate glass, making it easy to see him, but also Tweak was a Type 1 diabetic. Insulin dependent, Tweak was almost never seen indulging in the shop's specialty, but instead sipped endless cups of coffee that left him with such a caffeine addiction that it had earned him his nickname.

I was watching the shop for nearly twenty minutes when I heard the movement behind me. I dove to the side and rolled, pulling my Glock to see what it was. "Amateur."

"I really wish you wouldn't call me that," the other man said. "By the way, I almost snuck up on you."

"You were a whole building away," I retorted. "What the fuck are you doing here?"

"Same as you, it looks like," he whispered, kneeling next to me. He was carrying a large duffel bag, which was what had made most of the noise, slapping against his back when he jumped. He had something large and either metal or plastic, or a bit of both, in there. "So what is Tweak up to?"

Something in the amateur's voice tickled something in my brain again, but I dismissed it temporarily. Other things to focus on. "Normal night's work for a gang leader," I said, "but I just got here. You going to do anything stupid?"

The amateur shook his head and set his bag down. "Not this second. You can put the gun away."

I holstered my Glock and looked back across the street. It took a little while, but a pattern became evident. A donut shop, even one that was open twenty-four hours a day, tends to have very clear peaks in business, especially in the morning hours as you'd expect. It was rare, even at a Krispy Kreme that had fresh, hot samples, to have a line after six at night.

While the donut shop Tweak was sitting in never quite got packed, there was a constant line of young men coming in. They'd buy a single donut or sometimes two, then while they were waiting, they'd talk with Tweak for a minute before leaving. It was much higher than normal; the last time I'd spied on Tweak he had maybe a dozen visitors in a night.

That night, however, the visits were almost constant, and Tweak was busy issuing orders directly to the street level. "This is weird," the amateur said. "He shouldn't be talking directly to the soldiers, but his lieutenants. What the hell is going on, Snowman?"

"I have no damn clue," I said, reaching into my leg pocket. "If you shut up, maybe I can find out."

When I'd caught the amateur before, he was using a standard parabolic mic that you can get in any of a hundred stores or websites. About a hundred and fifty bucks, it works well if you have line of sight on your target and there is nothing in between you, like plate glass. What I pulled out was much smaller and higher technology, using a laser to pierce any window and allow me to hear what was being said. The set I was using cost somewhere in the five-thousand-dollar range, and while great, wasn't perfect. I had to be able to get a surface that I could bounce the laser off of that would reflect back to me, or else I wouldn't be able to detect the changes in the light.

I was slowly trying out potential surfaces when I heard something next to me. Turning my head, I gawked as the amateur clicked something together and stood up. "Fuck it," he said, bringing the device to his shoulder. "Take out Tweak, we wear down the GDs."

He pulled the trigger on his device, and I realized he had a compressed air rifle of some type. The front window of the donut shop shattered as whatever the amateur was shooting impacted and GDs scattered like rats from a fire. In the dim night light I was able to see what the man was holding, and I ducked back. I was willing to help the man, but if he was suicidal, I couldn't do much to help him. "Stop, you fucking idiot!"

"Fuck that," he said, a smile on his voice as he pulled the trigger. His rifle was the grown up version of a paintball gun, with a larger shoulder tank and firing something I guessed was a lot more damaging than just plain old paint. I snuck a look over my shoulder as I saw about half the rounds smash into dust, causing the GDs to start hacking and coughing, and I knew at least half of the rounds he was using were filled with a variant of pepper spray, common with certain SWAT teams for crowd control as it was a lot more accurate and longer range than standard sprays. The other rounds I wasn't sure about, but they looked solid. One GD took a round in his shoulder, spinning him to the ground. He grabbed his arm in pain, but there was no blood that I could see.

Pulling my Glocks, I dropped back as the idiot finished emptying his air tank before dropping to his knees and looking over at me. "Pretty fucking wild, man!" he said, right before the first rounds started being fired back from the GDs below. "Oh, shit!"

"Yeah, dumbass," I commented, scrambling back as an automatic rifle chattered below. "What you forgot was that the nearly full moon was behind you and you were kneeling like a fucking *Call of Duty* player busting shots for fifteen seconds. They know you're up here."

"Not for long," he said, breaking down his rifle in smooth, easy movements before throwing the pieces into his pack. He backed up and threw the bag over his shoulder, grinning like a madman at me. "You coming, or are you going to wait for them to come up the fire escape?"

Shaking my head, I led the way, leaping from rooftop to rooftop, away from our pursuit. Still, I could hear the GDs below us, their cars and other vehicles fanning out to find us. "What you didn't fucking think about," I grunted in between jumps as we ran, "was the tactics of the gang you just decided to hit. The GDs Zerg their opponents when they're attacked. What you did was like taking a stick to a fire ant hill. Problem is, they're faster than we are."

It was true. Each of the groups in Fillmore Heights responded to attacks in different ways. The 88s tended to roll in small, highly disciplined squads that would take an attack, but then counterattack with almost berserker ferocity. They'd kill their attackers and about half their family if they needed.

Meanwhile, the Latin Kings were damn near ninjas, working from behind the scenes to get their business done. As long as you didn't publicly insult their machismo, they were the most laid back of the gangs, although they would strike back. If they had to kill someone, they did it quietly, in the middle of the night, and melted away before you could respond. They also conducted themselves by a strict code of honor, which gave them the most support and street cred with the non-criminal residents of Fillmore Heights. If you had to rent to a gang banger, you prayed it was a Latin King.

Meanwhile, the Gangster Disciples were like I had told the amateur, the *StarCraft* Zerg. They swarmed their enemies with more guns and more response than anyone else. You knew they were coming, and you only hoped they ran out of adrenalin or ammo before you got shot.

It was this rolling, firing wave of criminals that I was attempting to outrun. Reaching the alleyway that my bike was in, I looked over the side of the building, yanking my head back as I saw a GD lowrider roar by on the street. "Fuck!"

"What?"

"My bike is down in that alleyway," I said, looking as another car roared by. I knew what the GDs were doing. Sending out cars first, they'd set up a perimeter around their territory, while behind them would be chasers on motorcycles and slower cars who would crisscross the streets until they had their prey. I'd heard about it too many times.

"My car is six blocks that way," the other man said, pointing. "If we can get there, we can get out of here."

"Your car is too far outside GD turf. They're sweeping now, and we can't stay up on rooftops the whole way. Unless you have a way to cross a major street without touching the ground," I said. "Can you ride on the back?"

"You mean on your cycle?" the other man asked. "How big is it? Five hundred, six hundred cc?"

"It's electric," I replied back. He looked at me incredulously, and I nodded. "Great for stealth. Listen, I'm serious, can you hold on well enough so we can get the hell out of here? We get to street level, I bust us through the GD line on my cycle. If they pursue, we high tail it out of Fillmore. My bike's still got another forty miles of high speed juice in the battery. If they don't, I drop you at your car, and if I catch you again doing anything that stupid, I shoot you myself."

The other man looked like he was about to argue, but he shut his mouth and nodded. "We can discuss that later," he said, reaching for the fire escape. He scrambled down the ladder, with me right on his heels.

Reaching my bike, I was happy to find that it was still undisturbed. Yanking the cover off, I grabbed my helmet and passed it to the man. "You're on back, they'll be shooting at you once we bust through," I said. "It's not bulletproof, but it's better than nothing."

He grabbed my helmet and jammed it on his head over top of his balaclava, and snapped the eye shield down. "Let's go."

"Hold on tight," I said as he mounted the bike behind me. "This thing doesn't accelerate like a normal bike. It can jump like a bat out of hell."

The other man squeezed tight and I slammed my bike into action, whipping around the corner, already going more than thirty miles an hour. The advantages of a motorcycle are enhanced with my bike in that I'm quick as a flash, and before I even reached the next corner, I was already going sixty-five. Even better, being nearly silent meant I wasn't announcing my presence.

Unfortunately for us, the GD barricade was quick and it was tight. Less than thirty seconds after taking off, I saw the first GD car blocking the road, a giant early eighties Chevy sedan that was roughly the size of an elephant. The bangers inside were strapped and ready, and in the instant I had to look, I saw two shotguns and an

Uzi.

Immediately, I started swerving side to side, my motor whining in protest as I twisted the accelerator even harder. The lead GD saw us and fired a round, which I avoided easily, but that was when things went to shit.

The last GD, the one with the Uzi, decided the best way to stop us was to spray the entire street from side to side. I heard a long, ripping sound, kind of like a denim tearing, and suddenly the man behind me groaned loudly. Rounding the corner, I abandoned my idea of getting him to his car and took off, knowing I could lose pursuit in the maze of streets between Fillmore Heights and Mount Zion.

What followed was some of the tensest riding I've ever done. My battery, which should have been good for forty miles, started to drain at an alarming rate, which told me that something had gotten hit, either my battery or somewhere in the system, creating a short that was draining juice too quickly. I was just happy that nothing mechanical was hit and pressed my bike as fast as I could.

"Hold on, dude," I yelled over my shoulder as we passed into a safe area. I kept my throttle maxed until I felt him start to slip behind me. Coming to a screeching halt, I grabbed his arms and pulled them tight.

Reaching into my pocket, I pulled out my phone and hit the speed dial for Sophie. "Hello?"

"I've got the amateur with me. He's been shot, I don't know where."

"Where are you?"

"Warehouse district. I'm maybe five minutes from MJT HQ."

"Is he conscious?"

"Nonsensical," I replied. He sagged again, and I pulled his arms tight. "I need your help."

"Get home, ASAP. I'll have the surgical kit ready in the bell tower. We have plasma here."

"Roger," I replied, closing the line and thinking quickly.

Reaching into another pocket on my vest, I pulled out my familiar roll of electrical tape. Not as useful as duct tape, but it was a lot more compact. Grabbing the guy's arms, I slung them over my shoulder and pulled.

"Hold on a bit, man, come on," I encouraged him. He didn't answer, just muttered something while deep in a delusional state. Grabbing his wrists, I quickly

92

looped five or six wraps of tape around his hands, leaving the rest of the roll dangling as I leaned into the controls. It shifted some of his weight onto my back, kind of like wearing a huge backpack, but with his butt still on the seat. I couldn't ride at full speed, but I could ride.

It took me nearly twenty minutes to get back to Mount Zion, and more than once I nearly lost my balance going around curves. We were plain lucky that I didn't run into any of the cops, but we got home unmolested. I pulled into the garage, where Sophie and Tabby were already there, both of them in surgical masks, both as a precaution against infection and as a way to hide their identities. If he woke up, he wouldn't know who we were.

"He's unconscious," Sophie said as I staggered, trying not to collapse to the concrete as I dismounted. Getting off a motorcycle with two hundred-odd pounds of dead weight on your back is hard. "Come on, quickly."

Tabby and Sophie both grabbed one of his legs as I headed through the house toward the bell tower. My lower back was on fire, but I kept going, adjusting him as best I could. Each step was agony and my legs trembled, but I reached the top where Sophie had laid out the foam rubber mat and her surgical kit.

I knelt down, letting Tabby and Sophie maneuver the guy onto the mat. Slipping his arms over my head, I sagged down and gasped, sweet, cool air flowing into my lungs. "What happened?" Tabby asked.

"Genius boy over there started shooting the Gangster Disciple donut shop with a goddamned hopped-up air gun," I said, "not knowing their tactics. But he didn't complain, took one in the back as I drove us off."

"He's been shot in the right lung," Sophie said, her voice icy and tense the way I knew she was when she was in her doctor mode. She rolled him onto his stomach after checking his chest. "It's still inside, I need to get it out. Then I need to stop the bleeding."

Reaching for her bandage scissors, she started at the neck of the guy's shirt, cutting down the back and pulling it open. I looked up at Sophie, who was intent on her patient. "How can I help?"

"Plasma, two units on the table, get me a line ready to go. Green IV needle, that's 18 gauge. Tabby, grab that pole and bring it over here so Mark can hang those bags."

Tabby didn't move, and I glanced up at her. She was frozen, staring at the man on the mat as Sophie peeled his shirt back. "Tabby?"

She didn't say anything, and I ignored her, grabbing the pole and setting it up. I set up the plasma line as best I could, and knelt down next to Sophie. "Want me to run the line?"

After my last bit of surgery, I'd told Sophie that I wanted to learn the basics of medical treatment. Starting with dummies and mannequins, she had worked with me up to doing some techniques, including running IV lines and even some basic stitching. I wasn't even good enough to call myself a nurse's assistant, but I could help out.

"Yes. Right arm," she ordered me. I found the arm, and pulled the sleeve down, exposing a series of tattoos. Whoever this guy was, he had some impressive ink on him, stuff I wanted to look at later. I found the large vein on the top of his forearm and tied it off, sinking the IV in on the first try. The large gauge needle would allow us to feed him plasma as quickly as possible, and I loosened the tourniquet.

I turned my attention to Sophie, who was working hard to find the slug. She had spread the entry wound open and was working with forceps. She found the round and pulled, withdrawing it from the wound and dropping it onto the floor. "Mark, over here, I need light."

For the next forty tense minutes, Sophie used her skills to patch him up. She had to put stitches both internally and externally, a task she had told me before she wasn't sure of, and twice had me wipe her forehead as sweat got in her eyes. Finally, sighing, she finished the last stitch on his back. "He'll make it."

We both were surprised when we heard a sob from Tabby, who I had tuned out after she had frozen. There wasn't time for concern at that instant, but now there was. Stripping off the surgical gloves that I'd pulled on when I was preparing the IV, I stood up and took her in my arms. "Tabby, what's wrong?"

"It's him," she said, sobbing. "It's him."

"Who?" I asked, stroking her hair. Tabby sobbed harder, and I looked down at Sophie, who shrugged. Reaching for her bandage scissors, she cut his balaclava off. The first thing I saw was black, slightly wavy hair, then stubble. Sophie kept cutting until his face was exposed and eased the mask up and off of him. "Oh, shit."

94

Lying on the mat, still unconscious, was Patrick McCaffery.

Chapter 12
Tabby

When Mark called Sophie while out on patrol, I knew something was wrong. He never used his phone while on a mission, not without coordinating it beforehand. If he had to talk with her, he preferred to use two way secure radios or a constant open microphone using a VOIP system. During those times, Sophie was always in the bell tower or in the home office, where she could access communication systems that the two of them had set up. I'd watched her a few times, and she was always intense, focused, with her headset on and her eyes constantly roving over the multiple screens. It was like watching an android at work.

This time, though, we were chilling out in the entertainment room. When Mark went out on patrol, we would often hang out there, mostly trying to distract ourselves from anything but the fact that her husband, and the man that I considered a brother, was out risking his life. It was the sort of thing that would drive you crazy if you let it. I could understand why police and firefighter spouses age prematurely.

We were watching a DVRed, day-old edition of *The Daily Show* when Sophie's cellphone rang. Her conversation with Mark was short and to the point, and when she hung up, her face had changed. It wasn't quite the look she sported when she was in the bell tower, but it was getting there quickly. "Mark's bringing a wounded man here," she said simply. "Follow me."

Following her into the bedroom, Sophie pulled open a drawer and tossed me some clothes. "They're a bit big for you, but they'll work. We can dispose of them later if we need to."

We stripped out of our pajamas and into clean light pants and shirts quickly. Sophie led me to the bell tower, where she and I set up the foam rubber mattress. Sophie got out her surgical kit and handed me a mask. "We may have to conceal who we are," she explained. "Leave it on."

The room set up, we headed down to the garage. The wait wasn't long, but in the few minutes between when we got down there and Mark came in, I could see the tremble in Sophie's hands. She was muttering to herself, most of it too low for me to hear, but in the cavernous silence of the four-car garage, I could hear some of it. She was wishing, or perhaps praying would be a better term, despite her professed atheism, that Mark was unhurt. Mixed in were some reminders to herself, like she was psyching herself up for what was to come. I understood, it'd been a while since she had done any serious medical treatment. I'd watched her keep her knowledge up to date with online simulators or other sorts of study materials, but that wasn't the same as the real thing.

Mark arrived with his passenger, who was loosely hanging on his back. For a few moments I thought perhaps he was awake until I realized that the reason his arms were so secure was because Mark had taped his hands together over his shoulders. Sophie and I helped Mark off his cycle and up the stairs, where we laid him down on the mattress.

"Genius boy over there started shooting the Gangster Disciple donut shop with a goddamned hopped-up air gun," Mark said, telling us about the incident, "not knowing their tactics. But he didn't complain, took one in the back as I drove us off."

"He's been shot in the right lung. It's still inside, I need to get it out," Sophie stated, her voice eerily calm and filled with command. I'd never seen her when she was doing her internship at University Hospital, but knew instantly where she got it from. It seemed like a lifetime ago, but it came back to her in an instant.

She used her scissors to cut open the man's shirt, and as she peeled the cloth back, I felt like I'd been hit in the stomach. The hole in his back wasn't that big; it looked like something I could plug with my little finger, but as she and Mark worked together to clear the space for her to work, they exposed his upper body. An upper body I'd felt and explored very recently. I'd felt those muscles, and had run my fingers around the two little moles there on the lower back near the waistband, so close together that you could loop them in a figure eight if you wanted to.

I didn't want to believe it at first, but when his right arm was visible in the light, my brain went into panic mode. There, I could see the designs I'd traced after we'd made love, and I was sure if he was turned over I'd see the gryphon on his right pec. I lost all sense of time, paralyzed. I heard Sophie ask me to do something, but I couldn't move, could barely breathe as I watched her and Mark work.

I've said before that I love Sophie. She's my sister, but I've never been in awe of her before. I'd seen her do some pretty cool stuff, but never anything awe inspiring. For example, she was great in the gym, but she wasn't on the level of an Olympic athlete. Her skills in martial arts and stick-fighting were impressive, but I was pretty sure Ronda Rousey could still kick her ass. What made me love Sophie were her mind and her soul, which, while amazing, aren't exactly awe inspiring.

Those forty minutes, though, she was a goddess, a primal force of nature that could not be denied. She was as forceful as the lightning that tore the sky apart when I was a little girl in Florida, as calm as an iceberg. She was Artemis, Apollo the Healer's sister. She was Eir, the Norse goddess of medicine. She was unstoppable, unflappable. She held life and death in her hands and commanded both with the pure force of her will and her skill. In my entire life, I'd never loved, feared, and revered a person as much as I did for those forty minutes. She held his life in her hands.

Finally, she was done. "He'll make it."

I felt like the entire world crashed on me with those three words. Tears and sobs tore from my chest, racking my body. Mark and Sophie looked over at me, Mark getting up while Sophie finished up her work. He pulled me into an embrace, his blood-stained surgical gloves quickly marking the t-shirt I was wearing.

"Tabby, what's wrong?" he asked quietly, his voice full of concern and comfort. He was another rock, a strong rock that lent me quiet strength, enough that I could at least form an answer.

"It's him. It's him," was all I could say, burying my face in Mark's chest and sobbing like a child. I heard Sophie cutting with her scissors some more, and a gasp from Mark.

"Oh, shit."

They understood now, too. Lying on the mat was the man I'd made love with just the night before. Lying on the mat was Patrick McCaffery.

* * *

We were still in the bell tower, Sophie downstairs showering after cleaning up her ad-hoc surgical area. We'd transferred Patrick onto a cot, still lying on his stomach to keep pressure off the wound. She'd given him a shot of a broad spectrum antibiotic to ward off infection, and then went off to shower. He didn't need a

97

ventilator, as the bullet had just nicked a lung, not collapsing it. He'd almost bled to death, however, and was taking another bag of blood that Sophie and Mark kept on hand for such an emergency. I was getting a first-hand inventory of just what all the two of them had prepared for, and I was shocked while at the same time thankful. If not, Patrick could've died.

Sophie was almost staggering herself, the stress and exhaustion finally overcoming her. Mark told her to get some sleep, and he'd watch Patrick while she did. She kissed him on the cheek and headed downstairs, leaving the two of us up there.

I was too wired to sleep, as all I could do was look at the still unconscious Patrick. He looked like he was sleeping, and Sophie said she'd given him a mild sedative to let him rest through the night. I looked over at Mark, who was sitting on top of a footlocker that contained some of the bell tower's arsenal. He said something, and I shook my head.

"Sorry, what?"

"I asked if you knew," Mark repeated, concern in his eyes. "Did you even suspect?"

I shook my head. "Mark, how can you suspect someone of something like this? I mean, the odds of this are . . . astronomical, aren't they?"

"Yeah," Mark replied, sighing. "I guess so. But still, you didn't suspect him of anything?"

"No," I said. "He's been a good couple of dates, and well, yes, we had sex. But while he's not been too forthcoming with his past, considering what he told me, I can see why. Did you brag to Sophie when you were first dating about your past in the Confederation? How long did it take for her to know most of the gory details?"

"Months," Mark admitted. "Some details that, well, I don't even tell myself happened sometimes. Over eighty deaths, even more injured . . . you don't tell people about it unless you have to."

We sat in silence, watching Patrick, both of us lost in our heads. As I watched, I thought. Why did I panic and freeze up? Was it because of the sight of the blood? Was it because of the surprise that Patrick was the other vigilante? Or was it because of how I felt about him? I could deny it publicly, and I wouldn't be willing to say anything to Patrick yet about it, but in my heart I knew I cared for him. The days we

98

weren't able to see each other, I was filled with a pleasant ache thinking about him, his smile and his wit. I missed him, and even talking to him over the phone helped. Even still, if this revelation would've been before I met Mark, I would have told Patrick to get lost. But my life has been opened to a world I never knew existed, and all this craziness has almost become *normal* to me.

It wasn't just the sex with Patrick, either. While amazing, the best in my life, actually, we'd only had that one night. My memories of him were filled with other things, little details like how his green eyes sparkled in the evening lights, or how he had been like a little kid enjoying the Spartans game we'd gone to.

Was I in love with him? At that time, I honestly would say no. Was I falling in love with him? There was a niggling voice in my head that insisted yes, despite all the problems that could arise from that fact.

"So what now?" I asked Mark. "I assume you've been thinking about that."

"On which front?" he asked. "Patrick's public life side or this new side of him that we've discovered?"

"Both, I guess," I said. "And us, too. When he wakes up, what are we going to tell him? I doubt you can transport him back to his apartment right now, and I don't know his address."

"He lives in The Playground, I know that," Mark said, "but you're right, I don't know his exact address right now either. Not off the top of my head. On the vigilante side, not much is going to need to change. He's stirred up a hornet's nest in Fillmore Heights, but with the sight of me there and the evenness of his attacks, we won't see a cook off in gang warfare—at least I don't think so. The Latin Kings might try to take some advantage; they weren't hit like the others were, but they've always been slow moving compared to the others. The 88s and GDs are both hurt, but not to such an extreme that it would invite invasion from the others. I'll probably do a surveillance run Monday night, just to see what's going on. The cops will be heavy around there too after this, but since I don't think anyone died, I suspect they'll be there to keep the gangs away from each other more than to try and arrest anyone."

"What about Patrick?"

"It depends on his personal schedule, and if he has an assistant yet. If he does, he can give them a call tomorrow, tell them he got food poisoning or a nasty cold or something. I've worked with people who've had gunshots to the chest before. He'll be able to talk as soon as he wakes up. He's not going to be able to leave here, though, for close to a week, not unless there's an emergency. Which leaves us with the big problem."

"What do we do with him here in the bell tower?" I said, looking around. While there was nothing inside the tower loft itself to identify us or where we were, the slatted sides where the bell sounds used to go out were a big hint, along with the vaulted ceiling that clearly showed the massive beams that used to support the bells. It was enough that a smart man could piece together where we were, even if we wore masks and full sleeves the entire time.

"Exactly. Tabby, I'm going to ask you a very simple question, but one that's not simple at all," Mark said. He looked at Patrick, then at me. I thought he was going to ask me about my emotions for him, but he surprised me. "Do you trust him enough to reveal yourself to him?"

I understood Mark's point. If I revealed who I was, it was the first domino in a chain. There'd be no way we could prevent Patrick from learning about all three of us and who we really were. I was risking more than just myself. I was risking all three of us, and honestly Mark and Sophie stood to lose far more than me. I thought for a long time, about the consequences if we were wrong, and about the man I'd come to know in the past few weeks. Finally, I looked back at Mark and nodded. "Yes. Despite it all, despite what I don't know about him yet, I trust him enough for that."

"Okay," Mark said simply. "I'll talk with Sophie, but if that's how you feel, then we'll go with it unless she objects."

I sat there, stunned. "Just like that?"

"Just like that," Mark replied, giving me a bit of a grin. "What, you didn't think I trust your judgment?"

I shook my head, then shrugged. "Well, after Pressman, and since you guys are the ones with the money and expertise, I guess I've always felt like Alfred to you two being Batman and Batgirl. A sidekick, a minor character—maybe quirky, and sometimes giving good plot points, but not vital."

Mark shook his head. "You've never been minor to me, Tabby. Not to Sophie either. You're the reason she wanted to come back to the city after Sal Giordano sent men after us. We could have disappeared, you know. Marcus Smiley and Sophie Warbird were clean identities; we could have gone anywhere. We could have

100

disappeared into the South Pacific, lived on Fiji and sipped coconut smoothies for the rest of our lives. But Sophie wanted to come back. She talked a bunch of stuff about the city, about making things right, but she wanted to come back because of you and how much you mean to her. After we got you out of that nightclub and I got to know you, I understood why."

"You . . . I didn't know," I said softly. "I mean, I know you guys care about me, but I didn't know."

"We're a team, Tabby. A triangle, three people who are all equal. You're just as important to this team as I am or Sophie is. If you trust Patrick enough, that's all we need to know."

"And if I'm wrong? Not trying to put a crimp on things, but I've been wrong about men before," I said. "My recent track record isn't so good."

"Then we'll deal with it," Mark said simply. "We've got enough money for the three of us to disappear if we need to, and I've already got a new identity being set up for you as well as Sophie and me. Although with a third person coming along, we might need to be a bit more frugal on our living arrangements."

"Oh, so no coconut drinks on Fiji?"

Mark grinned and shook his head. "Of course there will be. We're just going to need a serving girl to bring me and Sophie our drinks."

"Wise ass."

Mark and Tabby told me about their conversation the next morning as we ate a quick breakfast in the bell tower. I still wasn't ready for Patrick to be left unattended, and I didn't have a bunch of medical electronics up there that I could hook him up to anyway. We were lucky his lung hadn't been punctured, just nicked, or else things would have been a lot trickier. Mark had turned him over in the night, and he was resting comfortably so far.

"Okay," I said, munching on a spoonful of Cap'n Crunch. Not the healthiest breakfast in the world, but the overly sweet, processed corn nuggets were a comforting reminder of happy childhood memories. "When he wakes up, then, we'll tell him. We need to get him downstairs anyway. He shouldn't be lying down more than a little bit. Sitting up will help lower the risk of pneumonia and other secondary infections."

"What about the drugs you gave him?" Tabby asked, worried.

"They'll do their job, but still, it's best to keep him up. He should even be walking soon, but only limited amounts until the wounds heal more. He's not going to be going into work for a few days, that's for sure. Your idea of a cold is better for that. If he's as strong as I think he is, he'll be able to gingerly move about outside by about Wednesday, but Friday would be better. That's a solid week, provided he doesn't have any setbacks."

"After that, he'll have more work to do," Mark interjected. "Either he needs to stop his nighttime activities, which I doubt, or he needs some training. He's got guts, but he's also almost gotten himself killed multiple times. We can't have that."

I could see Tabby wanted to object to the idea of Patrick ever going out again, but she shut her mouth. She had seen the way Mark and I were, and she knew that even with my pregnancy, even with the love we shared, Mark was still out there doing his thing. Oh, Mark could tell you a thousand reasons why he did it, from defending the city to atoning for his numerous misdeeds in his prior life, but the reality is much simpler. Patrolling, being the Snowman, that's part of who Mark *is*. To deny him that would be like telling Tabby to deny who she is, or for me to deny that I loved both of them. It just isn't possible.

Patrick stirred, mumbling sleepily on his cot, and the three of us hurriedly finished our breakfasts and set them aside to be taken downstairs later. I went over and checked his heartbeat and lung sounds, which were both clear and strong. We had gotten lucky, I thought. Very lucky indeed.

Patrick's eyelids fluttered, and I hurriedly sat back. He opened them slowly, his eyes still dazed. I'd given him a pretty good dose of sedative. I wanted to make sure he stayed down. "What . . . what happened? Where am I? Who are you?"

"You got shot, you're being treated here, and I'm the person who pulled a nine millimeter slug out of your back," I replied. "But I assume you want more details than that."

Patrick nodded and wiped his hand over his face. "Yeah," he said, blinking. "I could use a lot more details. Like how I got here and why I'm not in a hospital and—"

"That's going to become very clear in a second," I answered. Turning, I waved Tabby over. "Tabs?"

The shocked look of recognition on Patrick's face was worth the misleading answers, and he was even more surprised when Mark stepped closer as well. "Wait . . . you guys . . . you're?"

"Matt Bylur, Marcus Smiley, Mark Snow. Pleased to meet you," Mark said. "Although you and I need to talk seriously later. But for now, I'm going downstairs to get some sleep; it's been a long night."

Patrick nodded, then looked at Tabby. "So . . . Marcus Smiley is the Snowman?" he asked, still perplexed.

I guess being shot, losing a lot of blood, and then having very ad hoc surgery done on you, only to wake up in a bell tower surrounded by your girlfriend and her, well, difficult to properly explain companions will fry anyone's logic circuits for a while.

"Yes," Tabby said, leaning down and kissing him on the cheek. "And like Mark said, there's a lot to talk about. But Sophie's right, you're safe, and you're being treated well. But we need an answer. Do you have any events you have to be at for the next few days?"

"No," Patrick replied after a moment. "Next thing is a meeting on Monday morning. My new assistant, Gwen, has the full schedule."

"Do you have her phone number?" I asked. "We can give her a call for you, or you can try later."

"In . . . in my phone, I think," he said. "My bag."

His eyelids fluttered, and he closed his eyes. His breathing deepened, and he was soon snoring lightly. Tabby looked at me, concerned, and I nodded reassuringly. "It's normal after surgery and sedation. You look exhausted. Did you stay up with Mark all night?"

Tabby nodded and yawned. "I couldn't sleep with Patrick just lying there. I closed my eyes, and each time I did, questions just kept whirling through my head."

"You need your rest," I said, giving her a hug. "Now go, lie down and close your eyes. If you want, you can up here, but it'd be best in the entertainment room. Close the doors, it'll be dark and quiet for you. Go, and I'll make sure to get you up for lunch. He should be coming out of it by then."

Tabby sighed and nodded. "Thank you, Sophie. I . . . I . . ."

"I know. Go get some sleep."

* * *

Patrick came out of his nap just before I was going to run downstairs and wake up Tabby, so I decided to let her sleep. Mark would be up soon anyway. He had most likely set an alarm to be sure. I came over and checked his pulse again and looked in his eyes. "How are you feeling?"

"Like I got clocked in the back by a baseball bat," Patrick said, a lot more clearly than he had that morning. "Is it going to hurt that way for a while?"

"Yep," I said. "You took a bullet through some of the biggest muscles of your body, which diffused the energy. Muscles aren't meant to do that, by the way, but they do it admirably well. They'll be stiff for quite a while though. Actually, you're lucky. It didn't hit any bones and barely clipped your lung. I was able to patch you up pretty cleanly."

Patrick nodded, accepting the situation. "Then unless I'm like seriously screwed up, don't give me any pain meds. I'll deal with it in my own way," he said. "In the meantime, think you can talk with me for a bit?"

"Sure," I replied. "Just to know, though, it's been a while since I practiced my bedside manner."

104

The little joke earned a smile, and Patrick chuckled before grimacing. "No laughter though," he gasped. "That hurts too much."

"Yeah, that might not be the best idea," I agreed with him. "So what's on your mind?"

"So you're *the* Sophie Warbird, the girl who caused the Snowman to go straight?"

"Trust me, he's always been straight," I replied before grimacing. "Sorry, we said no humor, right? Anyway, yeah, that's me. Although I'm officially Joanna Bylur now, Tabby still calls me Sophie around the house."

He looked around, thinking. "And he . . . the Snowman. Damn. I mean, I'm sure he can tell, and I told Tabby, I ran with some lower level Confederation guys when I was young, and I heard stories about the Snowman, but . . . wow. What's he like?"

"He's a good man," I replied. "He loves me, he loves Tabby, he loves our daughter. I guess you'll find out soon enough that I'm a little over four months pregnant."

"Congrats. You must be quite the woman yourself. I mean, from what I know of him, he's like a total savant. Smart, athletic, skilled . . . and now you tell me he's a business genius who is also a loving husband and, well, what is Tabby to you guys?"

"I think I'd rather let her explain that part to you," I replied. "The big thing is, though, if you're going to be given the level of trust we've placed in you, you're going to have to earn it."

"What do you mean?" Patrick asked. "I'm not going to go blabbing that my girlfriend's house staff, or whatever you guys are, were the couple that brought down the Confederation and Owen Lynch. I care about Tabby too much for that."

"Oh really?" I replied, raising an eyebrow. "I think that's something you might want to talk about with her too, but not right this minute. In the meantime, think you're up for walking downstairs? Lean on me, but you'll do better if we can get you into a semi-reclined position."

"Are you sure I won't start leaking on your living room rug?"

"I'm quite sure, Mr. McCaffery," I replied primly. "It might have been a while since my last set of stitches, but I stay in practice. The only way you'll bust a stitch is if you do something against my orders. I don't have an M-D, but I'm your doctor for this."

Patrick smiled and put his hands on the sides of the cot. "Sure you're up for it? I weigh about two ten."

"It's fine. It's not like I have to pick you up, just lean on me."

We made our way downstairs, Patrick leaning on my shoulder for most of the way. Walking slowly, we got all the way to the kitchen area before I led Patrick over to one of our dining nook chairs to sit down. "Looks rather middle class, no offense," Patrick said, looking around the space. "Although that gym was certainly sweet enough. I didn't get a very good look last time I was here."

"No, your eyes were fixed on something very different, and understandably so. By the way, you seriously had never seen *The Princess Bride* until the other night?"

"Never. I know, it makes me a bit of a heathen. But I can make up for it. I'm sure you're going to want to keep me here at least a while if Tabby's asking about my assistant. From what I saw on the walls of your entertainment room, you've got quite the movie collection."

"We do, and if you listen and follow directions, we'll see what we can do. If you're really good, I might even let Tabby sit on the same bean bag as you," I joked.

Patrick's face lit up, and I knew everything I needed to know about how he felt about Tabby before it clouded and he shook his head. "Probably not a good idea. You want me to not strain myself, and well, Tabby kind of inspires that in me. I'm sure you understand."

"She is very inspiring," I agreed. "Still, use these next few days. I'm not going to lie to you, Patrick, you put quite a shock into all of us when we took that mask off. To be honest, you were actually starting to tick Mark off with your antics."

Patrick sighed, and I went into the kitchen, getting the beginnings of a sandwich together. "Mark's the gourmet around here, but I can get you started. Nothing too fancy, but you won't be on rice porridge either."

Patrick

For the next three days, I focused on recovering my strength. While I understood Sophie's admonition that I try to take a week for recovery before going back to work, I doubted I'd be able to do it. First off, while I was the new council member, I was still expected to show up. If I was gone for so long, there'd be questions asked about where I was, especially since I wasn't at home or in any of the local hospitals. I couldn't risk that leading back to Tabby or my new friends.

For the rest of Saturday and Sunday, I was able to relax, slowly walking around the ground floor on Mount Zion when I had the energy, and sitting down with Tabby when I didn't. In a lot of ways, it was mundane. We didn't do much, a lot of her showing me around the inside of the house and such mostly. I was amazed as we did the tour, and I found all the ways they had hidden high tech devices for Mark to use in daily living and working areas. The most impressive had to be Mark's pocket sized computers, which could be plugged into any of a half dozen monitors around the house.

"So MJT really is a three-person operation," I said after dinner on Saturday. "So what's your super power?"

"What do you mean?" Tabby asked, a small smile on her face. I found that I had spent most of the day smiling too, a condition that was quite common around her. Maybe it was the hair, or the beautiful eyes, but I doubted it. I think it was Tabby as a whole that had that effect on me.

"Well, Mark's the super warrior, Sophie's the doctor and, from what I guess, a sniper too, so what's your super power?" I replied.

"I don't really have one," she said, blushing. "I guess every team needs a plain old Jane."

"You're hardly plain or regular," I countered, causing her to blush. "In fact, I think you're special in a lot of ways."

"Patrick," Tabby said, her voice trembling. "This . . . this is hard for me. My last relationship didn't end so well."

I knew more about it than what Tabby knew, but I didn't think it was the time to talk about that just yet. Instead, I answered from my heart. "Tabby . . . I'm here. I'm not saying you have to rush into anything. I was honestly surprised about the other night. Wonderfully so. It's not that I'm saying I want to sit around twiddling my thumbs, but you are special, and if it means we go slow on certain things, then I'm okay with that."

My face felt hot as I finished my statement, and I heaved myself to my feet.

The wound in my back ached, but it held. Sophie had done a good job. "Uhm, I'm going to walk around some. Sophie said I should do that often."

Leaving her, I turned right down the hallway, not really caring where I was going. I soon heard the sound of music coming from the gym and entered slowly. I needed to clear my mind, and I figured nothing I saw there would be in any way challenging to my thought processes. I was in for a surprise.

I had first thought, from the sounds that came out as I opened the door, that I'd find Mark alone. There were some pretty impressive weights being lifted by the sounds of things. Instead, when I opened the door I found Mark and Sophie both working out. Mark was stripped down to only some compression shorts, while Sophie was dressed in running shorts and a sports bra.

They were doing circuit training, although Mark was using weights that most men, well, I guess what you could call most normal men, would have considered heavy. He was practically jumping up and down with two hundred and twenty-five pounds on his back, while Sophie was doing the same with a hundred and thirty-five. They would go from there to swinging a kettle bell, to pushups, to pull-ups, and back to the squats with barely enough of a rest to move from one station to the next. I was tired just watching them.

Sophie noticed me first, dropping down from the pull-up bar and coming over. "I think I've hit my limit for today," she said, barely audible over the music. "After all, I'm in my second trimester. Mark's about halfway done."

I nodded and she left, patting me on the shoulder as she did. I found an empty box against the wall and sat down. My bullet wound ached, so I leaned back against the plaster behind me and watched as Mark finished his circuits. From there he moved on to rope climbing, which was pretty impressive considering they had set the gym up in the main sanctuary of what had been the church. The vaulted beam ceiling went all the way up to about twenty, maybe twenty-five feet, and Mark climbed it over and over again using just his arms.

As he climbed, I could sense that he noticed me, even though he never looked my way or said a word. As he finished up, he went over and grabbed his towel and bottle of water. Still facing away from me, he started speaking.

"You had guts, I'll give you that," Mark said, popping the top on his water and taking a deep pull, "but guts runs out very quickly. You damn near got yourself killed last time. And you almost got me killed in the process."

"I'm sorry about that," I said, humbled. "When you called me an amateur before, I thought you were just being an asshole. I didn't realize how right you were."

"Which is why I'm shocked at what I'm going to say," Mark replied, still facing away from me. As he talked he gestured with his free hand for emphasis, looking out the windows at times. "Out there, I need a partner. Someone I can depend on, someone I can work with. I'm limited in what I can do, mostly to small work, surveillance and information gathering, only doing direct action when I have to. The streets need more. I need a partner. But it has to be a partner I can trust, someone I know is going to have my back and I know can get the job done. If I can't have that, I'm better off working on my own. Before this, I had Sophie when I took down the Confederation and Lynch. Your guess earlier was right; she was the person who took down Petrokias. But she's pregnant, which means that for at least a year, maybe a year and a half, maybe even forever, she's off the streets. If she comes back, it'll be limited duty only, because I will not have my daughter grow up with both her mother and father killed in this fool's crusade. So, despite what you've shown me, despite my better judgment, I'm going to extend you the offer. Before you answer, it's going to be a lot of work before you step foot out there with me. Do you want to train, become my partner?"

"You mean your sidekick? The Robin to your Batman?" I asked. "And what about my day job?"

"That's a big part of why I'm even considering this. It'll be just as important as anything we do at night," Mark replied. "Just like what Tabby does with the money I make is just as important, if not more important, than every criminal I take out with my hands or my guns. And no, I'm not looking for a sidekick, although you'd start in a similar role. If you know your comics, you know what happened to the first Robin. He grew up and became Nightwing, and for a while, he was Batman himself."

I considered his offer. "What do I need to do?"

Mark chuckled. "First, you have to recover from that wound. Then you're going to have to survive something even more painful."

"What?" I asked, a bit worried. "Martial arts training with you? Knives? Guns?"

Mark finally turned to me and shook his head, a sardonic grin on his features.

109

"You're going to have to survive my wife."

Chapter 14
Patrick

That night I slept fitfully in the entertainment room. I would've loved to have had Tabby with me, but I'd been honest when I told Sophie that having her with me would have been too difficult for me. Despite the nearly constant pain I was in and the stiffness in my back, having her nearby was so distracting I barely felt it. I knew that if she was in the same room as me, dressed for bed, I would never have gotten any sleep, not without sex. And sex was not what my body could tolerate.

As I tossed and turned, the pain in my back increased. Sophie had checked my sutures after dinner, declaring that they were looking good. She even showed me a photo taken with her cellphone, and I couldn't really tell. I mean, how good is crusty, tied up skin supposed to look, anyway? It was still stained with the topical antiseptic she'd used for the surgery, even; it looked like a golden carrot surrounded by large, purplish black rings of bruising or something. The thing hurt.

Sighing, I sat up. Slowly rolling to the side, I made my way over to the rack of DVDs on the side, surprised that Mark hadn't had a Blu-Ray put in. Then again, maybe he had and I just hadn't seen them.

As I was flipping through, I heard a click behind me as the door to the room opened. Turning my head, I saw Tabby, thankfully wearing a robe on top of her silk pajamas. Even in the plain robe, she tugged at my heartstrings. "Hi."

"Hi," she replied, coming in and closing the door. "I heard you tossing and turning, and I wanted to see what was up."

"How'd you hear?" I asked her, slightly confused. "I thought this room was soundproofed."

"It is, except for the baby monitor we put in here," she replied. She pointed to the bottom shelf of the cabinet next to the screen, and I saw the red glowing light of the monitor. "Sophie wanted us to split up sleep shifts again tonight, just in case you needed help."

"I see," I replied. I mean, it was on one hand somewhat insulting to be subjected to a baby monitor, of all things. On the other hand, it did show that they cared a lot about my health, which was better than I could say for the last doctor I'd seen. "I just couldn't sleep. I was thinking of maybe trying to watch a movie. Any favorites?"

"I'm sure I can find something."

Tabby fumbled through and took out a disc and dropped it into the player. Grabbing the remotes, she pulled over one of the smaller bean bag chairs and sat down next to me.

"I know I want to be up there right beside you," she said, looking over at me with her beautiful eyes, "but I'm worried I'd jostle you too much if I did. I've wanted to hug you all day, really, but I can't."

"Maybe Monday," I said. "I'm sure the stitches will be nice and secure then. I'll even ask Sophie tomorrow if I can give you a hug after she checks me out in the morning."

Tabby gave me a small grin and nodded. "I'd like that. Now, before we begin, let me just tell you, this is a very special movie to me, so no wise cracks, okay? Only very special people get to watch this with me, so if you screw it up, I'm going to jam a remote up your butt."

"Sorry, not into remote controlled sodomy," I countered. "But thank you."

"For what?"

"For letting me watch it with you."

Tabby looked at me with unspoken words on her tongue for a moment, then she shook her head. "Come on, let's watch the movie."

Using the remotes, she dimmed the lights and turned on the film. "*People once believed that when someone dies, a crow carries their soul to the land of the dead. But sometimes, something so bad happens that a terrible sadness is carried with it . . .*"

For the next hour and forty minutes, I let myself be sucked into the emotional, action packed story that meant so much to Tabby. I kept most of my attention on the screen, but I also paid attention to her, watching her as she was moved by different scenes and different characters. As I did, I saw a lot of insight into Tabby, and everything I saw made her even more precious and special to me.

As the final music played, I felt strangely at peace. I understood my role in this little grouping more than I had when I woke up that morning, that was for sure. "Thanks," I said to Tabby when she brought the lights up. "I'd seen it before, but it's a good film, and it'd been a while."

"You're welcome," she replied. I growled lightly in my throat when she got off her bean bag to crawl on all fours across the carpet to the player, her butt wiggling at me the whole time. Glancing over her shoulder, she saw what she was doing, and simultaneously blushed, giggled, and looked apologetic. "Sorry."

"You didn't mean to," I said, "but yeah, it's very enticing."

"I'll remember that," she teased lightly before getting to her knees and at least knee walking over to the player, taking out the disc and putting it away. "I know you still aren't tired though."

"Not really. After all, I slept until nearly noon again. It's kind of nice having a vacation—haven't gotten enough of those lately. I have a question, though, if you don't mind."

"Go ahead," she said, sitting cross-legged on the floor like a little girl at a slumber party. It was innocent and cute, and her smile lit up the room. "What do you want to know?"

"When I went to the gym on one of my walks, you know Mark and I talked."

She nodded. She hadn't been too happy about the idea, but she understood Mark's point. At the same time, she didn't want Sophie out there risking her life alongside Mark either, so in a lot of ways her feelings were torn. "Yes, I remember. Go on."

"At the end, when I said I wanted to do the training, he said the first thing I would have to do is survive his wife. What did he mean by that?"

Tabby grinned and smacked her hands together, again increasing the youthful factor in her appearance. "Okay, well, I don't know the whole story, but here's what I know. When Mark and Sophie first came back as Marcus Smiley and Sophie Warbird, one of the things they did was put Owen Lynch on notice. I'd found out that Lynch had brought in a couple of Russian mercenaries. Mark and Sophie came back into town, and in the end, they killed the two Russians. But, Mark ended up getting shot two times, once in the leg and once in the shoulder."

"Yeah, I saw the scars today," I replied. "The one on his leg is pretty nasty, all twisted up and stuff."

112

"That was just a flesh wound," Tabby said, "Anyway, after that, Sophie took over his rehab. I don't know the exact details or the numbers or anything like that, but she pushed that man harder than he'd ever been pushed before. You know that gym downstairs from my office? If you check their numbers, Marcus Smiley's name is up on their record board in quite a few places. I'm not saying that Mark's not a great athlete, he was beforehand too, I bet, but Sophie . . . Sophie's got a side to her that she turned loose on him in the gym that took him from a good athlete to world class. She wasn't like that before, but Mark brought it out in her, and I love it."

"Yikes," I said. "Is she that tough with you? You told me once you did workouts with her."

"I do. She's obviously not as hard on me, but she's still tough. And that's the man she loves. What do you think she's going to do to a guy she doesn't even like that much?"

"She doesn't like me? She barely even knows me."

Tabby got to her knees and knee walked over next to me. "You nearly got her husband killed, and you're seeing me. After my last breakup, she's very protective, and I can't blame her. The guy really fucked with my head. But, she loves me, and she loves Mark. Give it time; she'll come to see the part of you that I do. Until then, though, a nice daily dose of Tylenol and a good glass of shaddap before workouts will be just what you need."

I smiled at the light joke and reached out, taking Tabby's hand. "I'm looking forward to tomorrow, when I get a chance to put my arms around you again."

Tabby leaned down and gave me a soft kiss, her lips caressing mine, until both of us were on the verge of losing control and pressing our luck further. Breaking contact, she looked into my eyes and smiled.

"I'll console myself with that until then," she said. She got up and went to the door, turning to look at me one last time with those beautiful eyes of hers. "Good night, Patrick."

"Good night, Tabby."

The following Thursday, I was sitting in my office twirling my pen around my fingers when Vanessa came in, carrying a large file. "Here you go," she said, setting it on my desk. "Have fun."

"What the hell is this?" I asked, thumbing the folder nervously. It had to be at least an inch thick and had little Post-It flags sticking out of it in more places than I could count.

"Forms from the city inspector's office on the community centers," Vanessa replied. "These will eventually be the job of the center managers, but as we don't have those yet . . ."

"They fall on my shoulders," I replied with a groan. Looking up, I grinned feebly. "Want a promotion?"

Vanessa shook her head. "Not until those forms are finished, thank you very much."

"Come on, it fits your personality type," I mock-whined. "Although I'd be out one hell of an assistant."

"Nope, sorry," she replied. "Remember, I'm the person who likes to work behind the curtain. Besides, I've got my hands full enough right now, again, thank you very much. With helping Gwen, that is."

I blinked, surprised. "You're helping Patrick's new assistant as well?"

"She's a friend of mine, and I trained her long ago," Vanessa replied. "And having your boss come down with a bad chest cold not even a week after starting work is hell on anyone. I'm just glad that Gwen's one of the better apprentices I've trained."

"You know, I never thought of administrative assistants having a mentorship sort of thing going," I commented. "I mean, in hindsight it makes sense. Executives learn from their mentors, so why not their assistants?"

"You'd be surprised how many people don't figure that out," Vanessa said. "In any case, have fun with the documents. I put the Post-Its by the important parts."

"It's all important parts!" I complained, rifling the stack. "You've got at least half a pack in here!"

Vanessa grinned, disappearing from my office. I looked down at the light brown cover of the file and made a mental note. From now on, I'd have Vanessa purchase pink file folders with images of My Little Pony or Minnie Mouse on them. If I had to slog my way through that much hell, at least the files would look cute while I did so.

I saw a pattern developing as I started reading, one that I could even put a name to. That name, of course, was Berkowitz. The double checking forms, the lack of transparency, and why the hell did we need to fill out a form for a check on the use of raw fish in the kitchen? We were opening a community center, not a sushi bar. We didn't even have the buildings cleaned out yet. I still needed to confirm contractors for that first before I could go further.

Sighing, I went through the file, dividing it into three portions. The first portion were forms that I needed to sign and have Vanessa return to the city immediately. They were ones specifically associated with the clearing and renovation of the buildings, and applications for building permits. The second pile, ones to be signed later, I set back in the folder. It wasn't that they didn't need to be signed, but I couldn't answer them yet. For example, a form on water usage and the use of low flow toilets. How in the hell was I supposed to know that?

The third pile quickly became the largest, and that was the, to put it politely, the bullshit pile. Applications for renovation of historical buildings (we'd chosen four buildings that were all less than forty years old, and had been office space or warehouses). Applications for request for historical status. Applications for the use of caustic chemicals, etc., etc., etc. It took me the rest of the morning, and about half of the afternoon, but at just before three o'clock, I carried the now much thinner pile out to Vanessa. "Here. Send these back to the city, with my thanks. The others will be filled out as needed, in a timely fashion."

"You caught it too, huh?" Vanessa said. "You should have seen what I waded through. Whoever set it up thought they'd try and bury us by including a lot of the forms in triplicate. I had to empty the paper shredder twice to make room for it all."

"Thank you then. I'll have another load for you to shred here in a bit, the ones that I'm just calling bullshit on. Speaking of the community centers, though, I think I'll give Gene over at the Spartans a visit, see if they're catching flak on this as well."

"Want me to give his office a call?" Vanessa asked.

I shook my head and turned to go back into my office. "No thanks. I'll handle this one myself."

I heard Vanessa get back to her work, and I closed my door. Going to the phone, I looked up Gene's phone number and dialed. "Gene?"

"Hello, Tabby. How are things at MJT?"

"Great. By the way, I didn't take the chance to thank you yet for the tickets a few weeks ago. We enjoyed the game very much."

"For Patrick, anything. What can I do for you today?" Gene asked.

"Do you have some free time this afternoon? I had a massive form dump on my desk from the city office on the community center project, and I wondered how the Spartans are doing on it, and maybe see if I could pick your brain for some advice."

"I've got some time at about five o'clock. The team's at practice and a lot of the office staff have left. If you want, we can even watch from the stands; they're doing walk-throughs in preparation for Saturday's game."

"You're playing on Saturday? Isn't that college time?" I asked, surprised.

Gene laughed. "I see you're an even bigger fan than I thought. Yeah, the league did it because the NCAA scheduled nothing big for this holiday weekend. So the league is getting double TV coverage, including a Saturday prime time game. We're kicking off against Oakland at seven."

"Sure, I'll be there. Mind if I wear my suit?" I asked. "I don't have my Spartans t-shirt right now."

Gene laughed. "Sure. Although I should say no. I know how you look in those. You'll distract half the team."

I got to the stadium just before five o'clock, and a security guard let me through the entrance. I found Gene in the main rotunda, near the entrance to the Spartan Hall of Champions, a sort of Hall of Fame at the team level. He was dressed in what I guess could best be called office casual, a Spartans polo shirt and slacks.

"Gene, thanks for finding the time," I said, offering him a handshake. "How's the team looking?" I asked. I usually try not to get right down to business. Of course

116

I was a fan, but business was my main concern. I just didn't want to jump right to it.

"The preseason went well, and I think we've got a shot at a playoff run. A lot's going to depend on our line play—we're pretty thin on backups there. If some of our rookies continue to develop, Coach thinks we can go deep."

"Good to hear," I replied. "So, you said we could watch some of practice?"

"Sure, I doubt you're a spy from Oakland," he said with a laugh. "Come on."

It was pleasant inside Spartans Stadium as the late summer-slash-early fall weather was taking hold. It was warm enough that I could feel it on my face, but not the stifling heat of mid-summer. Still, I knew why Mark was wearing warmer tops under his vest when he went out on night patrols. The early morning hours were starting to be chilly.

Down on the field, I saw as the players were stretching out in helmets, t-shirts and shorts. "Reminds me of a high school boyfriend," I told Gene as we took a seat on one of the benches that made up a lot of the so-called cheap seats. Spartan Stadium had been built with a very old-fashioned feel, but it still had a lot of high tech and modern conveniences. "He played football when I was a junior."

"Oh? Knowing you, he was the star quarterback."

I chuckled and shook my head. "Nope, wrong there. Actually, my boyfriend at the time wasn't even a starter; he played backup defensive end and a lot of special teams. We first started talking because of a time like this."

"What do you mean?" Gene asked. He sat down on the bleacher bench next to me, his eyes on the field. "Wasn't paying attention at practice?"

"No, actually he was the most dedicated guy on the team. Showed up early, made every off season lift, everything like that. But we had a pretty stacked team that year, and the guys in front of him were two seniors who both ended up going on to play Division I ball. So Alex sat the bench a lot. Anyway, a couple of my girlfriends and I used the stadium to run back then, and he and I started talking after one of these Thursday walk-throughs. We dated for most of my junior year."

"What happened senior year?" Gene asked curiously.

"Simple. Like I said, he was the most dedicated guy on the team. When it came time to choose between football and me, I was always second. I couldn't deal with that anymore, so we just broke it off amicably," I said. "But enough on me. Gene, have you been catching flak from Francine Berkowitz?"

117

"If you mean have we had Union reps around here trying to get everyone from the janitor to the popcorn vendor to join the various unions, then yeah, but nothing different than usual," Gene replied. "They've been trying to crack us ever since the strike back in '99. The owners are standing pat though, no unions other than the Player's Association. They don't care if it costs us twice as much to do things. I assume you don't have quite that much leeway in your operations budget."

I tilted my head, chuckling. Mark had plenty of money, but he didn't have the operating budget of a professional football team backed by a textile manufacturing powerhouse. Then again, we didn't have shareholders to answer to either. "Not quite. I'm trying to take a balanced approach to this. I've told her, I'm not outright rejecting any participation by union workers. Hell, if they do good work at a good price, I'll have nothing but union workers. But I'm not going to hamstring the non-union companies with the Union's bid-rigging crap either."

"So she's trying to drown you in paperwork," Gene replied. "She did the same to us last year when we renovated the bathrooms on the upper deck. Simple enough job, just going to modern urinals and toilets, should have been a simple two-month job from start to finish. City inspectors and everyone else turned that thing into a six-month headache. We barely got the damn thing finished less than a week before the first preseason game."

"But you kicked off on time," I said. "So is that a pattern?"

Gene nodded. "Pretty much. If you have power, she'll hamstring you, delay you, try and just wear you down until she can expose a weakness to exploit. Thankfully the league is supportive of us, and the players are fine with it as long as we take care of them. The stadium workers know that, by law, we can't prevent them from unionizing. Did you know that the security guard who let you in the door, he makes fifty-six thousand a year with full team benefits? Guy goes to the same doctor I do. Anyway, my advice is to continue the same way. Treat your contractors well, and you'll find workers for you. The Union works off of public perception just as much as the Spartans do. They know this. As long as they can harass and frustrate you without coming off looking like assholes, Berkowitz is going to be a bug in your ass the whole time. But as soon as she thinks that public light will make them look bad, she'll have the Union guys fall back until the next fight."

"And how long will that fight go on?" I wondered.

Put it like this: I'll tell you when ours is over, and that might give you an idea. So far we've been fighting them for nearly two decades."

"Damn."

Gene nodded, and we watched the field for a while longer. It was a lot simpler, football, that is, compared to the headaches I was dealing with at the time.

* * *

I got home late that night, nearly nine pm, as I wanted to start looking over contractors for the first of the community centers. The first building, in the heart of The Playground, needed to be cleaned out, and I wanted to find a general contractor to get that done as soon as possible. If Francine Berkowitz was going to continue to be a thorn in my side, I might as well damn the torpedoes and go full speed ahead, after all.

I was surprised when I arrived to see Patrick's car parked in front of Mount Zion. I knew that Mark had recovered it from Fillmore Heights earlier in the week, discovering as he did that Patrick had not only painted the old Civic, but he had tuned it up to the point it was a cheetah under the hood, but I hadn't expected Patrick to be back so quickly. We hadn't talked that day, and I figured he was overloaded with catching up on what he had missed at City Hall. Parking my Mercedes SUV, I made my way inside, curious.

I found Patrick and Sophie in the gym, sweat dripping off his face as she pushed him through a workout. "God's sake, woman, I'm a week removed from getting shot!" he groaned as she pushed on his back, his legs stretched out in front of him. "You trying to kill me?"

"The gunshot has nothing to do with the fact that you've got hamstrings that are weak and stiff, along with enough knots in your hips you should be a Boy Scout merit badge," Sophie replied matter-of-factly. "Now be quiet and breathe out."

I suppressed a chuckle as Patrick tried his best to comply, Sophie pushing more until his body wouldn't go any further. "I think I saw God there as the air left my body."

"I'll remember that. I've been called a lot of things, but never God before," Sophie replied, dressed conservatively in sweatpants and a t-shirt. She was being no-nonsense, but I could tell by her facial expression that she was amused. He must have worked hard, because if he hadn't, she wouldn't have replied except to push him

119

harder.

"You're terrible," Patrick groaned, "my legs feel like about a hundred pounds of fried rubber right now."

"They'd smell a lot worse if they were. But I think I see something that might put some energy in those muscles," Sophie said, seeing me and waving. "Hey, Tabs. How was work?"

Patrick rolled over, his face breaking out in a silly smile that I couldn't help but return as I came in and gave Sophie a hug. "Good. How about you?"

"Mark's on the computer doing some things right now. We were holding off on dinner until you got back. I was just putting Patrick through a light workout after he got done at work."

"How'd it go?" I asked, leaving my arm around her shoulder and looking down at Patrick, amused. "You first, Sophie."

"Not bad. he did okay with what we could do. He's stiff as a board, though. I'm going to have to work on that."

I gave Sophie a wink and stood over Patrick, straddling his chest. I knew what I was doing, giving him a very nice look up my skirt. Looking down and crossing my arms over my chest, I arched my eyebrow. "Is that so? And any complaints about Sophie, Patrick?"

"None at all," Patrick said, "although if you insist on standing there, she's going to be right about me being stiff as a board."

Sophie groaned melodramatically and rolled her eyes. "I'm going to go find my husband. You two, no leaving bodily fluids on the mats, okay?"

I bit back a jibe, considering I'd caught her and Mark doing just that once, but nodded. "We'll behave."

Once Sophie was gone, I sank down to my knees, straddling Patrick's waist. Leaning down, I kissed him softly, our lips molding together electrically. "I missed you today," I said as we parted. "I thought you were so busy with work you didn't have time to call me."

"You were on my mind all day," he replied, his hands resting on my skirt. "But I knew I was coming over here tonight and knew I could see you, though I didn't expect you'd be so late. Anything wrong?"

"Just some work on the community center project," I said, "but now

120

everything's better."

"Problem solved?"

I laughed and ran my hands over his sweaty t-shirt, feeling his muscles. "Not really. But having you here, it's much, much better."

"Tabby," Patrick moaned, his cock hardening in his workout shorts. "You're teasing me. You promised Sophie we'd behave in here."

"No," I said, sliding down his legs and freeing his cock from his shorts. I wrapped my fingers around the thick shaft, still surprised I'd been able to fit him inside me so wonderfully the last time. I couldn't even close my fist around him, and it's not like I have tiny hands. "I promised her I wouldn't get any bodily fluids on the mats," I said, grinning.

Patrick sat up on his elbows to watch as I licked his cock from the base all the way to the tip, his moan of appreciation growing as I reached the tip and circled around his head. It'd been a while since I'd done this, but it wasn't my first time either. Licking slowly, I worked my way up and down, relishing the clean sweat taste of his skin. He was warm, even warmer than normal after his workout, but not funky at all. Instead, he tasted sexy and masculine, and my panties started to get wet. There'd be time for that later. After all, I wasn't going to break a promise.

Going back down, I found Patrick's balls, heavy and full. Sucking one into my mouth, I swirled it around, sucking lightly on the heavy orb before switching and bathing him with my mouth and tongue. Patrick reached down and brushed my hair out of my face, which probably wasn't for my comfort but rather for his own visual benefit, but I appreciated it.

"Tabby . . ." he said softly, his voice shaky. "You're so beautiful."

I smiled at him and pulled my mouth away to look him in the eye for a second, then I swallowed his cock, slowly letting him inside my mouth until he brushed against the back of my mouth. I wasn't ready at the time to try and deep throat him, so I pulled back, letting him feel my tongue swirling around him, flickering over his tip until I was just sucking on the head. Licking one more time, I looked him in the eye again. "How long since you came?"

"When we were together," he whispered, blushing. "I was kind of holding out until we were together again when I got shot."

"Poor baby," I mocked, my hand pumping his spit-slick shaft. "Well, right

121

now is about you. Later tonight you can return the favor."

Before he could answer I swallowed him again, bobbing my head up and down with intense purpose. I wanted his essence, I needed it. That day, not hearing his voice after having him nearby for so long—it was horrible. It wasn't even the stress or the work, which at least acted like a distraction. It was that I wanted Patrick nearby. I wanted to hear his hum as he thought, and feel the weight of his eyes on me as we watched movies or looked out at the sunset from the front steps of Mount Zion. I was happy that he was now back in public, if only that we could actually go out again. I'm not one to be cooped up all the time.

It was these thoughts on my mind as I sucked and pleasured him, pouring all of myself into having him feel so good he couldn't help himself. His hand rested in my hair, and I knew he wanted to push me, to take control, but he restrained himself, trusting me and letting me guide him this time. When his fingers tensed, I knew he was close, but still he didn't push or grab at me. I buried myself as deeply as I could, and at the same time I massaged his balls, rubbing them in the way I knew would drive him even higher.

"Tabby . . ." he warned me, and I pulled back a little. Vacuuming my lips around the head of his cock, his first squirt coated my tongue, warm and sweet and salty and delicious. I relished his taste for a moment before spitting it into his gym towel.

I looked at Patrick, who was struggling to say something, his mouth gaping and closing like a fish. He looked pained, and I grew worried. "What is it?"

"I . . . I love you," he said.

I heard a crash from the kitchen, which echoed the crash in my stomach.

Chapter 16
Patrick

I didn't mean to say it, not yet anyway, but the words were honest. I knew what had been done to Tabby, and I knew that the longer we could go without saying the words, the better it was for both of us. Besides, there was no need to say the words I felt. The feelings inside were what counted. And my feelings were definitely true. Still, I didn't need to say them. In fact, saying them was probably more hurtful than helpful.

But there I was, covered in sweat with my cock in her hand, dropping a goddamn bomb on things, sounding like some dumbass high school nerd who'd just gotten laid for the first time.

Tabby blinked a few times and let go of my cock, getting to her feet and leaving the gym . . . if not at a run, then certainly at a fast walk. I sat there for a moment before tucking myself back into my shorts and sighing, getting to my feet. I was just gathering my things when Mark came into the room.

"What did you say to her?"

I turned to look at Mark, who was standing, his fists clenched, a look on his face like he wanted to tear my head off. I could understand, personally. "What did she say?"

"Neither of them are saying anything, actually. I heard Sophie drop something in the kitchen and I came in to find our casserole dish in about a hundred and fifty pieces on the floor, Sophie staring at the baby monitor with shock on her face. Tabby comes in before I can even ask her what the hell is up, and she looks like someone just kicked her in the crotch. The two of them retreated to Tabby's bedroom, not letting me in, and I'm still not getting any answers. Now what the hell happened?"

"I . . . I said I love her," I whispered, looking down. "It just came out. I knew right when the words came out that it was a mistake."

"You said you loved her," Mark repeated. "You dumb sonofabitch."

I sighed and nodded, changing my t-shirt quickly and grabbing the warmup pants I'd worn to Mount Zion. "I know. If it's any consolation, it's the truth."

Mark shook his head. He surprised me then by starting to chuckle, then putting his head back and laughing, trying to keep his voice down. "I swear I have nothing but mentally irregular people in my life. Drama, man."

"What do you mean?" I asked.

"I mean that Sophie and I pretty much said we loved each other over some pretty drastic, not exactly romantic circumstances too. If you hang around long enough, I may even tell you the story. I guess what I'm going to say now is not exactly what I should be, but Tabby's last man she was with . . . it didn't work out well."

"I know," I replied. "She said as much, and I'd heard some stories when I was working the bar. Lot of Confederation guys would come down around there, and you know how stories get passed around. In hindsight, I realize she wasn't ready for that."

I shook my head "And now I'm afraid that I've screwed things up with Tabby. I can't lose her."

Mark nodded, interlacing his fingers in front of him. "All right," he finally said after a moment. "Get out of here, and I'll talk with Tabby and Sophie. For the record, I don't think you screwed everything up, but I'm not a psychic. Go get some rest at home, and maybe Tabby will give you a call tomorrow. I don't know. She was probably just shocked, that's all."

I nodded and grabbed my bag. "Snowman . . ."

"Mark, please."

"All right, Mark. Thanks. I know I shouldn't be asking you to intervene for me, but thanks."

Mark nodded and I headed out the back door of Mount Zion, which ironically was the front door of the sanctuary. They'd changed things around a lot. Mark walked with me, unlocking the door and letting me out that way. As I walked through, I felt his hand clamp on my wrist, iron hard and unforgiving. "Patrick."

"Yeah?"

"This is a warning from me. I know what you did wasn't intentional, and you meant well, but if you intentionally fuck around on Tabby, you won't make me happy. Don't make me unhappy with you, okay? She can't take much more."

I saw in his eyes the ruthless man he could be, and I nodded. I knew the story of Scott Pressman, even if Mark didn't know that I knew.

Scott deserved everything he'd gotten, but he got off lucky.

* * *

The next morning, Gwen brought me a coffee as I sat at my desk. I still wasn't wearing suit coats in the office most of the time, but I was at least wearing shoes that needed to be polished and not cleaned with an old toothbrush like I did with high tops.

"You look distracted, Boss," she said. Gwen had called me 'Boss' from the moment I hired her, a term that I took as a positive. At her interview, I was 'Councilman McCaffery.' Now I was 'Boss.' It was a definite improvement. "Anything you want to talk about?"

"No, just personal life," I told Gwen. "What's the schedule look like for the rest of the day?"

"You've got a meeting with the mayor at one o'clock, and then a local Boy Scout troop is coming by at four. They've got a bunch of kids who want to interview you; it's part of their promotion requirements. Oh, and don't forget that tomorrow you've got the city engineers coming by. They're bringing you the updates on their building inspections in your district."

"That sounds like fun," I muttered under my breath. "Thanks, Gwen. By the way, any calls from Bishop Traylor or Ms. Berkowitz?"

"Not today, Boss. Are we expecting a call from them?" Gwen's little smile told me that she was familiar with my feelings toward those two particular scoundrels. She was much bubblier than the few times I'd met Tabby's assistant, Vanessa, but so far she had been a great help. I could actually see getting on top of things around the office. "Also, before I go, any idea on if or when you want to hire another assistant? You've got the space in your budget."

"Not yet. If you want to look at what would be best, I'll be happy to talk about it later. Maybe in between the mayor and the Boy Scouts you can give me some ideas. You've got some political experience."

It was the biggest reason I'd hired Gwen. While not an active campaigner, she had worked as an administrative assistant for a PAC in college, according to her resume. She was also very insightful in the short time she'd been working for me, and she had handled things well during the time I was out after being shot.

"Of course, Boss."

125

Gwen left, and I felt my mood dampen again. I had left my phone near me all day, hoping that Tabby would call or text me. Instead, my phone sat silent, and with every passing minute, I knew I was getting more and more into a funk.

Telling myself I was acting like an idiot didn't help. I'd been doing that ever since the words 'I love you' came out of my mouth. I knew that Tabby was busy, perhaps even busier than I was. In our city, being a councilman wasn't as difficult a job as you'd think. The mayor and deputy mayor held most of the power, and the various city departments were more or less self-contained. The police and fire commissioners were elected positions, so while I and the rest of the Council could drag them into a meeting and yell at them, there really wasn't a lot we could do. Most of our work was to look over different department reports from our districts, voice our opinions on matters to the mayor or deputy mayor, and then finagle budget ideas. We did have that much power, over about half of the total city budget, with the rest locked up through various other means.

All in all, I had a rather cushy job, with most of it being answering gripes and complaints from citizens in The Playground and Fillmore Heights. It was one of my secret weapons against the gangs, because many times I got lots of information from the very people they lived among because I was seen as a powerless politician rather than the police.

I was just about to run across the street from City Hall to grab a quick lunch when my phone rang. I looked at the number and saw it was from Mount Zion. "Tabby?"

"Sorry to disappoint, but it's just me," Sophie answered. "No call from her so far?"

"Not yet," I replied. "Although I'm feeling a bit more confident. You called me, at least, and you two are closer than twins."

"Mark came in and talked to us. I'll be honest, I was ready to give you a good sock in the face last night," Sophie said. There was still a hint of anger in her voice, but behind it I heard a lot of forgiveness too. "All things considered, I've forgiven my husband for more. Don't worry about Tabby; she just needs to get her mind calmed down. You shocked her and gave her a little scare. I was calling about you."

"What can I do for you?" I asked. "I hope you don't want to ask how my legs are doing, because I could barely walk up the steps of City Hall this morning."

126

"Good," Sophie said gleefully, "then you can get here tonight for your next step. That back of yours isn't ready for heavy back work, but I can start you on something else. When are you done with work?"

"According to my assistant, as soon as I finish talking to a group of Boy Scouts. Say, five thirty or so?"

"Hmm, no, that's not going to work. Be up here at six thirty tomorrow. I've got free time then. If Tabby's not pissed at you still, you can perhaps stay for dinner."

I smiled, the first real smile I'd had all day. "I could do that. By the way, I owe you a casserole dish."

"Don't worry about the dish, councilman. Remember, six thirty."

Sophie hung up, and I felt a bounce in my step as I dashed down the steps of City Hall and grabbed a hot dog from the cart in front of the building. I was halfway back when I realized I was moving a lot easier than I had coming in that morning, and I wondered if it was just that my soreness was wearing off, or if some of it had been due to my emotions. Either way, I scarfed my dog on the steps and went back inside.

I was a few minutes early to the mayor's office, and I found him sipping at a weight gainer shake—at least I suspected, judging by the smell and the logo on the shaker bottle. "Hey, Joe," I said, remembering from the first time he'd stopped by my office that he preferred that form of address. "Stomach still bothering you?"

"Yes, but at least the weight has stabilized out," he said. "All it takes is one of these disgusting things a day. Seriously, how do guys built like you choke these damn things down?"

I shook my head. "I don't know. I had a hot dog from the cart out front for lunch, and my diet is usually just regular food."

"You're lucky," Joe said. "Anyway, have a seat. How're things downstairs?"

Joe always referred to the City Council offices as 'downstairs,' like it was some other zip code or something. Ah well. "Not too bad. I've got myself an assistant now, Gwen. She used to work for a PAC."

"Really? I'd heard you had someone, but I didn't know that. Do you remember which PAC?"

I shook my head. "I remember she worked for a pretty conservative group, but so far she's been really apolitical with me," I said. "Other than some advice on

127

how to work the systems around here, she's not made a particular stand on any policy issues or anything like that."

"Sounds like a keeper then," Joe replied. "I've had a lot of challenges with that myself recently. So you're getting a feel for your district?"

"Same as when I came in, really. They need community investment, jobs, and someone to break the gangs up. Unfortunately, the city's got its hands full with everything but," I said, taking a seat across from him. Joe liked to sit at his desk for our meetings, but only for convenience's sake. He kept his hand busy, writing down anything I said that needed his attention, and the coffee table in the front of the room was just too low. "Those community centers are going to be vital for us. That, and MJT continuing to invest."

"Not to mention the vigilante up in Fillmore," Joe replied. "You're getting lots of non-governmental help, it seems."

"It would be better if I had some official government help instead," I said. "Joe, what's the status on getting more cops over to my district? I asked about it last month, but when I ask the Commissioner, I'm getting a lot of run around about manpower shortages. Which is strange, since the department's been growing in size for the past four years."

"Which was slashed recently when a lot of cops were caught up in the Fed probe," Joe countered. "The rest are honest cops—at least I hope they are—but the power structure of the department was screwed royally by this. I've got five Captains that weren't even Lieutenants a year ago. On the good side, they're hardworking cops, but a lot of them are struggling to just figure out their jobs. They're even worse off than you are downstairs."

I had to agree, but still, with the second largest police force in the country, there should have been enough cops even with the problems. "How much of this is Union too?" I asked quietly. "I noticed that the manpower shortages in those areas have gotten worse since the community center project was launched."

"It's not helping," Joe admitted, "but there's nothing that could be proven. The PBA is a strong part of the Union. Same with the City Workers Association. Unless you happen to have a way to break Francine Berkowitz in your back pocket, you just have to work with what you have."

"Bullshit," I muttered to myself, although apparently much louder than I had anticipated as Joe nodded. "You can't do anything about it?"

Joe shook his head. "I'm hanging onto this chair by the skin of my teeth as it is. Now, that was my own damn fault. I'm not going to quibble on that. But right now, Patrick, I've got enough on my plate just trying to make sure this entire goddamn city doesn't crumble and turn into Detroit or something. I'd love to fight the Union, take them down and get another brick out of the wall that's holding this city back. But you know what I learned in close to twenty-five years of being in politics?"

"What?" I asked, both angry and intrigued. Joe had never been this open with me before, and while not exactly a slimy politician, he had played his cards pretty close to the vest. I wondered what had him so damn talkative, but I decided I'd figure that out later.

"The wall that's holding the city back—it's part of a larger structure, one that steers and controls the raging river that is the will of the people. Now, some of those bricks you need. They're the flood gates, the channels that prevent damage. If you go in there and start smashing the whole damn thing, pretty soon you're going to find yourself up to your neck in a raging torrent, and that same flood is going to be destroying the good bricks along with the bad, going hell-bent for leather and sweeping everything, good and bad, out of its way. So sometimes, we have to do these things slowly."

"And hope that the next generation who follows in our footsteps agrees with us and is better than we are." I sighed, looking up at the ceiling. "And if they're not?"

Joe laughed and took a drink of his weight gain shake. "From what I see, young councilman, the generation following me is on the right track. You're making the connections you need to get things done. I know working around the Union isn't what you'd like, but if anyone can get it done, I suspect you and Tabby Williams can do it."

"Yeah," I said glumly. Joe looked at me askance, and I shook my head. "Nothing."

"All right. Well, Patrick, I've got Bill Franklin coming in about twenty minutes. Apparently, one of his executive vice presidents recently blew his own head off, and now Bill wants me to look into the circumstances around his death. It might tie into your district, by the way. Know anything about a place called Mistress Blood's?"

"Yeah," I said with a shiver. I had met Blood once, and that was enough. "Hard core, and I mean illegally hard core, things went down there. Place had Confederation ties, and if I remember right, Illuysas Petrokias acted as Blood's patron. It got shut down about a month or so ago. From what I read, Blood got herself a fatal case of nine millimeter lead poisoning."

"I assume the local detectives aren't expending a lot of energy in finding her killer?" Joe asked. I shook my head.

"With what she was involved in, most of my district is counting it as chickens coming home to roost. She wasn't as bad as the top heads of the Confederation, but she was a sick, twisted woman. I don't even know what sort of crazy to classify her."

Joe nodded. "Okay, well, I'll talk with Bill. You want to sit in? You being the council member from The Playground and all."

"No thanks, Joe, I have some Boy Scouts coming by my office at four. If you don't mind, I think I'll try and keep my soul at least somewhat clean for the rest of the day. Thanks for the talk."

"Let's do it again in about two weeks or so," Joe replied. "I'll have Hank get in touch with your new assistant . . . Gwen, right?"

"Yeah, Gwen. And that sounds just fine. Thanks again, Joe."

* * *

Mark

The night sky was cloudy, which helped as I made my way through the Park at nearly ten pm. Not the safest thing to do, but I wasn't worried. The Park was a lot better than in the old days, when it had been the realm of street gangs and the Confederation after dark. Now, at least the Confederation was out of it, and the street gangs were too busy seeing if they could get some more profitable turf for their activities. The junkie problem was still bad, though.

Thankfully, I wasn't going too deep into the Park, just over to the World War I Memorial, near the southwest entrance to the Park. I had my mask on, but the hood was pulled up, and I had skipped my tactical vest in favor of a belly holster for the one Glock that I was carrying.

My contact was late. The bells of the big clock started to toll, and I was still

130

waiting. I was just about to move off when I saw the approaching shadow, and my contact arrived.

I didn't even know his name, just his handle. We had first met through a website that catered to so-called hacktivists, and we eventually came to know one another. On the website, he went by the screen name Captain Zappy. Who knew where he got that one from.

"Captain."

"Snowman," he said. "Nice to see you in person again."

"It's been a long time. Nice beard."

Zappy stroked his beard, which was a good eight inches long and pretty well kept. Last time he and I had been face to face, he'd been clean shaven. "Nice eye mask. Although I'd have gone with more of a domino mask than the whole Kato thing. That thing has to be hot as fuck in summer."

"We're coming into winter though. It'll help then. I've got something for you."

"Oh? Anything interesting?"

I reached into the pocket of my pants and pulled out a flash stick. "You still got connections in the media, right?"

"Some," Zappy replied. "But with so much of the media being corporate nowadays, it's not as easy as it was to get on the air. Online's the way to go nowadays if you want to take someone down. Who you got dirt on?"

"Bishop Gerald Traylor," I replied. "Video and audio, plus documents."

"Oh? Anything juicy?" Zappy said.

"You could put some of it on Pornland," I replied. "In multiple sections."

Zappy grinned. He was a self-professed militant atheist and loved the idea of taking down a supposed man of God. I didn't necessarily agree with his religious views, but Gerald needed to go down. "Nice. Anything else?"

"Take a look. The documents aren't exactly as juicy as the audio or video, but you can connect the dots. I turned a lot of it over to Bennie Fernandez at the DOJ already; he said he'd forward it on to the IRS. But I think you can get me the results I want faster."

"I gotcha," Zappy said. "Can I ask, why do you want this done, Snowman?"

I shook my head. "November fifth is coming up soon enough. I figure you

131

guys can make hay to really kick that off."

Zappy grinned. As a member of the online hacker community, Anonymous, among others, he knew exactly what I was talking about. He loved breaking big scandals on or around Guy Fawkes Day. "Well then, let's see if we can make it come a little early this year. All right, I'll get this posted tonight. Question though. Why not you?"

"Don't have the media connections you do," I replied. "You know a lot of my style is more direct than that."

"Damn right it is," Zappy said. He pocketed the flash stick and turned around. "Hang loose, Snowman."

"You too."

With Traylor's trap now slowly closing around him, I turned to the next objective I had for the night, namely making sure Fillmore Heights was still staying calm. Police response to the area was dropping off, and I wanted to make sure that with the patrols lessening, the neighborhood wasn't going to see more gang violence.

I stopped by one of my strike bases, where I kept full kits of my tactical gear in standby. The vest wasn't quite as comfortable as the one I kept at home; it was a little less broken in and a little less perfectly tailored, but it would do the job for the night. As a precaution, I took the one with body armor panels incorporated into the webbing. While not as protective as a full on vest, it did cover my vital areas while still allowing me maximum flexibility and mobility, essential to my methods. I had another two levels of body armor available, just in case, but I wouldn't need it that night.

Like before, I made sure to leave my bike in hidden areas. My first stop was Gangster Disciple territory, where I saw that, despite the damage to the donut shop, Tweak Petersen was back in attendance, a brand new plate glass window already installed, with lettering on it and everything. Gang money got work done quickly, after all. On the other hand, the GDs were working at least a little less out in the open than before, and I only saw maybe four or five people say anything to him as he sat at his table, nodding his head to music and occasionally messing around with a handheld game system.

I made my way over to Latin King territory, where a unique opportunity presented itself. The Latin Kings were almost the antithesis of the Gangster Disciples,

132

in a lot of ways. Reserved where the GDs were loud and public, this extended all the way up the ladder to their leader, who was known on the streets as El Patron.

Part of it was that El Patron didn't even live in Fillmore Heights any longer. While Tweak Petersen still lived in the same streets that he came from, Edgar Villalobos had escaped the streets of Fillmore to live uptown, near the Park. I actually knew him from meetings with Sal Giordano, and while the past year hadn't been easy on him, he hadn't come up on my list of people to worry about just yet.

Still, seeing him on the streets of Fillmore worried me. Traditionally, Villalobos sent his lieutenants instructions from the safety of his condo near the Park using text messages. Ditching my bike quickly, I barely had time to get to the rooftops before he and his crew came around the corner.

"Patron, I'm worried," one man said. "The vigilante, he listened in, but he hasn't moved on the information our boys said he overheard."

"Perhaps the Dogs did the work for us," Villalobos replied. "They claim they shot one of them."

"*Si, Patron*, but you know how those donut eaters like to brag. Also, there were two, according to them. The other seemed to ride off with no problems. I have a cousin in The Playground. He says that bike belongs to The Snowman. If so, we might have big problems on our hands."

"Why do you think I'm down here? The men need to see that I'm not scared of any myth. If The Snowman wants to bring his little game up to Fillmore Heights, he's going to find that we're a lot harder to scare than those Confederation bitches. They were strong, but soft in a lot of ways. We're the ones on the edge of the steel every day. We'll see. But the boys need to relax. We'll take care of business."

I'd heard enough and thought it was time to see if Villalobos was willing to back up his words. Sneaking my hand down into the leg of my pants, I eased one of my backup weapons from its holster.

Blowguns are one of the world's oldest stealth weapons. The darts are light, and in the hands of a skilled user, very accurate. The main problem with them is that they're limited range, obviously.

I had gone with something a little bit more high tech, but still old-fashioned. Using high tensile strength rubber and the tube, I combined the ideas of a slingshot with a blowgun. I'd seen similar devices online and from talking to old prison

133

veterans, but mine was certainly stronger than something made from rolled up newspaper, cardboard, and the rubber out of someone's underwear. I could hit with accuracy at up to fifty meters with the device, and best of all, it was totally silent.

Sighting carefully, I loaded my dart and sent it into Villalobos's leg, right above his knee. I could have killed him if I'd used some of the darts that I keep on hand, but that wasn't my purpose. I wanted Fillmore to stay even until Patrick and I could work together to take all of the groups down. Instead, the drugs inside temporarily paralyzed his leg, making him tumble to the ground with his next step. I took off and was a rooftop away before the Latin Kings below knew what had even happened. Still, I could hear some yelling, and I hightailed it as hard as I could. I wasn't going to repeat the same scene as last time.

I was still clearly ahead of them when I got to my bike and twisted the throttle, flying out of Fillmore Heights at full speed. I streaked through The Playground before looping the Park area once again and hightailing it up toward home.

The bells of the clock towers around the city were just ringing one o'clock.

Chapter 17
Tabby

I could feel sweat trickling down my back as I waited for Patrick. I'd changed into workout clothes, and looked over at the spot where I had last been with him, the mats where I'd taken him in. My body yearned for him, but my mind still reeled at what he'd said afterward.

I knew I was still screwed up inside from Scott Pressman. If I had ever needed more proof, it was in the way I'd fled from Patrick after he'd said he loved me. Seriously, what person does that? He hadn't been growling or trying to hurt me. In fact, he'd never hurt me, hadn't even raised his voice to me once. When he'd told me, he struggled, and I knew he was telling the truth. He was as surprised by what he'd said as I was.

Even still, it scared the hell out of me. Sophie held me for nearly an hour as I went through hysterics that night, and since then I'd still felt cold sweats every time I went into the gym. Sophie had even changed my workout the day before to outside, taking the time with Mark to haul the weights I was going to use into the backyard of Mount Zion, just so I could get through it.

Today, though, I wanted to face my fears. Why should I be chained by the mental fuckery of someone who never cared for me? Should I let Scott Pressman's screwing with my mind forever prevent me from hearing the words that any person should yearn to hear? Determined, I changed into my exercise clothes and stood in the middle of the gym, tapping my foot while I waited. It was nearly six thirty.

"You know, you don't have to do this," Sophie said to me quietly as she waited with me. "I didn't call him over for this purpose. I called him over to do some training."

"I know," I replied, "but I can't just go hide in my room or something until I get over it. Besides, we both know he didn't do anything wrong."

Sophie nodded. It'd actually been touching, considering how much he was annoyed by the man, that Mark came in later that night and talked with me about it. He'd been convinced that Patrick had meant no harm and was genuinely broken up by the whole thing. Even Vanessa had done some surreptitious inquiry, giving me a

135

hint into just how widespread the executive assistant network ran. I wondered if I could tap into that somehow.

"You really think he's a good guy?" I asked Sophie. Six twenty-nine. He'd have to get there soon or else he would be late.

"Mark seems to think so, and he's got good taste in women, at least," Sophie told me, earning a smile from me. I heard the front door of Mount Zion slam and feet running through the house.

"Sorry I'm late!" Patrick said as he burst into the gym. Seeing me, he stumbled, thankfully near the mats where he could fall instead of near the weight racks. "T-Tabby."

"Patrick," I said. He looked so cute down there, with his tie askew and his one shoe off, that I had to smile. "You all right?"

"Uh, yeah," he said. "Just that at the last minute when I was leaving work, I had a phone call from someone, and it just delayed me a bit. Sorry about that."

"You should be apologizing to Sophie, not me," I teased. Sophie rolled her eyes and shook her head, walking past me to help Patrick up.

"Patrick, go change. Tabby's going to be doing her own thing today, but you're stuck with me." Patrick nodded, but his eyes were fixed on me, which I had to admit put some warm butterflies in my stomach. Sophie grabbed his jaw in her left hand and turned him toward her, pulling him down to look her in the eye.

"Eyes on me. It's time to work, got it? Don't you so much as look at Tabby until we're done." It was actually cool, seeing her get strict like that. If Sophie ever got tired of being a super friend, homemaker, vigilante and whatever else, she could have always been a damn good drill instructor.

"I understand," Patrick replied. "I'll do my best."

"You better," Sophie said. "Mark's not the only one who can kick your ass."

"Where is he, anyway?"

"Shopping for a few things," Sophie replied. "He'll be back by dinner time. Now, get changed and be back here in five minutes for warm-up."

Patrick nodded and disappeared, never once looking at me again. Sophie turned to me with a grin. "I think I'm going to like this workout. Now, do me a favor."

"What?" I asked, my nervousness evaporating under the light of Sophie's

136

smile. Seriously, having her around makes life so much easier.

"Do your thing, but don't tease him. I don't need him dropping something on his toes."

"So no hip extensions or toe touch deadlifts?" I asked.

Sophie rolled her eyes and shook her head. "No, and they're called Romanian deadlifts."

While I'll admit I enjoyed blowing off a little steam, not all of that came from what I was actually doing. Instead, there was a certain sadistic pleasure that came from watching Sophie put Patrick through his paces. She wasn't mean, and after that first time, she never even had to raise her voice except in encouragement.

But she wouldn't let him slack off, and she wouldn't let him stop. I was amazed as she knew exactly what psychological buttons to push and how to get him to keep going. She stopped to check his back twice, peeling off his tank top the second time to allow her to keep track. His stitches had come out nicely, but the skin still wasn't fully healed. He had a bright pink line that blazed against his skin as he worked, getting darker and darker as his skin flushed. Because of his new work and the need to hide his wound, he hadn't gotten any sun on his upper body in weeks. Trust me, if you ever want to prove that a man is of Irish heritage, just have him stay covered up in an office job for two weeks. Actually, it'd probably been more than that, considering how long Patrick had been working at city hall.

Despite his paleness, he was so handsome it made my throat close up. I kept losing count during my own exercises. I finally just went until my muscles ached before I said screw it and sat back for another half hour and watched.

Finally, Sophie called an end to it, and Patrick collapsed onto the mats, dry heaving into the convenient plastic bucket Sophie kept on hand for just such purposes. "You did good. Next week, we can really begin."

Patrick nodded dumbly, unable to form words because he was still sucking air so hard. Sophie came over to me and leaned in. "He did do well. Even if he did keep looking over to you."

"Did not."

Sophie looked at me, smirking, and nodded. "Just during the tired bits, when he needed a little extra motivation, I saw his eyes flicker over. You want to get out of here and get washed up for dinner?"

"Sure. Thanks, Sophie."

She shook her head lightly. "Don't thank me, thank Mark. I'd have put a bat upside his head, you know."

I laughed lightly and patted her on the cheek. "I know. That's what makes you so awesome. All right, I'll get washed up for dinner."

After a quick shower, I came into the dining area to find Mark serving up plates. "I heard Patrick survived," he said with a smile as he used a spatula to serve up large squares of lasagna onto our plates. "What did you think?"

"He's got a long way to go," I replied, "but like you said, he's got guts. He never gave up."

Mark heard the tone of my voice and smiled. "I see. Well, have a seat, everything should be ready soon."

After such an intense workout, Mark had been generous with dinner, making sure that Patrick got the largest serving of food. Like a couple of nervous parents, Mark seated Patrick across from me, with Sophie on one side of me and Mark on the other like a pair of guardian sentinels. Conversation was light, and we avoided both business and politics. In fact, for a lot of it, Sophie asked Patrick about his childhood and how he'd grown up in the city orphanage system.

"Well, Tabby knows most of it, so I'm sure you guys do too," Patrick said after setting his fork down. "But here's a story that you guys don't know yet. I was thirteen, and had just transferred from the Patterson Youth Home to Goldwell Hall, which is where they house the junior high school and high school aged kids. It's a rougher place than Patterson, where there was always the hope for some of the kids of at least getting foster parents. By the time you reached Goldwell, you were pretty much assured of only staying a ward of the state for the next five years. Nine out of ten kids who left Goldwell before eighteen did so because they were doing stints up at Juvenile Corrections."

"Sounds horrible," I said, taking a deep drink of my lemon water. After a large glass of fruit juice to make sure my body had some sugar after my workout, I always shifted to lemon water. "How did you survive?"

"At first I really struggled," Patrick admitted. "A lot of the kids fell into gangs, and as you know, I did as well, but never as hard as some of the other guys did. Part of it was because of Leon."

"Who was Leon?" Sophie asked, intrigued. She'd obviously already forgiven him, and I could tell she could see in him the same qualities I did. Twice she'd given me a sideways glance during dinner, smirking around her fork. She liked him, and was giving me her opinion again.

"Leon was the boxing instructor who came by twice a week to pick up guys and take them over to a dingy local place. I tagged along the first time mainly because I had just gotten my ass kicked by a couple of seventeen-year-olds who were the floor bosses for my area, and I wanted to at least put up a fight. Leon could see a lot of anger and rage in me and felt sorry for me I guess."

"Did he ever put you in the ring?" Mark asked.

Patrick leaned back and laughed, long and hard. "Yeah, but he wasn't happy about it. I may have had a lot of anger back then, but I had the technique of a gorilla. I put my head down and started swinging for the fences," Patrick said, laughing.

We all had a chuckle, and by the end, I was feeling better. Mark and Sophie glanced at the two of us, and Mark put his hands on the table. "Well, I think I'll go ahead and clear the table. Sophie, if you'd help me, I think Tabby can walk our guest to his car?"

Sophie and I nodded, and Patrick thanked Mark before following me out to the front door. We didn't say anything, but there wasn't a need to. Pausing at the open door, Patrick turned to me. "Tabby . . ."

"It's okay," I replied, putting my arms around his neck. "I know you were just saying what you felt."

"I've been in pain for days, worse than getting shot," he murmured, looking into my eyes. "I kept waking up at night, thinking I'd never have you in my arms again."

"I've missed you too," I told him. His arms went to my waist, pulling me closer, and we kissed, healing the pain in our minds and in our hearts.

There, on the entryway to my house, I gave him entry to my heart, saying with my lips and my hands what my voice just couldn't quite do. Not yet. He held me, and we spoke a silent language to each other that was beyond time, beyond anything except that of the heart.

For the rest of the month, things fell into a good regularity. I would have said comfortable, but the training program that I'd been on was anything but comfortable. I didn't even have the benefit of using the clearly awesome bathtub that Sophie, Mark and Tabby could use, restricted to only using the shower after my workouts when they invited me to eat with them. I measured time not so much by the calendar, but by the size of Sophie's belly, which went from flat to definitely starting to bulge slightly. I wondered just how big she would get before finally having her baby.

The month was basic training, plain and simple, and I loved it. Sounds weird, but I did. Four days a week, Sophie put me through workouts that left me aching and nearly staggering back out to my car every time. At least once a week, but often twice, either she or Mark would lead me through martial arts practice. I thought I knew a good amount after my years of boxing and the things I'd picked up in the streets. That notion was quickly put to rest after having a woman nearly five months pregnant hand me my ass. Admittedly, we weren't going full strength, but still.

Working with Mark was a lot rougher and a lot more full-contact, but also more fun. I didn't have to hold back with him at all, and in fact, I couldn't. If I did, I was more than likely to end up twisted into a very uncomfortable position with my toe trying to be jammed into my ear. I think Mark enjoyed it too, since I was big enough that he could go harder than he did with Sophie.

Best of all from all this training with Mark and Sophie was that I was able to spend time with Tabby. There was a brimming sexual tension between us, but for both of us it was an undercurrent. Part of it was that I was so damn physically exhausted that I doubt I could have had sex even if Tabby had danced naked through the gym after a workout. Instead, we found more and more in common, which was unexpected considering the difference in our backgrounds.

I think the reason we connected was that we both were orphans in our own way. Toward the end of the month, Tabby told me about the way her parents had reacted to her sexuality, basically making her emotionally an orphan from her teen years. Afterward, I had excused myself to go vent my frustration, Sophie finding me twenty minutes later in the gym, beating the hell out of a punching bag. "At least you're doing better than Mark the last time he got this pissed off," she noted. "He didn't wear any gloves."

I ignored her, pounding away until the tide of my anger subsided. "Why?"

"Why what?" Sophie replied. "Are you asking why he didn't wear gloves? Why I'm here? Why the Spartans are only two and two, despite having one of the better defenses in the league this year?"

"You know what I mean," I replied, peeling the gloves off and throwing them across the gym in a final spurt of defiance. "That someone like Tabby is left feeling as alone and abandoned as I did? Fuck, I can at least understand, if not like, that my mother was a drug addicted fuckup. But to do that to your own flesh and blood while they live with you? How could someone do something so shitty to someone so adorable?"

"Welcome to the question I've asked myself for most of the time I've known her," Sophie replied, still leaning against the wall with a bemused expression on her face. She did that a lot when she was in her teaching mode, like the answer was clear, but she was still taking the time to explain it anyway since I wasn't connecting the dots. "I still don't have an answer, but I don't think one exists. It doesn't stop me from trying to answer it, though. You know what I do instead?"

"What?" I asked, wiping my face with a small towel that had been hanging on the wall. I realized it was one of Sophie's and folded it up. "Sorry. I'll wash it."

She waved it off. "Forget it. But what I do is, I love Tabby for who she is. If you want my advice, do the same. Not that you aren't already. But her own family was stupid, and she can't take more heartbreak."

I nodded firmly, which said all that needed to be said.

Sophie left, and I followed back into the main house after putting Sophie's now dirty towel into the laundry. Tabby met me near her room, taking my hand. "I didn't mean to upset you," she said, giggling when I pulled her into a hug. "Although I guess you weren't that upset."

" I could never be upset with you," I answered, inhaling her clean, subtle scent. She didn't wear perfume; she didn't need it. "I just don't want to see you in pain. Ever."

Tabby let go of me and stood back. "You know you can't prevent that.

141

Nobody can."

"Doesn't mean I don't want to try," I said. "I just want to see you happy, no matter what."

Tabby stood up on her tiptoes and kissed me. I was surprised at first, then I kissed back, her lips and tongue soft and wonderful. I wanted her so badly, but I was already exhausted even before my burst on the bag. Despite her body being pressed against me, despite the soft swell of her breasts against my chest and her hips pressed against me, my body wouldn't respond. I was so damn exhausted. We parted, and she chuckled when she saw my hangdog expression. "Don't worry about it," she said, rubbing her hands over my chest. "First of all, you're drained from today. You've been going through so much stress physically and mentally that I'm surprised you even think of sex with me."

"I dream of you more often than you'd believe," I said honestly. I shook my head, realizing how I sounded. "Wow, that was creepy. Not over-obsessed stalker-type at all."

Tabby laughed and kissed my chest through my shirt. "That's okay, I know that what's here is clean enough. Listen, let me talk to Sophie and Mark. You don't have anything late night tomorrow, do you?"

"No, why?" I asked, a thread of hopeful anticipation making my pulse quicken. Or maybe it was just feeling Tabby so close to me in the privacy of the hallway, knowing her bedroom was so close that I could imagine it.

"Because tomorrow is date night, just you and me, Councilman McCaffery. And not here at Mount Zion, either. We've had enough chaperoned dinners with the rest of my real family. We're going to go to a perfectly normal restaurant down in your district, and have a perfectly normal, public date night. If it gets out that you've got a girlfriend, I'm more than happy to be known as that too."

It was the first time Tabby had ever brought up the public potential of our relationship, and it touched me. "I'd enjoy that very much. Although the cynical part of me, or perhaps the side that's just gotten used to being a politician, is thinking about the potential press situation with that."

"Oh, it can be spun the right way, very romantic like," Tabby chuckled, kissing my neck again. She knew just where to kiss, and I felt a surge between my legs that I didn't think I'd have the energy for. It was good to have this side of her back.

142

"We just need to keep a good public relations person on speed dial."

I could barely muster a reply as Tabby's tongue traced my neck and jaw, sending arrows of arousal through my body and straight to my cock, which surged to full hardness in my pants. She giggled when she felt it pressing against her hip, and reached down with her right hand to cup me, rubbing slowly. "My, you just might be Superman," she cooed, looking up at me. "Because your recovery is amazing, and I'm definitely feeling a man of steel."

"That's your doing," I said, biting my lip as she squeezed and massaged. "You're so sexy you could probably bring someone back from the dead with a kiss." My God, I sounded so corny with that one, but Tabby didn't seem to bat an eye at it.

"Well then, tomorrow maybe you can show me how far back from the dead you are," she said, letting go of my cock and kissing me again. I was glad, because if she hadn't, I most likely would have come in my pants; she was that arousing.

I think my hard-on finally relaxed somewhere near downtown, but I wasn't sure.

* * *

The next morning, I was in my office when Gwen came in. "You're going to love this."

"What?" I asked, looking up from the document I'd been reading, a statement on recent street repairs in Fillmore Heights. I had to grin as some of the damage caused was the side effect of my earlier activities. Despite the price tag, after a month of training with Sophie and Mark, I was feeling the itch to get back out there.

"You've been sued," Gwen replied, handing me the file. "I just had to sign with the process server."

"You're fucking kidding me," I replied, taking the folder. I opened it up, feeling my blood pressure rise. "You've got to be goddamn kidding me."

"Nope," Gwen said. "They're saying that you and MJT used illegal means when you divvied out the contract on the HVAC for the first center."

I could feel my rage building and nodded. "Thanks. Let me give MJT a call, see if they have a legal team working on this already."

"You want me to handle it, Boss?" Gwen asked. "Vanessa and I know some law groups we could get ahold of if we need to."

I shook my head. Law offices were the last thing I needed involved with all of this. There were just too many potential problems with that, considering what MJT really was. "I'll talk with Miss Williams directly, but thanks. Can you clear my schedule for the rest of the day?"

"Up until three. You've got your meeting with the mayor then."

I'd have to take it. "Thanks."

I dialed up Tabby, indigestion growing in my stomach. She picked up, and I could hear it in her voice. It was the shakiness, the insecurity that I hated to hear. "I take it you got the paperwork too?" I started, sighing.

"Yeah," she replied, still shaky, but handling it. "Pressman Contractors is suing MJT with you as a co-defendant. Fucking Pressman."

"I know," I said. "Tabby, I know this is a hard thing to ask, but does MJT have a law firm it works with that can handle this?"

"I'll have to talk with Marcus, although most likely Sophie will know more," she replied. I noticed she did that whenever she was referring to Mark in terms of business. Any other time, he was Mark to her. "But I think so. They might not be in the city, but I'll have to check. Patrick, you know this has nothing to do with the contract."

"I know. We can talk about it tonight, if you want. Although I guess this ruins our date, doesn't it?" I said, shaking my head.

Tabby's answer spoke to me about her strength and how hard she was trying to get past her traumas. "Fuck no. You and I are going out. You're going to take me to some decent little eatery in your neighborhood, and I promise you we're going to have a good time. We'll see what happens after that."

"I can dig it," I replied. "Listen, we'll get this taken care of. I know that."

"Okay," Tabby said, her mood brightening. "So, any plans for tonight?"

"Well, my neighborhood isn't exactly known for the high quality of its restaurants, so don't expect five-star steakhouses." I laughed. "But yeah. What do you think of Cuban food?"

"I can do that. I assume jeans and a sweatshirt are better than a suit and skirt?"

"For sure. Okay, let me make a few calls, see what I can accomplish work-wise before tonight."

"Okay. And Patrick?"

"Yes, Tabby?"

"I'm so looking forward to this," she said after a moment, and I knew she was struggling to say something different. Fucking Pressman and his fucking games.

"Me too."

Tabby hung up, and I sighed, not looking forward to the next call I had to make. I dialed up Mark's cellphone, the one he'd given me for emergency matters. True to the nature of the number, he picked up after only one ring. "What's up, Rook?"

"I really wish you'd stop calling me that," I said, a smile still coming to my face. "Although I guess it's better than *Amateur*. Listen, Mark, I need to talk with you. Tabby's going to be on the phone with you in about two minutes, and there's information that you and I need to discuss about it that she doesn't know."

"Are you telling me this because you don't want Tabby to know, or because she isn't in a need to know position?" Mark asked.

I chose my words carefully. "A bit of both. It has to do with my old life, and a connection to the Knave. Think you can get some time away from the house for a lunch?"

"Not at City Hall, I hope," Mark replied. "This scar isn't that much of a disguise."

"No, I was thinking the Park," I replied. "It's a public enough place, we could both blend in."

"Deal. One hour?"

"Deal. And Mark?"

"Yeah?"

"Thank you. Uhm, I'm going to need your advice on this one. I've let it go a while without bringing it up, and I don't know how to do it right," I said, feeling my face burn. "Jesus, I didn't plan this at all. Just, there's shit in my past."

"Shit that is hard to bring up to special people," Mark completed. "Yeah, that's a challenge. Okay. One hour."

I hung up my phone and sat back, just thinking. Fucking Scott Pressman.

I made it to the Park with a few minutes to spare and went over to the bandstand that Mark had texted me to meet him at. In my hands was a bag from Burger King, a guilty pleasure that I hadn't indulged in all month. I saw Mark coming and waved, having ditched my work sport coat for a Spartans hoodie. We looked like two normal working class guys having lunch, with him wearing a jean jacket along with black denim. He was carrying a plastic bag that, when he got closer, I saw was from a sub shop nearby. "Sophie's going to want to kick your ass for that," he greeted me with as we slapped hands. "But I won't say anything."

"Thanks. Honest, though, I haven't done this in weeks," I replied. I took out my burger and began. "So Tabby talked with you?"

"Don't worry about that," Mark replied, "I've got a Boston law firm that I've used for a lot of my contract stuff before. They're good enough to keep anybody that Pressman can hire off our tails, and they're just shady enough that they know how to protect our ass. But I doubt that's the reason you called."

I shook my head after taking a huge bite of my burger. Cheese, mustard, pickles, mayo . . . pure heaven. "I know Pressman," I said bluntly, "or at least I did."

Mark nodded slowly and started on his lunch. "I figured as much. With some of the things you've said, you have more knowledge on the Knave than what a simple former bartender would. How do you know him?"

I blinked and shook my head, frustrated. "Back in my high school days. Hell, this would have been before you even moved here, I think. I was just thirteen, Scott was fifteen, sixteen maybe? Anyway, he was already into being a player, although back then it was being a player more than what he turned into. All of the guys in our little group thought he was so damn cool. Did you know that by the time he graduated high school, he'd already slept with half the female teachers, including the Vice Principal of the school? And they talk about that shit on TV nowadays like it's some sort of scandal. Scott Pressman was a walking scandal, and nobody said a damn thing."

"I'm not surprised. I never met him except for that one time."

I laughed, remembering when the news broke about the Knave's 'injury.' "Yeah, I was working the bar back then. Pressman himself came in, pissed off and so fucking depressed he could barely talk straight. I hadn't seen him in at least five years, not since he and I had a falling out, but for some reason he came in that night, already half-drunk. I cleared out the bar. I didn't want some Confederation guy talking enough stupid shit to get the place shot up, and he proceeded to dump his whole story in my lap. I was damn near pissing my pants laughing until he put the forty-five on the table. Pressman might not have been a normally violent man, you know, but you'd just taken away his dick."

"So what's the problem?" Mark asked. "I mean, Sophie knows about my history with Anita Han."

"You and Han?" I asked. "Really? I knew you made the hit, but there was more?"

Mark nodded. "For about a year I was one of her boys. Never emotional, mind you, but she taught me a few things I still use to this day. Sophie was fine when she found out."

"Anita Han didn't mentally screw Sophie up," I replied, chewing on a fry. "I just didn't know how to talk with Tabby about this. I mean, how do you tell your girlfriend that one of your former buddies was the guy who had turned her inside out and screwed with her heart and head, and oh, by the way, he was the last person you were with before me?"

"Can I ask, how close were you and the Knave?" Mark asked.

"For a while there, we were part of the same crew," I said. "I mean, we worked game together, and I'll admit we talked a lot of shit about girls together. That continued until Vince got shot."

"Who was Vince?" Mark asked. "You haven't mentioned him before."

"Vince was my best friend through junior high and high school. We lived in the Hall, and we started running together soon after I got there. He and I were buddies, and when Vince met Scott, we all became part of the same clique. Pressman had the money and the moves, Vince was the athlete, and I was the smooth talker to get us out of trouble. There were a few other guys who kind of rotated in and out. We tended to run in a group of four or five most times. The other two, whoever they tended to be, were kind of the groupies."

"I understand. What happened to Vince?"

I sighed and ate the rest of my burger. "Vince was always the best athlete of the bunch. That kid could ball like nobody's business. Unfortunately, his grades were terrible, and after high school he was unable to qualify for a decent school. Still, he was able to talk his way through our Confed connections into a local juco that had a team. I did my best to keep Vince shielded. I wanted at least one of us to get out of the life."

147

"I can understand that," Mark said. "But I'm guessing others didn't?"

"No," I replied. "There were a couple of bookies who did action on the local sports, even at the juco level. When Vince started lighting up the scoreboards and getting attention from big name schools, they let things build until the odds were greatly in their favor. Then they called in their marker."

"Did they want him to lose?"

I shook my head. "No, just point shaving. They wanted him to look like shit, basically. Just one game, mind you, but it turned out that it was the night that three different D-1 coaches were coming in to look at him. It was Vince's best shot at a top flight program, and he knew it. If he did what the bookies said, he'd lose his shot at a scholarship. If he didn't, he'd be pissing off a whole lot of Confederation bookies."

"He didn't do what the bookies wanted," Mark said gravely. "I remember the name, actually. It was before my time, but I heard the name."

I felt tears spring to my eyes. "He went out there, and I swear afterward that he knew what he was doing. He knew he was finished either way, so he was going to show one time how damn good he was. That night, he was Magic Johnson, Michael Jordan, and LeBron James all combined. Vince had forty-four points by halftime, and he got even hotter in the second half. The final buzzer sounded, and he had a hundred and eight points, fifteen rebounds, ten assists, and five steals. It was the damndest thing I'd ever seen. Walking off the court, he flashed me a smile and a thumbs up, tears streaming down his face, utter exhaustion and exhilaration written on his face. It was the last time I'd ever see him conscious."

"They hit him in the locker room?" Mark asked. I nodded.

"They waited until the rest of the team had supposedly cleared out, and the coach was out talking to some of the Division I coaches who had come to visit. The first bullet took him in the leg, the second took him low in the spine."

"So they didn't kill him outright," Mark commented. "Paralyzed?"

I nodded, "If he'd woken up, yes. But the way he fell, he hit his head on the bench, cracking his skull. The doctors did what they could, but between the gunshot wounds and the hit to the head, he went into a coma. He died four days later."

Mark sighed and finished his sub. "That's when you started peeling away from the Confederation."

"And Scott," I said. "He never admitted it, but he was the only other person who knew that Vince wasn't going to go along with the plan. Of course, afterward he denied it, but after that, well, things changed. It took me three years to really drop out of the life and move on somewhat. That was the catalyst though."

"I see. I'm guessing with all of this, you never thought of talking about it with Tabby," Mark commented, bringing things back to the initial conundrum, "and now you don't know how to broach the subject."

"Not after the last screw-up I had," I replied. "I just don't know."

"Well, in any case, good luck with your date tonight. I'd say you need to talk about it tonight with her. Tell her the truth, see what happens. She's stronger than she thinks. That girl's been through a lot and she keeps bouncing back."

Chapter 19
Sophie

I'd spent most of the afternoon coordinating with Mark's Boston lawyer on the whole situation about Pressman Contractors. The lawyer, a guy nicknamed *The Squid*, promised me he'd be able to take care of things. Mark had total trust in the man, and he'd apparently done work for him before.

I was standing in the bathroom, staring at myself in the floor to ceiling mirror as I pondered my reflection. I was gaining weight, that was unavoidable. My biggest concern, however was that I'd been gaining weight too fast. My baby bump was becoming a full on potbelly, at least in my eyes.

I heard the front door close, and I knew that Mark had come back from his meeting with Patrick and his shopping. He hadn't told me what he had gone shopping for, so I was surprised when he came in with his hands behind his back. "What do you have there?" I asked, smiling. "Don't tell me you spent money on some trifle or something."

"Not a trifle at all," Mark replied, coming behind me. He wrapped his arms around me from behind, looking at us in the mirror, and he showed me a single rose. "Gifts for the most beautiful woman in the world are never trifles."

He felt so good with his strong arms holding me from behind that I could barely breathe. "I'm hardly beautiful right now," I said, running my hands over the bulging stomach through my shirt. I took the rose from him and sniffed it, letting my arms dangle afterward with a sigh. "I feel like a damned cow. And I still have three and a half months of this."

Mark nuzzled against the nape of my neck, his breath tickling and at the same time raising delicious goosebumps on my flesh. "Have I been that inattentive to you?" he asked, trailing little kisses over my neck.

"You haven't been inattentive," I said with a half-groan, half-laugh. He felt so good, and it had been nearly a week since we'd made love. Twice, our plans for intimacy had fallen through because I was too exhausted by the end of the day to do much more than fall asleep in the TV room. "I just . . . I'm not feeling very feminine."

"Well, that is something I shall have to remedy then, isn't it?" he said, nuzzling some more. He kissed my ear, his tongue following the curve down to nibble at the tip, my laughter evaporating as desire filled me. "Because I think you're the most beautiful, wonderful woman in the whole world. Look."

Stepping back just an inch or two, Mark eased my shirt up and over my head, leaving me in just my bra. My tummy already poked out, and I unconsciously went to cover it. It just brought up so many memories of my heavier days. It was hard to not feel self-conscious.

"Stop," he said, taking my hands in his. "Look at yourself in the mirror. Look how the light bathes your skin, glowing with health. There's no need for makeup or lotions or anything like that, because you're naturally beautiful and healthy."

Hearing those words from his lips sent ripples through my body, my heart fluttering. Looking into the mirror, I was captured by the intense fire in his eyes as he looked at my reflection and the way his hands hovered over me, showing without touching just where I was beautiful to him. Kneeling, Mark continued his words, pulling my shorts and panties down. I stepped out of them, my legs rubbery from the desire building inside me.

"Look at your feet," Mark said, "with five of the cutest little toes I've ever seen, but with a hidden strength within them, the strength to serve as the foundation for your amazing self."

My breath was husky and dripping with want. I knew what Mark was doing, and oh my, was he doing it well. Seduction has always been as much about the mind as about the body with the two of us, and it thrilled me.

"Then, of course, my eyes travel to your thighs, which are shaped perfectly, sweeping out to your hips that you know inflame my passions for you. Your hips that lead around to your delectable, beautiful backside, the backside that I love to massage and kiss . . ."

I groaned, my lust taking over for me. Mark responded by literally kissing my ass, his hands pulling my hips back and toward his eager mouth.

After the mental foreplay he'd given me, I reveled in the feeling. Putting my hands on the mirror, I looked myself in the eyes and smiled, both me and my mirror image knowing we were in for exactly what we needed. Looking back down, I spread my legs, letting Mark have access to everything. He reached around, cupping my pussy with his right hand while he continued to kiss and lick me, his fingers working in slow, languid circles. I was so wet that I knew he was already coated, but I didn't care, it felt so wonderful. "Oh Mark, I need you so much."

"I need you," he replied. His left hand reached down to unbutton his pants and push them down, at least to his knees, which were on the floor. "I want you more than I know how to say."

Part of me wanted him to take me right there in the bathroom, looking in the mirror as my man, my husband, filled me over and over until we both came. But another side of me, the bigger part, wanted to be carried to our bedroom and made to feel even more beautiful than I felt at that instant. Now, I felt desired. I wanted to feel beautiful too.

I swear it was times like this that Mark transcends from human to superhuman. He read my mind, picking me up in his arms and carrying me through the house in his arms. Like a princess, he carried me through the halls of Mount Zion, having somehow kicked off his pants when he stood up, carrying me all the way to our bedroom.

Laying me on the bed, Mark kissed me, starting with my lips and working his way down my neck to my shoulders. He worked down my left arm, kissing the inside of my elbow and causing my breath to catch as he kept going, all the way down to my fingertips.

"I love you," Mark said, his eyes wide and soft, expressive with more than just words. He sucked my index finger into his mouth, licking around it and letting me pump it in and out of his mouth. I pulled it out and he kissed back down my arm, finding my lips again in a searing, passionate kiss. His hands roamed over my body, stroking over my stomach, hips and breasts as our bodies entwined on the mattress.

I could see it in his eyes, clear to his heart and soul. I was beautiful, that day, the next day, a decade, a thousand years from that moment. To Mark, I was always going to be beautiful, regardless of how much my stomach expanded, or if my breasts sagged under the weight of having one, two, or a dozen children with him. I would always be beautiful to him until the last moment his heart beat, and the last sight in his eyes would be me, his beautiful Sophie.

"Show me how much you love me."

* * *

152

"You know, you didn't have to be so damn good at it," I joked lightly later as we lay in bed, still gloriously nude. "I mean, I still don't want to move."

"Then don't," Mark said. He'd pulled on a pair of sweatpants, but that was it, just in case Tabby and Patrick's date ended early. I was of two minds on the matter. I hoped on one hand that it would, but was at the same time afraid. If they came home early because the bubbling desire that had been building between them for the past month was boiling over, I'd be the happiest woman in the world, even if I'd need ear plugs. On the other hand, if Tabby came home early by herself, I'd be crushed.

Mark had told me about his conversation with Patrick in the Park. Once I got past my initial shock, I understood his dilemma. It's never a good time to bring up former associates, and it wasn't like Patrick was still friends with Pressman. Mark had told me about Anita Han, after all, and our relationship was stronger than ever.

Then again, it was still different, and I was worried. "What do you think will happen?" I asked as Mark came in, carrying two mugs of hot chocolate. "Tears of joy, or tears of heartbreak?"

"I think it depends on what fate has in store for them," Mark said, handing me my mug. He'd put cinnamon in it, just like I liked, along with three big, puffy marshmallows. Have I mentioned he's perfect?

"What do you mean?" I asked, and took a big drink of my cocoa. He'd even made the temperature perfect, allowing me to take a deep drink without burning my tongue.

Mark grinned and leaned in, giving me a kiss. "You're cute when you have a cocoa mustache," he smirked after we parted, "but as to your question, I guess I'm just saying that it's all in the hands of fate. I think Tabby is a great woman, you know that. Hell, she's the second most perfect woman in the world to me."

I teased him just a bit, knowing his answer. "So if I didn't exist, you and Tabby?"

Mark just rolled his eyes. "You know the answer to that," he said. "Anyway, I think Patrick's come around a lot too. He's impressed me the past month. He's done his work with you with barely a complaint, just keeps coming back for more, and that's after putting in his work at City Hall. He's got a way to go before I let him out on patrol with me, but he's come a long way."

"That doesn't mean he's a good match for Tabby," I countered, seeing where he was leading but wanting Mark to say it himself.

"I know. I'm just saying, we both see how they feel about each other. I personally think that their bond is strong enough to not even be deflected by this information about Pressman. If I'm wrong, then I'm wrong. I know Patrick won't betray us, and I'm willing to move on from that. If he's not the right person for Tabby, then we'll be there for her until the right person comes along."

"But you think he might be?"

Mark shrugged. "I have hope. Isn't that enough, right now?"

We waited, with Mark spoiling me via sublime massage, a little bit of chocolate, and a thousand little other things that made me feel beautiful and desired. Most of all, it was his eyes, and what was contained within them.

I was just considering the idea of having him take off those sweatpants when the front door of Mount Zion opened and closed again. Mark, who was just wiping his hands clean from the oil he'd been using to massage my skin, paused. "They're home."

We heard two sets of footsteps on the entryway tile, which I took as a good thing. However, what I didn't hear were the giggles or other sounds that told me they were engaged in foreplay or other amorous activities. I sat up and looked around for my panties before I realized that I had left all my clothes inside the bathroom. I guess I could have blamed Mark, but that was beside the point.

Getting up, I quickly pulled a fresh pair of clothes from my dresser and pulled them on. "What are you doing?" Mark whispered, curious.

"I'm going to see what's going on," I replied. "I'm confused."

Mark looked like he was about to object when he caught the look in my eyes and nodded. Reaching into his drawer, he grabbed an old workout t-shirt and yanked it over his head. "They'll have to forgive the lack of underpants and socks," he muttered to himself. "And I was having so much fun, too."

"That might not be over yet, stud," I teased him, giving him a kiss on the cheek. "I was just about to ask you to make love with me again when they came in."

Mark's expression changed, brightening up, and he nodded. "Okay, I might just hold you to that."

"Oh, you want to tie me up now?" I teased. It was a credit to Mark, how we could tease each other about things like that, even after his intervention with Mistress

154

Blood.

"Not tonight, but we can definitely do it some time."

We left our bedroom and made our way silently toward the kitchen and dining area.

I was surprised by what I found. Tabby and Patrick were sitting in side by side chairs, holding hands and just whispering to each other. It didn't look like anything I'd expected. If I had to compare it to anything, it looked like something from a sitcom from the nineteen fifties, where two teenagers considered it risqué if they actually kissed anywhere within yelling distance of their homes, and the epitome of a hot date was going to the drive-in after the sock hop. "Guys?"

Tabby looked up, smiling. "Hi, Sophie. Hi, Mark. Come on in, you're not interrupting anything."

The two of us came in, perplexed. Looking from Patrick to Tabby, I was absolutely confused. What the hell was going on? "Uhm, who are you, and what did you do with my Tabby?" I asked, a nervous smile on my face. "I expected passion, I expected tears, I expected tears and passion at the same time. What I didn't expect was this pod person act."

Patrick looked at Tabby, who looked back at him. "We've had that already," Tabby said, and I realized her tone of voice.

She was over the moon happy. I'd heard it before, but never to such a degree. You see, when Tabby gets truly, absolutely happy, she gets this strange calmness to her voice and body that it almost never, ever shows otherwise. In fact, in all the years I'd known her, the only other people who could get her in such a mood were Mark and me. "And?"

"We've got big news for you guys," Patrick said. "We had our date, and I told Tabby about my history with Scott Pressman."

"Which was the tears," Tabby interjected, "and a few slaps, which you'll be happy to know, Mark, your student here took quite well."

Mark flashed a quick smile before tilting his head again. "Okay . . . continue, before I blow a few brain cells thinking too hard."

Tabby laughed, a light sort of twitter that confirmed my suspicions. I still wanted her to say it, though. I had to hear the words.

"After I told Tabby, we sat and talked," Patrick continued for us. "In fact, we never even went to the restaurant. We just sat in my apartment, talking about things. A lot of it was about my personal history, and how it might affect our relationship. In the end, though, it came down to my ink."

Tabby saw my confused expression. Actually, looking over, Mark was also confused, and I was beginning to wonder if Tabby and Patrick had taken something mind altering. Tabby chuckled and reached over to Patrick, taking his hand. "I think we're being a bit too obtuse. How about we show them?"

Patrick smiled and let go of Tabby's hand. He reached for the top button of his shirt and began opening his shirt. He reached his belly and opened his shirt, showing the gryphon on his chest. "Do you guys know about gryphons?"

"Just that they're on a lot of churches and they are on a lot of old European flags," I replied. "Why?"

"There are a lot of mythical things about gryphons," Patrick replied, "but the reason I have it is because there is something about them that was common regardless of their cultural background. They mate for life."

Mark blinked, then shook his head before putting it in his hands. "I needed to read more classical mythology or something, because I'm getting lost."

"What it means is that Patrick and I have talked, and we've decided to move deeper in terms of our relationship," Tabby said.

"As in?" I asked.

"As in I asked Tabby to marry me, and she said yes," Patrick said.

I've been in a car crash once. I was nine years old and riding in the back seat of the car while my dad drove me to piano practice, when he was sideswiped by a guy who ran a red light in a pickup truck. I wasn't injured, but it did jar the hell out of me.

Patrick's words shocked me just as much. I looked from him to her, then to Mark, then back, my head moving in a sort of weird triangle. "Engaged?"

"Now, don't worry, we're not running off to Vegas like you two," Tabby said, reaching over and taking my hands. "We want to take our time. We haven't even talked about a date yet. It's more of a declaration of our wanting to spend the rest of our lives together. We know it's fast, and we know that it sounds strange."

Mark shook his head and walked over to Tabby. She stood up from her chair, looking up into his eyes. They had bonded nearly as close as Tabby and I had, and they looked at each other for a long time before Mark opened his arms and wrapped her up in a hug. "Okay," he said, her head tucked under his chin like he was protecting his little sister or his child. In fact, the mother growing inside me could see him doing that with our own daughter someday. "Okay. I love you, and I trust you. Congratulations."

He let go of Tabby, who turned to me while Mark turned to Patrick. "You know this doesn't mean I'm backing off on your training. If anything, I'm going to push you harder."

"Damn right, you are," Patrick said. "I've got something more to come home to than just a couch and two goldfish now."

Tabby watched the two men shake hands, then she looked at me. "Are you okay with this?" she asked me.

I pulled her into a hug, the woman that was most important in my life. "You've never been one to waste time when you want something. The real question is, are you happy?" I whispered in her ear.

"Yes," Tabby said, squeezing me tight. "Maybe I'm greedy or needy or whatever. But I need all three of you in my life."

"Then we'll be there," I said, squeezing tighter. "I love you, Tabby."

"I love you too, Sophie."

I know what Mark and Sophie expected of me and Patrick after we declared that we were engaged. After all, I'm supposed to be the hypersexual redhead, the girl that can't wait to get her itch scratched. And considering that I'd already gone over a month since Patrick and I had last had sex, I guess that assumption was a safe one.

But part of what Patrick and I had talked about—the thing that it took a couple of days for us to get used to and talk about—was that, at least for the first part of our engagement, we wanted to actively avoid sex. It wasn't that we were in a total no-touch scenario, but rather that we were just not actively seeking physical intimacy.

It was the emotional depth we were looking for. It had come to me after Patrick told me about his past with Scott Pressman. I realized that, despite the wonderful side effects of sex and however much I love it, the two people I was closest to in my life, I'd never had sex with. Sophie was closer to me than anyone else in the world, the yin to my yang, the woman who held more real estate in my heart and soul than I had even known I had. I would die for Sophie, but even more importantly, I lived for her too.

Then there was Mark. If Sophie was my match, Mark was just as much hers. It sounds so fucking weird, but it was true, and there was never any feeling of being shortchanged or jealousy in any of it. Mark was my brother, my mentor, my guide and my advisor. If Sophie was my heart, Mark was my strength. And it was the same with Mark and me. He'd come to me so many times for guidance, second only to Sophie herself. If I was the third wheel of the relationship, I certainly didn't feel like it.

So that was why Patrick and I made a conscious choice not to have sex for at least a little while. We knew we were a match sexually; we'd already proven that. Nobody had ever satisfied me as much as Patrick had, even though it had only been one night. We'd found something there that was precious, and I wanted it again and again, I knew. But I also wanted more than that, and Patrick agreed with me.

"Tabby, the thing that was most painful to me was that I'd caused you pain," he had said to me while we sat in his apartment. He was about ten minutes from asking me to marry him, and we'd just finished the fighting.

"You didn't do anything intentionally," I said. "Although not telling me about Pressman is your fault."

"For which I'm very sorry," Patrick said, rubbing his jaw.

I smirked and reached over, patting his knee. We were sitting on the poor excuse for his couch, which, from what I could tell, tripled as his dining room and sometimes bed too. A true bachelor pad. Most people didn't keep a pillow for a couch cushion, at least. "I understand, though. But it can't happen again."

"I know. Tabby, my life's an open book to you now. I promise, no more secrets. I'm not saying something might not come up and bite me in the ass; I have a lot of crap in my past, but I promise, no more hiding anything."

Later, we formed our plan. Part of it was to move in together. It sounded weird, sharing a house but not a bed, considering we were engaged.

Mark and Sophie hadn't blinked when I told them, however. Instead, they merely shifted their office into their bedroom, leaving Patrick with a small but adequate place to temporarily sleep. I could've just stayed at Patrick's place until we found our own, but I think we both silently agreed that Zion was leaps and bounds better. "Hey, it's bigger than my living room already," he said when Mark showed him the empty space. "I'm just glad you didn't stick me in the bell tower."

"Can't yet," Mark replied. "Don't trust you with the automatic weapons yet."

Patrick looked sideways at Mark, then he just shook his head. It was the sort of thing you got used to around here. Instead, he merely used the paycheck that he wasn't spending from the city to buy a simple twin-sized mattress and set it up on the floor. It wasn't much, but it sent the right message. He was willing to wait a long time if need be, but he didn't want to wait forever to be invited to my bed again.

The whirlwind nature, at least to the public, of me and Patrick was probably the biggest side effect we hadn't counted on. I knew I'd gotten in the newspaper a few times. Sure, there were the occasional comments, but I mean, I wasn't a *celebrity* or anything. I didn't go to red carpet events; I didn't try to get on TV or anything like that.

Still, somehow Patrick and I ended up on the front page of the society page and the local politics page more than once over the ensuing months. When we went to a Spartans home game again, there we were, in full color. When Mayor Joe had a fundraising event for one of his favorite charities, Patrick and I had attended—not to gain attention, but because I actually liked Joe, and his cause was worthwhile. The pledge was because I agreed with him, yet somehow, it ended up getting more press than Joe's actual speech.

One morning, as the first light snows swirled around the trees that lined the driveway up to Mount Zion, I got in my car to drive to work, and Patrick tapped on my window. "What's up?"

"I just wanted to remind you that I'm going to be late tonight," Patrick replied. "Council meeting. I probably won't be home until at least ten."

"I remember. I'll miss having you for dinner," I said. Patrick smiled and leaned into the car, kissing me quickly. Now, you'd think that two people who had said they weren't going to have sex wouldn't be affectionate at all. Instead, we were more affectionate than ever. We kissed almost constantly, to the point that Sophie had instituted a rule with me that when Patrick and I used the gym at the same time, I had to remain on the other side of the room from him at all times.

After our kiss ended, I smiled up at him. "I look forward to dessert," I told him, rolling up the window and putting my car into gear.

I knew I was distracted as I drove into the city, but when the police flashing lights came on behind me, I was absolutely shocked. I'd never gotten a ticket, and a quick check of my speedometer told me that I was still two miles under the limit. Pulling over, I turned off my engine and waited for the officer.

The guy who came up was your typical police officer, white, clean cut if a bit militaristic in his grooming, and carrying about fifteen to twenty extra pounds under his body armor. "Good morning, officer, how can I help you?"

"License, registration and proof of insurance, please," the cop stonily replied.

"Of course," I said, "it's in my purse, is that okay?" I was worried he was going to think I had a gun in there or something, even though it was a small purse.

He nodded, and I took out my license and car insurance card. The registration was in a little document holder clipped to my sun shade, so I got that out too. "Here you are."

He leaned in, and sniffed the air. "Ma'am, I'm detecting the smell of alcohol in your vehicle. Have you been drinking?"

160

So it was going to be like that then. "No, officer. It's not even nine in the morning. I'll be happy to take a breath test if you like."

What proceeded was perhaps the biggest jerk off job I've ever seen. His device, which curiously powered up just fine, didn't get a reading at all, and kept giving him an error message. When I offered to do a field sobriety test, in full view of his dash cam, of course, he stated that the conditions were unsafe for doing so, as apparently a tenth of an inch of snow gusting around by the wind was too dangerous to let me walk in a straight line. I wasn't even wearing high heels, those being in the passenger seat of my car. I drove in running shoes.

I knew better than to reach for my phone to call anyone, or to try and make a scene. I might have been a local media attraction, and I might have been dating the best looking member of the City Council, but that didn't mean I couldn't catch an old-fashioned police beat down if the cop wanted to. Instead, I waited the extra forty-five minutes while another cruiser was brought in and a police Sergeant got out. He had his dog with him, and I inwardly groaned.

Of course, as you'd expect, Rover started barking like hell and nearly pissing himself as soon as he got within sniffing distance of my car. "Open the trunk, ma'am," Sergeant Super-Cop said. "This is not a request."

"I understand," I said, keeping my temper in check as I shivered in the cold. I hadn't worn a jacket, and I was damn near freezing. "Just, do you mind if I call my house? I'm really cold, and they can bring me a jacket or something."

"Sorry, no phone calls," the first cop said. At least he said sorry.

My trunk was empty except for some dry cleaning that I didn't get out of the trunk the day before. Still, it was nearly another hour before the two cops decided that they'd hassled me enough. The first cop wrote out a warning for, quote, "not approaching a red light at an acceptable level of caution" and let me go on my way. As soon as I was in the office, Vanessa looked at me questioningly. "I was beginning to wonder if something happened to you, Tabby."

She'd gotten a lot better at calling me Tabby in the past few months. "Yeah, something did. Two of our local cops decided it was time to play 'screw around with the local supposedly anti-Union business leader'," I grumbled. "Tell me, what am I late for?"

"Nothing I couldn't handle," Vanessa replied. "The general contractor dropped off a cost update of next month's renovations on the first center, and he wanted the check for him to distribute out. I cut him a check; sorry, I had to use your autopen."

"No problem, I trust you," I said, distracted. Vanessa did have access to one of the public MJT checking accounts for specific purposes like this, where she could make online payments for different things. She rarely used it since we kept the level relatively low, mainly for accounting purposes. "Anything else?"

"Gene from the Spartans called, but he said he'll be out of the office for the rest of the day. They're in the playoff hunt, you know, and I think he wanted to offer you and Patrick first dibs on playoff tickets if they get a home game."

"Okay, thanks. I'll try and reply. If I can get a box, do you want to go? You know you and your . . . Vanessa, I have to apologize," I said in wonderment as the fact hit me. "I don't know what your social life is like at all."

"I've got a husband and a ten-year-old boy," Vanessa said with a smile. "If you're offering, I'd love to come. Although I have to warn you about my son. He's got a crush on you."

"Isn't he a little young for that sort of thing?" I asked, amused and flattered.

"He's mature for his age. We're thinking of getting him a razor as a stocking stuffer for Christmas this year," she said. "I'm just saying, if he gives you the puppy dog eyes, you'll know why."

I shook my head in amazement. "Ten-year-old boys need to be fantasizing about Katy Perry or something, not me."

Vanessa laughed. "Oh, what about your house staff? You know I've been working for you all this time and I've never met them."

"I'll see. Joanna is getting a lot closer to delivery. If things go according to schedule, we're going to have a new baby in the house by Super Bowl time. But I can ask."

"Thanks. I've talked with her on the phone a few times, and she sounds quite nice."

I smiled, thinking of my Sophie. "She is. By the way, any word from the attorney?"

"Not yet."

I sighed, my only sign of frustration since getting in. The Squid had been doing his job, using private investigators and delaying tactics to wear out Scott Pressman. If it had been just him or his family, he should have folded up by that point. Instead, his legal team was nearly as sharp as he was, constantly counter filing motions and things. I'd already had two depositions, and I hated them both.

The evidence was clear; Scott Pressman was being backed by the Union. It was our best opportunity for busting him open. If we could make a connection between Scott Pressman and the Union, Mark had enough dirt on Pressman to tie him to the now defunct Confederation. There was no way that Berkobitch would want that to come out in the papers.

"All right, thanks. Let me get to work and try to make up for some lost time. Patrick's got a council meeting tonight, so I should be able to catch up."

Chapter 21
Mark

I was really starting to get too familiar with crawling around unobserved, and it was beginning to bother me. I'm a man of action, not dirty shirt fronts. When Tabby called me to tell me about the harassment that morning from the cops, I added another stop on my list of night visits.

Thankfully, in neither of the two visits I had on tap for that night did I plan on having to use anything other than my stealth and observation skills. Of course, that didn't mean things couldn't change on a moment's notice, so I went prepared.

"Be careful," Sophie said to me as she lay back on the bean bag chair. Her stomach bulged like a soccer ball was under her shirt, and yet she was still beautiful to me. We'd even experimented on ways that we could still be intimate even after the doctors had told us that regular sex was not a good idea until about a month after the delivery. "Tabby's getting home late, so I'm going to be cold."

"She and Patrick will be home by ten," I said, giving her a quick peck. "You'll be fine until then. By the way, after the baby, I was thinking that maybe Patrick's ready for a patrol with me?"

163

"We can talk about it after the baby," Sophie said, "but I'm fine with it. He's better than I was when I started with you."

"Don't sell yourself short, beautiful," I countered, kissing her again. "See you soon. I'll have coms up if you need to get in touch. And go to bed early; no need to try and stay up until I get home. Remember what's most important."

My first stop was Pressman Contracting. After the last time we'd spoken, Scott Pressman had apparently tried to turn over a new leaf, at least until his long-nursed hatred against Tabby came out in the lawsuit. He'd worked hard when I checked in, and he had even used his illicit bankroll to finance the expansion of his family's business. His little brother was now in college as well, studying business out west at UCLA.

I had thought Scott had finally let things go until the lawsuit. Thankfully, The Squid had kept his lawyers from digging too deeply into MJT, while at the same time stalling the system. He knew me from my previous life, and he knew that going to court was the last thing I wanted. I'd be willing to pay a settlement first.

Still, civil law is a lot like poker in situations like this. We weren't playing the facts; we were playing the man. I knew Scott Pressman, and I knew some about Francine Berkowitz. The one advantage I had was that they didn't know me very well. Hopefully it was all the advantage I needed.

Setting up across the street, I waited while Scott closed up shop for the night. He'd gained about twenty pounds since I'd last seen him, most of it muscle. I guess when your dick didn't work any longer, and your wife was accustomed to what you were, you did what you could to keep interest where you could. He finished up a chunk of computer work, nothing that I could see, then closed the top on his laptop, leaving it behind. Not a good idea, in my opinion, but I only noted it for future reference. Tonight was about the observation of Scott himself.

He locked up the shop and got into a used pickup truck, driving off. I quickly followed, keeping enough distance between us that I was hopefully able to remain undetected. I was surprised when Pressman left the city and headed toward the suburb town of Kingsville, about a half hour outside of town. Kingsville was mostly upper middle class—not quite gated subdivision level, but it was the sort of town where you could let your kids play outside without fearing for their lives.

Pressman drove to a rather routine looking, ranch-style house and parked. I

164

stopped my bike a block back and watched him go inside before I followed, stashing my bike in between two SUV's that were parked on the street.

I'd learned stealth by practicing in urban environments, and of course growing up as a country boy, in the extreme rural confines of the woods. This suburban stuff was totally different to me. I decided to go with the old standby, just walk up like I was part of the neighborhood, hoping my hood would cover my face enough to prevent people from wondering what a masked man was doing walking through their neighborhood at nine o'clock at night.

I listened carefully as I vaulted the fence to his backyard. It was only a short little chain link fence, so I wasn't expecting a dog or anything, but you never knew. Pressman could have had one of those little ankle biters, a Schnauzer or terrier or something. It paid to be careful.

Going around back, I saw Scott sitting down with what I assumed was his wife. She was beautiful, I had to admit, but in a way that was also ugly. Let me explain. I've told Sophie that she's the most beautiful woman in the world, but it's not just her looks. It's her spirit and her heart, coupled with a nice build that makes Sophie beautiful to me. Sophie could be bald and two hundred pounds, and I'd still think her beautiful.

Scott Pressman's wife, however, was different. Maybe when she was out being a seductress, she knew how to change her facial expression, at least enough to fool her mark, but to me, there was something just inherently evil about the woman. She was beautiful but cold, aloof. My suspicions were soon confirmed. Scott was sitting at the dining room table, a look of utter rejection on his face. "Are you really going out tonight?"

"Of course," his wife replied. "Unless you found some magic dick pills, there are only so many things you can do to keep me satisfied."

Scott sighed and ran his hands through his hair. "Melinda, this is the third time this week. You know, sending Nathan over to his grandparents' house isn't going to keep working as a cover. What are we going to tell him when he figures out that his mother is out working the game with men every time he goes to play at Grandpa's?"

"That's your problem," Melinda said simply. "I figure you can put that either right before or right after you explain to him how his father's a limp dicked piece of shit."

"Hey, you know why I did that! For you, goddammit!" Scott yelled, his temper getting the best of him. "You think I enjoyed it?"

"I don't know, did you? It certainly looked like you did," Melinda said calmly, snapping her purse closed. She wasn't dressed for going out, but who knew where she might have been stashing clothes? As physically attractive as she was, she probably could have shown up in most clubs wearing a high-necked potato sack and gotten five men within twenty minutes. "The way you were moaning, it sure sounded like it."

"Fuck you, bitch," Scott spat, sagging back into his chair, defeated. "Just fuck you."

"If you could, I wouldn't be going out tonight, now would I? Enjoy your pro wrestling," Melinda said, leaving the dining room. I heard the front door slam, followed by the sound of a car engine revving before driving off.

I gave it a few minutes before making my move. I was just about to open the window and sneak in when Pressman shocked the hell out of me. The son of a bitch, who'd broken more hearts than I could recall—most importantly to me, Tabby's— put his face in his hands and started bawling like a child. Great racking sobs tore from his chest, and I felt a momentary flare of pity for him.

Instead of slipping the lock, I made a quick decision and knocked lightly on the glass door. Scott reacted like he'd been shot before looking at the back door. I faded into the shadows and waited for him to approach, opening the door. "Who is it?"

"Come out, Pressman," I rasped, sticking to the shadows. "No threat, I just want to talk."

He remembered the voice and sighed, resigned. He knew from my reputation that I was carrying guns, even if he couldn't see them. "What the fuck do you want?"

"Just to talk," I replied. "Come on out; you know I prefer shadows."

Sighing again, he nodded, leaving the back door to his house open. "How long have you been there, Snowman?"

"Long enough," I replied. "Is she the reason why you're doing it?"

"Doing what?" he asked, sitting down at a small picnic set on the patio. "The lawsuit against MJT?"

166

"I told you last time to stay away from Tabby Williams. Did you really think I'd let you keep this charade up? It's not like you need the business, Pressman. From what I've seen over the past few months, you can barely keep up with the expansion of your business as it is."

I was standing farther back in the shadows than he was, just outside the dim triangle of light that was cast by his windows and his open door. With the crescent moon and partly cloudy skies, he couldn't see me clearly, but I could still see him well enough.

Pressman shrugged, his face pointed in my direction, focusing mostly on the sound of my voice. "Why the fuck should I tell you, Snowman? All this shit is because of you. You were the one who drugged me, you are the one who taped those damn earbuds in and turned that shit on that fucked up my brain for eight hours. You're the one who tore my life apart, man. I'm just trying to pick shit back up."

"Bullshit," I replied. "Come off it, Scott. If you wanted to just pick shit back up, as you put it, you'd be spending your free time in counseling trying to get that mental block broken down. Hell, any damage the drugs did physically should have been mostly repaired by now. You're not physically incapable of getting it up."

His shoulders trembled, and Pressman looked like he was about to get up out of his chair, but he slumped back down. "That's not it."

"Then tell me. If anything, you know I'm not going to lie to you, there's no need."

It was true. I was perhaps the only person in Scott Pressman's life he could actually trust, the one person he knew the consequences of telling something to. Strange. "She . . . Melinda's behind it all," he admitted, sagging into his chair. "She and Berkowitz go way back, back to when Melinda was more active in the game. They've stayed FWB since then—nothing I minded before, but after what you did . . . Berkowitz told Melinda she knew how to cure me, to undo what you did. I know it's bullshit. I think Melinda does too, but Berkowitz, she knows she needs an in somehow. She goes through a normal union shop to get to MJT, all of that shop's shit comes out into the light. Pressman, though, we've been hiding more skeletons than a graveyard for two generations now."

"Then why keep going with it?" I asked quietly. "You know you can't be quick fixed. I'm better at what I do than that. Besides, you also know what I'd do if you actually came within sight of Tabby Williams."

Scott lurched, and I realized I'd seen it before, when I had said her name the first time. "The conditioning is stronger than I planned. I thought they'd have come and gotten you in four or five hours, not eight."

"Yeah, well, it's only in the past two months that I've been able to even hear her name without wanting to puke. If this case goes to trial, I'm probably going to piss myself and go blind as soon as she walks into the courtroom."

"So why do it? Fuck, I gave you an out. That doesn't happen often with me."

"Because of my son," Pressman replied, anguish in his voice. "She knows the deal. Divorce laws in this state give custody to the mother over eighty-six percent of the time. And she's got dirt on me, man. Video, not only of me before, but me since. She's taunted me for weeks, breaking me down mentally. I mean, all of us in the seduction game, or at least most of us, have gone the other way for a mark at times. I didn't need to often, but I'd done it before, always topping. This time, I bottomed for some cuckold fantasy mark she was honing in on. Or at least, that is what she told me."

"What happened?" I said, a hollow ball in the pit of my stomach. "She set you up?"

"You think? It was all a trick by her. She got me in the worst position, and only afterward showed me the video. Christ, I was acting, man! But she's got it on video, me being someone's bottom bitch while she isn't in the filmed part at all. She's held that goddamn file over my head ever since."

"Why is she coming after Tabby so damn hard?" I asked, curious. "It wasn't her who put you out of action."

"No, but she can't get to you. You don't get it, Snowman. She doesn't just hate you, she hates everything about you. She hates that you pulled me out of the game, took me out of it. I had over three million dollars in seductions going, even without Marcus Smiley's money, you know that? I had Gina Franklin riding me twice a week and this close to giving me the account numbers I needed to clean Bill Franklin out. You know how much we're talking there, even if it was only a few of the accounts?"

"A lot," I replied, trying to not puke. Even with his injury, even with his own trauma, he was still a self-centered asshole who thought of sex as merely a weapon to

168

use, like I use my Glocks.

"Understatement of the fucking year. And Melinda, she wanted it all. We were going to get away from it, away from the air conditioning contracts and the games, just get away and find a new life. We were going to pull a ghost job, just like you were probably going to do at first before Sal fucked you over. So, she's going after MJT. Notice I still can't say her name without feeling nauseous. I put up with it because, despite the fact that yes, I'm still an asshole. Despite the fact that I'm a total scum of a man who hates most of the fucking world, and most of all hates you, there is one thing that I do all this shit for."

"What's that?" I asked.

"The same thing that has kept me from climbing the Financial Tower and jumping off, or going over to Central Station and stepping in front of the Silver Bullet Express to Washington. My child. He's still innocent. I'm trash, I'm a motherfucker, but he's still innocent. And I swear, as God as my witness, I'll keep him innocent. I may have my own little plot in the seventh circle of Hell all ready to go for me. It might be right near yours, all things considered. But my son? No. It ends with me, and it ends with Melinda. She's at least agreed with me to that much."

I could tell even listening to him then, he was lying, to himself as much as to me. He knew his wife was going to screw him over, and most likely bring his son into the game as soon as he was able. I'd never seen the boy, but if he was at all as good looking as his mother and father, he was going to be a heartbreaker if he wanted to be. I could see it in the way Pressman held his shoulders and the tone of his voice. He knew it. If I could have seen his eyes, I would have seen it there too.

I considered for a moment what to do. I looked at Pressman and then thought about his wife. There was an option I could choose. I could kill Scott Pressman, wait for Melinda Pressman to come home, and kill her too. It was tempting. It would solve the problem with the lawsuit as well.

My fingers itched with the idea. But my hands didn't move. Maybe I was getting soft, but I didn't think so. Killing Scott and Melinda Pressman wasn't going to solve all of their son's problems. He'd be sent to live with his grandparents, the King and Queen of Hearts, grand thieves in their own right.

It wouldn't stop Francine Berkowitz, that was for sure. She was a vulture, who'd just find another front for her crusade against MJT. She was just as much of a

169

seducer as Pressman was, just in another fashion.

Another option came to my mind. It was risky, but it could end things quickly. "Give me what I need, Scott," I said simply. "Let me take Berkowitz down. It won't solve all your problems, but it'll at least prevent your wife from fucking over another innocent woman. Tell me, didn't you ever love her?"

Pressman made a sound that was halfway between a laugh and a sob, and I knew the truth. He still did, he probably always would. Love is like that sometimes. "You think it would change her?"

I shook my head. "I don't know. But there's a chance. You know Berkowitz, she's as much of a fucker as you and Melinda are. I can't guarantee you anything, except a chance."

Pressman thought about it for a moment, then looked toward me again. "Let me think, Snowman. How can I get in touch with you?"

It was an opportunity. I'd take it.

Chapter 22
Patrick

I was nervous when Mark told us about his activities. The second part, about tracking down the cop who'd harassed Tabby, was pretty boring. There was nothing much we could do at the time about the cop. He'd technically done nothing illegal, and while I was plenty pissed off, even I knew that sticking my nose in would do nothing useful. It'd only give him the satisfaction of knowing he'd succeeded in pissing her off.

It was his earlier visit with Scott Pressman that gave me my opportunity, however. Ever since getting shot, I'd worked hard, not only in being a member of the city council, but in training. I was in pretty good shape before—at least I thought I was—but now I was in better shape than I'd ever been. With such a beautiful girlfriend, the public just kind of assumed I was getting in shape to keep up with her. It had even garnered one comment from a morning radio jock calling me the "Hot City Council Stud." Tabby had insisted the station send us a copy of that show, and I

170

found out that her ringtone on her phone for me was now "Hot City Council Stud."

But that wasn't the reason I was working so hard. Okay, not the *only* reason. Instead, I was busting my butt because I wanted to earn Mark's trust and be allowed back on the streets with him. I knew that he could probably handle it himself, and that I could be of use with my City Council position, but I wanted to do more than that. I'd trained for months now, and as Christmas approached, I felt the itch inside me.

It was my desire to make the city better that fueled me through the workouts and the study sessions with Mark and Sophie. I learned more about the city, about tactics and urban combat than I had ever imagined. I learned how the different criminal groups in the city operated, far beyond the basic understanding I had from my teen years. I studied how economics, social structures, and even cultural conflicts were used and exploited by the different powers in the city to feather their nests while sucking the blood from the very people they were alternatively cozying to and exploiting.

It was a crash course on how to become one half of a two-man wrecking crew, and how to be a walking disaster by myself if needed. I was also taught how to be a manipulator, a shadow, the ghost in the walls if I needed. As I looked back on how I'd acted the first few weeks by myself, I agreed with Mark. I was lucky to not be a corpse in the graveyard. Still, I wasn't ready yet, despite the itch I felt inside. It was that frustration that was fueling me when I was lifting that Friday night, just a few days before Christmas.

"Slow down," Sophie said, sitting inclined against a soft pad. She was so close to giving birth that I didn't think she should be in the gym, but she insisted, saying that sitting around the house all day left her feeling like a lump. Still, I insisted that she at least relax, and that I do all the loading and unloading of my equipment. She could talk, she could offer coaching and motivation, but I wasn't going to have her lifting weights. "You're not giving yourself enough rest."

"Out there, I won't get a chance to rest," I grunted in reply as I tightened the wrist strap on my gloves. "There are no rounds out there."

"And if you're throwing punches for that long, you're going to be in deep shit anyway," Sophie replied.

I huffed and nodded, wiping my forehead. "Fine. I'm warmed up enough anyway."

Sophie kept her silence as I started my workout, only talking in my rest periods. "What's biting at you? I know it's not you and Tabby, you two are doing better than ever."

"No," I admitted. "Things are great there. We've even talked about moving on to becoming physical again."

Next rest period. "So what is it?"

"I'm tired of being on the sidelines."

Sophie waited for me to shift to a less intense exercise, then continued. "Do you think you're ready?"

"No. That's what is most frustrating," I replied. I was able to talk while I lifted, although the words came in between little grunts. "I know I'm not as good as Mark."

I was surprised as Sophie started laughing. "Patrick, you probably never will be," she said, not unkindly. "But there are things that you can do better than Mark. In case you forgot, you're a city councilman. He's a groundskeeper. You really don't need to be on the streets to do good. You can do things that he can't."

I had to laugh at Sophie describing her husband as merely a groundskeeper, considering everything the man could do. Sophie saw my improving mood and smiled herself. "See, you do have talents, Patrick. The whole point of this team, this family, is that we each bring something unique to the table. There will come a time for you to use your unique position and skills to help out."

"That could be very soon," Mark said, coming into the gym. "I just got a message on a blind email that Pressman has some information for me. He said it was something to do with another member of the city council."

"Sounds good. Any name?"

"Not on the email. We'll see what develops."

* * *

I didn't have many colleagues on the council. First off, as an independent, I didn't have a party affiliation that lent power to one side or the other. I didn't even vote consistently with one side or the other, instead going with my conscience and what I thought would do the best for the city as a whole.

Because of that, I'd pissed off a lot of people. Still, there was one member of the council that I could at least consider a colleague. Shawn Northrup was the second youngest member of the council. At thirty-six, he was also considered one of the rising stars of city politics. He was a conservative Democrat, which allowed him to pull votes from both sides of the ideological divide during elections. He'd been on the council for six years.

Politically, he and I aligned more often than we disagreed. He was big on increasing education and social services, while at the same time we didn't endear ourselves with the social justice warriors either. I don't remember who got more flak when the both of us were caught laughing our asses off during a Halloween party when Tabby and I dressed up as Belle and Beast from Disney fame, with Tabby making sure that her dress more than showed off her amazing figure. The trouble happened when Tabby and I danced, and my tighter pants showed off a bit too much when photos were posted online. Combined with the angle of the shot, which showed off a very impressive amount of Tabby's creamy, silky smooth cleavage in her yellow dress, both of us had laughed. That we were doing so while with a group of radical feminists wasn't helpful.

Shawn topped me, though, the time he had gone off on a religious group who'd come before the city council to make a proposal that we pass a resolution asking for God's forgiveness due to the recent court decisions on marriage and healthcare. Shawn had gone off on a ten-minute rant against them, even telling another member of the council to shut up as he lit into the group. He was gaining friends and pissing off people on both sides of the aisle.

In fact, the only area he and I seriously disagreed on was the Union. Despite his normal position of being strongly anti-corruption, he'd always been strongly for the Union, stymieing me every time I tried to put a knock into the armor of the Union. He had plenty of reasons why, but I still didn't like it. I kind of liked him, though. He was an okay guy.

That said, it pained me when I knocked on Shawn's office door, late at night. I had waited until most of the staff was gone, because while I wanted to put pressure on Shawn, I didn't want to humiliate the man. It wasn't the time for it then.

"Patrick? Come on in," Shawn said, setting his paperwork aside. "Just finishing up a letter to a Lion's Club that had me in to speak to them last week. What can I do for you?"

"Just wanted to see how you're doing, and to talk about a proposal I wanted to bring before the council tomorrow."

"Tomorrow? Damn, can't it wait until after the New Year?" Shawn said, his face breaking out into a grim. "It's not the sort of time to make big proposals. Everyone's trying to get home or to the airport to go see family."

I shook my head, setting my face. "Can't wait. I know it's going to create some headaches, but this is the best time to do it."

Shawn chuckled good naturedly and leaned back in his office chair. "I was a crusader like you, about six years ago. So I guess it's unavoidable. All right, what's your proposal?"

I handed him the proposal over. Two pages long, it was simple enough. "I want to open up the city contracts again."

"No way," Shawn said, handing it back to me. "You know I'm not for changing the bid process for city contracts. The Union gets first and last dibs on bids. That isn't going to change any time soon."

I nodded. "I thought you'd say that. Fuck, Shawn, you've seen the figures just like I have. The Union bid system is costing the city nearly a hundred million dollars a year. That's a hundred million dollars pissed away on second-rate road repairs, shitty civic buildings, and a heating system that leaves me wearing wool socks to the office and thinking of adding a damn hoodie to my typical work wear. I don't want to spend half the winter walking around City Hall looking like Bill Belichik."

"I don't care about the fashion, Patrick. I'm not changing my position on the bid system. The Union has a long, strong history in the city, and I'm not going to . . ."

I sighed and looked at him, shaking my head. "Melinda."

Shawn's flow of words cut off like a speaker that suddenly had its power cord pulled, and he stared at me, open mouthed. "Melinda? What do you mean?"

I reached into my jacket pocket and pulled out the SD card, handing it over to him. "Don't worry, I have copies of it. You can pull it up if you want, but it shows you and a woman named Melinda Pressman, and another girl, and what looks like an impressive pile of either heroin or maybe cocaine. How old is she, the other girl, Shawn? Only reason I'm asking is because if she was over eighteen, I'll leave this between us. If I find out she was under eighteen, I'm taking it to Bennie Fernandez. City Council isn't as high profile as deputy mayor, but I'm sure there's someone in his

174

office that's more than willing to add your scalp to the DOJ's wall."

In fact, I knew the girl was over eighteen. Mark had tracked her down. It was only her look that made her look like she was in junior high school, but I didn't know if Shawn knew that or not. His fingers trembled as he picked up the card. "I know that Roberta and Jack are going to support my proposal, they've been against the Union as much as I have. Mayor Joe will sign off if the council approves it, I know that too. That leaves me needing one more vote."

"And you came to me . . ." Shawn said, his voice quavering. "Asshole. Why me?"

I sat back, knowing I'd broken him. "Just bad luck, Shawn. I need just one more vote, and you were the first person I had leverage on. I couldn't let it wait any longer."

Shawn's hands still trembled, and I knew he had thought that 'Mary Sophie Collins' had actually been fourteen. I felt bile rise in my throat and swallowed it down hard. Shawn looked at the card and dropped it into his front shirt pocket. "You do this, and you're going to have very powerful enemies, Patrick. They'll eviscerate you come next election."

"They might," I agreed. "You know a lot of my skeletons. But I have an advantage on that. Most of the people in the city know my background. Hell, it was part of my campaign, remember? They know I ran in the streets, even if they don't know exactly what parts of the Confederation I was running with. They know that I worked in bars, and that I don't even have a college degree. What else do they have? There's not a lot of dirt left out there on me."

Sure, I had one large, very large skeleton in my closet, but that was not something to worry about. After all, I was doing this exactly for that reason. "So what do you say, Shawn? You going to tell Berkowitz to fuck off, or are you going to fall on your sword? You know this could be in Fernandez's inbox about thirty seconds ago, and I'm sure Channel Four would love to make something like this their lead story on tomorrow's five o'clock news."

Shawn blinked, and I saw tears in his eyes as he looked at the ceiling. "Her husband was your source, wasn't he?" he whispered, so low I could barely hear it. "Dammit. She told me she was leaving him, that we'd be able to be together once the lawsuit against MJT was over."

"And you believed her," I said quietly. "You believed *her*."

Shawn nodded, then looked at me. "We've been at cross purposes for the entire time we've known each other, you know that, Patrick? I couldn't believe it when you moved in with Williams. The one guy on the council I actually liked, and we were working at loggerheads."

I nodded. "Shawn, I actually like you as a person. That is, until I saw that video. But we've all fucked up in life. Just think about it, and tomorrow, don't let what Melinda Pressman and Francine Berkowitz have on you stop you from voting your conscience."

I got up and left. As I was at the door, I heard Shawn clear his throat. "Patrick?"

"Yes, Shawn?"

"You realize they have the same dirt on me, of course."

I turned back and looked at Shawn. "That's the thing, Shawn. If they knew, they'd try to get further leverage. I'm just leveling the field. You can upset them, or upset me. Either way, you are in a minefield of your own creation. If it were me, and I was going to be blown away regardless of which direction I stepped, I'd make sure that last step was done because it was the direction I wanted to go, the statement I wanted to make. Do the right thing, and who knows? There's a chance you might not get blown up immediately."

I left Shawn in his office and left City Hall, my hands shaking in my pockets as I made my way to my car. My keys chittered against the side of the door when I tried to unlock it. It was that little bit of noise that distracted me enough to not hear anything until it was too late, and all I could feel was a prick in my neck.

Chapter 23
Sophie

I was just scrubbing the last of the dinner plates with Tabby. "Are you worried about Patrick going to talk to Shawn?"

176

Tabby shook her head and wiped down another plate. To be honest, she was doing most of the washing, I was so damn swollen. I couldn't wait for the next few weeks to pass so I could get my daughter out of me. "I know he's ready. Besides, he's just going to talk, not to do anything else. How about you? You didn't exactly eat a lot at dinner."

I rubbed my tummy and shook my head. "I'm fine. I'm just running out of room down here, and I need to shift to a lot of smaller meals. Guess I just need to start grazing. I'm the size of a small cow anyway." I smirked and looked over at Tabby. "You know, I'm actually a bit disappointed."

"Oh? Why?" she asked me, taking the scrub brush to the spatula we'd used, which was crusted with cheese. "Wanted to have the baby before Christmas?"

I shook my head and looked at her. "After you told me that you and Patrick were engaged, part of me was kind of hoping we'd have some overlap to pregnancies."

Tabby snickered and looked over at me. "Really?"

I shrugged. "It was just a little fantasy of mine. I wanted to hand down some of these pregnancy clothes to you, that's all."

"Maybe you still can," Tabby said. "I kind of got Patrick a Christmas gift, one that he gets to open early if he wants."

"Oh?" I said, smiling. "Anything you can tell me about?"

Tabby blushed and leaned over, whispering in my ear. "Red satin teddy, trimmed in white lace, thong, and a Santa hat."

I growled and then chuckled. "Really?"

Tabby nodded. "It's time we got a little more physical again. A girl can only hold off so long."

I couldn't help it, I felt like when Tabby and I were back in college, giggling and dreaming occasionally about our dream guys. My grin threatened to split my face in half, and I could only want it to grow. "Really?"

"You're saying that a lot in the past minute," Tabby replied, her grin also growing on her face. "But yes, really. Sophie, the past few months have been a revelation for me. I'm not just falling too fast this time. Patrick is the one."

I thought about it, then nodded in understanding. "All right. As long as you're sure. So you're planning on rocking his world and your own as often as you like after Christmas?"

Tabby laughed, her green eyes sparkling in the light of the kitchen. "Oh yeah, babe. That poor man's going to be walking funny from Christmas straight through to Valentine's, perhaps. Just tell me when you're doing a leg workout with him, so I know when to back off a little bit."

"That sounds more like my Tabby," I said. "Uhm, I know this might be jumping the gun with Mark and all, but him and I, we were kind of talking. I don't mean to rush it or anything, but once our families start growing, this house is going to start getting small real fast."

"I know," Tabby replied. "I didn't want to think that far ahead, because I didn't want to even consider that you and I would be living apart again. I didn't think I'd like it so much, but I've gotten so accustomed to it. I don't want it to end, but it's not fair having Patrick keep living in a converted broom closet."

"I know," I said. "So what Mark and I were thinking is a couple of options. The first one was to expand this building, kind of turn it into a two-wing complex with a shared common area in between."

"Or?"

I grinned. "This property is big enough that you could certainly have a full-sized servant's quarters on the grounds. Knowing how generous and eccentric Marcus Smiley is, it'd certainly be bigger than a two-bedroom cottage, you know."

Tabby grinned and wrapped wet hands around my shoulders, hugging me as tightly as my belly would allow. "I love you so much, Sophie. Thank you."

I returned the hug, kissing her forehead. "I love you too, Tabs. Now, tell me more about this red satin teddy. Think I might fit into it after I lose the baby weight?"

"Hell no, it'd be too short, and you'd be spilling out of it with those big boobs of yours. Although . . ." Tabby said, before the phone rang. She held up her wet hands and smiled. "Think my servant can get the phone?"

"Yes, milady," I teased back, before grabbing the handset. "Hello, Williams residence."

"You must be the maid," a raspy voice said in my ear. "Where's Tabitha?"

"She's not available right now, may I help you?" I said, immediately tapping Tabby on the shoulder. She turned to me, and I covered the mouthpiece. "Phone call,

178

strange voice asking for you. Go get Mark; I have a strange feeling."

Tabby went without a single complaint, and I uncovered the mouthpiece again. "I'm sorry, I must have missed what you said, this isn't a very good handset. Can you say that again?"

"Tell her that if she wants to see her boyfriend again, she needs to come down to Pressman Contractors by midnight. Or else she's going to have a dead city councilman to mourn in the morning."

The line cut off before I could say anything else, and I stared at it, horrified. Mark came in, toweling himself off, his face clouding immediately in concern when she saw me. "What was it?"

"Male voice, calling saying they have Patrick. They want Tabby to go to Pressman Contractors by midnight or else he's going to be killed."

I saw Tabby tremble, but then she found a core of steel, a strength that I hadn't seen before in her. It hadn't been there when Scott Pressman broke her heart, that was for sure. That Tabby would have crumbled, collapsing to the floor.

Instead, I saw the new Tabby, the one who had grown stronger somehow. Maybe she just needed the love of family to be close by, I don't know. But she trembled for a minute, then turned to Mark. "You can get him back."

Mark nodded, but his face was still dark. "Tabby, if they want you, they could anticipate me. They know the Snowman keeps an eye on you. I've intervened a few times on your behalf. They can't expect you to show up by yourself. In fact, you won't be showing up at all."

"What? Like hell I won't," Tabby said, her spirit rising up.

Mark looked at her calmly, but without any wavering in his eyes. I had expected sternness, but instead he responded with almost heart-wrenching gentleness. He cupped her cheek with his hand and shook his hand. "Tabby, if I have any chance of getting him out of there alive, I need to go in there not having to worry about anyone else. You, for all of your brains and all of your spirit, don't have the training. I'd be worried about you, and I can't have that. I have to go alone."

"Would you have taken Sophie?" Tabby asked me, and Mark looked at me before shaking his head.

"Nine months ago, yes. Six months ago, maybe. Not today," he answered. "I need you here. I need you and Sophie to act as my intel and feed me information.

179

We're tapped into the city traffic cam network; I need eyes on target. When I hit, I'm going to hit hard and fast. If I do, I'll have a chance to get him home safely. But Tabby, it's only a chance. I can't give you a guarantee."

Tabby nodded, her eyes hardening as she accepted her role in the mission. "I know. Then one thing," she said, taking his hand off of her cheek and clenching it in hers. "You kill each and every one of them you can."

Mark looked her in the eyes for a moment, then nodded. "I'll be in the bell tower, getting ready. I want to leave within the hour. They won't expect a fast reaction."

He turned and left, heading for the front of Mount Zion and the bell tower. I watched him go, my worry mixing with my love. I mean, seriously, how many men would be willing to lay it all on the line like he was for a woman who wasn't even his blood? Just because of how much Tabby meant to me and to him? Still, I knew what he was going into, and I didn't want a repeat of what had happened last time.

Tabby read my face and licked her lips, trying to know what to say. "I'm sorry, Sophie. I should have asked you too."

I shook my head. "You didn't need to. I would've told you that it wasn't something to even debate. We'll get him back, that's for damn sure. Come on, let me show you how the computer system can work."

I could do more with the computers than just the traffic camera system. Using the specialized hacker computer that Mark had put together, and bouncing it off of a satellite uplink, I quickly hacked a weather satellite, which would for the next four hours tell NASA that it was having telemetry problems. While it wasn't as high resolution as a military Keyhole satellite, nor did it have quite as many tools, it would still give me live overhead feed of the entire outside of the Pressman building.

"That's gotta be a few felonies," Tabby noted as I showed her how Mark had access to a weather satellite that he could use for monitoring under special emergencies. She fell into her normal relaxed demeanor. A lot of people took it to be Tabby not caring, but I knew from years of experience that when Tabby was joking, she was focused. It was her way of dealing with the stress.

"You can add it to the laundry list. I think we're on notebook number two of them," I replied, firing up the systems. "All right, we are up and loaded, checking communications. Mark?"

"I'm good," he replied over the circuit. *"I'm just getting the last of my gear ready now. Leaving the normal Glocks behind tonight."*

"What's your load?" I asked, more for curiosity's sake as I pulled in the rest of my systems. I looked over at Tabby. "I want you on the monitor. Tell me as soon as you have an image, and I'll redirect it to zoom in on the city. It's run like you'd do Google Maps, so you can type in your destination and it'll take you right there. So what's your load, Mark?"

"One Glock 18s, four clips for it, along with the MP7."

"Not the MP5?" I asked, surprised. Getting ammunition for the MP7 was difficult; there weren't too many places you could buy the exotic 4.6 mm ammunition.

"I'm going to need the armor penetration of the MP7. These idiots will have learned from the last time they tangled with me. They should be in full armor."

I looked over at Tabby, who nodded. Just then, a rumble went through my stomach, and I looked down at my belly as a tightness spread through the muscles. I didn't have time for this right now. "Ready. Tabby's going to be patched in, she's got eyes on the building."

The system went silent for a bit as Mark left Mount Zion, and I heard him peel out in the SUV. He'd have the license plates covered, that was easy enough, but still, it wasn't his bike. I really wish we could have gotten another all electric, multi-person vehicle to augment his bike, but Mark had worried that if we did, it would give Mount Zion too much of a similarity to his signature as the Snowman. So, while the SUV was a hybrid, the engine did roar on occasion. I only prayed it wasn't going to happen on approach to Pressman Contractors.

My belly tightened again, and I glanced at the clock. Nine minutes. Shit. "Tabby."

"What?" she said, her eyes still glued to the screen. "I've got what looks like four trucks, but that's the same as last time. I see two men outside, no damn clue what's going on inside."

"Tabby."

"What?" she said, glancing at me. "What do you need?"

"I'm contracting," I said, looking down at my belly. "Nine minutes apart."

"Shit," she said, blinking. "Uhm, what the hell should I do? I mean, this is so

181

not part of the birthing plan."

"Don't tell Mark," I immediately said, "he's got to focus on the mission."

"Okay. Here, give me the headset," she said, holding out her hand. Putting it on, she squeezed the send button. "Okay, Mark?"

"What're you doing on the mike?"

"Sophie wanted me to take over because I'm looking at the scene directly from the weather satellites," Tabby explained. "Where are you?"

"Seven minutes out. What do you see?"

"Traffic cams and overhead show four trucks, all but one of them Pressman contractor trucks. There are two men outside, one looks like he's carrying something, maybe a rifle or something. The other I can't see anything yet. Roof and backside of the building are clear."

"They'll expect an attack at the rear then," Mark replied. *"You can't get a visual of inside the building?"*

"No, bad angle for the cameras. Most I get is that the lights are on."

"Understood."

Another wave of pain rolled through my stomach, and I gritted my teeth. My daughter wanted out, and she wanted out *now*. The only problem was, while we had made plans for a home delivery with a local midwife, Mark was currently planning an assault on a building full of people, most of them carrying automatic weapons, while Tabby's fiancée was being held hostage. "Tabs."

"Yeah babe?" she asked, turning. "How are you doing?"

"This baby's coming," I replied. "Help me down onto the floor?"

Coming over to my chair, the two of us kept an eye on the traffic cameras projected on the main wall of the room. My keyboard and touch pad were wireless, so that wasn't going to be a problem, I could still help in between contractions. This wasn't exactly the way that I'd wanted to have my daughter.

Another contraction gripped my stomach in a steely grip, and suddenly the floor beneath me was wet. Tabby sat back, her face an open O of surprise, and looked at me. "Uhmmmm . . ."

"Get my pants off, get a bath towel from the hallway, and get back here quick," I said between short little breaths. "Looks like you get to be the nurse that delivers your goddaughter."

182

Chapter 24
Patrick

My tongue felt thick, and the first thought that came to me was that I'd fucked up, yet again. Blinking, I tested my hands, which were bound behind my back. I was sitting in an office chair, but at least my legs were free. I was in the corner of what looked like an appliance repair shop, my back against the wall. Looking around, I saw five people, four men carrying automatic rifles, one paying attention to the large glass front, the other three focused on the steel door off to my left.

The fifth was one of the most physically striking women I'd ever seen. She looked like every teen's fantasy from the pages of *Playboy* or the Internet come to life. Still, there was something in her eyes that said despite the beautiful exterior, this was one evil bitch. I figured it was time to do what I could to keep her talking. If anything, it was better than sitting there looking scared shitless.

Smacking my lips to clear my mind, I just let my inner wiseass come out. "Hmm, you're not the Spartans cheerleader I'd expected."

"Very funny, asshole," the woman said. "Know who I am?"

"I'm thinking you all are part of an elaborate international plot, headed by a large headed genius lab mouse, bent on taking over the world."

One of the guys with guns looked like he was about to hit me, but the woman held up her hand. "Don't worry, let Mr. McCaffery talk all the foolishness he wants. He gets to talk a bunch of crap, then I get to get my revenge. I figure the better condition he's in, the better my reward."

"What the hell are you babbling about, you crazy bitch? I've never seen you before in my life," I said. Part of my mind said I had, though, but I couldn't place it. Perhaps it was the tranquilizers they'd shot me up with. I wasn't thinking too clearly yet. "What, did I piss you off at a campaign rally or something?"

"You? Oh, you're more or less an innocent bystander," the woman replied. "I'm more interested in your girlfriend and her protector."

So this was about Tabby. "If you have a beef with Tabby, you don't need

183

firearms, I think."

"Oh, but I do," the woman said. "It was her friend, the Snowman, who took my husband away from me. Well, I guess not took away, but took away the thing that I loved most about him. It certainly wasn't his choice of careers."

I nodded, the face clicking with my brain finally. "Melinda Pressman. I'd say it's a pleasure to meet you, but I don't do that when I'm tied to a chair with four armed men looking like they want to shoot me. Patrick McCaffery, but I guess you already knew that."

"But of course. By the way, I heard from Shawn about your little threat to him. Guess that won't be an issue, so Francine's going to be happy about that. He's too valuable exactly where he is on the council," Melinda said. "Too bad about my husband, though. Scott's the only other person who had that video file. Looks like he's going to have to be taken care of too."

"You'd kill your own husband?" I asked, only semi-shocked. She looked like that sort of person.

"Why not? He's useless to me as a man, the only way he can even climax is by having his prostate massaged. He's a pathetic husband, only wanting to spend his free time with his son. Never mind me, the woman who put up with his limp dicked ass. And now, he can't even do a simple job of sitting back and signing the goddamn paperwork." Melinda laughed, sitting back in her chair. "But don't worry. Soon enough you're going to be joining Scott in the limp dicked department. Too bad it won't be the same way it happened to him, though."

"What do you mean?" I said. "You planning on just killing me too?"

Melinda leaned back and laughed. "Oh, hell no. That would be too easy. The Snowman? Oh yes, he's going to die. I'd love to just cut his balls off too, but the fact is he's just too dangerous. You neuter that tiger, and you still have a man-eater on your hands. But you, my dear councilman? You're going to have your balls cut off in front of your precious Tabby. Fake haired bitch."

"Oh, like nothing on you is fake," I taunted. "Those tits had to cost what, eight, ten thousand dollars?"

"Motherfucker, these are real, and they're spectacular!" Melinda spat back at me. "But you can probably tell that already. You know, it was pretty hard getting my body back in shape after the baby. It's going to be a few years before I'm totally ready

184

to get back into the game, but when I do, I'm going to be better than Scott ever was."

"What do you mean?" I asked. I knew, but I figured it was better to keep her talking. If she was talking, she wasn't trying to cut off my balls. Also, the four men in the room, despite whatever their jobs were supposed to be, couldn't help but be at least a little distracted by our conversation. I wanted to exploit that and pushed the conversation in a more intriguing direction. "You're going to go back into the seduction game?"

"Even more than I am now," Melinda replied. "You know that the number one search for porn by straight men is for MILFs? Well, give me a year or two, and I'm going to be the hottest one out there. All those young bank execs and business grads, those boys straight out of their MBAs who are getting in on their Daddy's company . . . I'm going to have them eating out of the palm of my hand."

I rolled my eyes and turned my head away. I didn't have to fake much at being repulsed by the idea.

She started to get up, and I needed to keep her distracted. If what she said was true, then Tabby and most likely Mark would be coming. I needed the people inside not paying attention to the outside. I played a gamble. "I know why you really hate Tabby, though."

Melinda stopped and looked up at me, one finely sculpted eyebrow arching. "Oh? Please educate me."

"You're jealous," I said simply. Melinda sat back down, and I could see one of the men by the window turn his head in our direction. I decided to play it to the maximum.

"You're jealous because somehow, even though she was only with him once, Tabby captured your husband more than you ever have. I can understand though. She's more beautiful and sexy, and when we're making love, it's like nothing else in the world. You, for all your outer beauty, could never compare. Remember, I've seen you in action on tape. Hell, you needed a wannabe junior high girl to even get Shawn off. If you were as good as you say you are, you could have had him without needing a prop."

"Asshole, you have no idea what you're talking about," she seethed, but I could see her fingers twisting in her lap. She was pissed off, and I pushed it further.

"What was it that first told you? Was it when he was asleep, maybe having a

185

dream and her name came out? Was it during those first few weeks after Snowman had done what he did, and you were using every little trick you knew? You obviously are skilled, but it just wasn't doing anything. He was probably trying to do his best to make up for losing his cock by using his hands and his mouth. A mumbled word as he caressed you, as you were trying to convince yourself it was still good enough, but then he said her name. That was it, wasn't it? You hate Tabby because your husband knew he'd never have better than her anyway. Huh, I wonder. Maybe his mental block would evaporate if he just thought it was her. Why not try putting on a red wig, losing the fake n' bake tan, and you might find that Scott's got a little more steel in the rod than you thought."

"Motherfucker!" Melinda screamed, leaping to her feet and slapping me as hard as she could. Thankfully, I'd anticipated it, and could roll with the slap somewhat. With that, and the fact that Sophie and Mark both had hit me harder in training, I barely felt it.

I could taste some blood in my mouth though. I started chuckling, forcing the blood out to dribble from my lips. "Tabby even smacks harder than you do."

She raised her hand again, when one of the men raised his voice. "Ma'am. Remember, Berkowitz wants him alive. We need to stick to the plan."

Melinda's hand froze in mid-swing, and I saw that this time there was a knife in her hand. Grinning through bloody teeth, I shook my head lightly. I wanted to taunt her some more, but I knew I was pushing my luck as it was. I had her distracted and angry, but if I pushed her any further, she might just not give a damn about Francine Berkowitz's orders.

"Fine. I'll still have his balls for Christmas dinner," Melinda replied. "How's that for Rocky Mountain oysters?"

I was about to reply when suddenly the night exploded, and gunfire rattled through the air. I dove to the side, hoping that whoever the hell was shooting wouldn't aim at floor level. The office chair tipped over, and I impacted hard on my right shoulder, groaning when I felt my arm pop out of socket. I think getting shot hurt less.

I couldn't see who was attacking, but I had my suspicions. Turning to the front of the store, I saw one of the gunmen down, while another three were already beginning to return fire.

"Fuck it, I'll still get my prize," I heard, and I turned to see Melinda Pressman coming toward me, the knife in her hand and a gleam in her eyes.

Chapter 25
Patrick

I was lying on my right side, my shoulder dislocated from when I crashed into the hard, unforgiving vinyl tile, gunfire going off all around me. I should have been panicking, or at least worried about getting shot, despite my low profile. I should have been thinking about my shoulder, and if I'd broken or torn something on top of dislocating it. I should have. But I wasn't.

Instead, those were far from my mind. My focus was centered about four feet in front of me as Melinda Pressman approached me, murder in her eyes and insanity written on her features. She was as beautiful as she was pissed off. And she was very, very beautiful.

"Fuck it, I'll still get my prize," she said, a long knife in her hand. It looked wickedly sharp and glittered in the fluorescent lights overhead. I was torn between looking at the knife and looking at her face, both of which were filled with deadly intent. She stepped closer, a growl rising in her chest. It was paralyzing and hypnotic, and I found it difficult to move. "That bitch, Tabby, can't have you ever again."

Her words were like a splash of cold water. At the mention of Tabby's name, I knew what I had to do. With my arms tied to the chair behind my back, I couldn't use them to defend myself. At the same time, the wide base of the office chair that they'd used didn't allow me to rotate my body in any meaningful way. Besides, the same rope that tied my wrists to the chair also looped around my waist.

However, they'd made one mistake when they tied me up. My legs were free, a grave mistake. Perhaps they only had one piece of rope to tie me with, or perhaps Melinda Pressman had some other sort of plan in mind when she'd originally had me tied to the chair. In either case, I wasn't going to let the opportunity pass me by.

As soon as Melinda came closer, she started to kneel, intent on my junk. When she came within range, I kicked out with my left leg, wishing I'd landed on my left side, since my right leg is my stronger leg. Either way, I had to kick as hard as I could and hope that I caught her off guard.

In all of my training with Mark, we'd worked kicks from a variety of angles and situations. After watching my footwork and style, he had me focus mostly on what he called *Thai-style* kicks. It was one of these that I unleashed now, bringing my legs up to my chest like I was defending myself before shooting out with my left foot, aiming for the bottom of her kneecap with the flat of my shoe. She was leading with her right leg, which was helpful since it was at a slightly downward relative angle to where I was lying, making the kick easier.

I'd never kicked a woman before in my life before that point, other than light sparring with Sophie. She and I had kicked each other plenty of times, but it was always with light force and wearing shin guards. She was five months pregnant at the time, and I was just learning what to do. There was no purpose to unleashing a full power kick on a pregnant woman, even with shin pads on.

That kick against Melinda, however, was the first time I'd actually kicked out at a woman in anger and with the intent to hurt her. Considering the so-called *ladies* I'd grown up with in the orphanage system and living in The Playground, that was a pretty good run of nonviolence.

I was lucky that Melinda wasn't a trained fighter. Her weapon of choice was her sexuality, which while being much more esoteric, meant she didn't know what to expect. As it was, I connected with the inside of her knee, not hard enough to damage it, but enough to knock her to the ground. Her knife, which was clenched in her right fist, clattered on the tile but was still in her grip. Gunfire rattled around us, and I knew that the counter I'd fallen behind wouldn't stop heavy caliber bullets. I was just grateful that nobody had decided to start aiming low. Melinda looked surprised as she fell, her brown eyes widening in shock more than pain, before her lip twisted in a grimace of hate.

"Fucker," she spat, baring her teeth at me. She leaned over onto her left hand so she could raise the knife up from the floor, and I used the opportunity to kick her left elbow, connecting on the inside with a soccer kick that collapsed the limb. She rolled, unfortunately moving out of my reach, but she also lost her knife, which bounced on the tile a few feet away.

I could only stare as Melinda skittered along the tile toward the knife while the massive gunfire continued. I heard short, measured bursts within the general rattling carnage, and I knew that Mark was still alive. I'd heard him too often when he'd taken me out to the woods outside of the city to train to not distinguish his strictly controlled style. It gave me some hope that I might actually get out of the mess alive and possibly with my balls still attached. I had a great fondness for them; they'd been good friends of mine for many years, and I didn't want to part with them so early in my lifetime.

However, at that moment I couldn't waste any of my energy worrying about Mark or my balls. Melinda had scrambled to her knife and recovered it, turning to grin at me. She'd busted her lip when she rolled, a little trickle of blood running down her chin and filling her eyes with madness. "No more games, boy."

I'd expected her to come at me low, recognizing that there were a lot of bullets flying around the room. Instead, she sprang from her low crouch, springing high and quick through the air. I tried to pull my legs up as quickly as I could, but I knew in the position I was in, there was no defense for my side or my torso. She was on the upward curve of her leap when the burst of gunfire took her in the side, once near the hip and another in her left shoulder.

I got to see firsthand one of the great myths of movies clearly busted then. In movies, when someone gets shot, they usually end up flying through the air like they just got thrown at least a few feet backward (exceptions made for the hero, who still gets driven to their knees and grunting in pain). The reality is much different, and I guess grounded in science.

I'm no math genius. I barely pulled a 'B' my last year in high school, mostly because I spent more time worrying about Carrie Brickshaw, who sat one row over and three seats in front of me, than class. But when Mark took me out and showed me using watermelons on strings, gel packs, and even a dead pig, and combined it with an episode of *Mythbusters*, I believed it. When people fall down or collapse at being shot, it's due to their own bodies' motion. They see and anticipate the shot, trying to jerk out of the way.

In Melinda Pressman's case, she was jumping through the air focused on me. The bullets didn't affect her motion at all, except in one critical way. She reacted to the pain, and her right hand, which was holding the knife, relaxed. The handle slipped from her grasp and she landed on me with a thud, the side of the office chair cracking into her chest before she hit my shoulder. While it was my uninjured arm, the force still jarred my dislocated one, and I groaned deeply, trying what I could to get her off of me.

Melinda was seriously hit, but still conscious. Pain and rage mixed on her face as she tried to claw at me, only the pain of her wounds compounded by falling onto the chair and my shoulder preventing her from immediately clawing out my eyes.

That's when I got lucky. Melinda rolled off of me, her legs tangled up with the legs of the chair I was tied in, twisting her body just a little bit. I kicked, connecting square in her chin. Her teeth clamped down on her own tongue and her head jerked back. Her eyes rolled up and she fell to her back, unconscious. I wasn't worried until I saw the bright red blood flowing out of her mouth and heard the choking sounds.

I tried what I could, reaching with my legs and trying to kick her body to roll her over, but that final fall had spread her weight wide and onto her back, making it impossible. My shoves and kicks just thumped against her lower legs, not doing anything except making her thigh move over a few inches. I watched helplessly when she went into convulsions, choking on her own blood, never regaining consciousness. It was the first time I'd killed someone, and while it was self-defense, I couldn't help but feel bad for her.

It wasn't until Melinda stopped shaking that I noticed the gunfire had stopped. I looked around at what little I could see. My world consisted of a three-foot-wide, partially obscured window as well as the ceiling, and I could see nothing. I did, however, hear someone walking over the glass-covered ground at the front of the store, and I only hoped it was Mark and not one of Melinda's gunmen. I twisted my neck to see what little I could, knowing that if a gunman actually was the one approaching me, there was little I could do to stop him.

When Mark's masked face came into view, I swore I could have kissed him, full tongue even, and I've never wanted to kiss a man before in my life. He was covered with dirt and his cheek was scraped up pretty badly, but he looked more or less uninjured. "You okay?"

"Yeah," he answered, coming over and kneeling next to me. He found Melinda's knife and quickly cut the ropes binding me. "What about you?"

"Right shoulder's out of socket," I groaned as I rolled out of my chair. "Think we can pop it back in?"

"Let's get out of here first. The cops won't be far behind. This isn't Fillmore Heights where they wait until they have three cars before doing anything," he said, helping me to my feet. "Besides, Sophie's probably better at doing it than I am."

Getting up to my feet, I got my first look around the room. Broken equipment and bullet casings littered the ground, along with the bodies. "Jesus. How many did you take out?"

"Five, three in here and one outside. The scrape came from diving after getting the outside guys," Mark replied. "Let's get out of here. Can you jog?"

"Motivate me enough, and I'll outrun you," I said through gritted teeth. "But I have no fucking clue how I'm going to hang on to you on the bike."

"You won't have to," Mark said as we exited the ruined store. We turned left and jogged off, disappearing into the night. We were a block away when we first heard the wail of police sirens approaching. "Come on, I brought one of my other vehicles."

"You must have been planning on dragging me out of there."

"There was a chance, and I had to plan for it. Tabby . . ." Mark suddenly blinked like he'd forgotten something. He touched his ear, triggering the ear bud and microphone I hadn't noticed earlier. It made sense, Mark was the sort of guy who tried to use his tactical tools as much as he could. "Tabby?"

Just hearing that word from a friendly mouth made some of the pain disappear as Mark and I jogged off again. While we moved, he spoke again. "I've got him. Dislocated shoulder, but other than that okay. Tabby? Wha . . . what?!?!?"

Mark took off running, and despite my earlier boast I struggled to keep up, each step jarring my right shoulder and causing me to gasp. Thankfully, Mark's SUV was close by, only about a hundred meters ahead, because it felt like nearly a mile with the pain magnifying my every step. Still, I didn't even have time to close my door and fasten my seatbelt before he had the engine going and was driving down the street. Mark, who'd been listening to his earpiece the entire time, nodded and spoke again. "Gotcha. We'll meet you there. Give us time to change."

"Mark, what's wrong?" I asked, concerned. His expression was confusing me at first. It wasn't quite worry, and it wasn't fear, but it was so intense that it burned on his face like a flare. It took me a minute to realize that we weren't headed toward

191

Mount Zion, but toward one of his strike bases that he'd pointed out to me on a map but hadn't taken me to yet. His face was a mix of simultaneous joy and worry. "Mark, come on, man, what's wrong? Is it Tabby? Sophie?"

He glanced over at me and grinned. "Sophie's having the baby. Tabby said she's going to shut down the computer stuff, lock up the bell tower, and call for the doctor. So change of plans."

"How so?"

"We're going to one of the bases nearby, where we can change clothes and stash this stuff. I have a car there that I can drive. It has a clean license plate as well. Then we drive to the clinic. Sophie's still a few weeks early, so Tabby wants to be cautious and have her admitted rather than just the home delivery that we'd originally planned. We're going to avoid the University Hospital where people may remember what Sophie White looked like. The doctor has his own private clinic. We won't have any problems there. But we need to get cleaned up, we can't show up like this."

"Yeah, that scrape on your cheek doesn't look good. What's the cover story going to be?" I asked, excitement creeping through me as well. I mean, I'd known Sophie for quite a few months, and I considered her a good friend. Mark thought about my question while he drove the rest of the way to his base, a twenty-four-hour self-storage garage in the industrial district, just a half-mile from the MJT headquarters. Mark tapped in the security code and the gate slid over silently. We drove through the lines of units, Mark looking for his. "Didn't think you'd have one so close to your old office."

Mark nodded absently as he found his spot and put the car into park. He left the engine running and turned to me. "I needed a spot I could stash things close by."

The base was small, only the size of a two-car garage. Along the wall was a metal locker, which Mark led me to. I had my thumb tucked into the waistband of my pants; it helped the injured arm not bounce around as I moved. "Tell me about how you got the shoulder popped out."

"I lurched to the side when you started shooting up the place and landed on my right shoulder," I said. "It popped backward, if that helps."

Mark nodded and grabbed my wrist and elbow. "This is going to hurt, but we can get it checked out later if you want," he said. "Grab onto something with your free hand, and try not to scream or pass out. This place isn't soundproofed, and there are people in the area almost all the time."

It actually wasn't as bad as I thought it would be. I mean, sure, Mark rotating my arm as he pulled was about as pleasant as chewing glass, but he didn't have to yank too hard. Instead, after rotating, he lifted and twisted. My shoulder popped back into place with a muffled clunk, and an almost orgasmic wave of relief came over me.

"All right," I said, slowly moving my arm around. It was going to be stiff, but it worked. "Let's get changed and get to the clinic. Let's go meet your daughter."

Chapter 26
Tabby

When Sophie told me that she was going into labor, the first thought that crossed my mind was that fate could not have picked a worse time for it to happen. I mean, my fiancée had just been kidnapped by a criminal element that was most likely one of the strongest left in the city. The man I considered my brother was mounting a vigilante rescue mission, and my sister was still nearly three weeks before her due date.

"Grab a towel and help me get these pants off. You're probably going to end up delivering your goddaughter," Sophie told me when her water broke. I was glad that the carpet in the room was Scotchgarded, although I figured we'd still end up renting one of those steam cleaners by the end of the weekend. But that was the least of my worries.

First things first. Rushing out of the room, I clutched my wireless headset to my ear as I ran to the hallway closet, grabbing three of the big and fluffy Egyptian cotton towels that Mark bought for the house, along with the first aid kit just in case. I loved the fine texture and material of the towels, and I was glad our finances meant there was no regret in using them. If I was going to deliver my goddaughter, I was going to swaddle that baby in as much comfort as I could. I carried everything back into the entertainment room, where Sophie was already gritting her teeth and bearing down as another contraction hit. They were coming a lot faster than I'd expected.

193

This little girl was in a rush to get out and say hello to the world.

"How's it going?" I asked as I arranged one of the towels in front of Sophie. She used my arm for support as she worked her way onto the towel, leaning against the small bean bag chair she'd been using.

"Glad that I chose this chair instead of the big one," she said, her face already flushed with effort. "How about Mark?"

"I'm sure he's fine," I said simply. Mark had gone radio silent, which I knew from what Sophie had told me meant he was focused and intense. "Just watch the monitor, you'll be able to see when he does his thing. Focus on that and the baby. Come on, you know he's a one-man ass-kicking crew. It'll be better than watching a movie while giving birth. Not that I know anything about giving birth."

Sophie grinned and put on a fake Southern accent. "Why, I don't know nuthin' 'bout birthin' no babies!" she said, imitating the line from *Gone with The Wind*. It was nice to see that she still had a sense of humor.

Switching back to her normal voice, she chuckled. "Don't worry, I'll coach you though the tough parts. Most of it is sitting around waiting for the baby to crown. I see you grabbed the first aid kit. Nice job."

"Don't I need to go boil water or something?" I asked. "Whenever I see this done on TV, the doctor sends someone to go boil water."

"The water's to wash your hands," Sophie replied, then smiled. "And I think it gives the fathers a job to do too. Just when I tell you, put on some gloves from the kit and wash down with a damp cloth soaked in peroxide, it'll do just fine. Other than that, right now I need you to hold my hand during the contractions. I need something to bear down on."

I sat down next to Sophie, my attention torn between the monitors and the woman next to me. Taking her hand in my left, I tapped my microphone with my right. "Okay Mark, where are you?"

"*You can't see me?*"

"No. The traffic cameras aren't pointed in the right direction to catch you, and the satellite imagery isn't refined enough to pick you out against the shadows," I said. I grabbed the wireless keyboard and took it over next to Sophie, waiting for Mark's reply.

"*I'm across the street, looking at the two men you told me about. No other movement visible.*"

Inside, I can see through the windows. Three gunmen, a woman who I can assume is Melinda Pressman, and Patrick. He's alive, tied to an office chair. He seems to be doing what he does best."

"What's that?" I asked.

Mark's light chuckle told me more than his words. He was feeling confident. "*He's talking. I swear, that boy never does know when to shut up sometimes. Alright, I'm going radio silent, time to go to work.*"

"Okay. Good luck, Snowman." It was a little weird calling him that, but given that was the persona he was taking on, it felt *right*.

The radio clicked in my ear, and I reached over, taking Sophie's other hand. She squeezed hard, her body contracting again, her grunt of effort sounding eerily similar to how she sounded when she worked out in the gym. "I thought there was supposed to be more screaming and wailing?"

Sophie chuffed through her gritted teeth and shook her head. "I think that comes later. Besides, never underestimate the ability of television and movies to over-dramatize something to do with women's health. At least that's what I'm hoping."

I laughed. When the contraction passed, I got up and ran to the kitchen, getting her a bottle of water. "Here, you look like you could use a sip or two. Sorry I couldn't grab the Evian; we're going to have to slum it with the Poland Springs."

"Thanks," Sophie said in between small huffs, smiling as I returned her attempt at humor. "This is harder than I thought it would be, but I think I'm doing pretty good so far. A lot better than some of the ones I've seen."

"How many have you assisted with?" I asked. Before Sophie could answer, the traffic camera feed we had exploded in a hail of gunfire as Mark made his move. In two tight bursts he took out the gunners outside Pressman Contractors and shattered the glass-front. He then dashed to the side, diving and taking cover behind a dumpster before unleashing another burst.

"I've watched it done three times, once in person," Sophie said before her voice raised as a wave of pain hit. It felt like she was nearly crushing my hand she was squeezing so hard, and I could see the cords of her neck and forearms standing out against her skin.

I had to turn my attention away from the video screen, focusing instead on Sophie and her immediate situation. I couldn't help Mark, but I could help her.

"That's it, babe, come on. Come on, you can do it. Just bear down, push as it comes. I'm here for you."

By the time Sophie's contraction passed, Mark had moved again, and I couldn't find him on the screen. It took me a moment to see him across the street, this time behind one of the Pressman trucks, firing in short little spurts. "Why isn't he firing more?"

Sophie huffed and gasped from the efforts of her labor. "He . . . automatic rifles are impossible to control with just your hands in long bursts," she said. I unscrewed the top of the bottle again and gave her a sip. She used the water to calm herself, getting her breathing under control. "You can't aim properly. That's why the big guns all have bipods and mounts. So he shoots in small little bursts that he can aim."

"Some time, you're going to have to teach me about all this crap," I replied. Mark dashed forward again, firing as he ran, and disappeared from the screen as he ran into the building. We both held our breath as another burst of gunfire flashed against the light, and then there was silence.

"Mark?" I whispered into my microphone, only to be greeted with silence. I tried again, before remembering that Mark had said he was going radio silent. While my unit could stay on, he had probably muted his end totally to allow him to focus on the task at hand.

"I'm sure he's okay," Sophie said. "Both of them."

Another contraction started, and I turned my head away from the screen as Sophie's eyes slitted and she pushed as hard as she could. The contractions were coming closer and closer, worrying me. I thought this was supposed to take hours; she'd been in labor less than thirty minutes.

"*Tabby?*"

"I'm here, Mark," I said, smiling at Sophie. "What's going on there?"

"*I've got him. Dislocated shoulder, but other than that, okay,*" Mark said. I grinned and gave Sophie a thumbs-up.

"Good. Now get your ass back here, on the double, mister, or else you're going to miss it."

"*Tabby?*" Mark said, clearly confused.

"Your wife is in labor, and I think she's a few minutes from giving birth to

196

your daughter."

"*Wha . . . what?!?!?*"

* * *

As it was, I was the one to deliver Andrea Tabitha Bylur into the world. According to the clock on the wall, it was eleven thirty-seven pm, December twenty-first. A winter solstice baby. Sophie had told me her name as soon as she was out, my vision doubling momentarily as I cried in happiness. The honor of being named not just her godmother, but to even have her share my name? Perfect.

The ambulance to take Sophie to the clinic arrived less than two minutes after she had delivered Andrea in a rush of blood and fluid that more or less soaked the towel beneath her, and I had barely wrapped up the beautiful little girl in another clean towel to hand to her mommy when they came in. "Well, we missed all the fun," the first paramedic said, carrying his large bag. He'd come in through the back door, which I had told them would be unlocked. "How long?"

"Just a minute or two," I said, while Sophie was so enraptured by her daughter that she didn't even act like she'd heard anything. I could understand why. Despite being a little early, Andrea was shockingly beautiful, with a pale mound of straw-colored hair and eyes as arresting as her mother's. She was still messy and red, but nothing out of the ordinary from the pictures Sophie had shown me, and I knew that she'd be a beautiful little girl once she got cleaned up and used to the world. Sophie had pulled open her shirt as soon as the delivery was complete, and at the moment the medics came in was holding her daughter against her chest so that the baby could hear the familiar sound of her mother's heartbeat. After squalling for only a few seconds, Andrea had calmed down to look at Sophie.

Despite knowing that a newborn's vision is very minimal, her face had an expression on it I'd never forget. "Hi," it seemed to say, and the barely minute-old baby blinked. "I love you. So, what's next for us?"

"Well, let's get some of the basics done, and we'll get mama and baby to the clinic safely," the medic said as he was joined by his partner. "Now . . . it's Mrs. Bylur, right?"

"Yes," I answered. Sophie was still pretty exhausted and shook up by the whole experience, and I didn't want her to blank out and say Sophie White. "Joanna Bylur."

197

"All right. Mrs. Bylur, can you talk, or are you still wore out?" medic number two asked, opening her case and pulling on gloves. "May I give your daughter a quick once-over?"

"Quickly, please," Sophie said, her voice still wrung out. Andrea wiggled as the medic took her, but she put up with the poking and prodding pretty well, all things considered. The medics clamped the cord about five inches away from her belly and then snipped it off before wrapping her back up in her towel and handing her back to Sophie. Andrea squalled a little bit, but she quieted again when she felt Sophie's warm skin against her cheek.

"Okay, here's what's going to happen," the first medic said. He pointed toward the rolling gurney they had brought down the hallway. "You still have one more thing to push out, Mrs. Bylur, your birth sac and womb lining, but that can take fifteen to thirty minutes. We're going to get you on the gurney and into the ambulance where we can monitor both of you there. Your doctor's been contacted; he'll meet you as soon as we get to the clinic."

The second medic turned to me. "I'm sorry, you are?"

"Tabitha Williams," I said. "Mrs. Bylur's, ah, employer."

"Bullshit," Sophie said. "She's my sister. She rides with us in the back."

I wasn't sure who was crying more: Andrea, Sophie, or myself.

Chapter 27
Mark

Four days later, our new family celebrated Christmas with Sophie coming home from the clinic. While we had originally wanted it to be a home delivery, Andrea's rush to get out into the world made the doctor want to keep mother and baby in the clinic for a few days. It's times like that when it's useful to have a well-padded bank account that could pay for a private room where the two of them could rest together. In fact, most often when I came in, I found Andrea lying on Sophie's chest, either feeding or resting her head on the warm comfort of her mother's skin.

The biggest challenge of coming home was bringing Andrea out of the clinic, and in hindsight, understandably so. A stiff winter wind had picked up, and while it created the effect of a (barely) white Christmas on the ground, it meant that Andrea was now faced with the daunting task of wearing clothes and having a cold wind in her face for the ten yards we had to walk to get her in the car. Add to that the fact that she had to ride in a car seat, another cold and uncomfortable first, and I was glad that Tabby drove. I certainly wouldn't have wanted to put up with the fifteen minutes of infant screaming that came from my daughter.

"Well, at least we know she has good lungs," Tabby quipped when we reached the house and got everyone inside. I nodded and rubbed my temples, thinking that I also knew that my daughter was very strong-willed, some might say stubborn. I wondered if she got that from her mother or myself, and then I grinned. It didn't really matter.

Sophie had immediately taken Andrea back into her arms as soon as we had her inside, and Andrea calmed down almost immediately. Cooing, she snuggled against Sophie's chest and yawned, already tired and wanting another nap. "See? All she wanted was Mommy."

Sophie and I were both shocked when we came into the entertainment room and found Patrick. I had spent the night before sleeping at the clinic with Sophie and Andrea, so walking into the house to find it so changed from what I had left it the morning prior was happily pleasant. The far corner of the room, which normally contained some spare bean bags, had been converted into a total Christmas tree wonderland, complete with a six-foot-tall tree bedecked with lights, ornaments, and just about every other little thing you can think of. There was even a star on top that glittered in the light. Around the tree were at least two dozen various boxes, including a few that I recognized from the little bit of holiday shopping I'd done earlier in the month.

"Merry Christmas, and welcome home," Patrick greeted us, holding up a tray with three steaming mugs on it. "Cocoa?"

I'd never been one for holidays. As a child, my father spent too much time drunk around them. Presents were few and far between once my mother died, and I often ended up eating nothing more than a peanut butter and jelly sandwich while watching football on the TV. Once my father died, I was already into the Confederation life leading up to being a hitman, and until I met Sophie there hadn't

199

seemed a point. Christmas was just another day on the calendar. I'd even done work on a Christmas five years prior, although it was only a setup for something I did later. Despite not having stepped foot in a church since I was ten, unless you counted the chapel Sophie and I had our Vegas wedding in, there were some lines I didn't want to cross.

So at first, having the whole Christmas spread was a bit strange. As I relaxed and got into it, though, I enjoyed myself. "This whole thing was Tabby's idea," Patrick said after Sophie had settled in with Andrea, and he handed Sophie the first wrapped present. "So don't blame me if we went overboard."

"I'm just happy you got the carpet steam cleaned already," Sophie quipped. "That had to have taken you guys a couple of hours."

I was impressed by everything Patrick and Tabby had done over the week, actually. Tabby had handled communications for the rescue while at the same time helping Sophie with the delivery, and I owed the woman more than I could ever repay. After all, she'd brought my daughter into the world. "I can't blame you for anything," I said instead, smiling. "So, Sophie told me she ruined the surprise about our gift to you?"

"What gift?" Patrick asked. Sophie looked at me and smiled. I conceded to her.

"Well, we were thinking about one of two options: either expanding this building to put in another full-sized wing, or maybe building another separate house. This is supposed to be the house of one of the wealthiest people in the city, remember? It might as well start looking it besides just being eccentric. We'd give you guys the option of either one to live in, of course."

Patrick blinked, stupefied. "Really?"

"Really."

"Wow, that's going to make your first gift seem like crap," he muttered, then grinned to himself. "I've gotta start upping my gift-giving game."

In fact, the first gift opened was adorable, three sets of easy to open infant pajamas, all in feminine pastels. "I figure she's going to know how to kick my butt by the time she's eight, so I've got to work on her girly-girl side immediately," Tabby commented. "That's my job, after all."

I only mock groaned, knowing that regardless of how feminine or tomboyish

200

we raised Andrea, she'd always be her own free spirit. Besides, having influences like Tabby and Patrick as well as Sophie and myself was important to our parenting plan. Our daughter was going to have more than just Sophie and me as parents if I had my say-so.

The rest of the gifts ran the gamut, from useful (Patrick got me a set of weightlifting shoes I'd been eyeing) to frivolous (Sophie gave me a coffee cup that read "World's Sexiest Dad," much to everyone's laughter) to the outright humorous (Patrick got a t-shirt that read "I'm the sidekick. Shoot me!"). Andrea, for someone only four days old, enjoyed it all, smiling and watching in amazement before dropping off for a nap on the cushion.

"It's perfect for her," Sophie commented as she tucked her brand new Winnie-The-Pooh fleece blanket around her. "The cushion supports her well, and she has no risk of rolling off or out. She can't sleep here overnight, but it is perfect for naps."

"I'll try not to make too much noise while I clean up," Patrick said, grabbing the first of the papers we'd strewn over the floor. Getting an armful, he headed out toward our garbage cans, only to hear me behind him. "Relax, man, I've got this. Your arm must be killing you."

"It's not that bad, I got it checked out two days ago at a drop-in clinic just to be safe. Doctor there said I probably stretched the tendons some, but that nothing seemed torn. I told him I fell doing martial arts practice."

I balled up the paper in the kitchen, the rattling covering about half of what I said next, and I had to repeat myself a little louder. "Nice cover. But still, take it easy until after the New Year. I think you earned it."

"I'm trying, but to be honest, I'm kind of having trouble letting it go," he said. We went out the back door and went over to the flip-top rolling canisters that the city insisted we use. Lugging those down to the curb once a week sucked. At least sorting the trash was easy. We usually did that in the kitchen. Cans in one, plastic in a second, food and paper in a third. "I haven't been sleeping well."

"Good," I replied, causing Patrick to do a double take. I nodded, reaffirming my point. "You should be upset about it. Patrick, I saw her injuries as much as you did. You know Melinda Pressman didn't die from the gunshot wounds. And I don't think she got knocked out from just landing on the chair wrong, did she?"

201

Patrick shook his head. "No, but still, I mean, I was defending myself. Shouldn't I feel at least a little less guilty about it?"

I sighed and shook my head. "Did you know that night I reached a milestone? One hundred people have died by my hands. One hundred people's blood stains my soul. That's a mark that a lot of hitmen never reach, and those that do, well, usually they're the sort of person that I wouldn't trust within ten miles of my daughter.

"I told Sophie when we met that I have always refused to kill innocents, but that doesn't mean all one hundred were total bastards deserving of the death penalty. Jail, sure. A bullet in the head, or poison, or a bomb in their cars? No, not all of them. And I've injured or even crippled dozens more. Before you ask, the answer is yes, most of them were before I met Sophie, so they weren't in pursuit of a good cause."

It was good to unload some of my burden to Patrick, who watched me with somber acceptance in his eyes. It wasn't that he was a man and that Sophie was a woman. It was that Sophie was my wife, my soulmate, and she'd always accept me. Patrick wasn't, so to have him accept what I was saying meant something a bit different, and in its own way a bit more relieving. I guess that's why, for millennia, men have gone down to the local bar, pub, tavern, or whatever not so much to drink, but just to unload their mental burdens with others who think like they do.

"So does it get easier?" Patrick asked me, his eyes carrying a shadow I had grown all too familiar with. His question caused me to pause, and to shake myself out of the rapidly darkening funk I was getting into.

"God, I hope not," I finally replied. "I guess what keeps me going is that there is something to fight for now. They're inside, waiting for us to finish cleaning up. Although you and I have another way to fight, too."

"How's that?" Patrick asked. He looked so earnest, yet so unaware. While only by a year or two, it was hard to believe that he was older than me. I guess experience had aged me more than I wanted to admit.

I chuckled, thinking about the hours I'd talked this subject over with Sophie and even Tabby. "I've got to get you reading more. Von Clausewitz. 'War is the continuation of politics by other means.' You and I, we have other means. You have politics, in case you forgot. I have money, a lot of it. Combined, it makes the four of us very, very powerful."

Patrick nodded, then thought. "You know, next year's mayoral election might be too early, but five years from now . . ."

I clapped him on the shoulder and smiled. "Exactly. Think of what MJT money and your politics can do in those five years. But for now, let's go enjoy Christmas. I think there's another gift in there for you—at least Sophie mentioned it to me."

"Really? What, a new car?"

I shook my head, thinking Tabby's gift would be a lot more memorable than a new car. "Nope. We'll check around, see if we can find it under the tree or something. Just no waking the baby."

Chapter 28
Tabby

I actually gave Patrick his 'present' five days later, to preserve the surprise. I'd set things up precisely as I wanted, decking out my bedroom with scented candles and changing the sheets to a set of black satin that I thought would look wonderful against Patrick's pale skin. On the pillow, I set a small box, while I wore my lingerie underneath a plain looking bath robe and cotton pajama pants, although I did brush out my hair and style it up a little bit. Checking myself in the mirror, I thought I still looked "plain" enough to fool Patrick for a little while. I didn't normally wear a lot of makeup around the house, and Patrick didn't feel the need for me to wear it anyway.

I found Patrick in the entertainment room, happily playing with Andrea, who was lying on her back in the middle of the carpet. It was heartwarming to watch my future husband smiling blissfully while tickling the little infant and allowing her to grab his fingers and yank. I watched for a minute until I felt a presence behind me, and I turned my head to see Sophie, who was still wearing the same style of casual house clothes she'd worn the entire time she'd been home. She had told me that she was going to get back into shape, but that it would wait until after the holidays. Considering she'd just had a baby, I thought it was a well-deserved vacation.

Sophie leaned in and rested her chin on my shoulder, watching the two in the room. "Hey, little early for the bathrobe and PJ's, isn't it?"

203

I smiled and shook my head, turning around to face her. "Not quite," I whispered, pulling one side of my robe out a bit to show her what I had on underneath. "Think I can pull it off?"

Sophie laughed quietly and leaned in. "Just go easy on the poor man. He's not going to last long after he sees you in that."

"Then I'll just have to take some time and let him recover for rounds two and three," I responded. I wasn't lying either. I was more than ready for it. "You want your daughter back?"

Sophie nodded and placed her hand on my chest, just above my heart, looking into my eyes to confirm something, then smiling. "Sure. Just, give me a minute before you two get started. Mark was planning on getting into the gym. I don't want your evening ruined by pounding heavy metal, and I doubt he wants to lift to Barry White songs. I'll make sure he takes his iPod."

"Thanks. Who knows, maybe we can make magic tonight, you know?"

Sophie nodded and arranged my bathrobe, making sure the surprise was hidden well. "Maybe. But don't worry about that and just enjoy yourself."

I nodded and the two of us went into the entertainment room, getting Patrick's attention. "Hey, Patrick, having fun?"

"She's amazing," Patrick told Sophie, a simple expression of joy on his face. "That hair, those eyes, she's just so cute."

"She is, but she's also due for a bath," Sophie said, "especially since we had a missed poop this afternoon. So I'll need to take her from you if you don't mind."

"Not at all, go ahead," Patrick said with a chuckle. Turning his head to me, he just kept grinning. "The advantages of being the uncle-ish. Playtime is mine, diapers and bath time aren't. What's up, sweetie?"

"I have something for you; can you come with me?" I asked. "A late Christmas present."

"Sure," Patrick said, his smile staying easily on his face. His arm wasn't stiff any longer. He'd been stretching it and working it lightly in the gym, one of the reasons I'd waited the extra few days. That and to let him forget after Mark kind of half gave it all away. I understood why—he needed a decent segue to get Patrick off of his guilt trip, but it did slightly tick me off for half a day. Only half a day, though, considering Mark did save his life.

Taking Patrick's hand, I led him through the halls of Mount Zion. "Have you enjoyed the holidays?" I asked. "I know you wanted to get that vote in on your motion, but after what happened . . ."

"Yeah, I didn't mind at all," Patrick said. After his kidnapping, we'd used Andrea's birth as an excuse to delay his motion on the Union bidding scam until the first meeting of the new calendar year, on January fifth. We couldn't exactly say it was because he'd been taken hostage and rescued by a masked vigilante who happened to be my housekeeper. "As for all this, it has been like a dream come true. All those years in the homes and living in orphanages, Christmas was both the best and worst time of the year for me."

"How so?" I asked. We were in the kitchen and I paused to grab a glass of water.

"During the Christmas season, a lot of what we called the do-gooders would come around, handing out gifts or taking us kids on outings, stuff like that. It was about the only time of year until I got to running with the wrong crowd that I was able to wear new clothes or sometimes new shoes. One year I even got a sweet pair of Nikes for all of five hours until one of the older kids robbed me for them. There was lots of good food. You could check out the malls and not feel like a bum because there was a chance you could actually get something there, stuff like that."

"But it was the loneliest time also. It was like that period, from about December fifteenth until the twenty-fourth, was hectic, full of things to do. Christmas morning the staff would hand out the gifts that they'd been saving from the biggest charities, and we'd all have a big meal at lunch time, ham and mashed potatoes, gravy, the whole works. It was even bigger than Thanksgiving. But then after that, it was like all the adults and charity people said to themselves, 'Well, we checked off that box, on to more important stuff,' and the place emptied out. Minimal staffing, and lots of kids just sitting around bored. It was lonely as hell, and after the staff left, things always went a little *Lord of the Flies*. The good stuff was stolen by the older or stronger kids, while the weaker ones ended up with little or nothing. I got good at sneaking a marker out of the laundry room during the run up to Christmas in order to write my name in anything I got in someplace I could then point out but hide later when I went to school. Shirt tails, inside waistbands of jeans, stuff like that."

205

"I didn't mean to bring up any bad memories," I said, putting my glass away. I wrapped my arms around him, laying my head on his chest. My heart was near breaking, and I knew that I was making the right decision.

"Don't worry, it made me who I am today. And I guess it was what made this holiday so perfect," Patrick said, brushing the hair out of my face and kissing my forehead. "Tabby, in this house, I have a family. I have you, I have Sophie and Andrea and even Mark. I couldn't imagine a more perfect holiday, one filled with love and warmth and happiness. Only thing missing was a fireplace. Maybe we can have one in the new place. Have you decided if you want it to be an extension or a separate building?"

"Not yet," I said. "Come on, I really do have something to show you."

We walked the rest of the way to my bedroom, where I opened the door. Patrick noticed the new sheets, but he didn't say anything as the candles weren't lit yet. I wanted him to be blown away, but I disguised the situation as best as I could prior to my reveal. "There, on the pillow," I said.

Patrick went over, and I quickly closed the door behind me and undid the belt of my robe while his back was turned. He picked up the box and opened it. Inside was my first gift, a one of a kind creation. Black anodized titanium gave the foundation for inlaid polished jade.

"What's this?" he asked as he turned, his mouth dropping open and the ring tumbling from his fingers as he saw me in my lingerie. "Tabby . . ."

"That, my love, is your engagement ring," I said, walking over. I knelt on the carpet in front of him, picking up the ring and taking his hand. "I know you already did this, and this is a bit out of tradition, but Patrick McCaffery, would you marry me?"

Patrick could only stare at me, his eyes filling with happiness, and something else was filling as well that was currently right in my face. "Yes, of course," he said. "I want nothing more in the whole world."

I took the opportunity to slide the ring on his finger, where it was a perfect fit. Thankfully, having a 'brother' like Mark who is hyper vigilant and also very intelligent, allowed me to get Patrick's ring size without having to ask him. Taking his hand, I placed it on my hair before reaching for the waistband of his pants. "Now, last time I did this I made a huge mistake," I said, undoing the snap and working his zipper down. "I don't want to make it again."

"Never," Patrick said. I was surprised when he knelt down in front of me, despite his cock already trying to push out of his underwear. "Tabby, before we do this, promise me something."

"What's that?"

"Don't hold back on me," he said, taking my hand and placing it on his heart. "I can't always promise I can be everything you need, but I will promise you every bit of me."

"That's more than I need," I replied, kissing him. My hands squashed against his chest, and I let my desire fill me as we kissed, closer to being married than we'd ever been before. I was trapped, unable and unwilling to move as he embraced me, his strong arms holding me helpless on my knees. We'd been denying ourselves the release of intimacy with each other, and while it had been worth it, it also meant there was a lot of pent-up passion involved.

Patrick lifted me up like I weighed nothing, his arms holding me tightly as he turned and set me on the bed. "I want to look at you," he said, "before I tear it off."

"Don't, please," I asked, covering myself. "I want to save this one."

Patrick grinned down at me, his eyes full of fire and smoldering lust. "That's fine," he said, lightly taking my hand in his and laying it next to me. "I'm sure we can find something I can tear off another time?"

"Deal," I said with a light giggle. It was sexy, feeling myself under his eyes. I've had lovers look at me before, in so many different ways. I've had ones that looked at me like I was a piece of meat. They never got a second shot. I've had ones that looked like someone on the beginning of a great adventure. I've had lovers who even looked at me like I was some sort of divine being, which is actually a lot creepier and less sexy than it sounds.

Patrick looked at me instead with warmth, love, affection, admiration, and yes, a big heaping measure of desire thrown in. He took in all of me as I pulled my heels up on the bed, butterflying my knees so that he could look at everything. "I bought this just for you," I said, my nipples already aching and pushing against the silk of the top just from the kiss and our bodies touching. "I don't know anything else I could give you that means as much."

"It's all I ever want," Patrick said, reaching out with a finger to trace the swell

207

of my breasts against the silk. "The imperfect, beautiful, crazy you."

I'd never been called imperfect and crazy at the same time and had it feel like such a turn-on. "So I take it you like it?"

"Should I show you?" he asked me, reaching for his shirt. I nodded, smiling as he peeled his shirt over his head. His work with Sophie and Mark for the previous four months had paid off. He was in good shape before, but now he was ripped. My heart hammered in my chest as he pushed his pants the rest of the way down, his cock bouncing as it cleared the waistband of his shorts. "As you can see, you have quite the effect."

"I can appreciate that," I said, reaching out with a foot to fondle him with my toes. I'm not a foot fetishist, but it was fun to trace his cock with my toes. "How about you get some oil from the dresser?"

"You prepared well," he teased, going over and getting the oil. "Hmmm, odorless and hypoallergenic. High quality stuff."

"Only the best for the sexiest man I know," I teased, squeezing some into my hands. I let it warm for a little bit before I massaged it into his cock, looking up expectantly at him as he closed his eyes. "If you need to come, go ahead. I know we've been waiting for so long—I'm not planning on stopping until the sun comes up or we are both fulfilled."

"Tabby . . ."

I knew what I was doing, but I wanted it so much. I knew that while Patrick had masturbated—we both had over the past months—it was nothing like the feeling of when we made love. It's kind of like eating at a multi-star restaurant, and eating your home cooking. You can have chicken both ways, but let's face it, eating at the restaurant is so much better sometimes.

I couldn't believe he lasted as long as he did. I stroked and pumped his cock in my hands, occasionally leaning forward to lick the head, but not too much. The massage oil may have been hypoallergenic, but it wasn't tasteless, a thing to remember for the next time. Still, when his hips started twitching under my hands, I knew he was close. I'd have let him cover my face; I know a lot of guys like that, but the angle wasn't quite right for his pleasure. Instead, I pointed him in between my breasts, into the deep cleavage created by the silk, and let him go. He came in what looked and felt like torrents, splattering all over my upper chest with seven strong spurts.

"My, what a strong cock you have," I teased, looking up at him. "I'm so messy. I need to clean up real fast," I said, scurrying off to the bathroom to quickly wash up.

As soon as I walked out of the bathroom door, Patrick grabbed me into an embrace and carried me to the bed. He kissed down my neck and to my breasts, sucking and nipping at the tender spots near my pulse points that had my hips trying to lift off the bed if he hadn't been pinning my legs. Instead, my hands stroked through his hair and across his upper back as our eyes met. I wasn't sure how he'd react, given that he'd literally just come there minutes beforehand, even though I did just wash myself. But it didn't seem to faze him. "You are the perfect man," I whispered as he kept kissing. "Never, never doubt that."

"Not perfect, but maybe together we can make perfect," he replied, finding the edge of my top and pausing. "Do you want it on or off?"

"Off, please," I replied, scooting back and arching my lower back. He pulled the top off, dragging the silk over my skin so that my nipples were erotically tortured under the slow progress of the slick fabric. I was left in just my panties, which were already soaked with my anticipation of what was to come.

"Flawless," he whispered to himself, almost too low for me to hear as he looked at me. Lowering his head, he kissed my right nipple, sucking it between his teeth and rolling it around with his tongue. I was in pure heaven as he stroked and sucked, his hand not letting my other breast feel neglected at all. His right knee shifted, demanding access between my legs, and I submitted, the strong muscles of his thigh pressing against my mound as he nibbled and sucked.

I'd told him he could come quickly, and here I was, not even nude yet and fully ready to explode. "Patrick, you're going to . . ."

"Not yet," he said, pulling his lips away. "I'm not ready for you to come yet."

There was a tone of command in his voice, not harsh, but undeniable. He wasn't going to tease me or deny me. Instead, his command was for my benefit, I could tell, and he wanted to bring me to a climax that would make me see stars. It was a loving command, not a greedy one. I took a deep, shaky breath and nodded. "Yes . . . sir."

"Maybe another time we can explore that more," he replied, looking me up and down. "But never Master. I'm not your Master, Tabby."

"No, not Master, but my husband . . . that you will be," I said, running my fingers over his face, tracing the contours of the face I loved so much. "I promise you my heart and soul."

"You have mine already," he answered, kissing my left breast over my heart, claiming it for his own.

With a raised eyebrow, he asked his question and I answered it, nodding and pushing down as I spread my legs more. Patrick paused once in a silly display of humor as he tickled my bellybutton with his tongue until I was nearly out of control, giggling and trying to roll away from him before he kissed me lower, finding my panties. "Mmm . . . very nice."

"I feel sexy in them when you're around," I replied.

"Then wear them as often as you want," he said, rolling them down my hips. I'd carefully trimmed the hair that I had, leaving just a light patch of my natural red, darker than my colored flame red, more of a rich auburn. "I do have one request though."

"What's that?" I asked, shivering when he touched and circled my lower stomach. "You want me to change down here?" I'd had some laser treatments, so the hair was fine and not too thick at all, but I'd never taken it all the way to bald, except through waxes or razors. However, I thought Patrick would like the color, so I had kept it. I was worried, until he shook his head and smiled.

"No, I love it. It's beautiful. Actually, I was hoping for our wedding, you could maybe have your natural red up top too? It's such a beautiful auburn, like burning coals, embers of passion and love. I dream of it."

"Then we can let it grow out, or something like that," I said, not really knowing. I'd need to make a hair appointment, but if Patrick asked me to be bowling ball bald, I'd have gotten a razor two minutes later.

"Thank you," he replied, lowering his mouth. Just before he made contact, he looked up at me. "And you can come any time you want now."

"Yes, sir." I grinned in reply, my words drawing out when he kissed my lower lips. With feather light caresses of his lips against mine, he teased me open, cupping my ass when my hips lifted up, needy and demanding, wanting his tongue to reach deeper, fulfilling my dreams.

The first time we'd made love, I had marveled when Patrick licked me to an intense orgasm. This time, though, I was blown away as I watched him stroke and lick my soft folds before teasing my clit and alternating between licking my pussy and higher. I grabbed his hair, pulling hard as my first orgasm ripped through me, but still he didn't stop. Knowing I was multi-orgasmic, he kept up his loving oral assault, his tongue lashing my clit over and over, broad strokes followed by rapid strumming with the tip. I was soon on the edge of another orgasm when my eyes caught sight of something I wanted even more. His cock was barely visible when he adjusted himself on his knees from my angle, but I could see it was already hard and ready. "Patrick, stop."

"What?" he asked, looking up at me with worry in his face. "Did I go too fast?"

"No, but I need something," I said. I lifted my leg up over his head and got on my hands and knees, my ass pointed at him. "I need you inside me."

I felt a moment of worry as his strong hands grabbed my waist and his thick cock pushed inside me. Nothing was as good as feeling his warm, hard cock spearing me open, filling me up and making me his. He was huge, masculine, and powerful, maybe even more so than last time.

Throwing my hair back, I moaned when he wrapped it in his right hand, his cock pulling out to thrust hard inside me again, driving me face first into the mattress. He pulled back and pushed, his hand never yanking on my hair but at the same time letting me know who was in control, and I lowered my face, putting my hands behind my back for him to take if he wanted. He held my wrists in one hand as his hips pounded into me, hard and fast, my body quaking with every powerful stroke of his amazing cock. I didn't hold back, letting my voice cry out whenever I needed, until I lost all sense of where I was or even who I was. All I knew was that it was pure pleasure, and that Patrick's cock was the instrument of my deliverance. He filled me over and over, my body, heart and soul, until I screamed, burying my face in the mattress. In the throes of my climax, I could hear him bellow again, and I blanked out for a moment, coming to later to find him holding me from behind.

"Don't tell me you're done yet?" I teased him as he panted lightly in my ear.

"Don't worry about that, *my wife*," he replied, his last two words filling me with newfound energy and emotion. "Just let me get my breath. We still have hours until morning."

The New Year's holiday was capped off by me and Tabby going back to the jeweler's where she'd gotten my ring for its partner in her size, this time in black and ruby to match her hair. We'd toasted the New Year in with all four of us enjoying the scenery from the front steps, along with five snowmen that a New Year's Eve storm had allowed Mark, Tabby and myself to quickly build, working together in the fading light to get one for every member of our family. We'd decorated all of them with something to denote who the each was supposed to be, with the cutest being Andrea's little snow girl decorated with a blanket and a pacifier in place of a mouth. It was the perfect end to a perfect vacation.

Coming into work on the fifth of January, I surprised Gwen when I came in chipper and smiling. "Morning, Boss," she said. "How was your vacation?"

She saw the ring on my left hand and smiled. "I see."

I glanced down, feeling my face flush, partially with happiness and partially with embarrassment. "Yeah, political scandal of the new year already. City council member gets engaged to ultra-hot company president. Think we can get our political consultant in on it?"

"You still haven't hired one," Gwen reminded me. "You told me you'd do that after the holidays."

I slapped my forehead, wincing somewhat when my ring bounced off my skin. I had to remember about that from now on. "Oh yeah. Okay, well, first things first, we've got a council meeting tonight. You think we still have the votes on the Union issue?" I asked, heading toward my office door. "Give me a head count."

"You've still got the votes on the Council, including Northrup's, last I knew. Is Mayor Joe still on board?"

I nodded. "Pretty sure about it, but I'll confirm it this afternoon. Any last-minute advice?"

Gwen chuckled and nodded. "Make sure your car and house insurance is paid up. Although, if you're engaged, I guess you won't have to worry about that. I'd heard you two moved in together, but that's pretty awesome. Congratulations."

213

"Thanks, Gwen. Let me get some work done before the political horse-trading begins," I said, opening my office door.

"That is your job," Gwen shot after me as my door closed. She was right, and after the conversation I'd had with Mark on Christmas day, I was more than ready to get right to it.

By the time my lunch meeting with the mayor came around, the black and green ring on my finger was the talk of the entire building. I'd even had two of my political opponents, Dennis Fernandez and Maxine Carter, drop by. "Hey, just wanted to say congratulations," Dennis told me as he stuck his head in the door. "We might not agree on anything else, but you've got yourself one beautiful fiancée."

Dennis was a Tea Party Republican, and in a lot of issues he was pretty repugnant. The only thing he and I agreed on was that corruption was one of the most important issues facing the city. Unfortunately, he disagreed with me on how to go about it, favoring a slash n' burn mantra while preaching about the common good of the regular citizens. Perhaps he was right, for certain parts of the city. Dennis represented the area next to the Heights, another pretty affluent area. Maybe there, where the average income started in the high five figures and rocketed up into the six figures quickly, and children could play in the streets or the playgrounds all the time without their parents worrying themselves sick—maybe those people were more honest.

I'd grown up on the other side of town, however, where the average man had a criminal's boot on his neck and an exploitative boss's fist up his ass. I came from where getting home safely at night meant being meaner than an alley cat, and where the *Golden Rule* was modified into "fuck them before they fuck you."

Then again, perhaps Dennis wasn't as high and mighty as he seemed. After all, he was taking sides against me on this Union issue, and if there was one thing Republicans were supposed to agree with me on, it was being anti-Union. Roberta and Jack, the other two votes I had besides Shawn Northrup's, were both Republicans.

But Dennis was trying to at least be civil. "Thanks, Dennis. Hey, you got a minute?"

"Sure," he said, coming in and closing the door behind him. "But if you're going to try and get me to change my vote tonight, you're wasting your breath."

214

"No, I figured that much," I said as he took a seat. I shivered and wished I had been wearing my thermal top. It was true, the City Council offices were cold as all hell, and being the junior most, I got the crappiest office. I reminded myself to get two electric space heaters, one for me and one for Gwen, before one of us got frostbite. "I just wanted to ask you, if you don't mind, why? I mean, you of all people should be as anti-Union as they get. Yet you're opposing me on this. Come to think of it, since I won the election you've been against me. I swear, Dennis, if I say the sky is blue, you're going to oppose me until the sun sets and you can declare the sky is red. What's up?"

Dennis shrugged and thought about it. "Want the truth?"

"Why not? I doubt I could do much with it, anyway, if you're offering it to me." I leaned back in my office chair, waiting for Dennis to speak. Finally, he chuckled, as if he'd made an internal decision.

"Pretty simple, really. Joe's going to be gone at the end of his term. This city, well, it's ran pretty blue for the past generation or so. Most bigger cities are. I intend to change that. I plan on tossing my hat into the ring come election time."

"Then why not side with me?" I countered. "Being seen as pro-Union can't be winning you any favors in the party primary. Hell, even the State Repubs have got to be sweating your ass about it."

Dennis nodded. "They are. But, I have it very well planned out. You see, my appeal will pick up the Republicans without a problem. Roberta and Jack, they're happy where they are; they don't want the big chair. I'm sure I can win the primary even if someone else throws their name in. But, come election time, I'm going to be facing a Democrat, one that has traditionally counted on Union votes. They've put more than one Dem in office around here for quite a few decades. But, the Dems have a big problem right now. They've got no superstar to replace Joe. Shawn's got troubles of his own, and Maxine's never going to win enough of the Heights vote to carry the city. That leaves you, maybe."

I think I play poker pretty well, and my face was impassive. "So?"

"So, you're an independent that might get the Dem nomination if you go that way, but you can easily get onto the main ballot just as you are. You have the sort of appeal that will take some of my Heights voters, especially with your association with MJT and Tabby Williams. Pro-business, but at the same time you've come from The

215

Playground, so you're going to get a big chunk of their votes and the Fillmore votes as well. My best chance is to not only position myself to counter you, but to make sure that all those Union voters out there know that you were the guy who fucked them, while I was the guy sticking up for them."

"Even though they're as corrupt as anything you rail against?"

Dennis nodded. "Sometimes you've got to do what you've got to do."

I shook my head. "I understand. All right, Dennis, thanks for the honesty. I'll see you tonight. In the meantime, I have to have a meeting with Mayor Joe."

* * *

In the end, the vote on the measure itself was anti-climactic. While there was some debate, the fact was that everyone had their positions set well in stone beforehand. Francine Berkowitz even made an appearance at the meeting, giving us an impassioned plea for a good fifteen minutes before sitting down and glaring at me. If looks could kill, I'd have been dead and buried before we even had the vote.

It fell just like I had predicted, five to four with the motion carrying. A few of the other motions that were brought up were in fact more contentious, but those fell into the normal system of Republican and Democrat.

As the meeting wore on, I realized that while I may have been the most junior member of the council, I was in a unique position. For the most part, the people who belonged to one party or another tended to be very party line, if for no other reason than, as I'd mentioned to Dennis earlier in the day, to survive the primary season that was upcoming soon. I was an undeclared independent, however, on a divided council. More often than not, I was the swing vote, sometimes siding with one side, sometimes with the other. I pondered as the meeting wore on if there was a way I could use that position without endangering my conscience. To get some of the big issues I felt were important voted on, I'd have to do politicking. But to get a big vote, I'd have to give a big vote too, or at least a big vote in the eyes of the other person.

I didn't think I could get dirt on each and every member of the council. Maxine Carter was overwhelmingly boring, and although we didn't always agree on political issues, she wasn't a bad person. She had gotten her seat after her first husband died in a plane crash, and she had sat on the council for going on twenty-five years, happily representing the most liberal area of the city, centered around the arts and university district. She looked like everyone's hippie aunt, or maybe a young

216

grandmother who'd spent a bit too much time in her teen years following the Grateful Dead around.

Jack Park was also clean, a moderate Republican who'd started off in the banking world before running for city council. Big business to the core, he lived in the Financial District and had in fact been Mark's former councilman when he was Mark Snow and living near the Park. While I was happy to have his vote on the Union issue, he and I tended to oppose each other on a regular basis. But Mark had investigated him long ago. The man was as clean as a whistle, with his greatest crime being that he spent far too much time out at the Airport Country Club working on his golf game rather than doing his job. He had enough money and enough security that he didn't need to be dirty, and he was comfortable with the business voters who lived around the Financial District.

As I went back to my office after the meeting to drop off the papers I'd gathered, thoughts kept swirling in my head. The only two people I had real leverage on were Dennis Fernandez and Shawn Northrup. Dennis I could predict to try and stymie me at any turn. He'd made that clear enough already. While he might have put it in polite terms, he could have been slavering and growling earlier in my office. Shawn, I wasn't sure about. I could depend on my dirt on him to continue to possibly have some influence, but with Melinda Pressman's death, there wasn't as much influence as before. An affair with a woman who was now dead and a young looking but still over eighteen teenage girl wasn't quite as powerful as an actual living affair.

I was slightly surprised when Francine Berkowitz was waiting for me in my office, with Gwen sitting at her desk with a frustrated look on her face. I could tell she wasn't happy Francine was there, but she couldn't do anything about it. "Ms. Berkowitz, it's late. Think it can wait until morning?"

Francine smiled at me, a predatory smile that I knew from my time in The Playground. "Oh, I only needed a moment, Mr. McCaffery," she said, walking toward me. "Trust me when I say this. Your days in office are numbered. You've got just over a year before the next election, and mark my words, it will be your last. By this time next year, you're going to be looking for a new job slinging beers again."

She didn't wait for me to reply but stormed out, slamming the door to my office behind her. Gwen watched her go and then started laughing. I turned and looked at my assistant, perplexed. "What's so funny?"

"You're engaged to Tabby Williams," Gwen reminded me. "I doubt you're ever going to need a job slinging beers again. Unless she wants to put you to work doing that, of course."

Chapter 30
Mark

The vote against Francine Berkowitz and the Union cleared a few hurdles, and the community center project continued on. By Valentine's Day, Tabby had hired her first director, taking a lot of the weight off of her shoulders and letting her focus on what MJT was created for in the first place, investing and creating wealth within the city.

It was actually damn scary how easily the money flowed in for us. With even only a portion of the corruption and graft cleared out of the way, a lot of these companies flourished like never before. Profit margins were bigger than they had ever been in the company's history, not because of price raises or hurting their workers, but because they were able to be productive and not have to pay protection money or waste time on rackets run by criminals.

I agreed with Patrick on the idea building in his head that Dennis Fernandez had planted. Patrick was uniquely positioned as the swing vote, and he was a natural charismatic leader of the people. With a mayoral election coming up at the same time, Patrick's original shortened term as a council member was wrapping up. Maybe there was a bigger brass ring that Patrick could reach for. We had to do some serious thinking and strategizing. Patrick himself devoted a lot of energy to the idea, reading up on politics and political science theory.

Political ambitions aside, that wasn't the reason I was putting on my Snowman uniform that particular night, three days after Valentine's Day. Patrick watched me come downstairs and into the gym, where he was catching a quick workout. He was coming along well, putting down his kettle bell as he turned and shook his head. "You sure you don't want me to come along with you?"

"No, but I do want you ready for a patrol of Fillmore Heights tomorrow night," I replied. "I just want to check on Scott Pressman. I should be back by eleven, in fact."

Patrick nodded. "Okay. But be careful out there."

"That's Sophie's line," I replied with a laugh. "So what's your plan for the evening?"

"The three of us were going to go over blueprints the architect sent over," he said. "We're trying to decide the floor plan for the extension. Sophie's favoring the four-bedroom plan, but Tabby and I want to do the five. You guys never know, you might have a couple more kids, and still having a home office would be helpful."

"Perhaps. Then again, I could just take over your old bedroom here," I said with a chuckle. "Or just move the home office up to the bell tower. Probably safer with kids running around the house. By the way, Tabby . . .?"

"Nah, not this month," Patrick replied. He turned back to his kettle bell and picked it up, swinging it in smooth arcs. "False alarm."

I nodded. After they'd started having sex again, it didn't take long for both Tabby and Patrick to acknowledge to Sophie and me that they wanted to have a baby as well. They were going about it the old fashioned way, that was for sure. It had gotten so frequent, in fact, that Sophie had gotten me an early Valentine's gift, a pair of Moto Surround wireless in-ear headphones for my time in the gym. It helped. As much as I loved them, we really did need to get construction rolling for their house.

Going into the dining room, I found Sophie and Tabby with Andrea in her little carrier in between them sleeping soundly. Kissing my daughter on the forehead, I stroked her hair with a finger. It was still nearly platinum blonde, but I knew it would darken up as she got older. "Okay, guys, I'm going out to Pressman's."

Tabby's lip curled only a little bit, but having Patrick in her life had done more than time had for healing her inner hatred. Sophie took my gloved hand and squeezed it. "You want me on coms?"

"Nah, nothing you need to worry about," I said. I looked at my wife's face, just as awestruck by her as I was by my daughter. She was even more beautiful than when we'd first met. Leaning in, I gave her a kiss, which quickly grew hot and passionate.

"Ahem, there are children here," Tabby admonished us primly. "Oh, and

Andrea, too."

"Later," Sophie whispered as we parted. If I needed any more motivation to stay safe, I don't know what it could have been.

The ride out to Scott Pressman's house was refreshing, the frigid air clearing my mind and letting me focus. I found Pressman putting his son to sleep as I arrived, pausing in the doorway of his room to watch the sleeping boy. The expression on his face gave me hope for him.

"You should have waited," he said when he came out into the kitchen to find me sitting at his dining room table. "It's not like I don't have a winter coat."

"More comfortable in here. I wiped my feet though," I said. I'd turned off the overhead light, leaving the small light that was over his cooking range on to cast the room in shadow. "How're you doing?"

"He still cries at night sometimes," Scott said, looking back at his son's room and ignoring the main portion of the question, "but he's getting past it. Thankfully, the coverage of it was pretty low on details, so even if he goes poking around, he's not going to know the full details of what Melinda was into. Guess I was lucky that two of the gunmen she hired were Owen Lynch's former cops. The department didn't want another black eye on its hands so quickly, and the city DA has enough on his plate. Lucky for you, too, I assume. You know, I never asked you; did you do it?"

"Kill her, you mean?" I asked. It was one of the facts I hadn't revealed to Scott the last time I'd visited, checking if he'd set Patrick up. He hadn't, which was why he was still alive, son or not.

"Yeah. I mean, I read the coroner's report. She asphyxiated on her own blood from a severed tongue. That's the sort of thing that could happen by accident or on purpose if a man of training wanted it to happen." Scott went over to the cabinet next to his fridge and poured himself a scotch and soda, getting a tumbler from a wire rack next to his sink. He'd softened up some in the six weeks since Melinda's death, and was trending now more toward a so-called *dad bod* than before. I guess with his looks-obsessed wife gone, he didn't feel the need to worry about it as much any longer.

I pondered my answer. I could lie to him convincingly, I knew that. If I did, I'd take the brunt of his anger or rage, which I knew he still felt despite the hurt Melinda had inflicted on him. On the other hand, if I told him the truth, he'd want to investigate more into Patrick, which I didn't want. In the end, I took the blame.

"I did, but not quite on purpose," I answered. "She had a knife and was going after McCaffery. I had one shot. I kicked and caught her under the chin. I didn't expect her to bite her tongue off."

"I see," Scott said. He tossed back half of his drink then wiped his lips. "I suppose I should thank you, but I won't. She was a bitch, she was manipulative, she was more of a player than I ever was. But still, I loved her. I still do, I guess. I'm not ashamed to say my son's not the only one who still has tears at night."

I nodded, knowing what he meant. If Sophie was taken from me, I don't know what I would do. "Focus on your son," I advised. "He needs his father right now."

"Did you just come for parenting advice?" Scott asked, his voice gaining an edge. "Or did you want something else?"

"Two things," I said. "First, I want the lawsuit against MJT dropped. But also, answer a question for me. What's next for you? Are you staying in town or leaving?"

"I don't know yet," Scott replied. "I sank most of my money into expanding the HVAC work. Mom and Dad live here in town too."

"True, but if you're serious about your son not being drawn into the life, the farther away you get, the better it is."

Scott nodded. He knew his family's history, how his father and mother were two of the best thieves in the city for decades before their semi-retirement. "I know. What's your preference?"

"As long as you stay silent, I have none," I replied. "Although I do hope your son stays innocent."

Scott finished off his drink and rinsed out his glass, drying it before setting it back on the steel rack above the sink. "Me too. Okay, conversation done. Get out of here, if you don't mind, Snowman."

* * *

The next night, Patrick was almost bouncing with anticipation as we drove in our new car toward Fillmore Heights. It was matte black, all electric, and had a ton of other enhancements. The only thing it lacked was being bulletproof, but I couldn't have it all.

"Calm down, padawan," I said as we climbed out of the car. Driving with a

221

partner was more difficult in terms of parking than a motorcycle, but I wasn't sure that Patrick was ready for his own motorcycle yet. He did fine on normal driving, but I was waiting until spring and taking him out on a closed course to give him high-speed training. This car was more for intimidation patrols than recon, but we work within our limitations.

"I know, but it's been a while," Patrick said, wearing his new uniform. He kept the hood, but had also added a half face mask, adopting a cowl-like appearance that made sure his face was mostly obscured. He'd also changed the fabric, going with biker leather pants along with a top similar to mine. In typical flamboyant Patrick fashion, though, he'd picked a top with muted red stripes, not enough to really give him away, but noticeable up close. It was his tribute to Tabby.

"Just keep calm, stay at my side, and we'll accomplish the mission and get home safe and sound," I said. We walked down the alleyway we were parked in and into the neighborhood. We were in Latin King territory, and I wanted to check up on El Patron, Edgar Villalobos. The leader of the Latin Kings should have recovered from the dart I had put into his knee, but he was still more active in the neighborhood than he had been in years. I wanted to know why.

Thankfully, Villalobos's presence also meant he was staying more centralized. We had to avoid a few patrols, but we were able to mount the rooftops near El Patron's headquarters without being noticed.

It was there when we were slightly surprised. El Patron had expected us, it seemed, and had stationed men on the roof. There were four of them, all of them armed not with guns but with bats and nightsticks. They saw us as soon as I stuck my head up over the edge of the roof, coming toward us while taunting us. Game time.

I rolled to my right as soon as I got off the ladder, taking out one of the gang members at the knees. Patrick rolled left, taking out another before gaining his feet. He dropped a heavy knee into the back of the guy's head while I finished off mine with a stomp. The other two were already approaching us, and neither Patrick nor myself had time to pull our own weapons. Instead, I stepped inside the swing of my opponent, catching his wrists and turning at the same time.

I was faced with a split second decision. If I held on, I ran the risk of him staying on my back as we fell to the rooftop, possibly in a position to wrap me up or even choke me. I'm good, but I'm not impervious to attack. I'd taken my fair share of hits in my time, in and out of practice, and I knew the first lesson for any encounter was to not underestimate your opponent.

The other option was safer for me, but deadly for him. If I twisted my hip and let go, he'd go flying over the edge of the roof, falling the four stories to the asphalt below. Considering he would be doing it parallel to the ground, he was either going to hit on his chest or his back, guaranteeing death as his skull impacted with the blacktop of the alleyway.

I made my decision based not off of anything other than that I was tired. I already had a hundred deaths on my conscience, and I didn't want another one if I could prevent it. Dropping my knee, we tumbled together to the roof, a rock digging into my shin as we rolled. Thankfully, the impact of our bodies landing on the roof stunned the man on my back, and I was able to twist over and knock him out with a hard shot to his temple right after.

I got to my feet to watch Patrick close with his opponent, ducking the swing of a baton to catch him around the waist and lift him into the air before twisting and driving him down to the rooftop face first. Patrick dropped a forearm shot into the back of the man's neck, and he shuddered once before dropping limp.

"Nice work," I said, reaching into my pocket for the packet of zip strips I had originally brought along to attach a wireless camera to the building. That wasn't going to work any longer. As soon as the Latin Kings discovered what we'd done to their members, the rooftop would be swept. We'd have to get information now. "Bind them up."

"Why didn't you let him go?" Patrick asked as he got to work with his own strips. We had brought along an entire pack, fifty each, since they were easy to keep in our pants pocket that way, sealed in their own packaging. "You know, Babe Ruth over there."

"He'd have gone over the edge," I explained. "Didn't want that."

He nodded in understanding and quickly bound up the four men, along with taping their mouths shut. "We won't have much time to get info."

"Don't need a lot," I replied. "Come on."

We crawled to the edge of the roof and set up our directional microphone. El Patron was meeting with someone inside the apartment he was using as his headquarters, and I used a small periscope to see what was going on.

"You really are desperate if you want this," El Patron said to his visitor. Whoever it was, I couldn't see them. They must have been sitting just outside the view of the window. "You really hate this guy that much?"

"Just business," the other person replied, a woman's voice. "He's trying to undercut my group's power base, and my boss, she doesn't want that. Unfortunately, as he says, he's pretty much an open book. There's no skeleton that we know of in his closet that the public doesn't already know about."

Villalobos nodded and gestured with his hand. "Perhaps, but attacking a center for kids? That's low, even for us."

"Are you saying you won't do it?" the woman replied. "Because if you won't do it, I'm sure someone else will be interested. Perhaps the Gangster Disciples or maybe the 88s?"

I was surprised at El Patron's reaction. Any normal flunky, and he would have had them summarily shot. You don't go around insulting or threatening a man like that, not unless you had serious backup or a death wish. But Patron didn't do anything other than raise his hands in understanding. "Not at all. I'm just stating that such an undertaking can be very expensive. Are you prepared to compensate the Kings for it?"

"Of course," the woman said. "The Union has a bankroll that would make the Latin Kings the most powerful street gang in Fillmore Heights. With our financing, you'll easily be able to sweep the GDs and 88s out of the way."

"Interesting. And your members in the police department, they won't get in the way?" El Patron asked. "Not that we were worried about them before, but such a move would be quite public. The politicians, they enjoy getting publicity. Especially that new one, McCaffery."

"He won't be an issue. You give the community centers a black eye, and we defeat him in the next election. Problem solved in just over eleven months, and you can have Fillmore all to yourself afterward."

"Well then. It seems we have a deal," El Patron replied. "Okay. Tell your boss that we'll be willing to do what she asks. One thing, though."

"What's that?" the unknown woman asked.

"I want to meet her face to face on this. She can suggest the time and place, but I'm not sending my soldiers into battle without at least once looking my partner

224

in the eye."

"That can be arranged. Good evening, El Patron."

The men behind us started to stir, and I pulled our materials out and put them away. "We've got a lot to talk about," I said as I put the microphone back into my pocket. "And you're not going to like a lot of it."

Chapter 31
Tabby

When Patrick and Mark told me about the Union recruiting the Latin Kings to attack the community center, I was pissed. I was prepared to go right out and tear Francine Berkowitz's head off, but Mark calmed me down and talked me out of it.

"They're not going to just cause a plain accident," he said as we sat in the kitchen the next evening. Patrick was still at City Hall, and Sophie was getting her workout in. She was working hard to get back into shape after having a baby, knowing that despite Mark's assurances, her skills might be called on. Andrea was happily staring at her fingers, waving her tiny little arm in the air in her baby seat while the two of us talked on either side of her.

"What do you think they'll do?"

Mark pointed at the calendar hanging on the wall. "They know that the biggest time to make a splash will be as we approach the opening. We're going to be opening the first Saturday in April. It coincides with the local schools' Spring Break, gives us a good run up for summer vacation, and gets us a whole training course in on some of the job prep programs before the summer company hiring surge. If they're looking at trying to create problems for Patrick, they'll be looking to cause issues when they can make hay with the press."

"So you think they'll wait until they are closer to April?" I asked, still seething.

Mark nodded. "Remember, as much as she hates you and MJT, you're not really an obstacle to her except as a symbol against the system that the Union runs. She's confident she can destroy that symbol easily enough. Her first attempt failed when Pressman pulled his lawsuit. She's just going on to her next plan, although she's moving faster than I thought. She must really be worried about Patrick's rise in city politics."

I laughed. "It's funny, really. I love him, but he's no politician."

"It's what makes him so powerful, though," Mark replied. "He's not going to worry about being polite; he's there because he believes in what he's doing. He can capture the people's attention and imagination better than any stuffed suit politician. He's a demagogue, but in the good way."

I had never heard the word demagogue used in a good way before, and I tilted my head. Andrea cooed and dropped the rattle mirror that was in her left hand, which clattered to the table. I scooped it up and held it back out for her, turning it so that she could look at herself in the shiny surface. She was soon entranced, and she barely had the opportunity to make a frown before she was happy and smiling again. "You're a natural at that," Mark commented. "You'll make a great mother when it's your time."

"Thanks. It'll come when the time is right. But back to your point. Do you really think that Patrick can have a future in city politics? I mean, we're talking a man who doesn't even have a college degree."

"Neither do I," Mark pointed out to me. "Do you judge either him or me as unintelligent? You've never treated me as your intellectual inferior, even though you have an MBA."

Dammit, when Mark was right, he was very much right. "Honestly, I hadn't even thought about it. Most of the time I feel like the village idiot when you and Sophie start talking about so many things. Only area I feel like I even hold my own is on business."

Mark nodded, the teacher pleased as his student made the connection he'd been hoping for. "Patrick's the same way you are. He's got a natural feel for what is right and wrong, and he's a quick study. He picked up not just the physical nature of the martial arts I've been teaching him, but a lot of the verbal and situational cues as well. He's learned a lot about city politics very quickly, and if it wasn't for his gym work and the fact that he goes gaga over you, he could be accused of being a bookworm because he reads so much."

It was true. In the time he'd been living with us at Mount Zion, if Patrick wasn't at work, or training with Sophie or Mark, or spending quality time with me, I

226

most often could find his nose buried in a book or reading a tablet computer. Often his reading was based off of a comment we had made or something he had heard during the day, and invariably he'd research it. Depending on how important or vital he judged something to be, the reading could be as casual as Wikipedia, or as deep as a textbook. Sometimes I wondered how far Patrick would have gone in traditional schools if he'd had the means to do so.

"He is, but you're still somewhat dodging my point. Could he really become a major factor in politics?"

Mark tickled his daughter's belly for a moment until the beautiful little girl giggled and waved her arms and feet in joy. He studied her for a while, and I thought he wasn't going to answer me. Then he turned to me and smiled. "I think he could go a lot higher than mayor if he really wanted to. What do you think about living in the governor's mansion, or maybe even in Washington?"

The idea struck me dumb, and I watched Andrea wave her rattle happily until she made a face, twisting her mouth down at the corners. Mark and I glanced at each other, and I stood up to get the cleaning supplies. "Uh-oh, I know that face. Time for a fresh diaper."

* * *

The next day, I went down to the community center, making sure the manager and the construction foreman knew I was coming down. I didn't want to surprise anyone and cause a scene. I was there to see how progress was coming with less than two months to go until opening.

As it was, the manager, Helen Watters, met me. I'd hired Helen because I wanted her to be first the manager of the first center, then the overall program manager of the community centers. A former high school teacher, she'd been caught up in a scandal where one of the other teachers had been caught with a student. The school accused Helen of not reporting the affair and fired her. When Mark and I did a thorough background check, though, she was innocent of the accusations, and I wasn't going to waste the talents of such a dedicated professional. In addition to being a two-time teacher of the year, she'd volunteered, teaching the drama and glee clubs as well as heading her school's Future Entrepreneurs of America chapter. Unconventional, dedicated, and with a misunderstood flawed past. Perfect for an MJT employee.

227

"Helen, you don't need to meet me at the door like I'm some sort of VIP," I said with a smile when I came in and she was waiting for me. "I'm here to look around, not get the dime tour."

"You're lucky enough to get both," Helen replied. "First off, the foreman would have a fit if you weren't escorted; we've still got a lot of things to work on, and a lot of open wires, pipes, stuff like that. So, instead of sitting behind my desk and typing up emails or responding to complaints from your favorite representative of a large collective bargaining group, I can take an hour or two and let you look around."

"Okay. So how's the work coming along?" I asked. Since the heavy renovation was finished, I didn't need to wear a hard hat, which I was grateful for, although only slightly more than I was happy for the opportunity to wear jeans and a casual shirt to work that day. "Think you'll be ready on time?"

"The city inspectors are being a bit of a pain, but yes, we'll be ready. You hired a good general contractor, and he knows how to work the system. We might be missing a few basketballs, but the important stuff is going to be in. We're getting the computers in for the classroom next week."

We walked through the hallway toward the back, where I could look through the currently missing plexiglass windows toward the sports facility. While it wasn't big enough for a full-sized court, we could do half-court, and there were other games and sports we could do in there as well for children's activities. Our plan was to get at least two of the other centers with full-sized courts, more if possible. The big challenge was the size. There aren't too many buildings with the dimensions of full-sized gyms plus other rooms sitting empty in the middle of a city. "Nice. When is the board and other equipment being brought in?"

"Some of the last bits to go in, actually," Helen replied. "A volleyball net just needs ten minutes to set up. As per your requirement, there will be a wrestling mat brought in too. Are you sure on that one? It's going to take the insurance premiums through the roof."

"I'm sure," I said. Mark had reminded me about it that very morning, in fact, as he served everyone breakfast. "Mr. Smiley was quite insistent on that. There are a lot of kids out there who either need the skills, or more importantly, need a way to burn off all that youthful aggression while learning some self-control. Besides, according to Marcus, at least, after a good practice you're too damn tired to get into

228

too much trouble."

"He's got a point there," Helen replied. "I had quite a few athletes whose grades actually went up in season as opposed to off season. You'd think with the time they took for practice that it would the opposite, but I can see the theory behind it. If anything, they focused more because the consequences of their screwing off were more immediate. By the way, thank you for agreeing to the minimum grade code for any kid in our sports programs."

"It's just as important to me," I said as we turned away and headed toward the stairs. The grade code was one of the main approaches we were taking to try and motivate the local youth to work hard in school as well. For them to participate in any of the sports programs, they had to have at least a 75 average or its equivalent for elementary school. Anyone who was a dropout could qualify again if they enrolled in some of our other study programs, but life skills and academics were always to remain first.

With the gym being so tall, it was foolish to waste the extra building height, so we had classrooms and workshops on both floors. As we finished the stairs, I turned and emphasized my thoughts to Maxine. "You're here to create opportunity, not just keep them out of trouble."

The upstairs, besides the classrooms, also had one of the most important rooms to me. The nursery room. Designed according to Montessori principles, it would provide up to twenty mothers the opportunity to have a safe, professional place for their children to be watched while they worked or went through job training. We hoped that by starting children on a love of learning and exploration early, they'd be getting a leg up on the world before they ever entered even a preschool program.

Helen had already forwarded me the resumes of the teacher and assistant she'd hired, and I had to say I was impressed. Everything was tiny, and while the facilities were simple, they were high quality and encouraged the children to explore, strengthening the bodies and their minds. "Wow, this looks amazing," I noted as I looked over the child-sized sink and other materials. "And all of it is meant for usage by the children?"

"All of it works just like the adult versions," Helen replied. "The plumbing contractor really did a great job. I think there's a bit of personal bias in on it, though. His wife wants to go back to work, and they've got a one-year-old. He works here in

The Playground, and he already turned in his application for the first batch of kids we let in."

"Approve him," I said immediately as I looked everything over. "Another reason we started this place was to give local communities a sense of investment. If he sees he can get more than just the one job out of this place, he'll be more on our side."

The tour continued, and I got to see each of what would eventually become the first of our centers. There were general purpose rooms that could be a classroom, a meeting room, or really anything else the center needed. There was a dedicated computer lab as well as culinary arts room, and a room that would eventually teach tailoring and dressmaking. The theory was that each center would focus on certain areas of work training, with the first center being focused on so-called 'home economics.' The other centers would each have their own focus, including car and small engine repair, contracting and construction, and general business. We hoped that along with a strong college prep course, we'd be able to get the people in the neighborhoods out of the cycle of poverty they were trapped in. We were also going to offer counseling and guidance, although drug treatment programs and others would most likely have to be shopped out to other places that were better equipped to handle such cases.

"It looks good," I finally said as we went into Helen's office. It too was bare boned, but it at least had a temporary desk and her computer up and running. I made a note to replace her folding table desk with something more befitting her position ASAP. That would be a personal gift from me. If Sophie and Mark could build me a house, the least I could do is buy a center director a desk. "I also wanted to give you a heads up."

"More trouble from the Union?" Helen asked. Now that we were alone in her office, she dropped the pretense and polite talk. While most of the workers that were doing the renovations were non-union, we did have a couple of the subcontractors who were, which meant they were most likely pro-Union. "Thought we'd have been done with that."

"Not quite," I replied, not wanting to give away too much. "I received some good information that the Latin Kings might be coming down from Fillmore Heights to cause some trouble here as we approach the opening date. I've got people working on trying to get you details, but until then, you keep your eyes open. You know anything about them?"

"Not much," Helen admitted. "My school didn't have too many of that type, fortunately. Mostly prep kids and middle class kids. What should I look for?"

I took a flash drive out of my pocket. It had a copy of the local police department's gang task force file on the Latin Kings, along with a few other pieces of intelligence that Mark had compiled for me, things that the police didn't know about. It was scrubbed of anything that could tie it back to him or the Snowman, of course. "Here. Police file on the Kings. Again, don't ask where I got it, okay?"

"Don't need to. In this city, money talks and bullshit walks, and Marcus Smiley's got plenty of money. And of course, you've got some pull at City Hall yourself. Congratulations, by the way."

"Thanks. I'd invite you to the wedding, but we're thinking of going with a very low key, small ceremony type of thing," I replied. It had finally gotten out after someone in the local news hounds had put together the new rings Patrick and I were wearing, along with an 'anonymous source.' Of course, that anonymous source was my own assistant, Vanessa, who knew how to play the media game as well as Mark and Sophie did, maybe even better since she could do it with more finesse. She'd been doing it for longer, too. "But if you want, I can for sure bring you a souvenir from our honeymoon. We're planning on going to the Virgin Islands."

"Cool. Maybe something with a lot of coconut, and especially a lot of chocolate in it," Helen replied. "But don't sweat it if you forget. Set a date yet?"

"We're thinking later in the year. Kind of depends on Patrick's political future, if you know what I mean."

"I know. Rumors are making the papers. Anything you want to spill the beans on?"

I shook my head and smiled. The game of politics was as much about what wasn't said as what was said, I was learning. "Nothing I can confirm or deny."

231

Chapter 32
Mark

I yawned. The constant late nights were getting to me. I was on the twenty-seventh floor of an upscale condo complex in the downtown area, outside Francine Berkowitz's place, after spending the past half hour penetrating the building and making sure I was so far undetected.

My work was easier when I could be a "business investor", or even in my hitman days as a "freelance troubleshooter". I could sleep until noon, shower, and roll out for an afternoon or spend a day getting my body clock adjusted again. Sophie was understanding, and we were able to cover for each other when I needed to be Marcus Smiley. Nobody cared if I went into work at noon, as long as it was just the two of us.

Being a father demanded more. A baby negates all that. Sophie needed help with our daughter, and I couldn't be so greedy as to monopolize all the time I was awake for just my work. So in addition to being a masked vigilante (I refused, no matter how often Tabby joked, to refer to myself as a superhero or a costumed avenger), I had to be up by eight o'clock in order to catch the morning stocks, as well as give Andrea her bottle while Sophie got her first workout of the day in. She was doing workouts twice a day, pushing hard, knowing the fight that was coming. I didn't like it, but there was the possibility of getting back on the streets for her. I was hoping that it would never come to that, and that we could find a way for Patrick to fight the battle on another front with his increasing political influence. But we had to be ready just in case.

After her workout, she would routinely take Andrea for a quick bath while I did some cleanup around the house and prepared lunch and dinner for our growing family. We were getting used to lots of casseroles. I just didn't have time for freshly cooked meals as often. A casserole could be put together quickly and then just tossed in the oven later to be ready at six or seven whenever we needed it.

With my evening work often going until two or three in the morning, I was running short on sleep, and I was starting to feel it. Sophie had even let me take a nap that afternoon after finding Andrea and me asleep on a bean bag chair together, my daughter snuggled against my chest. It was the best hour of my month, at least until Andrea peed on me. We enjoyed letting her sleep nude as often as she wanted except at night. It prevented diaper rash, but it didn't help with having a wet, stinky t-shirt on me.

I shook my head and focused on the task at hand. I was good at breaking and entering, but I wasn't the best around. I was more adept at industrial type buildings, which tended to use a lot of armed guards. Private residences couldn't afford such things and used more electronic devices. You'd think those are easier to defeat, and they often are, but there is a drawback in that if you don't know one is there, you're easily screwed. Many of them had battery backups or other systems in place, so you had to scan for them individually.

I anticipated trouble, though, and was taking my time. Francine Berkowitz was not only rich, but corrupt as well. Before, she'd only used her corruption and power in what could be called quasi-legal means. Lots of blackmail, some arm twisting, but at least nobody had a gun held to their head. By contacting the Latin Kings, however, she had crossed a line, one that took her out of just being countered in the political and legal arenas and into my line of expertise.

My sensor flashed and I pocketed the small computer. There was one final system that I could expect, and it was one that I couldn't detect. I needed assistance. "You there?"

"Yeah," Patrick replied in my ear. He was back at Mount Zion, working the computers. Sophie was ready to assist, but she was resting with Andrea. The mission tonight didn't require quite as much knowledge as some, and it was good practice for him. *"You sure we need this much area?"*

"I'm sure," I said. "Even if the sensor has a battery backup, we need to cut out the power to the cell towers in the area. I've already taken care of any hard-lines."

"Okay. You've got five minutes to get in and get out," Patrick reminded me. We were tapped into the city power department through a backdoor hack that Captain Zappy had given me months ago. It would take them that long to reboot their system once we crashed it, fully blacking out a couple of city blocks. Fortunately, there were no hospitals or other emergency care centers nearby.

233

I listened, and as soon as the click in my ear told me the power was down, I went into action. Slipping the lock, I had to move silently and quickly. It was the most dangerous type of breaking and entering, because Francine was at home. I couldn't move during the day, and she was unpredictable as to when she would be at home or at the office. I had to wait until she was asleep and hope that she wasn't having a bout of insomnia. She was divorced, her husband and children having moved out years ago. My sensor sweep and casing had at least shown that she wasn't moving around and talking, but you never knew for sure.

The condo hallway was pitch black, but my night vision goggles let me see clearly enough. I made my way silently to the living room, looking around for something to hide my little presents in. By the television, under the Blu-Ray player, I hid one, a super thin passive microphone that would go active only on a trigger.

The second bug was more traditional, and was active, using a burst Wi-Fi signal to send constant audio and video to an offsite server in Malaysia. A program on the server would scan for target words in conversation and ping us back at home if certain words were said. We could also tap into it at any time we wanted.

The third sensor was like the first, passive. It went under the sofa, against the wood frame where it wouldn't be detected. Unfortunately, it would also be slightly muffled, but I only wanted it there in case bugs one and two were detected. My time running short, I made my way out, double checking to lock the door behind me. The unarmed security system could be attributed to the power outage, and I didn't think Francine would suspect anything.

* * *

The next night, I had another contact to make, this time for the first time meeting someone face to face. Or at least he thought so.

The roof of the Federal building was cold, but it was safe. It was just past eleven at night, and I hoped my meeting would go quickly so I could get home before one in the morning. Seven hours of sleep was a luxury.

"You up here?" I heard, then a stamping of feet and hands rubbing arms over a heavy jacket. Bennie Fernandez may have been a good attorney, but he wasn't prepared for the winter cold. He was dressed in a full-length heavy parka, looking for all the world like he was getting ready for a winter blizzard instead of just a conversation on a clear winter night.

"You look uncomfortable, Prosecutor," I said, keeping my voice pitched. "You should try getting a job in Dallas or something."

"Very funny," he replied. "You know I'm breaking about half a dozen volumes of the laws I'm supposed to be upholding just talking with you up here. What do you need?"

"Francine Berkowitz," I said. "You have your eyes on her?"

"My boss does, I don't," he replied. "She's a very big fish, like in Washington level. There are plenty in the DOJ who would like to see her taken down, but she's got a very tight game. Nothing that can be proven, nobody willing to talk. And she's got political allies. Why?"

"If I bring you direct evidence of her collaborating with a street gang to incite violence at the new community center that is opening up next month, think you can get something done?"

Bennie thought about it. "You're going to make me famous if you do. I'll take the case myself if the evidence is damning enough. What do you have?"

"You might have to wait for it," I replied. "I have a recorded conversation between Edgar Villalobos, the head of the Latin Kings, and someone claiming to represent the Union discussing a collaboration. But I don't have Berkowitz herself on tape saying anything."

"That would be helpful. You can get some heat on Berkowitz, but she's got enough connections and a high power team of lawyers. No way could I get even an indictment without either testimony, a confession, or her on tape, preferably high definition audio and video. You do that, I can get an indictment on at least a RICO charge."

"I'll see what I can do," I said. I turned away, but Bennie's voice called me back. "Yes?"

"You're doing more than just gathering information for me, I know that," he said. "But how long are you planning on keeping this up? Your luck has to run out some time."

I leaned against the side of the building and crossed my arms over my chest. "How long are you planning on trying to take down the corrupt assholes I keep bringing you? You know eventually one of them is going to get off on some technicality on appeal. You're making enemies just as powerful as mine."

"It might happen," Bennie agreed. "But I have the hope that I can be promoted out of here and in Washington or heading an office by that point. Hell, my luck holds up, you might be breaking in a new federal prosecutor soon enough. But as to your question, I'm not stopping. Cleaning up the streets, it's in my blood."

"I won't stop either," I replied. "We all have our reasons, Bennie. Someday, maybe years from now, we can sit down and enjoy a drink together and celebrate the fruition of our plans."

"And if we can't? What if you get arrested in the meantime?"

I turned and headed to the edge of the roof, where I pulled my black hang glider from out of the shadows and strapped it on. "Then I expect a pretty good case from the city DA. But it won't come to that. Good night, Bennie."

Chapter 33
Sophie

I looked down the sight, working to still my body and my heart. It had been nearly seven months since I'd last shot a firearm, and I didn't have time for any more rust to accumulate on my reactions.

The target was tiny, an empty Red Bull can a hundred meters away against the dusty bluff of dirt. There weren't too many places within easy driving distance of the city where I could actually go out and fire under real conditions, but there was only so much I could do with laser replications or pellet guns. Patrick and Mark might have been able to keep their skills up using indoor firing ranges, but I was practicing long range shooting.

The AR-15 felt light in my hands, and I knew I was stronger than I had been the last time I fired. I hadn't been sitting on my ass the whole time I was pregnant, and my hard work since having Andrea had paid dividends. My waist and hips were still larger than they'd been pre-pregnancy, but that was due to changes in my pelvis. I was in nearly the best shape of my life, and while we hoped it wasn't going to come to it, I was ready if need be to fight next to my husband.

236

There was only this one skill to work on still, one that took not aggressive energy, but patience and calmness. I caressed the trigger, and the gun kicked in my hands, sending another round down range. The can tumbled over, and I knew I had another hit.

"Good job," Mark said, taking his binoculars away from his face. Andrea was enjoying a day with her Aunt Tabby and Uncle Patrick, a bit early for a three-month-old baby, but necessary. "Think you're up for longer range shots?"

"Yeah, let's take it out to two hundred meters. If I can hit those well, we'll be ready for three hundred plus with the balloons," I said. It was one of the ways Mark had changed me, making me a stronger, better woman than I'd been before. The military might ask for soldiers to hit only torso sized targets, but I held myself to a higher standard. My goal was to hit balloon sized targets consistently at three hundred meters, which if you've ever tried, is hard as hell. They flutter in the wind, move around erratically, and demand pinpoint targeting to hit. Even a good sniper could miss them in a good breeze.

Mark had taught me how to find that place inside where snipers operated best, when emotion and doubt and confusion fell away, leaving just the mind and will. It took me a long time and a lot of training prior to having Andrea to reach a level even approaching his, but I used it often. Working communications for his missions, I had to go there in order to focus on the task at hand and not worry that my husband was potentially getting shot at on the other end of the line. It had even helped in delivering Andrea, allowing me to suppress the pain enough to let Tabby do her best to help take over communications.

By the end of my training, I was exhausted, mentally more than physically. Focusing on such precise control for so long is just tiring. Still, I was happy. It was a lot better than I'd done the week prior, and while I wasn't quite ready yet, I was making progress. "Let's go home."

On the drive back, I noticed that Mark kept looking over at me. "What?" I asked, smiling at how silly I felt. "Do I have some gunpowder on my face or something?"

"No," Mark replied huskily. "You're just so sexy, it's hard."

Suddenly, I felt it too. It had been a long time since we'd had sex, one of the side effects of his late nights and a very young baby at home. But that day, it was just

237

the two of us, and we were being who we loved to be. More importantly, we were with the person who was most important to us. "Can you make it home?"

"Hell no," he said, reaching over and putting his hand on my thigh. His touch was hot and arousing, and my hands twitched, the car swerving in our lane before I straightened out. "But don't crash."

We drove on in a silence that was heavy with anticipation, constantly exchanging little glances as we looked, searching for a place to pull off the highway. Finally, three miles down the road, I saw a turn-off onto what I knew was a mostly deserted country road. Taking it, I drove along until the highway was invisible in the rear view mirror, and on until the road slightly opened up on the left side. The woods were deep in this area, heavy old growth that earlier in the year would be heavier with hunters. The early spring sun was barely warm enough, but I couldn't wait any longer. I threw the car into park and reached into the back seat, grabbing a blanket that we had brought in case the wind had picked up.

"In here or over there?" I pointed to a small clearing in the trees, thick with fallen pine needles and clear of even traces of snow. It had been over a year and a half since we'd had sex outside, the last time being during my training in Eastern Europe, but right then I didn't care. I'd have stripped butt naked on the fifty-yard line of Spartan Stadium if Mark wanted me to.

Mark opened his door and got out, with me right behind him. Instead of heading for the clearing, though, he stopped me at the front of the car, taking the blanket out of my hands and spreading it over the hood.

"Warmer here," he explained as he turned, wrapping his arms around me fiercely and kissing me with unrestrained passion. I returned his passion with my own, clutching at his jacket and kissing him back as hard as I could. He pressed me up against the car, which I had to admit was warm, his hands busily working at the zipper on my jacket while I returned the favor.

In my haste, I jammed the zipper on his old-fashioned military field jacket, tugging uselessly until I grew frustrated and pulled as hard as I could. With a metallic *ping*, the teeth yanked free, the brass clasps destroyed as I pulled his jacket open to feel the slick, tight fabric of his thermal Under Armor top beneath. I noticed it was a new one, black with white patches rather than the all black he'd always worn before. "New duds?"

238

"Uh-huh, thinking of wearing them at night," Mark replied as he got my jacket open and pushed a hand inside, his strong hand roughly caressing my breast. It would have bordered on painful if I hadn't been wearing the exact same type of shirt he was, the slick fabric lessening the grip enough that it was amazing instead. Fire flooded my skin, my nipples aching under the warm fabric as we kissed again. I reached up and tweaked his nipple through his top while I spread my legs and wrapped them around his waist. Even through the heavy fabric of our pants, I could feel the heat and iron hardness of his cock. We rubbed together through our clothes, groaning as we reconnected.

I'd been naked with Mark since Andrea was born. We would take time to hold each other in bed, or to sometimes even shower together. But exhaustion or the cries of a baby had inevitably killed nearly every prior encounter. Even the ones we'd had felt rushed, the fumbling of two people who wanted more than what time and circumstances were permitting them, most often not even given the time to come to orgasm before being pulled apart by something beyond our control. Here, though, on this deserted country road that was barely more than a fire trail, I felt closer to him than since before our daughter's birth, even through thick layers of clothing.

Still I needed more. Pulling his shirt up, I slid my hands under his shirt, too impatient to let him strip, feeling and scratching my fingers down the hard muscles of his back and chest. He was as sexy as ever, each muscle perfect, his skin smooth and flawless except for his scars that told me the tale of his painful past.

While I traced my love's history written on his body, he found the soft tender skin of my neck and kissed; my head fell back and I offered myself to him. He nipped and sucked, harder and harder as his fingers reached for the button of my pants and quickly undid them. He pulled back from my neck and stared with nearly frightening intensity into my eyes. "How?"

"Here," I said, turning around and resting my chest against the warm hood of the car. There wasn't a lot of room to spread my legs with the way the pants bound at my feet, but it didn't matter. Mark pushed my jacket up to expose my ass, which chilled as the skin was exposed. My ass broke out in goosebumps for a moment before his warm hands ran over the skin, turning my shivers of cold into shivers of wanton lust. I lowered my head and said what came to my mind first, my voice thick and drawn out with need. "Oh, Mark, fuck me."

239

"As you wish," he grunted, pulling back just long enough to open his jeans. I felt my wetness increase with each muted click of his zipper being pulled down, until he pushed against me, his cock hard and hot against my panties. I was soaked, delirious with sensation as he rubbed his cockhead against the slick, wet fabric, my body nearly convulsing with the feeling. "Ready?"

"Fuck me," I growled, reaching back and pulling my panties to the side. We'd make love another time, but this was something different, something primal and needy.

The first push of his cock inside me was hot and again bordering on the fine line between pain and pleasure as he filled me up. I lost all track of time as Mark thrust all the way inside me, lightning detonating from my pussy all the way to my brain with each inch of his cock pushing inside me.

All I knew for glorious, eternal minutes were the dual sensations of the warm hood of the car against my breasts and Mark's cock hammering into me from behind. He filled me over and over, every cell in my body screaming in pleasure from the sensation. I couldn't get enough, pushing back into his thrusts and meeting him, desperate for more and more.

As we continued, it dawned on me the dual nature of what we were doing. We were growling and moaning like animals, perhaps not that much different than the normal residents of the woods, rutting and mating in an ancient pattern written in our very DNA. His cock plunged in and out of me with ferocity, making me his over and over, driving me wild with pleasure as my pussy clutched at him. I wanted my man and gave myself over to him. But at the same time, with all of the raw, base physical pleasure, there was still a connection, a tenderness and need that grew between us. We weren't just fucking because we both happened to desire it; we were doing so because we knew the other person wanted it as well. I was pushing back not only for my own pleasure but for Mark's, for the sensations I was giving his cock and the feelings I was giving him. It compounded my pleasure, almost as if I could feel from both sides of the situation.

My orgasm rushed upon me with the suddenness of breaking glass, shattering the endless pleasure of our sex with an even purer, more intense explosion through my body, so intense it was impossible for it to last more than a moment before I overloaded, just holding on as my body shook and spasmed. I felt Mark push me one

240

more time against the car, groaning deeply as he came. Finally, I was at peace. I had my husband, my mate, my perfect companion.

We stayed there for wonderful minutes, embracing as Mark's cock slowly softened until he slipped out of me. The creeping sensation of cold air on my ass again started feeling a bit too uncomfortable, and I pulled away with real regret. I pulled my pants up and turned around, pulling him down into another kiss, this one as soft and loving as the earlier ones had been passionate and heat filled. "We can't go this long in between sex." I sighed as he kissed me underneath my ear. "We'd both go crazy."

"I know," he mumbled against my neck, his arms pulling me close. I held him, and we stayed there for a long time, secure against the whole damn world. A sharp gust of wind came down the trail, and even with Mark around me my ears were tingling, so we folded up the blanket and put it back inside.

"Next time, let's do a five-star hotel or something, okay?" I asked as we closed the door. "Soft sheets, room service, the whole nine."

"Actually, I was thinking," Mark said as we got back into the car and I started getting us turned around. "Maybe that's something we can make a regular thing of."

"What, driving out in the woods to have sex on the hood of our car?" I said with a laugh. "Don't think so. Murphy's Law would eventually come to bite us in the ass."

"No, not that, silly," he said. I got back on the highway and headed for home. "I meant like date nights or just making sure we spend time together. Think Tabby and Patrick would mind having some more days watching Andrea while we get away sometimes?"

"As long as we're willing to return the favor, I don't see why not," I said. "Think the two of us could handle two kids for a couple of hours or even overnight?"

"I can fight five men at once, do combat reloads on over a dozen different types of firearms, and run five minute miles repeatedly," Mark replied confidently. "How hard could two kids be?"

"Two toddlers?"

Mark cocked his eyebrow, conceding. "Good point. Okay, together we might be able to handle that."

Chapter 34
Tabby

Toward the end of the week, I was spending an hour in the now re-established home office, Patrick having moved into my bedroom with me. He still had his apartment in The Playground, but that was merely for politics. He had to maintain a first or second residence in the district he represented to be eligible for office. In any case, I was spending an hour doing some research when one of Mark's computers beeped. Since they were set up to monitor things that were important to his vigilante work, I immediately saved and set aside the document I was working on, a letter to Gene and the Spartans requesting their input on the schedule of activities for the opening day of our first community center. "Mark?"

"Yeah?" he called back from the kitchen, where he was talking with Patrick. "What's up, Tabs?"

"Computer's beeping," I said as he stuck his head in the door. He looked, then pulled the HDMI cable out of my computer, sticking it in the slot on his. His face wasn't worried but intensely curious. While his bugs would record for later playback, there was something in his face that said he had a hunch about this time.

"Sorry, you can have it back in a minute," he said, watching the screen. The monitor flashed and kind of wiggled, then steadied as the computer registered and adjusted. Three notices were on the screen, as each of Mark's bugs from Francine Berkowitz's condo were sending notifications. The computer had detected the trigger words on the active bugs and sent signals to the passive ones to turn them on as well. "Well, well, let's see what we've got."

The video feed and audio feed were actually composites from two of the bugs, spliced and clarified by the computer on our end. Because of that and because the system was monitoring for key words, we were actually watching a feed that was about a minute old.

"Yes, that sounds fine," Francine said. She was sitting on her couch, a glass of white wine in her hand as she talked on her phone. *"No, no way in hell am I bringing you*

242

to my condo. Patron, you may live outside of Fillmore, but that doesn't mean you're material for this neighborhood."

"Bitch has got some balls," I noted while we listened. Mark nodded, not commenting until the conversation was finished. I could see in his face, he was studying every facial expression and vocal inflection, trying to make sure what we were overhearing was real and not just an elaborate deception from someone who had found our devices.

"No, I can't do it during the day either. Why? Do I really have to explain why I can't be seen with you? All right, all right. We can talk details tomorrow night. Where? I know you live near the Park, how about there? No . . . okay, I understand that. The docks? Why there? Fine. The Docks, eight o'clock? Pier thirty-two. I'll bring the deposit; you make sure the meeting is secure. No visits from the cops . . . or him."

"Sounds like Francine is expecting company," I quipped as Mark set the computer back to passive monitoring. It would still record, but only notify us if key words were tripped again. "What's this about Pier thirty-two?"

"The Docks are one of the areas that are very open," Mark replied. "And Pier thirty-two is one of the farthest out there. Approaching it is difficult at best, impossible at worst if the Latin Kings bring decent observation. The nearest buildings to thirty-two are over a hundred yards away, and the approaches are all easily defended. Two roads, both going deep into the warehouses near the Docks, and the ground area is crisscrossed with only tiny little alleyways that are barely big enough for a mini forklift. That area is also rarely used, because of how old-fashioned and out of date it is. Most of the sea traffic that comes into the Docks prefers to use the closer in, modernized berths."

"So they're preparing themselves to have a visit from you," I replied. "They wouldn't put their backs against the sea with so few avenues of escape if they were just worried about the cops."

Mark nodded. "The thing is, they're not going to be anticipating one thing."

"What's that?" I asked.

"I know the time of the meeting. They're meeting at night because they can move a lot of soldiers into the area once the sun goes down. But, if we're already there . . ."

"They're walking into a trap themselves," I finished for him. "What's your

243

idea?"

* * *

I was nervous as I walked into the Federal Building the next morning. While Patrick, Mark and Sophie would be in more direct physical danger that evening, I was still sweating. After all, I was revealing a lot to a man that I wasn't certain we could trust. He was still a federal prosecutor, after all.

"Excuse me, is Mr. Benjamin Fernandez in?" I asked the receptionist at the front. "I'm Tabitha Williams of MJT Holdings."

"I can see if he's available," the receptionist, who was wearing a security uniform and had a Glock on his hip, answered. It was a Federal building, and while I could dimly remember an era when government buildings weren't the target for terrorist attacks, it was a hazy memory at best. I waited nervously while the man made a phone call, speaking quietly into the handset. He took the phone away from his mouth for a moment. "Miss Williams, what's the nature of this? Mr. Fernandez doesn't have you on his schedule, and is supposed to be in a deposition in twenty minutes."

"I understand," I said. "Tell him it has to do with the roof problems he had a little while ago. I know of a contractor that can assist him."

The receptionist gave me a strange look, but repeated what I'd said. His expression grew even more confused as he listened to the answer. He set his handset down and blinked. "Mr. Fernandez is coming down right now," he said. "Would you mind waiting over there?"

I took a seat in one of the few chairs over by the window, people watching for a few minutes. It was pretty easy to peg people based off of their clothes and their walk, a skill Mark had been casually working with me on for most of the winter. The law enforcement agents all walked the same, their shoulders back and their heads on swivels. The FBI guys were the worst, putting off a visible air of arrogance. With the reputation they'd garnered recently with taking down Owen Lynch and the Confederation, many of them probably did feel like they were masters of the city, or at least that they were on top of things. How wrong they were.

In contrast to the law enforcement types, the hordes of regular workers, analysts, and other jobs were also easy to pick out, although their individual jobs were more difficult to detect unless they carried something in their hands that gave it away.

They walked like anyone else, half unaware of their surroundings, complacent in the security systems in place and in the common decency of their fellow man not to have anarchy break out at a moment's notice. After living with Patrick and Mark, both of whom had lived a life where complacency was a very risky option, it was somewhat off-putting. It's not that the safety and security of good people is a bad thing, but I could tell many of these people were missing the good details as well as the bad details of life. They lived in a world made up of muted sepia tones, when the world all around them was dramatic and full of color if they would just open their eyes and look. I wondered if I had been one of those people once, then shook my head. Of course I had been. It had taken being kidnapped, my heart and head screwed with, and then being put back together by the most important people in my life to wake me from my slumber.

I picked out Bennie Fernandez as soon as he stepped off the elevator. It wasn't just that he'd been in the newspapers, it was his facial expression. He wasn't as arrogant as the FBI agents, but he was confident. Also, he was aware. His eyes were taking in details with every step and breath. I could see why Mark had continued to work with him after breaking the information on Owen Lynch.

"Miss Williams, it's a pleasure to meet you face to face," Bennie said as he came over, shaking my hand in a firm yet still somewhat soft grip. I'd spent too much time with people who earned their callouses the old fashioned way, I guess, because as aware as Bennie was, I could tell from his grip that he still trusted things that I didn't have faith in—like the security measures of the building. He'd be the man who could pick out who the real killer was in a movie, or see details in documents that everyone would miss. On the street, he might be aware enough to spot trouble before it happened, but most likely wouldn't be able to do anything about it personally other than run away. "I know I came by your house months ago, but you were unavailable. I apologize that I never followed up with you."

"That's perfectly all right, Mr. Fernandez," I replied, remembering the visit Mark and Sophie had told me about. "I understand that you have big fish to fry, and my issue was small potatoes at the time."

"Well, it did seem to rise up again," Bennie said. "I was a bit surprised when a friend in the civil court clerk's office called me, telling me about it. I was glad it got dropped, honestly."

"Thank you. The guard said you have a deposition in a few minutes. I hope I'm not keeping you," I said.

Bennie shook his head. "I sent my paralegal ahead of me; they can get things started. It would be helpful if you and I could walk together, though. I can save a few minutes if I head toward the RIST station while we talk."

I had to give it to him, it was a slick move. By getting us out of the building, he and I could talk more honestly without worrying about being overheard. Of course, he could have been wearing a wire, but Benny didn't know that I was also carrying something useful in my soft briefcase, a portable jammer that I could turn on just by touching a button on the case itself. It had a ten-minute battery life and would shut down any and all transmissions within a two-meter radius, including cellphones and bugs. Mark had some pretty nifty gadgets.

"Sure," I said, turning to the door. I was wearing one of my suits and shivered slightly as we left the Federal building and walked out into the late winter sunlight. I didn't know if he was telling the truth or just being deceptive, but I was willing to play along. "I took the RIST down here myself."

Bennie gave me a quick glance of slight surprise. "Oh? I guess I had you pegged for that Mercedes SUV you've been seen around town in. Mechanical problems? Or worried about a ticket still?"

I laughed and shook my head. Within the city, the law enforcement community was simultaneously close knit and very tribal. Rumors like my troubles made for juicy passing around, while facts on cases were guarded like precious jewels. "So you've heard about that too, huh? No, no ticket worries, just having it taken in for a full workup. With MJT being all about being eco-friendly, I gotta make sure it's tuned up. The winter wasn't too harsh, but still, all that road salt sure can play hell with the engine and undercarriage."

"I understand. I'm just taking the RIST because parking over by the site of the deposition is hell," Bennie replied with a chuckle. "Once you get a parking spot around here, you hang onto it with a choke hold if you need to. So, what can you tell me about my roof problems?"

"Well, we have a mutual friend who is interested," I said. We were clear of the building, and I looked around. Quickly, I reached into my pocket, then pulled out a flash stick. "Here. A gift from said mutual friend."

246

Bennie took the stick and made it disappear into his pocket. "Can I confirm any of this?"

"It's video and audio," I said simply. "But this comes with a simple price."

"What's that?" Bennie asked, looking at me carefully. "I've learned in my years working in government, sometimes the price might be too much."

I nodded. "Don't I know it? His price is simple. Don't tell your pistol carrying buddies for at least twenty-four hours. You can still use the information to move against Berkowitz, but the other men on the file . . . they belong to someone else."

Bennie thought about it for a long time. Walking along silently, he pondered the price, and if it was worth it. I'd already given him the flash drive, so he had to assume there was some sort of catch to make sure he paid the price. We made our way all the way to the RIST station, where we paused on the platform. He was going downtown; I was going back to Mount Zion to help my family get ready for war.

There were consequences for his actions, he knew. He knew who Mark was, even if he didn't know his real face or name. He knew if he gave his word, there'd be blood spilled for certain, and most likely men going to the morgue. But he also knew the Latin Kings were one of the groups that were beyond the law. They'd survived the crackdown after Owen Lynch and the Confederation were swept away. They'd survived numerous gang wars. They'd done it through not only regular intimidation, but also the tacit support of certain members of the Fillmore Heights community. He was making a deal with the devil, but a devil that was at least trying to atone. "All right, he has until nine tomorrow morning. Just do me a favor, and try and limit the damage?"

"He'll try. To unlock the files, the password is *blizzard*, all in lower case."

Bennie got on his train, and ten minutes later I caught mine. I hadn't been lying about my normal SUV being in the shop for a tune up, but more importantly I wanted to have the time to think as I walked from the RIST back to Mount Zion. Vanessa could hold down the office at MJT for the day, and probably do a better job than I could in handling certain things. I needed to clear my head.

As I walked, I mentally prepared myself for the stress of the night. Sophie had insisted on going with Mark and Patrick, which meant that if everything went to hell, I could be the only member of our little group that lived to see the next day. I knew what I had to do if that happened. Mark had given me all the passwords and documents just the night before. Disappearing out West, probably Arizona or New Mexico, where there were large areas with few people and a lot of cactus, I'd use the fake papers on Andrea to get her a passport while the fake passport I already had would do. I'd get the papers I needed, buy tickets and then cash out, disappear anywhere in the world I wanted to go. I prayed that didn't happen.

I turned up one of the hills that gave the Heights their name, still thinking. In any other circumstance, there'd be no way I'd be able to go on. Before, I would have insisted to go too, even if only to act as eyes and ears. But there was Andrea to think of. My goddaughter, whose smile was magic and whose little chubby fists contained the strength of her father and mother. She would need me, not only to raise her, but to teach her who her parents were. It was a heavy burden to shoulder, and I wasn't sure if I was strong enough to do it by myself. But I had to.

I saw the driveway to Mount Zion and turned, seeing the bell tower rising above the trees. I knew they were up there, at that moment, preparing. I paused for a moment and just looked at the clear early spring sky, so blue it made my eyes water. The bell tower's peaked roof stabbed upward into the impossible blue, stalwart and resolute. I thought about the people it contained and my role with them.

I remembered talking with Sophie about how when she and Mark first got together, she told him she wasn't going to play Alfred to his Batman. But as I stood there, I realized that there was nothing wrong with that role. Alfred served as Batman's conscience, as his helper, and as the steady rock he could depend on. In the months of living with Mark, Sophie, and eventually Patrick, I'd read my fair share of Batman comics. Throughout his years, Batman had lost partners and had others leave him, but Alfred was always there.

I decided if that was my role, then so be it. Besides, more than once Alfred did his own little bit of ass kicking from time to time, and he was always good for an ironic observation or sardonic comment to break the heaviness of everything. I headed up the driveway and walked inside. Opening the door to the bell tower, I headed up to my family, finding the three of them hard at work assembling their gear, Andrea in her play seat looking around with big eyes. "He agreed."

"Great," Mark replied, "that means we can take out the Kings."

"He had one request, though," I continued, looking over the array of weaponry on the tables and work spaces. "He wants you to minimize casualties if you

248

can. Understandable, considering who he is."

I expected them to stop work, to at least be a little surprised or put off by my words. Instead, nobody missed a beat, not even Andrea pausing in her looking around and enjoying the new sights and sounds.

"It is," Sophie replied to my comment, running a lightly oiled rag over the inner workings of her rifle—her favorite, a heavy caliber AR-15 with magnifying scope. "But he knows that there won't be a guarantee of that. What can he expect?"

"Well, do you guys have rubber bullets?" I asked, and Mark stopped what he was doing, setting down his own guns to look at me. I blushed, feeling childish. "Sorry, stupid question."

"No . . . it wasn't," Mark replied. "Because I think I actually have something. In one of my old Snowman hideouts, I took in a crate of unique rounds. It was for a Confederation operation, where Sal Giordano wanted it to look like I made a hit on someone, but we were only making him disappear. So instead of real lead, the bullets were made of a lead and plastic powder polymer. When they hit, they basically vaporize, but the energy goes into the body, shocking the system if you hit someone in the right place."

"Where's the right place?" Patrick asked. "And what caliber rounds do you have?"

"If you hit them in an arm or leg, the whole damn thing goes numb for three to five minutes," Mark said, "leaving the affected area paralyzed and unable to move if I remember right. A hit to the stomach will paralyze the diaphragm for a good minute; they'll pass out from lack of air. But, there's also areas you can hit and drop them permanently."

"Like?" Patrick asked, biting his lower lip. He and I had talked, and I knew that while he'd kicked Melinda Pressman, he'd never actually intentionally killed someone before. He was nervous.

"A frontal or side head shot can kill, an unprotected hit over the heart too. That's the other problem. Even a heavy jacket can diffuse the energy enough to make the rounds useless. I remember shooting some of the test guys for it, and a guy wearing a leather jacket on top of a sweatshirt walked right through the rounds like I was shooting him with a Super Soaker. It wasn't until I put a round in his right thigh that he dropped," Mark said, touching his body to emphasize his words. "And the rounds were in nine millimeter Parabellum. We had to get a whole case of it to avoid the ATF tracking the job down. I should still have about a thousand rounds of that stuff over near Sophie's old apartment. I had a place near there."

"Then let's go in with a mix," Patrick said. "The Glocks carrying those, and a backup with real rounds. Sophie's going to have our butts covered up high with the heavy caliber."

I looked at them and nodded. "Thanks."

Sophie shook her head. "No need to thank us, Tabby. Mark wants to do it because Bennie Fernandez is a good ally to have. Don't want to lose him just to kill a few street level soldiers. Our goal is to bust up the gang, and if we can do that without killing some of them, the better."

Chapter 35
Patrick

The Docks were windy, which you'd expect from being next to the ocean. It was late afternoon, and the three of us were driving an old, grumpy sounding panel truck through the Dock warehouse area. We looked like any of a dozen different delivery companies in the city, which is exactly what we wanted. All of our gear was in the back, except for a single Glock that Mark kept under his jacket just in case someone stopped us and asked questions we couldn't answer—loaded with the special ammunition, of course. We were even dressed like delivery workers, and Sophie actually looked somewhat normal and slightly frumpy in an old denim jacket. Considering Sophie's physique, that was quite an accomplishment.

We weren't noticed as we made it all the way down toward Dock 32. I was at first suspicious of parking so close to our ambush point, but Mark's plan had multiple escape options. In fact, if our plan went the way we wanted, we'd not be using the truck at all, which is why we were all wearing gloves. There was little chance it would be dusted for prints, but we wanted to be sure.

The warehouse we selected was empty, and it had been a very long time since it had last been used. Formerly owned by Sal Giordano, upon his death it had gone into legal limbo. The probate court was unwilling to release it to the heirs, since there was plenty of suspicion that it was used in criminal activity. However, there was little direct evidence against Sal's warehouse, since it had been little used in favor of air and train delivery instead of sea. Bennie Fernandez and the rest of the federal prosecutors weren't worrying about digging up evidence of a dead man's crimes, except in terms of how they applied to direct prosecution of current, living criminals. Since most of the men swept up in the Confederation were guilty of much larger and easier to prove crimes than anything tied into the warehouse, the warehouse sat in a legal limbo. Sal's heirs weren't concerned, either, as they were living well enough on the money Fernandez and the Feds hadn't touched. Half of a crapload of money was still a lot.

Best of all, Mark had access to the warehouse, having been taught the security system codes by Sal Giordano himself back when he was just a delivery boy for the Confederation godfather. Using the chain operated backup system, he raised the door enough for the truck to be parked inside and then shut it behind us. Unfortunately, while the building security systems may have been active, the power to the lights and other utilities had been cut off, with the fuse boxes literally pulled out.

"Guess it's a good thing I packed a canteen," I quipped as I jumped out of the passenger seat. "Although I wish there was still a potty. So where are we deploying?"

"You and I will be in the alleyway, direct action," Mark said simply, ignoring my joke. "Sophie will be up top. Remember, we're leaving Berkowitz for Bennie Fernandez, so we hit before she gets here. The Latin Kings will follow their standard operating procedures and show up an hour or more before the meeting time. We let them come in, we close the gap behind them, and we move in."

"It's still dangerous," I remarked as I helped Mark and Sophie unload our weapons from the back of the van. In addition to Sophie's sniper AR-15, all of us carried handguns with the disabling rounds. For our backup weapons, Mark and I were carrying Heckler & Koch UMPs, one of the best nine-millimeter submachine guns in the world from what Mark told me. While Sophie would have her rifle in a nest with a few magazines lying nearby, Mark and I had to carry everything we needed on our persons. We'd be moving, most likely, and couldn't depend on an ammunition point. "You worried about the numbers?"

"Are you?" Mark asked, not grinning as I would have expected for such a rejoinder, but instead curious, questioning. He was trying to figure out if I was truly ready for this mission, or if he would have to pull out at the last minute and depend on another way to get the Latin Kings eliminated.

"Some, but I trust you two," I finally said in reply. "We can get through this."

Mark nodded, satisfied with my answer. He grabbed his stuff and headed off into the corner, while Sophie shouldered her own load and headed for the stairs. As she passed me, she stopped and looked up into my eyes. "Good answer," she said with a smile. "There might be hope for you yet."

* * *

The twilight shadows were deepening, and the Latin Kings hadn't arrived yet. The sun was already down, and the last of the day's sunlight was barely visible against the western buildings. Sophie was keeping an eye through one of her positions inside on one of the approach roads, while Mark had his eye on the other. I came up to Mark, making sure to keep myself low and out of sight of the road. "How's it looking?"

"Still quiet," Mark replied. "The meeting's supposed to kick off in ninety minutes. They should be here soon. What do you need?"

"Just a quick question," I said. "Have you given any thought as to what we're going to do with the other two gangs once this is done?"

"I have," Mark replied. "But aren't you thinking a little far ahead?"

"Like I said, I trust you and Sophie. You trained me well. I just hope I live up to your training. But we've been keeping the others balanced by having the Kings around too. What happens next?" I was surprised I was thinking so far ahead. Maybe I was getting a little ahead of myself. I did tend to do that sometimes. But maybe it was just that I was feeling confident. If I could even consider the problems of the future, at least a good chunk of me thought I'd live through the evening.

"We'll have to figure it out, but I have some ideas. If we live through this, I'll talk them over with you the day after tomorrow. Tomorrow itself is going to be busy enough as it is, and we should take a day to celebrate."

I heard cars in the distance, and our ear buds crackled. "Three cars coming in on the waterside road. They look full."

"Understood," Mark replied, then tapped me on the chest. "Go to the front, stay down. I'll keep eyes over here in case they come in from two sides."

I nodded and started to turn. Mark put a hand on my arm to stop me. "Remember, stay down, out of sight. We'll get through this just fine."

"I know. Like I said, you two are the best," I replied. Before Mark could say anything, I jogged down to the end of the little alleyway, staying low and out of sight. There was an old pile of wood pallets that we'd stacked up near that end, enough to provide concealment, but I wouldn't feel comfortable trying to deflect bullets with the cheap, thin chunks of wood. They'd work for an initial burst of gunfire, and then I'd have to move.

I was sweating hard underneath the heavy body armor that I was wearing, a choice that Mark had made based off the fact that he and I would be at street level. We were in full tactical gear, including a fully armored vest, Kevlar helmets, and even the shin and knee pads some SWAT teams wore. Cinched in tight to prevent gear rattling, I was sweating even though the evening light meant it was literally below freezing in the shade of the alleyway. I was glad I was in the best shape of my life, because even with that, my heart was hammering. Perhaps from nerves, perhaps from exertion.

I took a knee behind the pallets, looking out between two of the slots as the three cars slowed and came to a stop, two of them fanning out somewhat along the narrow road. The lead car continued on, driving halfway out onto the dock itself before coming to a halt. The two spread out cars opened up, each of them discharging five men, all of them pretty standard looking street gang bangers. The other car, about maybe another hundred meters further down the dock, opened up to have only two men get out, although I could still see a driver through the back glass. "Thirteen total, twelve out in the open," Sophie whispered on the radio circuit. She had moved her position and was settling into her spot. From the warehouse she was in, it was just over a hundred yards to the near cars. Well within her shooting ability, and I knew her handiwork. She wouldn't let nerves get in the way of a good shot.

"One minute, I'm coming up," Mark whispered. "Patrick, I want you to stay where you are. I'll loop around this building and hit them from the side. We should catch them in a ninety-degree crossfire."

"UMP's or Glocks?" I asked. The Glocks were loaded with what we were calling the neutralizer rounds, the UMP's with alternating neutralizer and regular nine millimeter rounds. The other clips I had in my vest for the UMP were regular rounds all the way. There just hadn't been enough time to reload all of the clips with the mix of rounds.

"What's your distance?" Mark asked.

"Twenty meters." It was just on the edge of a good shot for a Glock for me.

"Go with the UMP, I'll use the Glocks," Mark replied. "Sophie, you take out the targets on the dock first, then back us up. You have flash suppression?"

"I'm far enough back for the first two, but there's not enough flash suppression, no," Sophie replied. Before, I would've never known what the hell that meant, but they'd taught me well. She was firing from deep enough within the building that any flash from the end of her barrel wouldn't be visible from outside. "I'd have to go to ground level indoors if you want no flash."

"No, stay up there and fire down on burst from close to the window if necessary," Mark replied. I understood his thinking. With Sophie up there, not only could she provide heavy firepower with her larger caliber rifle, but she was safer too. She wasn't quite as armored as we were, foregoing the Kevlar helmet, and her vest was only standard thickness instead of having additional trauma plates, but she would have the additional protection of the building. He was protecting her, while at the same time trying to honor Tabby's request by using the Glocks himself. Regardless of his past, if anyone ever doubts that Mark Snow is an honorable man, I'll happily kick their ass.

"Understood," I said, slipping my UMP slowly out from behind my back and taking aim at the nearest group of Latin Kings. I aimed a bit low and to the left, knowing that when I fired it would rise and pull my shoulder to the right. Settling in, I waited for Mark's signal.

"I'm in position," Mark whispered over the radio, "Sophie, you have first shot."

"Understood," Sophie replied.

I waited, feeling my palms sweat and the blood rush in my ears. This was different from my attacks on the 88s or the Gangster Disciples. Hand to hand fighting against thugs or a paintball gun attack on the GDs is one thing. These guys

254

were carrying fully automatic weapons, as was I. People were going to die, regardless of the measures we'd taken to minimize the loss of life. It wasn't even like when my kick ended up killing Melinda Pressman. She'd been trying to kill me, after all. This was an attack.

In an instant, there was no more time to worry about it or to question things. "Sophie, you're up."

"Understood," Sophie whispered, and adrenalin flooded my system. Time stretched out, and I was beginning to wonder what was taking Sophie so long, when a crack pierced the fading light, and all hell broke loose.

Chapter 36
Mark

As soon as Sophie's first shot went off, I was around the corner of the warehouse, both Glocks firing. I'd told Patrick to use his UMP from his position because the Latin Kings were facing his direction. They'd react to him faster, and with at least half of his rounds being potentially lethal, he'd have a better chance to survive. Also, the firing rate of a UMP is actually a bit slower than most submachine guns, for good reason. It would allow Patrick to waste fewer rounds and maintain a bit better control of his bursts.

My first shot caught one of the nearest Kings in the back of his head, knocking him out instead of killing him. There was a chance there could have been major damage, but I doubted it. He looked like he was the type with too thick a skull for it to be life-threatening.

My next shot caught the person next to him in the shoulder, paralyzing his right arm and making him drop his Uzi. I knew he wasn't totally out of the fight, but I didn't have the time to worry about that. I had to move on.

Sophie fired again above us, followed by a quick succession of four shots. Someone returned fire on her, and I heard the distinctive rattle of an AK-47 and rounds impacting the side of the warehouse. I only hoped that she was safe. I didn't have time to let my mind think about the possible consequences of the rounds. I would only endanger her more by hesitating. Patrick's next burst silenced the AK-47, and I rolled deeper toward the two cars.

My first Glock was empty by the time I'd completed my roll, and two of the Kings on my side were down. Shoulder shot, the second guy I nailed, turned toward me and I lashed out with a thrust kick into his left knee, dislocating it and putting him on the ground for the rest of the fight. I kicked away his Uzi while I shot at another. A burst from above answered my questions about Sophie's wellbeing, and suddenly all of the Latin Kings were down. It had felt like minutes, but most likely the entire fight took less than sixty seconds.

I holstered my Glocks, which were both empty, and pulled my UMP around to secure the area. "Clear?"

Patrick, who had moved across the alleyway from where he started, darted out, slapping another clip into his UMP. "Clear."

"Up top, clear?"

"Clear." Sophie yelled down, her voice pure and strong. A knot that I didn't even know existed threatened to unwind itself in my chest, and I clamped down on it savagely. There would be time for the shakes later. I had one more job to do.

"Secure the area," I told Patrick, "keep an eye out for cops."

Before he could answer, I turned and jogged down the dock toward the car, which I saw was resting on two flat tires with at least three bodies around it. I raised my UMP and ran harder, looking for Edgar Villalobos. El Patron was crawling, a wound in his left leg, while his bodyguards wouldn't be getting up ever again. One was on the concrete with a neat hole in his chest, the other was still behind the wheel of his car, slumped over a crimson Rorschach blot that came from his chest.

Villalobos saw me coming up and turned onto his back and crab crawled with his right foot. He reached for the pistol in an underarm holster, but he stopped when he saw me tighten the grip on my UMP. "Fuck," he muttered through gritted teeth when he realized who'd attacked him. "You."

"Good evening, Patron," I said, looking down at him as I came up. I reached into his jacket and relieved him of his pistol, a pretty nice looking .357 Magnum, and chucked it into the sea. "Tell me why I shouldn't shoot you now."

"Like anything I say would change your mind," Villalobos replied. "You aren't the type to factor my words into your decisions. You know, I thought you'd been the

256

one to pull that shit to my knee in Fillmore, but damn my luck anyways."

I looked down at the man, my finger twitching on the trigger of my weapon. I knew what would be easy, putting a burst into his head. He'd probably thank me if I did, as it would be a lot kinder than what he'd get in prison. On the outside, he was in control of a street gang. On the inside, at least in our state, the Latin Kings weren't a strong presence. He'd most likely end up being someone's bitch.

I shook my head and lowered the barrel. "You're right, I made up my mind already. I don't care how much money you've got saved up, or what strings you think Francine Berkowitz is going to pull for you to get you off, it's not going to be enough to keep you out of jail for a long damn time."

"So that's how you found out. Who squealed? The Union or one of my men? Tell me that at least," Villalobos hissed, pulling himself up to a sitting position against his car. "Fuck, your sniper's good. Where the fuck did you find him? SEALs? Rangers? FBI?"

"Listening to movie music in a nightclub, actually," I replied, "but as to your first question, neither. I had Berkowitz's condo tapped. I've got resources too. But let me clue you in on something. Cops are going to come and interrogate you. Now, you and I both know you're dirty enough that they can pin you to probably a good dozen or more Class A felonies from tracking the guns around this car and down by your soldiers. And, of course, a bunch of them have outstanding warrants too. Despite what you may think, Berkowitz isn't going to spend Union money saving your ass. She'll save herself and let you rot down at Central Holding until they get done arraigning you, then send you to County. You'll never see a Union lawyer the entire time."

"So that's your game," Villalobos replied. "You want me to flip on her. Why?"

"She pissed me off, that's all you need to know," I replied. Time for a little bit of lies, priming the pump and sealing Francine's fate. "Besides, you know I've been trying to clean up the city. I would have left you and Fillmore alone longer. She was always my main target. That is, if she hadn't overreached."

"You motherfucker," Villalobos muttered to himself, cursing his luck and fate. "How many of my boys are dead?"

"Hopefully just the ones here," I replied. "Why, think you'll have a chance to carry enough soldiers in with you to protect your sphincter?"

"Never know," Edgar said, then he smiled. "But I ain't becoming no bitch. Might be perforated, but I am not going to be someone's bitch boy."

"Good luck with that," I said. I turned and walked away, leaving behind the fallen king of the Latin Kings.

"What's the view?" I asked Sophie over the radio as I approached the scene of the biggest portion of the battle. Patrick was using zip ties to bind the men he could, although three of them had bullet wounds so he was binding around the wounds. He just wanted to keep them from running away into the night.

"Scanner is saying the cops are on their way, I'd give an ETA of five minutes," Sophie replied. The Docks was the sort of neighborhood that wouldn't get a fast response unless it was to certain areas, and Pier 32 wasn't a high-priority response area. "We should move."

"Two minutes," I said. I knelt next to Patrick, who was using a chain of three strips to zip tie a wounded Latin King to the handle of his car. "How're they looking?"

"The wounds aren't life-threatening," Patrick replied. "How about over there?"

"El Patron is wounded, the others are down permanently," I replied. "They're bound?"

"Those that are conscious. Some of our playmates are going to be knocked out for a while longer."

"Then leave them. If they wake up before the cops get here, they can count themselves lucky, tell their homies what happened. Time for us to ghost."

We met Sophie coming out of the warehouse, her piece slung over her shoulder and the rest of her gear in a backpack on her back. One of the tied up Latin Kings, who'd been shot with just the neutralizer rounds and hadn't been knocked out, opened his eyes wide as he realized that the sniper who'd taken out his boss and his bodyguards was a woman. "A bitch? Fuck me, we got taken down by two *gringos* and a bitch?"

I was proud of Patrick's reaction. I was still turning when he already had his weapon out, shooting another neutralizer round into the man's shoulder. The man yelped and stopped talking, Patrick smirking with one side of his mouth. "I like these things. Great for just getting them to shut up. Think we can get more?"

258

Tabby greeted us at the door, her eyes shimmering with tears of relief and happiness as we walked in the back door of Mount Zion, unharmed. We'd had to wait until long after dark, partly to take the time to dissolve parts of Sophie's rifle and Patrick's UMP in acid. It wasn't strong enough to totally eliminate the thick metal of the barrels, but it would render both of them untraceable. While we left plenty of other evidence behind, specifically the brass of our spent rounds, it would be a lot harder to connect the attack to us if anyone ever came knocking. We'd dispose of the rest of the pieces later, scattering them in the ocean after again giving them an acid bath. Still, it took time.

"We told you we were fine," Patrick said quietly as she wrapped her arms around him, pulling him tight and burying her face in his chest. I couldn't hear her sobs, but her shoulders shook, and he stroked her hair, soothing her with gentle murmurs that I couldn't make out.

I put an arm around Sophie's shoulders, watching them. "She looks happy to see him," I quipped, smiling as Tabby pulled her face—which was, in fact, streaked with tears—away from him to smile at us. "Good, because I think Sophie wants her hug too."

"Get over here you damn fool," she laughed, pulling both of us into a hug. Patrick joined in until Andrea, who was in the dining area and had been sleeping rather soundly, woke up to figure out what was making all the noise. The four of us held each other, a family, only stopping when my daughter's voice demanded attention.

"How was Andrea, anyway?" Sophie asked Tabby. "I hope she listened to her Aunt Tabby."

"She's an angel, just like her mother," Tabby replied, sharing a look with Sophie that spoke more than words. I let go of the two women and watched them hug, a bond different but perhaps even deeper than the ones they shared with me and Patrick. I often said Sophie was my soulmate, and I know Patrick felt the same about Tabby, but those two, their souls were grand enough and deep enough that they needed more than one soul to share with. They needed two, each other and their men. They left for the dining room, and I looked at Patrick, offering my hand.

"What's this for?" he asked as we shook.

259

"You did good out there . . . partner."

Chapter 37
Tabby

The next day, Vanessa could see something in my eyes as I walked into the office. "What's up?" she asked, noticing the aggressive spring in my step. "Got someone's balls on a platter or something?"

"Something like that," I answered, thinking of how today was my turn to walk into battle and emerge unscathed. "We're going to have a visitor in about an hour. Then another set of visitors maybe ten minutes after that. Think you can make them comfortable?"

"I'm sure of it," Vanessa said, perplexed. "Going to tell me who these visitors are?"

"First one should be Francine Berkowitz," I said with a baring of teeth that was probably as far from a smile as a lion's. "Second should be Bennie Fernandez and a few of his friends from the Federal Building."

"So I guess fresh coffee won't be all that important," Vanessa quipped. "Still, I'll have some on when Ms. Berkowitz shows up. Although I think I'll use the cheap stuff, none of that nice blend you got me from Guatemala."

"That's fine. We can share a cup of the good stuff later, then. I have another bag of that and a bag of Colombian you can choose from," I replied. "Just make sure she doesn't suspect anything when she comes in. I want her to be quite surprised when everything goes down."

"Of course, Tabby. I look forward to it. Things have been far too regular and boring around here recently."

I grinned and went into my office, looking around. I wanted Francine to have her back to the door, so I decided that the best position for the meeting was at my desk. It wasn't like she was going to be in a friendly mood anyway. While the newspapers didn't have all the information out there, the initial reports of a group of Latin Kings being involved in what the police were saying was a "gangland-style hit"

260

had to have her worried. Of course, the cover story itself made us all laugh.

I did my best to busy myself as I waited for Francine to arrive. The meeting had been set up quickly last night, before the Latin Kings went out to the docks. In my message, I had insinuated that I was ready to strike a deal, but I didn't say so clearly. It was sure to confuse her, which was exactly what I wanted. I'd won the first round of our little war, and by the end of the evening she would have thought I'd won the second as well. Why was I doing this?

She'd find out soon enough. In the meantime, I sent off a quick email to Gene at the Spartans, along with another to Helen Watters about the grand opening of the community center. I had just clicked 'send' on Helen's message when Vanessa knocked on my office door. "Tabby? Ms. Berkowitz is here to see you."

"Please, show her in, and get some coffee ready," I said. Vanessa nodded, hiding her smile perfectly. She knew how to play the game, that was for sure.

Francine came in, and despite what had to have been a stressful past eighteen hours or so, she still carried herself like a cross between a bully and a queen. Practically shouldering Vanessa out of the way, she came into my office like she owned the damn building. I wondered if that was what Marie Antoinette was like before the French guillotined her. "Tabitha, it's nice to see you again."

"Good morning, Francine. Please, have a seat."

Francine started to sit down at the coffee table before realizing that I wasn't moving from my office chair. She played it off well, setting her purse down on the chair before coming over. "So to what do I owe the pleasure of your invitation?"

"I felt like we needed to clear the air between us, Francine," I answered. Under my desk, I tapped a button that was hooked up to my computer, silently beginning to record everything that was happening in the room. While I didn't know if I would turn over anything to Bennie Fernandez, it was always helpful to have a little bit of extra ammunition to offer. "You know, the past few months have hardly been profitable for the Union, and I'm quite frankly sick and tired of the bullshit that I have to deal with to get my business done. I think I need to make a major change in the city's landscape, and you are exactly the woman to help me do it."

"I don't know what you mean," Francine replied, looking for all the world like a child who had just gotten their hand caught in the cookie jar but still didn't give a shit. She was cocky, arrogant, and sure of her impending victory. It was so ludicrous that I was having difficulty controlling my smile. "I mean, I'm not sure how the Union could help you."

"Well, before I ask more, perhaps you could explain that more to me. Let me just say that I've gotten the impression that if I go along with the Union on certain things, the road toward getting what I want gets radically smoother. How is that?"

"That depends on what MJT can offer the Union," Francine replied. "I mean, how much more are you looking to invest in the city?"

"We currently have an investment fund in the eight figure range," I replied. "I'd have to check with Marcus directly, but my goal is to triple the amount of businesses that MJT is invested in within the next two to five years."

Francine blinked, momentarily given pause. It wasn't often when someone flatly said they wanted to buy stake in over ten percent of the businesses in a major city, along with also stating that they had an investment fund of at least a hundred million dollars set aside to do so. The best part was, I was understating things. If Francine knew exactly how much money MJT had access to, not even including what we could leverage or borrow, she'd probably have a heart attack. "That . . . that's quite a feat, Tabitha. Do you really feel that you can do all that with this two-woman operation running out of the top floor of a gym?"

"I think that if the road were smoothed for me, yes I could," I said. "But that's where the problem lies. You see, if I have to spend half my funds hiring attorneys and fighting the Union and the city in courts, I can't do nearly as much as I want to do. So, while it might hurt me a bit, I think in the long run I can do better working without the Union in the way."

"I wholeheartedly agree," Francine said, her grin growing triumphant. "I'm glad your viewpoint is coming around."

"But tell me, Francine, just how is it that you get it all done? I mean, it should seem impossible to get all of the various unions to cooperate under your banner. Some of them are diametrically opposed to one another, yet you somehow get it all done. MJT could take some lessons from you I think."

"There's a few areas where we can exert influence," Francine replied, "the least of which is having dirt on the right people in the city. Why, with what I know about some of the members of the city council along with the heads of some of the city departments, I could have myself declared God around here and nobody is going to be able to say boo about it."

"Those sorts of connections must go rather high. Tell me, just between the two of us, how high do they go?"

"All the way to Congress." Francine laughed. "I've got ten different members of the House and a Senator who all owe me their jobs and their secrets. You'd be shocked at some of the perverted shit politicians in Washington get up to if you just offer it to them."

"So if we cooperate, do you think I could have access to some of those connections?"

Francine laughed and shook her head. "I doubt it. You see, Tabitha, the thing is that I have everything I need. I don't need MJT in my corner, but you need me. This isn't going to be equitable. You're going to play by my rules, and in return, I won't crush you."

"I doubt that," I replied. I saw shadowy outlines against the frosted glass outside, and I decided it was time to turn the tables. "Francine, I called you here today to tell you that, despite your attempts, despite funding a frivolous lawsuit, and despite your hiring the Latin Kings to disrupt the opening of the community center in a few weeks, MJT has decided to continue in its current policy of not working with the Union. In fact, we're going to be rejecting the Union in general, and will continue to shop out contracts to individual companies regardless of their union status. Further attempts to interfere with our business will result in a lawsuit being filed against the Union by MJT."

"You called me down here just to throw down the gauntlet? Are you insane, or just rude as hell?" Francine spat, seething. After months of polite back and forth, veiled threats and restrained innuendo, here was the core of Francine Berkowitz, angry and exposed, a despot who thought that with her largest competition out of the way in the form of Owen Lynch and the Confederation, she was in a position to be an empress. "You think this is just a game, you pretty little bitch? I've crushed companies bigger than yours, hell, I've crushed whole city administrations. Got it? Your company, out of business. Your boyfriend, Patrick? He won't even get a job washing dishes in this state, if he even survives till the next election. Your pretty little house? I'll have that shit repossessed and torn down. Better yet, I might just make it my house by the time it's all over. I'll . . ."

263

Her words stopped in an instant as the door to my office opened, and two police officers walked in, along with Bennie Fernandez. "Ah, hello, Mr. Fernandez," I said with a tight little smile. "How's your morning been?"

"Very interesting. I woke up to find such wonderfully absorbing information that I read and watched along with my morning coffee. In fact, Judge Hawkins agreed with me, and when you sent me a message, well, I just had to come by with some of my friends to say thank you. Then I see that you've given us an even larger gift."

"You bitch," Francine said, looking from Bennie to me. "You conniving little bitch."

The rest of it was pretty standard stuff you'd see in any cop show. Francine didn't even fight except for a few snippy words; she just let herself be handcuffed and escorted out by the cops. They took the elevator, which I was glad for. Taking the stairs up from the ground floor was difficult enough. Trying to do it in high heels and handcuffed? Knowing Francine Berkowitz, she'd have thrown herself down the steps and sued the city as well as MJT for injuries. I wouldn't want that, as much as seeing her on crutches would be appealing.

"Bye, Francine," I dismissed Berkowitz as she walked out. Bennie Fernandez stopped at the door and gave me a look. "What? I've wanted to say that to her for at least six months."

Bennie nodded in understanding, then stuck his head out the door. "Take her down to the car, we'll take her to the Federal Building for questioning and process her there. Give me a few minutes, though. I forgot something I needed to ask Miss Williams."

The cops outside agreed, and Bennie closed the door, waiting until he heard the elevator start down to turn to me. "You've handed me another feather in my cap, Miss Williams. This is becoming a very pleasant routine."

"Tabby. Didn't I tell you that last time?" I replied. "But don't give me all the credit. I'm sure you know that."

Bennie nodded. "Yes, but you should give your friend some advice. First off, thanks for the restraint showed. Only two dead against thirteen Latin Kings, all trussed up? Very impressive work. But he needs to watch his back. The ATF is very interested in those polymer and powder rounds. They're poking around. I can keep

264

them distracted, but if he uses them again . . ."

"I understand," I replied. "You know, Mr. Fernandez, he's your friend too."

Bennie shook his head. "No. You and I both know, if I had to, I'd prosecute him too. He's guilty of at least four federal firearms crimes that I know of. Although that's minor, considering what the DA would want him for. Thankfully, the DA is a friend of mine. I clerked in his office when I was in law school. He's more than happy to just keep putting away the scum bags. The Latin Kings alone might guarantee him a judgeship if he wants it. But if the Snowman ever gets into the public eye, he's going to have to give him attention as well."

I nodded. "And your point of view on it?"

Bennie shrugged. "I just arrested the head of the Union, which happens to include the police and fire departments. And as much as I hate to say it, even with all the good cops out there, this city needs a lot of help. But tell him, don't push it too far. There's a lot to say for just investing money and driving a riding lawnmower all day. Take care, Tabby."

It was the closest Bennie Fernandez came to saying flatly that he knew who Mark was. I nodded in understanding, and Bennie left, closing the door behind him.

Chapter 38
Tabby

The night after the opening of the first of the community centers, Patrick and I were engaging in some private celebration. We were above the MJT offices, inside the strike base that resided on the fourth floor of the building. "You know, Mark would be annoyed if he caught us up here." Patrick chuckled as he poured me another glass of Castello Banfi Chianti Superiore. "Remind me to make sure we clean up before we go."

"Well, it just felt right, considering he just gave us the codes to this place today as a thank you for everything," I replied. We were about halfway through the bottle, a special gift from Vanessa. I hadn't taken her last name to imply Italian heritage, but she swore there was some in there. It was a touching gift, especially since she gave it before I promoted her to executive secretary of all the community centers. She would still be out of the spotlight, and still working for me, but able to apply her strengths more than she ever had before. I was glad she'd accepted the job.

I took a sip of my wine and chuckled at Patrick's comment about Mark. "I love the man, but his avoidance of alcohol all the time is sometimes frustrating. It's not even that he looks down on us if we did have it at home, but, well, you know how he is. He's just such an example to live up to, it's both inspiring and frustrating."

"I know," Patrick said, thinking about how living up to Mark's example was sometimes so damn difficult. If it wasn't for how much he'd seen us interact, he would have been jealous of Mark. A lot of lesser men than Patrick would have regardless. "So are you excited about tomorrow?"

I shook my head. "After all the stress of getting the centers open, giving up the in-house gym to move it all over to the outbuilding is nothing. And yeah, it'll be a bit tight while they get the wings started, but in the end, it's going to be awesome."

"Speaking about the centers opening," Patrick said as he sipped at his glass, "you looked amazing today. The Spartan girls were there in their sideline skimpy uniforms, and I don't think anyone looked at them once after you took the podium. How'd you pull it off?"

I blushed and took another sip of my wine. "I just imagined dressing up for you. After that, the choices were easy."

Patrick set his wine aside and leaned in, his lips brushing against mine. We were sitting on the floor, since the room didn't have any sort of decent table for two people. I was kind of reclining on my side, while Patrick had been sitting cross-legged. "You're the greatest thing to ever happen to me," he whispered as we parted lips. "Are you sure about the campaign?"

I nodded and set my glass aside. "I love you. I know you're great for the job, and Joe thinks so too. Besides, it's not the big chair yet, just deputy mayor. And it'll keep whoever takes over for Joe honest."

Patrick nodded, then sighed. "But I won't be able to go out on patrol as much. The deputy mayor has a lot more duties than a junior member of the city council."

I laughed and kissed him again, tracing my tongue along his lips, lingering on the aftertaste of the rich wine. I licked the last little droplet off and traced his jaw with my fingertips. "You know, there are other duties that I want you to have too," I said. "You can't neglect your husbandly duties."

"Speaking of which," Patrick said, stretching out and rubbing his hand over my arm, "did you do the test like you said?"

"Mmm-hmmm," I replied, smiling. It had taken every bit of self-control I had not to spill the beans early, but I wanted Patrick to ask, and I wanted him to be the first to know. "Congratulations, Daddy."

The expression that washed over his face was worth the wait, although I knew Sophie would need some convincing as to why I hadn't told her first. I love her, but Patrick did deserve to know first. Focusing on the man I would soon marry, I leaned in and kissed him again, pushing him lightly onto his back. "So you know what that means, of course."

"What?" he asked as he rolled over. I threw a leg over him, swiftly mounting him, even though he was still dressed in his suit pants and dress shirt. He'd actually gotten dressed up for the ribbon cutting ceremony, wearing the custom tailored Brooks Brothers suit I'd convinced him to purchase for political purposes. Although with what I had in mind, his new suit would need at least a dry cleaning, if not a replacement, by the time we were done that evening.

"It means, silly man, that you're going to have to make an honest woman out of me and marry me soon," I replied as my fingers worked at the buttons on his shirt. "After all, shotgun weddings don't go over well with the voting public."

"Wedding? For sure. Honest? Tabby, my love, neither of us are ever going to be all that honest." Patrick laughed. He brought his right hand up to cup my breast through my own dress shirt, stroking with his thumb over the silk. I groaned as he found my nipple through my thin shirt and bra, teasing it until it was hard and poking out even through the two layers of fabric.

"Your lips had better be able to finish what your fingers are starting," I growled, feeling warm pulses radiate through my body from my nipple before gathering between my legs. I had changed out of my work skirt into a pair of casual shorts that I kept in the office in a backpack in case I couldn't get home early and wanted to grab a workout downstairs, and I was happily rubbing myself back and forth across the large, hard bulge that was growing between his legs.

I kept unbuttoning his shirt, pulling it aside when I finally reached the end,

267

exposing his hard, muscular body. I traced the gryphon over his right side with a fingernail, grinning as he shuddered from the sensation. "You know, I was thinking, I'd like a gryphon myself," I murmured. "Maybe on my back? Or perhaps over my heart?"

"You don't need one, but if you want," Patrick said, bringing his left hand up to start working the buttons on my shirt. "I know where your heart is."

I leaned down and kissed him, ignoring my shirt as I pressed myself against the man I loved. He was right. I didn't need any ink to prove to myself or to him who my heart belonged to. I loved him, that was all that was needed. Patrick reached down and cupped my ass through my shorts, squeezing the soft skin and muscle while at the same time our lips danced and dueled with each other. He was raging hard inside his pants, lifting his hips and rubbing against me even though we were both wearing clothes still.

"Wait," I whispered, breaking our kiss. "Let's get these clothes off."

There's an art to undressing for a lover. So many people just tear their clothes off, like it's some sort of race to see who can expose their skin the fastest. Maybe it's just over anticipation of the actual sex, but for Patrick and I, we had months of learning how to entice and please each other without even making physical contact. We took our time, each bit of exposed skin coming after careful positioning and movements. We never got off our knees, yet we performed for each other. Patrick's movements were sinuous, showing each sexy swell of muscle while at the same time not posing. He wasn't a bodybuilder, but an Adonis, a perfectly put together man who displayed himself for the express purpose of pleasing me.

I reciprocated, swaying my hips as I unbuttoned my shirt the rest of the way and shrugged it off, giving him a little tease of my bra before working my shorts down. I was wearing just my panties, and I knew he loved my ass, so I turned to the side, getting down on all fours to work my shorts down and off, my back arching as I threw my hair back, letting him see the waves of my natural auburn. I had never felt sexier than when I was with him, because it was real, no play, no tease. Well, okay, there was a lot of tease, but it was for him that I did it. It was foreplay and fun combined, which is the best type.

Next to go were my panties and bra, lifting my toes up to hand Patrick my thong. I lay back, my knees spread, my heels pulled high up to my hips. I felt not so much sexy as sexual, if you can grasp the difference, and from the look in Patrick's eyes, it made me more aroused. I could feel my pussy, slick and heavy with need, pulsing with my heartbeat as he finished taking off his own clothes, pushing his pants down before kicking them off. He even somehow pulled off the impossible task of taking full length pants off look sexy. All I knew was that in the dim light of the room, he was everything I'd ever need.

Lying back, I pulled Patrick on top of me, wrapping my legs around him as his lips found my neck, kissing and tasting my skin. Each movement of his body against me gave unexplainable pleasure as he let enough of his weight settle onto me that I was held still, unable to resist his strength or his desire, but at the same time light enough that it wasn't stifling at all. I couldn't move, but I didn't want to. My nipples rubbed against the light hair on his chest, lightning sensations shooting through my body. I could feel his cock teasing at my entrance, and I ached to feel him slip inside me, but not yet.

Patrick kissed down my body to taste my breasts, sliding off to the side enough that I felt a moment of chill before his hand cupped my pussy, a strong, nimble finger tracing through my folds. I couldn't help it, my hips lifted up, impaling myself on his digit, not able to hold back any longer. "Patrick . . ."

"I know. I love you too," he whispered around my breast, sliding his finger in deeper. Pumping his finger in and out, he let go of my breast to encourage me to sit up, keeping his finger inside me. Curious to his idea, I did, and he slid behind me, holding me with his free arm.

"I wanted you from the first moment I saw you," he whispered in my ear as his finger slipped deeper. He added another finger, filling me more, and I leaned back against his chest, thrilled as I felt the thick heat of his cock push against my low back. "Remember, at that first press conference? You were so beautiful, so amazing, I wanted you right there and then. When I found out you were even more perfect than I'd first thought, I was in love by the end of our first date. Now, you're mine, and I'm never going to give you up. I'm going to stay by you, protect and cherish and take care of you. I'm going to rest my head in your lap when I'm tired, I'm going to hold your hand as we walk in the sunset, and I swear, I'll be there for the rest of your life. I love you, Tabby."

Patrick brought his other hand up, cupping my breast as his lips found my

269

neck again. I lost myself in his caresses, his fingers and lips combining to bring me to a blissful state that felt like it would go on forever. My pussy twitched in warning, and I shook my head. "No . . . I want you inside me first."

Patrick nodded, leaning back onto the floor while I pulled my legs up. Holding me effortlessly in his arms, he lifted me up and onto his cock, filling me with a single bold thrust, driving the breath out of me it felt so good. I spread my knees to let them rest on either side of his hips, riding him cowgirl style. Looking back over my shoulder, I smiled down at him, catching my breath. "Like the view?"

"Nothing better in the world," he replied, reaching down and lightly spanking my right butt cheek. "You know, we never have tried spanking."

"Next time, I'll wear a schoolgirl skirt," I promised him with a saucy grin. I slid my hips back and forth slightly, both of us shivering from the feeling of his cock sliding in and out of me. "Maybe some pigtails?"

"Keep it up. I'm going to be coming way too soon," Patrick promised me, both of us laughing. Nodding, I turned my head back, letting my mind focus on the feeling of Patrick's cock inside me. I lifted myself, impaling myself over and over again on him, his thick hardness stretching and filling me. I was so close, but I wanted him with me, to come at the same time I did; it was difficult. If I squeezed down like I wanted, I was nearly ready to come, but if I didn't, the fire built inside me anyway.

Patrick's hands found my waist and he pulled me back, again laying on top of him. "Shh," he whispered in my ear as I groaned and grunted in frustration. "You come as often as you want. I'll be right here the whole time."

Reaching around me, his fingers found my clit, rubbing it while his other arm pulled my legs up to my chest. Underneath me, he thrust, pounding me from beneath while my clit danced to his strokes. Within seconds I was groaning, my body awash with the relaxing heat of my first orgasm, Patrick holding me tight against him as I trembled and squeezed around him. "That's it," he said quietly. "I've got you."

When the sensation settled, I squirmed, wanting to turn over. Patrick let go, and I quickly dismounted for only a moment before laying on my back. Of all the positions we could have, this one, the supposedly boring missionary, was what I needed. I wanted to feel myself beneath him, submitting to him and seeing his face as he and I came again.

Even though he had just filled me seconds before, Patrick's cock again was pushing inside me, our eyes focused on each other. I gave myself fully to him, my body his as he plunged into me over and over, his body flexing and powerful. Our moans faded as our hearts sped up, sweat stinging my eyes and glittering on Patrick's forehead like diamonds. His pale skin flushed, his green eyes burning with love and desire, the only sounds in the room being the harsh gasp of our breath and the slap of his hips against me. He pounded into me, filling me over and over, hard and fast.

Patrick's breath rasped as he tried to form words, and I knew what was rushing up on him. I was close, too, and I could only smile, my hands clutching at his back, my fingers hooking into claws as my body clenched around him. With the sensations Patrick caused in me, I'm sure he was happy I kept my fingernails relatively short. He had enough scratches from his training. He didn't need more from sex.

The breath caught in my throat, my body already starting to convulse with my next orgasm. It was going to be big, and I was glad that Patrick was the man he was. I could see the slightest tremor at the corner of his sensuous mouth, and his own orgasm started. The feeling of him sent me over the edge, reality washing away as I held onto my rock, my Patrick.

Chapter 39
Sophie - Twenty-Three Years Later

I was in my best cocktail dress, coordinating the servants we'd hired for the night, which was a beautiful late January evening. The stars stood out, diamond pinpricks against the black velvet of the sky, and I shivered only a little bit as I greeted our guests. "Governor, it's good to see you again."

"Joanna Bylur, as always, you put on a great event," the man greeted me. He wasn't the sincerest man in the world, but he was well meaning. He had been by Mount Zion multiple times, usually alone. Sadly for him, his wife had died the year before, and he was still mourning. He tried his best to cover it up with a good smile, even though it never quite reached all the way to his eyes. "How's the family?"

"Amazing, sir," I replied, shaking his offered hand. "Matthew is still shocked by Patrick's offer."

"Chief of staff is a great position. And reading what I have about your husband, he sounds like the type of man who can help Patrick in any situation."

You have no idea, I thought before smiling. "Thank you. Enjoy the party, sir. Maybe next year we can have one for you?"

"We'll see," the governor said before heading inside. I turned to the next guest, smiling and shaking hands with the VIPs and those who I knew personally. I was the head of the house at Mount Zion, and it was important to make sure the house maintained its good reputation.

After the majority of the guests had arrived (these sorts of events always had a few late comers, but we had greeters and coat-check people to help with that) I made my way to the back and launched into last-minute instructions for the help. "First round of trays go out in three minutes. Remember to smile, and keep their glasses filled. If you see someone who you might recognize from the news start acting a little tipsy, don't give them another glass, and tell me. I'll handle it."

"Yes, ma'am," some of the staff replied, causing me to shake my head in good humor. Was I really getting old enough that people called me ma'am? I guess I was. At least, despite my job as head of the house, I still wasn't Alfred Pennyworth though.

While I pondered the passage of time, Mark came through the crowd. The years had been very, very kind to my husband, who still sported the lean physique that had turned me on when I saw him in that nightclub twenty-three years prior. We (and I mean, Mark and I, not MJT or any other front corporation) had bought that building and had it torn down, replacing it with a daycare center ten years ago. It had been part of the second cycle of community investment, after the community centers.

"Hey babe, how's things here?" he asked me, taking my hand. There was just a touch of gray at his temples, but he still turned heads on women in their twenties, and not just those with Daddy issues either. I am one lucky woman. "Need any help?"

"No, go and enjoy the party. There's plenty of handshakes out there for you too, Mister Chief of Staff," I replied, giving him a kiss on the cheek. "I'll be out once the first wave of stuff is on the way. But if you see your son, can you send him in here? His mom might need a hand with the cake later."

Mark grinned and nodded. "Of course. He's probably around here somewhere. There are quite a few pretty girls in the audience. He's going to have his hands full."

"Like father, like son," I replied. Mark chuckled and left, and I redirected my attention to the staff. One girl, a cute little thing who looked kind of like I did when I was twenty, with a lot of curves and just a hint of softness to them capped by a thick mane of nearly black hair, watched Mark leave with dream filled eyes. She was like me, I could tell, a lot prettier than she thought she was and suffering mostly from a giant case of insecurity. I smiled and tapped her on the arm. "You okay?"

The girl jumped, startled. "Yes . . . sorry, ma'am."

"It's okay," I said. Quietly, I leaned in and whispered in her ear. "You want to know the secret?"

She nodded, all big eyes and innocent features, and I smiled again at how much she reminded me of me at that age. "Just go out and try for them. They're not out of reach, although they are hard to find. Got me?"

The girl nodded again, a sheepish smile coming to her face as she realized I'd nearly read her mind. Her smile faded and her jaw dropped as the swinging door to the kitchen area opened again, and Riley came in. Named after his father (it was how all of us had finally learned his real name), Riley Bylur was the spitting image of his father when he was younger—sandy blonde hair, piercing eyes, smart and athletic.

The only thing he lacked was the soft Southern drawl his father could recall in an instant that still melted my heart. At nineteen, Riley was already a junior at Harvard. Like mother, like son, I guess.

"Hey, Mom, Dad said you needed . . . help," Riley said, his eyes stopping on the young girl next to me. I tried to hide my smile as I saw the two look at each other, and I made a decision.

"Yes, later. In the meantime, Riley, this is . . . sorry, I didn't get your name," I said to the girl next to me.

"Janet," the girl replied, blushing. "Janet Wayne."

"Janet Wayne. Janet, this is my son, Riley Bylur. If you need any help tonight, ask him. I'm sure he'll be happy to assist you. He can coordinate things back here," I said, patting my son on the shoulder. "I'm going to join the party."

Riley nodded and smiled at Janet, already dismissing me from his thoughts. I left the kitchen before I could overhear too much of their conversation. The celebratory gala was already going when I came out, followed seconds later by the servants, carrying trays around to everyone. I made my way through the crowd, smiling and exchanging pleasantries with people while I looked for Mark. Finally, I spotted him near the front door, shaking hands with Bennie Fernandez. Excuse me, Judge Fernandez of the Fifth District, a new position that had him in line for a Supreme Court spot if he wanted it later on. Still, he was just Bennie to us.

"So how's the new house?" Mark asked as he two took drinks from the tray, Mark's, of course, being non-alcoholic. Some things never changed.

Bennie, on the other hand, had. Balding, with a pleasantly round belly, he still had the fire in his eyes that had told me he was a good prosecutor years before. "We're enjoying it. Our son's getting married soon, so the extra room will be great. Can you imagine it? Grandkids running around the house. My wife is already planning on spoiling them rotten whenever they come over. I was glad the President was willing to relocate me down there after my son got a job in Miami. It's a good thing. Keeps me out of your hair at least."

Mark laughed and patted Bennie on the shoulder. "You know I'm getting too old for that type of stuff, Bennie. I'm not twenty-five anymore."

Bennie chuckled, knowing that he'd never, despite all the years of subtle probes, get a clear answer from Mark. "I see . . . and the urban legends, then?"

I chuckled and came up to Mark, wrapping my arm around his waist. "Are urban legends, Benjamin. Don't make us lie to a judge."

Bennie laughed and nodded. "Okay. Well, I'm still fighting the good fight myself. New playground, same trash to take out. You know how it is."

At the front of the room, Patrick's assistant campaign manager took the microphone in hand. "Ladies and gentlemen, thank you for coming tonight," the man said. He was young, just out of college and was replacing Gwen as Patrick's personal assistant after so many years, once Gwen had trained him in how to do things.

Gwen wasn't leaving us, she was just moving up, taking Vanessa's job as head of the community center project while Vanessa came over to Patrick's staff as press secretary. The old campaigner had finally found her niche, that was for sure. Meanwhile, Nick, the new assistant, smiled again as the crowd quieted. "Again, thank you. The speeches are more or less done for the day, and my boss, as you know, likes to keep things not so stuffy, so I'm just going to say, please welcome to the party, our city's new mayor and first lady, Patrick and Tabby McCaffery!"

The crowd broke out into raucous applause while Patrick's music, a lighter remix of the old Nolan *Batman* film themes (he'd picked that because of my Hans Zimmer appreciation), played over the loudspeakers. Patrick was also nearly as fit as he had been when the three of us had taken down the Latin Kings, his face still youthful, his scars from his battles hidden. He'd had a few losses over the years, including that first campaign for deputy mayor, but he had come back stronger than ever each time.

Tabby, for her part, was heart stoppingly beautiful, and even Mark hummed his appreciation. "How does she do it?" he asked. "Seriously, we saw her just this morning, looking like normal Tabby, and now . . ."

"Now she looks like an A-list Hollywood celebrity?" I remarked. "Who knows? I'm just glad she's still in our lives."

"Kind of hard not to be, isn't it?" Mark asked with a slight grin as another couple followed Patrick and Tabby onto the stage. "Andrea looks nervous."

"She takes after you," I said. "Never has enjoyed the spotlight. Much better in the dark."

Mark patted my hand. Patrick took the microphone and smiled. "Thank you, everyone. I wouldn't be here without all of your support, but I'd like to give special thanks again to my family. First of all, to my lovely wife, Tabby, who inspires me every day to reach beyond myself and find new light in the world. To my son, Carter, and his fiancée, Andrea, who I've known since she was born, thank you for being here. And finally, while she couldn't be here tonight, my daughter, Barbara, who is off in Europe studying at university. Without your help, I wouldn't be here tonight. I'd also like to thank everyone who helped us reach this goal. I only hope I can continue to uphold the dreams that you've placed in my trust."

The crowd applauded again, and the music started up, with the first dance being the exclusive dance of Patrick and Tabby. They had chosen "Music of the Night" from *Phantom of the Opera*, and it was beautiful played on violin, the crowd applauding a final time before the party swung back to normal. Patrick and Tabby made their way over, Patrick embracing Mark as soon as he could. "Sorry I couldn't say you too."

"It's okay, we know," Mark said, as Tabby hugged me too. "Hey, did you see? Shawn Northrup stopped by to offer his congratulations. He said he'll talk to you in the office Monday."

Patrick chuckled and nodded. For twenty years, the two had butted heads, agreeing while disagreeing, consistent rivals even as Patrick's star shone while Shawn's waned. He still was on the city council, but was never going to grow bigger than that. "Yes, we exchanged handshakes. I'm sure he has something up his sleeve. After all, he is Shawn."

Carter and Andrea came over, their arms around each other. Their wedding was in a month, and the two of them were crazy in love. With his father's green eyes and his mother's rich auburn hair, it was a shame Carter didn't let it grow longer. He was perhaps even more handsome than Mark and Patrick. Andrea, whose hair had darkened some to be halfway in between Mark's sandy blonde and my brown, was obviously happy. They had grown up together, and it had just seemed natural that they were to fall in love, even though the stories of how they figured that out can be a whole other epic in itself.

"I can't wait for this to be over," Carter said. Standing six foot three, he was even taller than his father, and I was glad that Andrea had ended up closer to Mark's height than mine at just over five eleven. "I'm practically itching to get out of this monkey suit."

276

"Oh, I don't know, honey," Tabby said, adjusting the bow tie of her son's tuxedo. "I think you look rather dashing. Don't you agree Andi?"

"You know it, Aunt Tabs," Andrea said. "Come on, Carter, let's show them what we can do on the dance floor. Our parents can't have all the fun. By the way, Mom, where's Riley? I can't find him anywhere."

"Your little brother is probably still talking to Janet, the staff member I introduced him to," I replied. "I'll tell you all about it later if he gives me a chance."

"Okay," Andrea said knowingly. Riley had a well-deserved reputation as a playboy. He took after his Aunt Tabby so much, but I had a hunch that Andrea's dismissal of this latest girl might be a bit premature. There was something in Riley's eyes that said he might be different this time.

Mark looked at me with a raised eyebrow, and I patted my husband's arm. "He's fine. She reminds me of me twenty years ago."

"That worries me more than assures me," Tabby joked, and we all laughed, enjoying the party.

* * *

That night, as the moon set and the last of the cleanup crew drove away, I went upstairs to the bell tower. Inside I found Carter and Andrea already suiting up, their outfits more high-tech than anything their fathers or I had ever worn. My legs had never been bulletproof, and I never had the sensors or physical enhancements they had.

"I read the manual on vigilantes. In fact, I wrote the manual, if I remember correctly. You can take a night off every once in a while," I joked, looking on enviously as Andrea zipped up the side of her outfit. Had I ever been that slim? I must have, at least Mark said so. Thankfully, even after nearly two and a half decades, he still loved me and still loved my body. Even still, Andrea's pinup figure had me wistfully recalling my days jumping rooftop to rooftop with Mark. "With Riley in town for the summer, you could even work out a patrol sharing system."

"Little bro? He's already gaga over that new girl," Andrea replied. "Come on, Mom, it's just a quick sweep and check of the Docks. You know it's nowhere near as dangerous as when you and Dad were running down the Confederation."

"Or even when Dad and Uncle Mark cleaned out Fillmore Heights," Carter

277

added. "Besides, Mark's agreed to work coms for us tonight. We promised to be back by one in the morning. He's got an early day tomorrow, so we can't tire him out. You know how age gets to you."

I shook my head in exasperation, then laughed. "Watch yourself, Carter, or else your Uncle might just take you out on the mat and kick your butt. All right. Just be careful, I read the files. New weapons on the streets, something military based?"

"Yep, and new toys for us," Andrea replied, putting on her mask, fully covering her hair in a black and white motif cowl. She came over, and with technology assisted strength, carefully gave me a hug. "We'll be fine, Mom. And I'll talk to Riley about taking a few patrols early. He already promised to cover when Carter and I go on our honeymoon."

The new generation of vigilantes, Ice Princess and Crimson Justice by their street names, left the bell tower, heading downstairs. I stayed up there, watching through the remodeled one way windows of the bell tower as the twin taillights of their matching cycles disappeared down the driveway.

Our city was in good hands.

The End.

Don't forget Book 3, Justice: An Alpha Billionaire Romance!

Also by Lauren Landish

Blitzed: A Secret Baby Romance
Relentless: A Bad Boy Romance
Off Limits: A Bad Boy Romance
Mr. Dark: An Alpha Billionaire Romance

See all my books at www.LaurenLandish.com